The Chronicles of Eden

Presents

The Prayer Circle

By M.D. Rhett

The Prayer Circle
by M.D. Rhett

Printed in the United States of America

ISBN 9781597811323

This is a work of fiction. Names, characters, places, and incidents either are the product of the author's imagination or are used ficticitiously, and any resemblance to actual persons, living or dead, events, or locales are entirely coincidental.

www.xulonpress.com

Acknowledgements

The Inspirational Series, **The Chronicles of Eden**, is inspired by so many wonderful and amazing people that have traveled together with me on this Life Enrichment Journey. Some have transitioned and are now resting with the Lord, while others, continue to walk with me as we explore a deeper relationship with Christ. Though this is not an exhaustive list, this series would never have reached the world without the influence, guidance and support the following people have provided to me: In Heaven: Bessie B. Edwards and Ruth Fields Garrett, my grandmothers; James Edwards, Mattie V. Morris, Charles Stanley Hobbs, and Kameela Lott.

On Earth: Malachi and Jean Rhett, my incredible parents; Malachi Eugene Rhett, Gregory D. and Constance Rhett, Prentiss and Ladiner Blaylock, aka..the extended Rhett PAC; Tracy "Nuke" Rhett, Captain Erol Rhett, Archbishop Alfred A. Owens, Jr., and Susie C. Owens, my pastors of 21 years; Arthur Morris III, Finis D. Creer, Jewel Flowers, Rev. Helen Harris, Glendora C. Hughes, Anita Marchitelli, Deirdre Cheek, Retha Beatty, Daniel and Angela Thornton, Daniel and Joycelyn Hatchett, Raymond and Nellie Rooks, Alfred and Barbara Reese, Dennis Hatchett, Rev. Timothy McFadden, Min. E. Carol Burns, Cheryl McGill, and my entire Greater Mt. Calvary Holy Church Family!

To my colleagues, and authors: Beverly East, S. James Guitard, and Amari Yarborough- Thanks for leading the way!!

To my Heaven sent Editor, Pat Barnhardt (Writing Down Pat)- we never met, but God sent you to me!! I love and appreciate all that you have done to make this story come together as a readable novel!

To my most faithful friend, big brother, and gifted accountant, James "Jim" Newby- You have been my inspiration from the start. Your belief that I deserved a better life has inspired me to dream bigger, reach higher, and fly solo knowing that God has it all in control. I love you to life!

Table of Contents

For Mom and Dad

In Loving Memory of Grandma Ruth,
Aunt Ida, and Mother Brown,
the real Prayer Circle.

Author's Note

Welcome to ***The Chronicles of Eden****! I invite you to explore with me the greatness of African Americans from the past and their relationship with an Almighty God. Even today, the church remains the essential foundation of African American Culture. It is where our faith was developed, and after years of oppression and abuse, restored. We are, as a people, as a human race, nothing without the power to survive that comes from God.*

The stories you are about to read are all inspired by real people who walked the earth. They were farmers, steel workers, Pullman porters, domestic help, business women and men who defied the odds to claim a piece of what was rightfully theirs, ownership in the American Fabric called Freedom.

I am a proud descendent of the very people you will read about. I am a privileged woman because of their struggles. In fact, we all are. Let us begin to embrace the greatness of America's past, no matter how painful, for the hope of our future lies in the many silenced voices from our past.

Get a cup of your favorite drink, have a seat, grab a box of tissues, and enjoy! It's storytelling time and I am so thankful to God that you are here! I look forward to chatting with you on line, Facebook, or in book II: Awakening the Dead.

With Godly Love,
Michelle

I

Ida Mae Wilcox Tilley
"Lil Anne"

ONE

September 1976

"Swing them hips, Ida!" Timmy yelled across the floor from the makeshift bar where he stood that warm summer night.

"Do that dance, Baby!" he chuckled.

Ida could hear him, but she kept her eyes closed anyhow. She fantasized while Ronald Isley belted from the speakers, *Living for the Love of You*, her favorite Isley Brothers' song. No one could reach her in this state of mind, and she cared not what anyone thought of the way her small hips glided from side to side.

Hands above her coal black curly locks, she snapped her fingers to the rhythm that pulsated through her very bones. She was lost in the music while she danced. Swaying to the beat, all alone on the dance floor, she looked as if she were in a trance.

Timmy kept one eye on the patrons seated at the bar in front of him, and the other on the front door. After he had a clear view of each person that entered the dark foyer from the outside, he would relax and await the next one, praying that this was a night that Johnny Law would not pay them a visit.

With a loaded double barrel shotgun placed on the middle shelf underneath the bar, arms length away, he occasionally glanced in Ida's direction, and each time he did, her dancing would break his concentration.

"Oh yeah, Tilley...keep it up...don't hurt nobody!"

The patrons seated around him slowly turned to watch Ida dance, but only after looking at Timmy carefully. He had to give them his approval before they too could gawk at the beautiful chocolate woman swaying to the music on the stained concrete dance floor.

"Ida sho' looks good. Still looks like she did when she was just a youngin," one man said.

"She sho' looks at peace...like she don't have a care in da world," a woman added.

"She shouldn't. She got a new car and just moved into that brick house down the road everyone is admiring," another commented.

"Must be nice," they all said in unison.

Timmy cleared his throat loudly to signify to them that it was time to stop talking about Ida before he was forced to respond. Jealously brews fast when aided by liquor; first admiration, then criticism, and next pure hatred for everything Ida Tilley stood for.

Ida kept dancing. She yelled to the DJ to keep the tunes coming. It was her birthday party and she was determined to enjoy it and celebrate the past year.

Suddenly the sounds emanating from the record player came to an abrupt end, as if someone dragged the needle across the vinyl, permanently scratching it. Ida stopped dancing, dropped her arms, and opened her eyes.

"What happened, man?" she yelled as she looked in the direction of Timmy's brother, Ronald, who played records for the club on Friday and Saturday nights.

Ronald stared at the dark entryway where a tall figure stood obstructing the view from the outside. It was clearly a man, but he did not step into the dance hall. Ida turned around and glanced at the doorway. She did not to look at Timmy, who had by now reached down and grabbed his shotgun.

"Come on in, Sheriff Bryant!" she yelled, and then laughed and said, "Everythang we doin' tonight is legal."

Moments later, the big man stepped into the dance hall and Ida could see that her assumptions were correct. It was indeed the high sheriff of Jasper County.

Charles Bryant stood six feet five inches tall, weighed about three-hundred pounds, and carried his weight like a registered weapon. Few people had the guts to step to the likes of him. As he walked in the direction of the bar, he surveyed the people seated around the room. Then he looked directly at Timmy.

"Evenin', Timetheous," the sheriff said, placing a meaty fist on the bar.

Timmy ignored him and slowly placed the shot gun back on the middle shelf.

Sheriff Bryant enunciated every syllable. "I says good evening."

"Heard yuh. What business yuh got heah tonight?" Timmy shot back.

"What does it matter? You run a public juke joint and, the last time I checked, I am a public citizen."

"Not tonight, Charles. I don't wanna deal wid yuh foolishness. Ida done told you that we behavin'." Timmy paused and then blurted out, "Ain't nobody drunk neither, so go on 'bout yuh bizness."

"Not yet," Bryant remarked as he walked toward Ida. "Let's see what happens at ten past midnight." He turned his full attention to her.

"My, Miss Ida, you sho' look good."

"Back away from her, Bryant," Timmy snarled.

"Ah, come on! You know she's a pretty woman. I'm just giving her a compliment. Yo' woman standing heah looking better than a ripe peach and you don't think another man is gon take notice?"

"Last I remembered, you had a wife! Go home tuh huh," Timmy yelled as he maneuvered his way around the bar and stood between Ida and the sheriff.

"Don't pay him no mind, Timmy. Bryant just being fresh. I give him some leeway tonight. That's how good I feel and I'm not about tuh let mean old Sheriff Bryant ruin mah mood."

Then, staring directly up into the sheriff's face, Ida cooed, "Wanna dance, Charles?"

He ignored her offer as he stood still, feet planted, in the middle of the small dance floor. Sensing the other's fear of him, he peered directly into the eyes of everyone in the room, one after the other. He rested his hand on his holstered pistol, then, slowly, he turned around and faced Timetheous.

"Now who's flirting? She asked me to dance. I have a right to accept this woman's proposal, since there ain't no proof down at the courthouse that y'all ever made it legal. Besides, I'm on official pohlice business."

Timetheous Tilley was not a tall man. He stood an average five-feet-eleven inches tall, yet he knew how to handle a bully, and to him the biggest bully he had ever met was standing directly in front of him.

"What now, Charles?" he asked.

"Nothing much. I'm just looking for someone."

"Who?"

"Now I just told you this is official poh-lice business." The sheriff kept his eyes roving on the thirty or more people congregated in the club. Last thing he wanted was to get jumped by some drunk with too much liquid courage in his belly.

"I could save you a lot of time. Don't nobody come into this club widout me seeing 'em," Timmy said. "Anyway, the club is closed tonight. Everyone know this is a private party."

"Private party? What y'all celebrating?" Bryant inquired.

"None of yo' business!" Ida interjected. "It's my birthday and I don't want to have to deal with the likes of you tonight." She clasped her fingers together and pleaded, "Can you just give us one night off?"

Sheriff Bryant looked down at her and rolled his eyes. "I gave you more than that, lady. Remember, I could shut this place down permanently."

"Yeah, we can't forget. Now either you gon' dance, or get the hell off the dance floor!" she shouted defiantly.

"Watch it now, Ida Mae Tilley! I don't want no trouble outta you."

"Then don't start none and won't be none," she yelled back.

"Can't you be a decent woman for one night?" Bryant asked.

Timmy could see this was going badly. "Charles, do yo' business and leave us be. Can't yuh see yuh're interrupting these good law abiding citizens' evening? You're not welcomed heah and yuh know it. So why…"

"Hush your mouth, Timetheous!" Bryant interrupted before Timmy could finish the sentence. "I am the law! I can come and go when and where I please!" His voice escalated while an enraptured audience listened to every word that emanated from his lips. "Beaufort County is a part of our jurisdiction. I don't care how far y'all keep moving...this is still my damn turf. Don't you fergit it!"

Ida ignored him and yelled to Ronald. "Put another record on. Something fast. I wanna move!"

Just then four people walked into the dance hall, but when they spotted Sheriff Bryant, they turned around and made a quick retreat.

"Where y'all going?" Timmy yelled after them. "Bryant done finished wid his business heah and was just leaving. If y'all come tuh celebrate Tilley's thirtieth, come on in! Yer mos' welcome."

Sheriff Bryant walked over to Timmy and whispered into his ear. "Looking for Edgar Carter...you ain't seen him, huh?"

"Hell no. What would he want around heah?"

"You tell me. You see him, give him a message: I'm gonna hunt him down and throw his black butt in jail," Bryant sneered.

Timmy just shook his head and backed toward the bar. The sheriff cracked a phony smile, raised the brim of his hat, and walked over to where Ida stood talking to some of her guests. He reached out and grabbed her by the wrist.

"Take your dirty hands offa me, man!" she screamed.

"I thought you wanted to dance." His eyes surveyed her voluptuous body, perspiring in a form-fitting yellow silk dress.

"Told yuh tuh go home tuh that wife of yearn. You pushing it tonight, Charles." Timmy grabbed the shot gun and placed it menacingly on top of the bar.

Without looking back, the sheriff said, "Don't even think about firing that weapon boy, ya hear?"

Timmy responded with a hiss, "Then I suggest you don't make me."

Sheriff Bryant stared at Ida, winked, and walked toward the door. Within minutes, he'd disappeared into the pitch black South Carolina night.

Minutes later, Ida turned around and stared at Timmy. "I can handle myself, Timmy." She rolled her eyes. "Ain't scared of Sheriff Bryant or no one else and you know it!"

Ronald played fast tunes from R&B groups like The Ohio Players, Confunction, Kool and the Gang, and The Bar-Kays. The floor was jumping, as more guests entered from the outside. As couples headed onto the dance floor, Ida commanded the center and danced among the crowd.

Timmy remained at the bar the entire time, his hand always close to the shotgun.

About a half hour later, Ida, fanning herself wildly, walked over to him. "What Johnny Law want?" she whispered, as she wiped her wet forehead with a paper towel.

Timmy stood looking at her, saturated in sweat, curls fallen, make up smeared in places, yet still beautiful. Then he turned his back to her and poured her a hefty drink of moonshine.

"Drink something, Tilley, befo' yuh pass out." He handed her the cup.

"I'm just getting started. This party is jumping now! Man, yuh see all dese people? Where dey come from? I ain't see Josette in years...and ain't that Laura's boy? I forget his name. He grown now. I wonder where Laura at?"

She stopped talking long enough to catch her breath and take a sip from the Dixie cup.

"Whew, this moonshine sho' nough strong! Yuh mixed it just right. Go on wid yuh bad self," she teased.

"Long as my Tilley is having a good time. I put my foot in that brew! That there our private stock. I ain't giving these fools none of this so they can go out o' heah and kill someone on these dark roads. No way, just give the sheriff another reason tuh shut us down...again." He gave Ida a look that needed no explanation.

"I hear ya. Now, what he want?" she asked impatiently.

"He looking for, of all people in these heah parts, Edgar Carter."

"Carter don't come around here and Bryant knows it. Why would he come heah looking fo' 'im?"

"He wasn't. I believe he just lying. He dropped Carter's name on purpose. He really checking on us. I was glad no one was heah and everyone was on CP time."

"Dunno man, yuh think Carter done gone and hurt somebody?" Ida asked cautiously. "I just pray tuh the good Lord that he ain't kill no one else."

"Hush ya mouth now, Ida Mae!" Timmy warned her. "No telling who gonna hear yuh talking stuff can't nobody prove."

"Don't have to prove the obvious...some things we just know."

Ronald walked toward them with a strange look on his face, interrupting. "Where is my drink? Y'all forgot all about me! I can't stop playing records long enough to fetch a brew. Y'all knows if y'all want to keep the music coming, you gon' have to keep the drinks coming." He smiled at Ida.

"Timmy, get this man two drinks...the private stock!" she screamed, slapping the bar for emphasis.

As Timmy turned to pour the liquor, Ida and Ronald watched the commotion on the dance floor. Folks were yelling and clapping their hands high into the air. Ida smiled and kept watching. Ronald watched the front door. No sooner than he had his two drinks in hand, he headed back to his post, but stopped when he saw another obstruction in the doorway.

It was the figure of a woman. Standing still, she did not enter the dance hall. Ronald signaled to Ida, who looked over her shoulder before turning her entire body around in the seat so that she now faced the front door.

"Timmy, who dat?" she leaned back and whispered.

"How I 'sposed tuh know, Tilley? That woman may be waiting fo' someone in the parking lot. You know ain't none of y'all fool enough tuh waltz in heah widout a man on yuh arms."

Ida kept watching the woman. Timmy was right. No woman in the Low Country was bold enough to march into a juke joint unattached. If she did, she neither knew nor cared about the rules of the Deep South. Whoever she was had Ida Mae Tilley's undivided attention.

After several minutes and no movement, Ida became suspicious about the woman in front of her. Although other people continued to walk inside of the club, the mystery woman still did not make one move. Suddenly, Ida arose from the chair, adjusted her dress, smoothed back her hair, and walked in the direction of the stranger.

As she passed the dance floor, several of her guests attempted to lure her back, but she motioned to them that they needed to wait, all the while never taking her eyes off of the figure standing alone in the foyer.

Walking directly toward the woman, the closer she came to her intended target, the more the glare from the lights in the parking light obstructed her view. Determined to get a better look, she marched directly into the small dark foyer. As she raised her hands above her eyebrows to block the glare, Ida Mae stopped dead in her tracks.

Stunned, she took two steps backwards, grabbed her cheeks with both hands and declared, "Well, God in heaven" she screamed, "it's gonna rain!"

TWO

Spring 1966

Ida stared at her wedding gown and admired the softness of the satin fabric and its elaborate details: Princess bodice, a-lined shape, scalloped hem, and hundreds of pearls and rhinestones. Just seeing it lying on the bed, lifeless without the contours of her small frame, made her teary eyed. The details were exquisite, like nothing she had ever laid eyes on before.

She sat on the bed staring out of the window as she recalled local gossip concerning her impending nuptials. Townfolks were outraged because it was rumored that her wedding gown cost more than an automobile.

Ida actually had nothing to do with the talk in town, she was completely innocent. In fact, she made no decisions regarding her wedding except the selection of the groom. The choice of dress, its style, and the New York City designer, responsible for its creation, were brought about by the tireless efforts of her mother, Eula Mae Wilcox.

Ida simply ignored the stares of the locals and continued planning what she prayed would be a small wedding. If truth be told, she did not want a large ceremony. All she wanted was to start her life as Mrs. Timetheous 'Timmy' Tilley. The scheduled pomp and circumstance was all a façade. All a part of a fantasy Ida never thought of or imagined. All a part of Eula Mae's lost childhood dreams.

Ida leaned over and grabbed a rhinestone-covered satin shoe from the shoebox. They had arrived by mail from the JCPenney Catalog. In fact, every item from the gown to the veil had arrived by special delivery. Eula Mae's careful attention to detail ensured that each piece perfectly matched the other so that anyone looking at Ida would immediately recognize that she was wearing only the finest.

There was no love lost between Eula Mae and the residents of Jasper County. Her relentless efforts to have the final word in everything she did made Ida the target of many wars, divisions, and schemes. The lastest involved the hiring a designer whose dresses graced the pages of *Harper's Bazaar* magazine.

There was just one significant factor that she overlooked: This was 1966 in Jasper County South Carolina and no one talked about fashion designers or cared who made a wedding gown. It was believed that wedding dresses were supposed to be plain and simple cotton garments, without much detail, nothing to brag about. They were not a subject of conversation and little significance to poor Negros living in the Low Country. No one even thought to mention the price of a gown because that was considered tacky conversation.

Despite her mother's constant theatrics, Ida adored her. She was a strong woman, and compared to the other seemingly docile women living around them, Eula Mae had guts. She stood up to whites, challenged racial unfairness, and proved she could handle the meanest of people in her path. That also made her ostracized from many family gatherings and local events, because of a belief that a woman who refused to submit to a man was more dangerous than the Ku Klux Klan. Besides, a mouthy woman, it was said, was a loose cannon and a threat to the cherished traditions of the Old South.

Eula Mae never conformed to the unofficial rules society placed on women of her generation. In fact, she spoke against them and fought to change ones that impacted her own life as well as every woman around her. This is the type of a woman Ida dreamed she could become and, for that very reason, she chose to wait until she had Eula Mae's nod of approval before getting married.

For many years, marriage, in the Wilcox household, was a taboo subject. In fact, Eula Mae warned Ida that marriage was an unnecessary noose around a woman's neck. It was simply something any smart woman would avoid at all possible costs, until she wanted to have children, that is. Eula Mae told her daughter to concentrate on developing ways to maintain her independence as a free woman, because, according to her, no woman should ever allow herself to be totally dependent upon a man.

1964

By the time Ida reached young adulthood, her mother had already made plans for her to go north and live with relatives in New Jersey. She would attend college so that her only option of employment was not working as a maid for a white family. Upon graduation, she could choose to do whatever she wanted, yet until then, Eula Mae was in charge. What she said was the law and Ida had learned, under her roof, never to break the rules.

On June 23, just days after her high school graduation, Ida Mae Wilcox, begrudgingly boarded a Trailways bus aimed toward a land of the unknown. Newark, New Jersey was as opposite of the South as ice was to fire.

After a few months, Ida found the big city too fast paced, always having something going on, a new thing to see, or something new to experience. There was no time for rest. No time for slow days; city folks behaved as if they were always in a rush to get somewhere, to see something. Ida found herself unhappy with the prospect of living in such a place for three long years. Jasper County was calling her home and its calls became louder each day. So in the summer of 1965, three months shy of her nineteenth birthday, Ida

Mae Wilcox boarded a bus and headed back to a place she knew her mother was not welcomed.

She loathed deception, but she felt there was no other choice. If she wanted to court Timmy Tilley, she would have to do it out of Eula Mae's sight. In the five years they had secretly been seeing each other, they only spent three days together alone and their one official date under her parent's roof almost never happen.

"What kinda name is that?" Eula Mae yelled toward the back bedroom where Ida was getting dressed.

"His people's!" she shouted.

"Now don't you raise your voice at me...you won't be going anywhere but into that back room to get me a strap!"

Ida was seventeen. She barely looked at the opposite sex without feeling as if she had committed a deadly sin. Besides, Eula Mae pumped such negativity into her head, all Ida learned about boys was that they were the scum of the earth...nastier than dogs. Never to be trusted.

"You lie down with dogs, you get up with fleas," Eula Mae warned.

"I didn't say we was getting married."

"What does that got to do with nothing?" Eula Mae screamed. "Men are dogs...lower than dogs, if ya asks me, and all they think about is getting between some young fool gal like you legs."

"I ain't trying tuh make no baby, Mama. All ah want's is tuh git tuh know 'im widout you makin' me feels as if ah'm doing somethang wrong."

"Chile, don't sass me! You best not be thinking any wrong thoughts or I will find out. All these little grown gals running around these woods with their bellies sticking out. Let me catch you lying down with one of these dogs and you sho' 'nough gon' die."

Ida memorized her mother's words as if her continued existence on this earth depended on them. She vowed never to become a Low Country statistic, at least not while Eula Mae Wilcox was still alive.

THREE

1956

Unlike most families living in the Low Country, the Wilcox family were never regular church goers. In fact, they rarely stepped foot in a church unless it was to celebrate a marriage, or to mourn the loss of a loved one.

There were no Bibles throughout their home as was expected and no pictures of a white Jesus hanging on the wall. Instead, the Wilcox home showcased few mementos of what was important to them. That left young Ida Mae in a world of make believe with one doll she played with for far too long, and a worn out book, *Little House on the Prairie,* that she read until she'd memorized the entire story.

That summer, her father purchased a record player. It was then that she heard a style of music called rhythm and blues. It was a popular genre often played during the week or in the local juke joints. However, families in Low Country South Carolina shunned secular music on Sundays, a day believed to be reserved by God as a time to purify man's soul and send messages of deliverance throughout the land. Everyone adhered to this unofficial rule, except the Wilcox family.

Ida fell in love with doo wop groups like The Platters, The Coasters, and her all time favorite, Frankie Lymon and the Teenagers, who belted out harmonious notes right into their living room. She and her brother, Frank, often fell asleep on the floor as they listened to the heartfelt and fast paced music that dominated the sounds in their home.

Listening to music became a normal routine for the Wilcox family. On the weekends, after she got dressed, ate breakfast, and cleaned the kitchen, Ida waited in anticipation for the first musical note played on the phonograph. That was her cue that children were permitted in the living room. It was also a signal that, at least while the music played, she could relax, knowing that her parents, who argued almost every night, had miraculously reached a truce.

Ida noticed the impact music had on all of them. She watched how her father used it to change her mother's often sullen moods. After work, Herman Wilcox strolled into the front door, and, upon seeing a dreadful look on Eula Mae's face, walked over and pulled out a vinyl album from its protected cover, placed it on the record player, and then put the needle exactly where he wanted the music to begin. It worked like a charm. Within minutes, it seemed Eula Mae had forgotten what had her so riled up, instead focusing on the blissful sounds that permeated the atmosphere.

In her innocence, Ida believed music could solve all of life's problems. The sound of music, at least in the Wilcox home, signified good times. It became the backdrop to the magic in her dreams. Over time, she would discover its limitations, and learn that there were some walls not even a good song could penetrate.

As if growing up was not complicated enough, life in the Wilcox home, like everywhere else in the early fifties, was especially hard for blacks, exacerbated by other problems that Ida would only understand once she became an adult.

1959

Everyone called him "Li'l Boy."

He had been honorably discharged from the Navy, but found it hard to live as a civilian on the outside. When Ida was twelve, he came to live with her family. It was evident that he was different from most people in town, evident that something troubled him deeply. When Ida asked what it was, Eula Mae simply warned her to keep an eye on him and never play alone in his room.

She normally obeyed her mother, but Ida ignored the warnings about Li'l Boy. To an innocent child, he seemed harmless, and unlike everyone else in the house, he made Ida the center of his attention, often waiting on her hand and foot just to keep her happy. Of course, the attention he gave helped to fill the void Ida felt was lacking in she and her mother's relationship.

Li'l Boy refuted much of what Eula Mae told Ida about life. For one, he said marriage was a good thing. According to him, everyone should try it at least once. There was nothing that prevented a woman from having her independence and being married too. The two did not contradict the other, as Eula Mae claimed. Happiness, he often said, was something that came from within; it was not something another human being could give to anyone else.

He attended church every Sunday. No matter the distance, Li'l Boy strolled out of the house in a freshly pressed suit, with a Bible in his hand, on his way to whatever church had its doors open that particular Sunday. When he returned, he carried a small brown paper bag filled with sweets.

"Sweets for the sweet," he always exclaimed when he saw her, rattling the bag.

Ida jumped up and down with excitement as he opened the wrought iron gate. She longed to go on that walk with him, but Eula Mae declared all church folks were bad.

"Why Mama won't let us step foot in a church?" she asked him one day.

"Some kind of superstition I suppose."

"What?" Ida stood up and began to rearrange all of the bottles Li'l Boy had on the dresser.

"Crazy myths, that's all." He stood looking out of the window as he held his trumpet. It was the one thing he carried with him everywhere he went.

"Why do people believe them?" she asked.

"Dunno. Some folks need someone to blame and God is the easiest. We can't see him and more often than not, he won't talk back, so we make him the scape goat for all our problems. Easier than blaming ourselves." He turned around and smiled as he watched Ida repositioning the medication that governed whether he would be in a good mood each day.

"But that's not fair. Everyone asks why we don't go to church. They say Mama is evil, straight from the Devil like my grandma was."

"Oh, that's foolishness. Your mama and grandma are not evil! They just seem strange to some folk. That's probably why my brother is so in love with Eula Mae. Her strangeness won't leave him alone!" He chuckled and turned back to stare out the window.

"Li'l Boy, why you always holding that instrument like that? Seems you want to play it, but I never hear a sound." She stopped fiddling with the bottles and walked over to where he stood.

"I can still hear the music, baby. That's what I love most about it. Music continues to play in your mind long after the record is over." His fingers were spread along the trumpet as if he were actually playing it.

"What kind of song do yuh hear? Is it a spiritual?"

When he did not answer immediately, she continued, "Does it make yuh sad? Daddy says you sad sometimes. Is it the music?"

"Oh no, baby." He snapped out of the trance he'd been in earlier. "The music is what keeps me wanting to live after everything I had in life been taken away from me."

"Like what? Who took everythang away from yuh, Li'l Boy?"

"Between the government and the white folks hiding under them sheets, I gots nothing left." He placed the trumpet back in its case and locked it.

"I don't understand. Why they take everything from yuh?"

"Because they said I had too much. Said I always thought I was like them." He began to walk out of the room. "Said I forgot that I was a low down nigger like the rest of y'all." His voice drifted down the hall.

Dexter "Li'l Boy" Wilcox was the illegitimate son of Ida's grandfather. When his mother was killed in an automobile accident, Ida's grandmother took him and his sister into her home and raised them as her own. She never let on about her husband's indiscretions, and none of her children knew the truth until she died.

Dexter enlisted in the Navy while it was still segregated. On a tour in France, he discovered the local jazz clubs and started playing the trumpet. That is how he met and fell in love with a French girl named Hannah. They remained in France for ten years, had three children, before Dexter, believing life in America had changed, decided to return home.

Four years later, the Klan found out.

On a crisp early morning with the skies generating enough fog to restrict anyone's vision for ten miles, Dexter and Hannah were awakened by the sound of their children's screams in the room next to where they slept. Moments later, the wooden door that gave them a small sense of privacy was knocked down, and in shock they looked at ten persons covered with white hoods.

Before Dexter could move to protect his family, one of the men reached into the bed, and yanked Hannah's one hundred pound frame onto the wooden beams beneath the bed. She screamed while three men grabbed her husband, held a two by four to his throat, and threatened to rape her if he moved. In an instant, he pleaded for her life as his voice became strangled.

Fire raged from his children's bedroom and he could hear their frantic cries as Hannah's face was pinned to the floor and Dexter lay bound by a sharp piece of wood and two shotguns pointed directly at his forehead. Eventually, everything went black.

He had no recollection of what the end of his wife's life was like and that absence brought him some consolation. He later discovered that she had died in the fire with his three children, while he was dragged through the house, whipped repeatedly on the front porch, stripped naked, and then hung from a tree.

He had no memory of the many knives that ravaged his torso, but later discovered he was nearly castrated, and a small piece of his left ear had been severed. There were jagged scars on his abdomen where he was repeatedly stabbed, but that was not the source of his pain.

His brothers, who lived on the adjacent lot, ran to their rescue, but they were too late. Unable to stop the Klan, they knelt behind a shed on the side of the house while they watched Dexter, near asphyxiation, cough up handfuls of blood, while his two hundred and twenty-five pound frame rocked from a thick cord that hung from a branch of the oak tree in his back yard. When the crowd dissipated, through tears, they cut his limp and bloody body down. Miraculously, Dexter Wilcox was still alive. Barely.

For three years, his presence changed the way Ida saw the world, leaving an indelible imprint on her mind that would last long after he was gone. It was a gentle way of living that she wanted to experience. A world without chaos, told to her by a man who knew firsthand the meaning of life and love. A side of life, before meeting him, Ida had yet to experience.

His stories freed her mind from the calamity in their home, and introduced Ida to the world he had known as a younger man. A man who fell in love at first sight, married his true love, and fathered three beautiful children. A gentle man who never held his tongue, but learned that silence was the greatest weapon of them all. He shared his triumphs as well as his pain, giving Ida a front row seat into his agony, yet showcasing the good in his life like his many travels, playing in a band, and acquiring a level of wealth few Negros had ever known.

Just shy of her seventeenth birthday, something about Li'l Boy's spirit abruptly changed. He no longer ate dinner with the family, opting to spend hours alone in his room. He became combative, often arguing with Eula Mae over insignificant things. His demeanor even changed toward Ida. Each time she knocked on his door, he was slow to answer, and if he did, he seemed preoccupied.

Gone was the fatherly advice he provided on every subject from how to survive in a racist world, to how to become a decent and respectful Negro woman in the Low Country. He even walked around without his trumpet, and eventually, a surprise to the entire house, Li'l Boy stopped leaving the house all together, even to go to church.

On the September morning she turned seventeen, Ida discovered a handmade box placed on the floor outside her bedroom door. She opened it and saw a beautiful fourteen carat gold locket. Inside was a picture of two people whom she did not recognize. She held the locket tightly in her hand and ran to Li'l Boy's room, but he was gone. Gone without a trace.

1962

There were other troubles that distracted Ida during her high school years. For one, her parents parted ways, as it was called in the South during that time. There was no mention of a pending divorce, and since her father came around just about every week, Ida thought it was a temporary situation. She was wrong.

"Can I go to the sock hop?" she asked Eula Mae, who was seated in a rocking chair next to the fireplace with a blanket covering her legs.

"Ask yo' daddy." She barely noticed Ida who stood before her holding a new dress.

"When?" Ida questioned.

"He's heah every weekend, Ida Mae."

"Is he ever coming back home?"

"That ain't none o' yuh business! Leave it be. He come around every week on Friday like he 'spose to and drop off the money. That's all he good for, and that's all I want," she shouted.

"Then can I wear this dress?" Ida said, changing the subject.

"Why yuh going tuh a sockhop? Yuh think that boy you got your eyes on gon' be there?" Eula Mae looked suspiciously at Ida through her black framed reading glasses.

Ida was too embarrassed to look her straight in her face. "I ain't got my eyes on no boy."

"Ah, hush yuh mouth telling lies! Yuh do so. I see yuh staring at that boy that work down at the docks in the back o' Piggly Wiggly. I seent ya grinning like a Cheshire cat!" Eula Mae laughed and rocked back and forth. "G'wan now, tell the truth and shame the Devil." She looked closer at Ida. "Where did yuh get that dress?"

"Daddy."

"Oh, Lawd, that devil's at it again. He tryin' ta buy your side against me."

"Un un. He always buying me thangs, even when he was living heah," Ida responded.

"You thank so? That man's the Devil hisself. Everythang he give, got a price tag around it. You just watch and see," Eula Mae cautioned.

"Well, speaking of the Devil, Daddy said he was gon' come and take me tuh church." Ida walked away, toward the kitchen in the back of the house, deciding she'd pushed her luck hard enough with her mama.

Eula Mae started again,"Lord knows he needs prayer. He going tuh da right place. Only hypocrites goes tuh these country churches. Which one y'all going tuh?"

"Second AB," Ida hollered back, pouring herself a glass of cherry Kool-Aid.

"Oh, Lord, you'll see. Them church folks too much fo' me. They'll grin in yuh face and cut yuh' throat at da same time. Never had much use for 'em myself."

"Did you get married in a church, Mama?" Ida inquired carefully, looking out of the kitchen window. She did not want Eula Mae to go off again about her father.

"No. Went down to the courthouse. Church folk would not let us marry in one of their buildings because I was already 'specting. That's how much they love everyone. One mistake and I was out in the street. Didn't matter that I had spent my entire life in the church, singing and being a part of Sunday school, no sir! To them I was a sinner. Since then I swore I would never step foot in a church again." She stood and walked toward Ida at the kitchen sink.

"Don't even think about having my funeral at one of them churches; just take me down tuh da Coosawhatchie River, roast a hog, and get drunk!"

"Why you talking about dying, Mama?" Ida stared at her mother, horrified.

"I'm not, Ida Mae. I'm talking about the likes of church folk. I can't stand 'em and I don't want nothing tuh do with the whole lot of 'em, alive or dead." Eula Mae turned and looked out of the window.

Ida grabbed a chair from the table, sat down, and studied her mother carefully. Eula Mae still had a girlish figure. She was indeed a beautiful Coppertone-skinned woman, with a unique feature rarely seen on Negros. Folks said that characteristic proved she was pure evil. They said it was an awful generational curse; Ida had become all too familiar with the stories of its origin.

It was bad luck to cross the path of a black cat, especially for a woman expecting a child. Seemed at nine months, Eula Mae's mother did just that. The extra weight, bloating, and swelling caused her not to see the striped black and white feline in the distance.

That night, at the stroke of midnight, Eula Mae Jamison entered into the world. Delivered by a midwife, she ignored the numerous slaps on her naked behind and refused to cry. When her tiny eyes finally opened, the midwife fainted and dropped her small body onto the bloody sheets.

After hearing the infant's grandmother wailing in shock, the midwife regained her composure, retrieved the baby girl, and slowly turned toward her distraught mother to watch her reaction. Eula Mae's mother fainted and her grandmother screamed, "Great God in Heaven. The Devil done cursed my grand! God help us all."

FOUR

1957

There were originally three Wilcox children: Anne, Frank, and Ida. Anne was killed three years after she moved to Harlem with a boyfriend. Eula Mae said he sold illegal things like marijuana and probably hashish and heroine. All Ida could remember were stories that Anne was pushed from a high rise building on Christmas Eve. Her body was discovered in an alley of the building she supposedly lived in. They never heard from the boyfriend again. Eula Mae said he was probably running from the law. Ida wondered if he was the one who'd pushed Anne out of the window.

Although she was still just a young girl, Ida never forgot the rumors that Anne was a prostitute. Folks said the boyfriend was really her pimp. They swore he killed Anne, despite what the police told her parents. According to them, Anne was dead before that Trailways bus left the depot. The rest was only a matter of time.

Ida thought of Anne as she watched her mother one day. Anne, at nineteen, had been a lot heavier than Eula Mae was at forty. Anne was full figured, and resembled women like Jane Russell in the Playtex commercials for large-busted women. Though both were petite in stature, standing no more than five feet tall, Anne, a chestnut brown complexion, looked much older than her mother, Eula Mae.

1936

Coveted since the day she was born, Anne and her father were always inseparable. Eula Mae suspected this and later discovered that still waters ran deep. Herman allowed Anne to have anything she wanted, and if Eula Mae refused to give her something, he snuck behind her back, and gave it to Anne in secret.

"She straight from heaven," he cried the moment she was born.

Eula Mae did not say a word. Instead, she focused on the careful way he held the infant's head with his hand. She watched how he was completely smitten, never stopping to look up even as the baby slept in the bassinet hours later.

"She sleep now, Herm. She'll be okay." Herman just stood there, staring into the face of his newborn angel.

"I know. I just don't want her to be alone," he said as he rocked the cradle gently back and forth.

"She sleep!" she screamed. "That's what babies do! She going tuh do a lot o' that so yuh better get used tuh it. You gon' wear huh out! She just got heah."

"I know, Mae. That's why I'm so concerned. She's so tiny. So precious. Straight from God Almighty into our arms!" he beamed. "What a God, what a God!"

"All right, Herm. That's enough and yuh know it! Not good tuh speak about a newborn like that."

"What do you mean 'like that'? Mae, she's our first born. That's a big deal and you know it! My daddy missed every one of our births. I promised myself I would be there. Most men don't care to see y'all women bring life into the world, but I think it's completely beautiful. Divine, I tell you, simply divine."

"You take things so seriously." She turned to face the opposite direction. "I needs my rest, too. So please find something tuh do fo' a while. We both needs rest right now. Go on wit'cha."

Herman stood there for another half an hour before he finally gave in and walked out of the room. He went into the adjoining room and looked around. The midwife was on the back porch cleaning out the basin used in the delivery. Herman stood in the door watching.

"You need some help?" he asked.

"Nawsuh. Ah finished now. Best be on mah way home if yuh can manage. She sho' lucky tuh have you by huh side. Never seen no man stand next tuh his wife and hold her hand during da actual birth. Most men long gone by then. Dey act like dey afraid tuh see a woman give life. It's natural, but dey don't think so." She carried on as Herman peered out into the back yard.

"It's the most natural thing I ever did see," he said.

"Well, I see it all da time and I tell yuh, dis God's handiwork! I am so glad just tuh be a witness tuh all these great moments. Now, I seen a few not make it into dis world and it's a strange feeling, yet a peaceful one. I can't describe it. One day when I have chirren, I'll know what da woman on the other side of my hands felt like."

"No kids yet?" He turned to face her, surprised.

"None. Always wanted chirren. Been a midwife since I was fifteen years old. John, my husband, say dis my purpose, but I disagree. I think it was a part o' what God called me tuh do, but I don't thank God mean enough tuh force me tuh witness half of da process widout ever getting tuh witness da other half."

"I agree. I want more children, yes I do. But if the good Lord only see fit to give us this beautiful child, it will be enough. It's just the way I love little ones that I believe he will give me more. He's going to give me and you the desires of our hearts, I tell ya," Herman said as he sat down in an old cane chair on the back porch.

"I keep believing it. I just hope every mother dat God bless me tuh help deliver dere child, send some prayers up fo' me. Be twenty-three next birthday. I be too old in a few years." She opened the screen door and walked down the steps into the back yard carrying the basin in her arms. Herman was resting on the porch by then, his eyes closed.

1948

At twelve years old, Anne stopped taking orders from her mother. She said she did not have to do anything unless her father approved. When Eula Mae mentioned the girl's demands to Herman, he just laughed and said it was nonsense; Anne just made it up to make her mad. For some reason, she did not believe him.

One day they stood together cooking on the Potbelly stove in the kitchen while the children played out on the front porch.

"You settin' her up!" Eula Mae accused, looking over at her husband.

"What do you mean, Mae? How am I setting up my oldest daughter, my first born?" he questioned.

"Oh, you know how! Don't play stupid, man! You give huh everythang! You let her do everythang! That child barely has manners. Whole town say she grown and sassy. I don't like it. Something bad gone happen tuh her wid all that mouth."

"Well, then the fruit didn't fall far from the tree," he countered.

"How the hell would you know?" she shouted.

"Don't go there, Mae! That's my daughter. I been here the entire time. Talked to her in your womb. I know that little girl. She just like you and me. She smart, street smart. Nothing is going to happen to her. You stop putting bad blood into the atmosphere!" he warned.

"Bad blood! You really crazy! Tell me this: Why yuh so involved in Anne's life, but barely take time fo' yuh son?"

"When can I get to him? You always in his face! You spoon feed *him* everything. What to think, what to say. I can't get a word in edgewise." He opened the pot to check the stew brewing inside.

"Ha! Yuh always got an excuse. Yuh gone pay for what yuh did tuh Anne. Got that girl so spoiled she can't wait on nothing and nobody! Stuff don't come when she wants it, she pitches a fit and destroys something. Yuh know that ain't right!" Eula Mae said.

"What's wrong with taking good care of my own?"

"Nothing! Yuh doing more than taking care o' yuh own though! Whatcha gone say when Anne grow up and 'spect everybody tuh treat huh like you do? She gon' 'spect everybody to wait on her hand and foot. When that don't happen, she going off, I tell yuh. Completely off!"

The front door swung open and the subject of their conversation walked inside and stood in front of them watching her parents' discourse.

1953

At seventeen, Anne Devereux Wilcox went to work on Hilton Head Island with her father. They both worked on an estate until it's owner, Mr. Lance Billingsley, became ill and later passed away. Anne then went to work for a new motel on the island, snagging a job that most negros could never get: working in an office handling billing receipts. Although the motel owners made sure she kept a low profile by limiting her comings and goings to the back door, her hire caused quite a stir on the island. It incinuated that times were changing.

Anne was quite popular on the marine base of Parris Island as well. Every weekend she had a date, and by that following Monday, she paraded around town wearing a piece of fine jewelry or a new dress. She swore they were friendship gifts, but rumors suggested they were payments for something more than a platonic relationship.

Then Eula Mae found out.

She was furious. She warned Anne that partying with the male persuasion all the time would result in a bad reputation she could not shake off. Reputations, according to Eula Mae, were all a woman had to hold onto. It was their proof of decency. It was how a woman commanded respect from a man. Anne simply ignored her.

A few months later, Anne showed up driving a fancy Studabaker, picked up friends in Hardeeville, and headed into Ridgeland. She was on her way out of town when she spotted Eula Mae walking along the sidewalk. Anne slowed the car alongside where her mother walked. Eula Mae, in dark shades, raised her arm, lowered the shades, and peered directly into Anne's face. Nothing was ever said. Moments later, the car spun off.

Eula Mae marched into the house and told Herman.

"What? That must be the car Billingsley left me." He shook his head.

"If he left the car to you, what is Anne doing in it? Why am I walking to fetch groceries and my no good for nothing daughter driving such a fine car?" she yelled.

"Mae, that car has been in the shop so long I thought Junior and them was using it for parts! Anne must have picked it up some way."

"With what license? That fool child parading around town wid no license. It will take all of five minutes tuh get stopped by one of these redneck cops and put in jail."

"You right there, Mae. I don't know what's gotten into Anne. I told her when I taught her..."

"Say what? You taught her to drive?" She ran toward him, hands raised to the heavens. "Herman, have you lost your mind? When did you find the time to teach Anne to drive since y'all suppose to be out there working?"

"There were times when we went on errands for Mr. Billingsley. Other times nothing to do, so I taught Anne how to drive in the driveway and 'round the back of the house. No big deal! She got to learn one way or t'other," he responded defensively.

"Why? When she gonna afford a car? You planning on giving her that one?"

"I thought about it. Look, the car was half done with by the time I got it. I didn't know Junior would be able to fix the darn thang! Never gave it much thought. Anne begged me for it and I said yeah. It was beat up and half running."

"Herman, I did not see Anne driving a beat up car today. You sure we talking about the same car? Anne was parading around town in a beautiful powder blue Studabaker. It look brand new to me."

"No way. I don't know anything about a new car!" He took his glasses off and wiped his brow. "Where would Anne get such a thing? Definitely not from me and you know it. No sir, not from me!"

"Then who? How come yuh never know what Anne up to?" Eula Mae walked up to Herman and spoke right in his face.

"Maybe because Anne is grown, Mae." He raised his voice. "She is a grown woman."

"A grown woman that lives under this roof. That puts no food on our table. That barely cleans her hindparts heah, let alone, any part of this house. Yep, that's a grown woman. All that running around! If she slowed down she could get a husband and move outa heah."

"You're the one who told her to be independent! According to you, no woman should get hitched less she knocked up."

"Or buck wild!"she interjected. "Anne just need something to slow huh fast butt down."

"Watch yourself, Eula Mae! A husband won't slow Anne down anymore than all that fussing you do around here. She has a mind of her own; she'll find her way in life, just give it some time," he pleaded.

"How much time, Herman? She almost twenty years old! She don't have a pot to piss in or a bucket to throw it out of. Yeah, she took care of Frank so I could care for Ida, that's all. After he got of age, she forgot her responsibilities around the house and flew the coop. She ain't good for nothin', but partying and laying up wid them soldiers on Parris Island. All that sleeping around ain't got her nothing but a bad reputation. I told her. Now she can't give huhself away!"

"Having a man isn't everything, Mae."

"Don't I know. Most men ain't worth nothing much anyway! I perfer huh tuh have a piece of man than no man at all. Serves her right. You got yourself to thank for that too."

"I knew it! I was waiting until you blamed me for everything that is wrong in Anne's life." Herman walked past Mae, opened the screen door, and walked out onto the front porch.

Ida sat in her bedroom listening to her parents' argument. She had grown accustomed to the weekly shouting matches between her father, mother, and sister. She could not recall a time when Frank was involved. That left young Ida as the sole spectator to what was clearly the best of a dysfunctional family.

FIVE

1954

They never had the type of relationship that most sisters share. Ida was just a young girl when Anne entered into adulthood. It was probably the age gap. Yet, Ida adored everything about her older sister. Anne, strikingly beautiful, stood more than five-feet-nine and walked with the grace of a ballerina. She loved high-heeled shoes and they added stature to her already voluptuous legs that were often on view just enough to capture the attention of both men and women.

The few times Anne permitted Ida to tag along with her in public, it was evident that the whole town was enraptured by Anne's elegance and style. Always wearing a pencil thin tightly fitted skirt, she glided along as if she walked on air. Wherever she went, there were numerous admirers of the male persuasion who pardoned themselves just to give her a compliment or to ask her out on a date.

Anne never allowed those interruptions to cause her to ignore Ida. In fact, she introduced Ida to each and every person they met while in town. Years later, long after Anne was gone, folks started calling Ida "Li'l Anne," never bothering to ask her name. Ida loved to be identified with one of the most beautiful women to ever grace the streets of Jasper County. It was, for such a young girl, a dream come true.

"Hey, Li'l Anne," someone shouted from behind her.

Ida turned around and a very tall man, the color of her favorite caramel candy, with the most beautiful, deep set, light brown eyes stood in front of her. He was over over six-feet tall and had the biggest hands Ida had seen in her young years.

She tried to remain calm. He obviously sensed her fear.

"Oh, baby, don't be afraid now. I ain't gone harm ya," he said gently, as he looked around. "Where your sistah?"

"Why you wanna know?" Ida asked, using the rude manner Anne had taught her to do when addressing strangers.

"Just thought I'd ask." He smiled and fixed his eyes on hers.

"Then ask huh. She live in her skin. She know where she at at all times," Ida replied smartly, laughing.

"You a funny li'l gal, just like your older sistah," he said.

"Excuse you!" It was Anne. She walked out of the Five and Dime to join Ida and the good looking stranger on the sidewalk.

"My, Miss Anne." He turned away from Ida when he heard Anne's voice, preferring the original to the weaker carbon copy. "Didn't mean no disrespect. Just thought I would ask ya younger self where you were."

"In my skin! Why ya asking?" She looked him up and down and then looked about the sidewalk in both directions.

"Just curious," he said. "Like you curious about what I drove heah in."

"Just curious, ha. Well, you take your curiosity and go on about yuh business! You know you ain't got no right questioning chirren out heah in the broad daylight for no reason."

"No reason. Why Miss Anne, I thought we were better friends than that." He reached up and tipped his hat to her.

"The jury is still out on you, Mr. Marcus. Still out. You seem to always show up in the strangest places, and every-time you do, you run into me. Now is that what they call a coincidence, or are you following me?" She handed Ida a bright red Charms lollipop, her favorite.

"I don't follow no women. I told you I was a married man. Folks know I look out fo' my sistahs in Jasper County. Too much happening around heah to y'all."

"And you gon' do what?" Anne started laughing. "My mamma told me the bigger they are, the harder they fall. So what you gon' do if I need help? Choke the daylights out of someone?" She laughed even harder.

"My hands are lethal weapons, Missy. I may have even broken some laws with 'em. Couldn't say I won't provoked." He looked at the two of them, smiling as he watched Ida enjoying her lollipop.

"So we know never to get on yuh bad side, right?" Anne whispered.

"Miss Anne, let's settle something right heah. I already told you I know yuh mamma and yuh daddy. They good people. Real good people. They know me too. Know my reputation. They know if I'm around, yuh ain't got nothin' tuh worry about. Safe and sound," he winked.

"Safe from what?" she interupted. "Why you always around talking about my safety? You think something bad gonna happen to me? Then you know something I don't."

"Can't say that I do. I just know you the daughter of a man I respects and you out and about alone sometimes, so I wanna keep an eye on yuh." He turned and winked at Ida.

"I just wanna know who paying you to be my bodyguard? Now my mamma crazy, but I don't thank it's huh. I thank this got somethang to do with my sweet daddy. That's why he never worry about me." Anne closed the distance between them and boldly peered into his eyes.

"Tell me, Mr. Marcus, is my daddy paying you to keep watch of me?"

Ida thought the entire exchange was odd. Here was an older man who claimed he was just looking out for Anne, no strings attached. Ida wondered was he looking out for her too? She wondered if Anne was right about Herman paying someone to watch over her. It even made since to a young girl. They had a caring father, one that would go to the ends of the earth to protect his daughters.

1955

"Where Mr. Marcus know you from?" They were standing in the backyard of their home.

"What ya talking 'bout, Ida Mae?" Anne stared at the oak tree in front of her.

"I jus' thought of him is all. He was so big! Big like this heah old tree. He had the biggest hands I ever saw!" Her young voice was filled with awe.

"You so funny. You always know how to take my mind off of thangs." Anne turned toward Ida and tugged at her dress. "Why Mama won't let you grow up? She gotcha in these short dresses like you a five-year-old. Yuh starting womanhood soon and she still won't let go. That woman need somebody to boss around all time a day."

"You and Mama like fire and ice." Ida looked away and laughed.

"Fire and ice! What you know about fire and ice? See, ya told on yo' self. That ya mama talking like that. She always got some saying that don't make no sense. She talk like she old as dirt!" Anne walked over to a tree stump and sat down. It was Ida's favorite place on Earth, but like everything else, Anne took it for her own when she chose.

"She is old as dirt!" Ida exclaimed, laughing.

"She need to let go." Anne pulled at her long black hair. "My hair is falling out messing up with Mama. She make me nervous all the time. Like she got witch's eyes in the back of huh head."

"I wish you two got along. I would love tuh go downtown with both of you on my arms. We could sing and skip and laugh." Ida walked over and sat next to Anne. "Y'all ever got along?"

"A million years ago we did. I idolized that woman. She strong, smart, and can do anythang a man can do." Anne looked down, grabbed a stick, and began to doodle on the ground.

Then she continued. "I don't know why she hate men so much. Don't know why she so bitter. She won't have a good time. I tried to get her to go out on a date with Daddy and she act like it was a sin. A sin! Can you believe that? This woman has three kids with this man, and she act like she can't even touch him. You ever seen them kiss?"

"Nasty!" Ida yelled.

"Oh, hush ya foolishness, Ida. It's okay to kiss someone you love. Let him hold you. It's okay for a woman to like a man. Even okay if she love him and she let him know. Sometimes he love yuh back, and sometimes he don't." Anne stared at the ground.

"You in love, Anne?" Ida put her hand on top of Anne's.

"Why you ask that? Oh no!" she yelled. "You don't thank I meant I was in love with old man Marcus?" She threw the stick and put her hands up in the air. "That ole man too big for me! I wonder what his wife looks like! No way, man. Mr. Marcus just a guardian angel. He help me out a couple of times when I didn't know who to turn to. I used tuh talk tuh Daddy. Tell him everythang, but that changed. Seems he think he owe Mama some sense of loyalty so he tell huh everythang I say. Say he keep it a secret, but that man can't keep his mouth shut, yuh hear me? Yuh tell him anythang, and he gone tell Mama," she warned Ida.

"I ain't got no secrets." Ida put her head on Anne's shoulder.

"Not yet. Yuh will one day. Like me, yuh gonna have many secrets. Just don't tell Daddy, whatever yuh do. Don't tell that precious man."

Those were the days. Years later, that was all Ida would say. She felt good all over when Anne was around. Seemed Anne had a way with folks. Those that knew her used to say she had a calm spirit. Just the opposite of what they said about Eula Mae. Ida never saw them call a truce. By the time one seemed close, everything came to an abrupt end.

1955

"What ya' doing, crazy gal?" Herman Wilcox stared into the barrel of the gun.

"Whatcha think, fool!" Eula Mae shot back.

"Hold on, Mae. Don't even think about putting a hand on Anne. She just rebelling and trying to sow her wild oats," he said.

"Yeah! That's what I'm afraid of. She sowing her oats with every Tom, Dick, and Harry in town," she screamed.

"You can't believe everythang you hear, Mae. Folks just talking, that's all. They just talking. Don't pay them no never mind."

"Well, there's some truth tuh every rumor. What's wrong wid you? Yuh own flesh and blood out all time a night and yuh ain't once tried tuh find huh and bring huh home!" She placed the gun on the couch beside her, close enough, that if her husband tried to take it away, she had a better chance of keeping it.

"Mae, leave it be. It's in God's hands," he said. "I trust God will send our baby home."

"There yuh go again...then tell me why God ain't keep huh in the house in the first place? Why didn't God make huh do what her mama and daddy tell huh to do?" Eula Mae shouted.

"Woman, lower ya' voice, I say. That child in there sleep and you're yelling like that." He stood in the front door and flipped the switch to turn on the front porch lights.

"I ain't care. I want huh tuh hear me just in case she grow up and try the fool thangs Anne try."

"So what you gon' do? You're sitting heah with a shotgun, yellin', acting like you yourself gone harm Anne." He turned around to face his wife.

"Just might. I'm gon' harm her, and whosoever she bring home tonight. Put an end to my misery and hers too."

"Woman, just calm down and let me handle it. I'll talk to Anne and we can come to an agreement about her curfew and the proper behavior of a young lady."

"You a day late and a dollar short, old man! What can yuh say now? It's a little late for that kinda talk. Anne done lost her mind. She ain't paying you no attention. What time did yuh tell huh to come in tonight?" Eula Mae asked.

"I said to come in at a decent hour."

"Which is what? Midnight..one..three...four in the mouning?"

"Anne knew what time I meant." Herman walked past Eula Mae who was still seated on the couch and sat in the worn out chair closest to the narrow hallway leading to two large bedrooms.

"Uh huh. Yeah, Herman, that's why she out close tuh sunrise. She really knew what yuh meant." She stood up, grabbed the gun, and went out into the blackness.

Ida Mae got out of bed and crawled over to the window. She tried to remain still and quiet. Even with both hands over her ears, she could hear them, her father trying to persuade her mother to release the gun and go back inside the house and, her mother refusing, claiming she would handle the matter her own way.

As they continued to argue, Ida heard the tires of a car as they crunched over the driveway gravel. She lifted her head to look out of the window and saw a big long automobile. She sensed trouble but, before she could catch her breath, she heard the car door slam. Just then she caught a glimpse of Anne as she exited from the passenger side, then walked around to the driver's side. Then she leaned into the front window.

A single gunshot split the quiet night air, then more yelling.

"Give me the gun!" Herman yelled.

"No! Get out of my way, yuh fool," Eula Mae shouted, then . . .

"Anne, who yuh out dere wid? Yuh crazy? Yuh think yuh can come in all times a night and just drive up and do yuh business heah in our yard?"

"Mama, are you crazy? Put that gun away! I'm grown, or have you forgotten?" Anne stood defiantly, hands on her hips, in front of the vehicle.

"Grown! Yuh ain't grown. Not while living under my roof! Yuh ain't got the sense God gave yuh!" Eula Mae shouted, waving the gun in the air.

"Mama, please!" Anne yelled. "Daddy make her go back in the house fo' she kill somebody!"

Ida knelt at the window and watched all the commotion. She did not have a clear view of her parents, but she heard everything that transpired. Just then the driver of the automobile stepped out of the car.

Eula Mae and Herman wrestled over the gun. Ida watched as they stumbled down the front porch steps, Eula Mae holding onto one part of the gun, and Herman holding the other. By this time, Anne had moved closer to them.

A second shot rang into the air. Ida screamed at the top of her lungs, then clapped her hands over her mouth. She hoped no one had heard her; the last thing she wanted was to become part of this scene.

"God in heaven! Mama, you done lost yuh fool mind! Let go of that gun and stop shooting all over the place like some wild fool," Anne pleaded.

"Turn me aloose!" Eula Mae screamed at her husband.

" Anne, yuh betta git away from me! Get off my property! Yuh wanna be grown! Then go in the house and pack yuh bags!"

Anne ignored her and walked over to where her father stood. "Can't yuh do somethang? She is out of control!"

"Mind your mother, Anne." He turned and looked at Eula Mae. "Your mother did not mean you have to leave. She just upset is all."

"Yes, I did too mean it!" Eula Mae interrupted. "When a child o' mine smells her own piss, it's time tuh get outta mah house."

"This my house, Mae! I say who stay or who goes. Anne can stay right here if she do what I say."

"Herman, shut the hell up!" Eula Mae yelled as she stood in front of him still holding tightly to the shotgun.

Their conversation shifted to a lower volume and suddenly Ida could see their lips moving, but could not decipher what was being said. She noticed the stranger as he walked over and stood next to Anne, protectively putting an arm around her waist. She strained to see his face, and when she could not, she looked again at her parents.

Anne raised her arm and pointed her finger at her mother. All of a sudden, Eula Mae swung a punch that landed straight in Anne's face causing her to fall backward onto the stranger. He caught Anne and lifted her body onto the hood of the automobile.

Everything became audible again. Ida felt as though she were watching a movie at the drive-in theater and the sound was going in and out.

"You! How dare yuh step foot on mah property? Yuh ought tuh be ashamed of yourself driving up heah at this time of the mouning with some young girl. Yuh know better!"

"Please, Miz Eula Mae," the stranger pleaded. "Let's all go into the house and talk about this calmly."

"Yuh not welcomed in mah house! Take Anne and git off my property! Take huh tuh yuh wife and kids and try tuh explain what she doing in yuh car this time of mouning! I sees Anne now messing with married men. She sho' picked a winner!" Eula Mae screamed.

"Ms. Eula Mae, I don't mean no disrespect. I drove Anne home tonight because she needed a ride."

"Yeah. Who yuh thank yuh fooling, coming up heah wid Anne in yuh car? I was born at night, but it won't last night." She looked back and forth between the man and her daughter.

Herman now had possession of the gun. He looked at Anne, his wife, and finally the stranger. He never said one word.

Ida felt sorry for Anne. Maybe she was telling the truth. There were of plenty reasons that even young Ida understood as to why a young woman should not walk the roads of Jasper County alone at night. Even Eula Mae, if she'd been in her right mind, knew that.

The commotion died down, and for several minutes, no one uttered a sound. Ida let go of the curtain, and stepped away from the window. Exhausted, she slowly walked over to her bed. Seconds before she could raise her feet to climb inside, gunshots again rang out into the air.

Too frightened to look outside, she jumped against the wall, and covered her face. "Lord, please!" she pleaded softly. "God in heaven, please don't let mah mama get hurt or hurt nobody huhself!"

For a long time, Ida just stood frozen in the dark room, her back against the wall. The outside commotion had suddenly ended. She heard the sound of an automobile engine as it revved up and spun out of the driveway, gravel flying.

Just then the sun cracked the sky, and the lives of the Wilcox family changed forever.

SIX

1962

Franklin Coles Wilcox lived on the other side of the railroad tracks just outside of Gillisonville, a small town on the border of Jasper County. Few negros lived way out there during the fifties, but some migrated there during the later part of the Civil Rights Movement in the sixties. Those who did were advised to live on the left side of the two-lane highway leading into Ridgeland, the former county seat. None dared venture to the right side. No one, with the exception of Frank Wilcox.

Frank lived on the right side of the road and dared anyone to question it. He had lived there for three years before one night a cross was burned in his front yard. A few nights later, that same cross was found in the yard of a well known Klansman with a pitchfork in the front of it. Superstition ran deep in the South and a pitchfork represented Satan, the father of all evil. Needless to say, no one ever messed with Frank Wilcox again. The message had been clear.

Ida often visited her brother during the holidays. He lived in a medium-sized clapboard house that sat a few hundred feet off the main road. A farmer by trade, Frank had a reputation for growing the most beautiful and tasty crops in the Low Country. He sold them on the side of the road, but later was allowed to sell them to just about every merchant along Highway 17. This is how he became known throughout the South. However, Frank Wilcox had another reputation that made him a hero in a time when few negros were celebrated for their courage.

Although she was his sister, Frank treated her like the rest of the ten or more workers he employed on his farm. He was strict, and he tolerated no playing around, negligence, or theft. He paid his workers more than anyone in that area, and even allowed them to grow a small amount of crops for themselves on his farm. Of course, he took a percentage of those crops, but at that time, no one allowed negros to own any portion of what they grew during the planting season.

Folks either loved or hated Frank Wilcox. Many swore he was mean as the Devil himself, while others professed he was sent straight from Heaven. He lectured his workers on the responsibilities of being a negro in the South, and taught many of them survival tactics he said he learned from his own experiences. Whether they liked him or not, everyone respected him, particularly after they witnessed the way white people referred to him as 'sir' or 'Mr. Wilcox.'

He was a mystery to most. Few dared to gossip about anything that pertained to Frank Wilcox, his business, and with the exception of his mother, his sister Ida. No one knew if he was married, had children, or exactly how he rose to such prominence while still a young man. He spoke few words, but boasted an intelligence that made everyone agree he was a wise soul, so much so that his advice became synonymous with the game of *Simon Says*.

"Are you rich?" Ida asked him one day.

"Watch ya' mouth, gal! Ain't nothing wrong with being rich. Though most saints think we s'posed to die broke and get buried in a pine box to go to a glory where we will wear shoes of gold!" he yelled, slapping his hands on his knees.

"What ya' talking 'bout, Frank, Jr.?" she asked.

"You're the only one that calls me Frank, Jr. and you know it, right? Ain't nobody fool enough to call me Junior or boy either, for that matter."

"Not even white people?"

"Specially them."

"I hear the Klan scared of you. What you ever do to them?" Ida stepped down from the porch to where Frank sat shucking corn. She hated finding the big green worms that sometimes hid in the corn tassels.

"Oh, I s'pose I remind them that Lucifer still reigns in the flesh right here in Gillionsonville. White people bold, but they respect the supernatural," he explained.

"They mess with you befo'?"

"Sho' 'nough. They gonna try ya. Only the weak die young though," he replied.

"You ain't 'fraid of getting lynched living out heah by yuhself?" Ida picked up a couple of ears of corn and placed them in her apron.

"Not really. I used to worry. But then I got me some collateral," he said.

"Co-lat-teral? What's that?"

"Insurance. The kind of insurance that white folks respect. Now it ain't much the Klan respect, but you just take something that they value and let them know that you ain't giving it back without a price...yes siree, I guarantee they gon' leave you be."

"What kind of insurance you got?" she asked, enjoying having such a grownup conversation. Her parents never talked to her other than to order her around.

"Grown folks business. When yuh old enough, I'll teach you the ways of the world." He reached over and pulled one of Ida's curly black locks behind her ear.

"I gets scared sometimes. With all the fuss Mama keeps going in town, I gets scared that some fool white man gon' snatch me and take me in these woods and have his way with me," she whispered, casting her big brown eyes toward the ground.

"Not gon' happen. They know you're kin to me. This ain't New York. Anne was foolish to go somewhere where she had no protection, except that fool Willie Hayes she run off with. He ain't got the sense God gave him. How he gon' protect Anne when he couldn't protect himself?"

"You ain't come around much after she died. You still mad at Mama?"

"Naw. I done spoke my peace with Mama." His voice faded as he looked up into the bright blue skies above.

"Ain't much to be said now anyways."

1941-1955

He had not thought of things gone wrong in his life in a long time. He preferred to focus on the here and now and allow old wounds to slowly heal. He would never forget how she left him twice. The first time to run off to New York City, and the second time when she left the Earth all together. He was still mad.

His entire childhood was consumed by his sister Anne. She was the only real mother he had ever known. She cradled him in the crib and for all he knew, it was her breasts that he'd been weaned from. A tight bond had formed from birth, and for eight years he believed she was his real mother.

The smell of her hair reminded him of the green crab apples he plucked off the tree in their back yard. She said it was shampoo, but to young Frank that meant nothing. Her scent represented the delicious fruit that he devoured and that meant she was good.

As a toddler he slept in her bed. They laughed together and played most of the night. She taught him to read, tie his shoe laces, brush his teeth, and even comb his hair. She bathed him daily, put his clothes on, and when he hurt himself, she was the one who nursed his wounds and comforted him. She walked him to school each day. She was the first person he saw when he awoke, and the last person his sleepy eyes focused on at night. His sister Anne.

In the fifth grade, he learned the ugly truth that she was not his mother, but his sister. He had come home with a permission slip to attend a field trip to Savannah and when he handed the paper to Anne, she immediately handed it over to Eula Mae. After listening to him cry for a week, Eula Mae moved him out of Anne's bedroom for good. Enough was enough.

Although he could not remember it clearly, Anne became his caretaker when he was three years old. It was the year Eula Mae suffered two miscarriages and was sick in bed for weeks at a time. It was supposed to be a temporary assignment, but when Ida was born a few years later, it was clear that she had severe respiratory problems, so once again, Anne became responsible for Frank's welfare.

Before he discovered the truth, he was a genteel angelic child who required little or no discipline, but that changed. After learning Eula Mae was his real mother, he began to act out on a daily basis, from temper tantrums to lewd behavior, which he even demonstrated in public. Anne simply ignored him, which made the situation worse, leaving Herman and Eula Mae responsible for disciplining a child with whom they'd never bonded.

Anne used Frank's misguided hatred toward their mother to her advantage. She loved upsetting Eula Mae, and just like Herman had taught her years before, when Frank was not given everything he asked for, she would sneak behind her parents back and give it to him any way just to spite her mother.

A petty thief by the age of ten, Frank stole from many of the local grocers, was often apprehended, and told to inform his parents, which he never did. One day a store-owner escorted Frank to his porch steps and knocked on the front door. To his surprise, Eula Mae answered and that evening, without Anne to plead his case, Herman Wilcox took an extension cord to his behind.

It was the first and the last spanking he ever received. It sent a revelation to him that Anne was not always going to be around to protect him. He would have to protect himself. He stopped going to school regularly, and by the age of fourteen, he had numerous run ins with the police and had become a noted enemy of the Klan. By his fifteenth birthday, he had stolen more cars than he could remember, driven across five state lines, and consumed enough moonshine to cause his liver to shrivel up like a piece of dried fruit.

Herman went to Anne. At first she acted as if she did not care, but eventually she too became alarmed by Frank's actions. She knew she had to get involved. She cornered him and made clear her expectations of him. He would not make the same mistakes she had made. Mistakes, she admitted, she would forever regret.

No one knew how she did it, but Anne succeeded in turning Frank away from a life of destruction and toward a life of promise. Everyone noticed the change and credited Anne for it. Frank's behavior also had a positive impact on the way Anne behaved. In fact, she stopped hanging with the soldiers on Parris Island, opting for clubs in and around Jasper County, closer to home. It surprised everyone. Eighteen months later, she moved to New York. She never told Frank why, but he knew.

He was there.

They could not see him as he squatted behind an oak tree, but he heard everything they said. They were behaving worse than in the past. On that fateful night, Frank Wilcox sat front and center to witness their anger, sensed their hate, and would later learn their shame.

"He's not your father anyway!"

Frank did not move. His eyes were totally focused on Anne. For a while she showed no emotion.

"I know yuh heard me! You might think you just alike, but he ain't no mo' yuh daddy than any of them soldiers you laid down wid." Eula Mae stood over her and spoke angrily, spittle flying from the corners of her mouth.

"You are pure evil, woman! How dare you say something like that?" Anne tried to get up off the ground.

"Because it's the truth! You tryin' tuh destroy this family. Yuh don't care about Herman. If yuh did you wouldn't make 'im look like a bigger fool than he already is. He believed your lies. You his baby girl, he say. He know everything you do. Ha! Those just lies he chose to believe. How he know? He ain't put a bit of seed into your body!" She watched as the look on Anne's face turned from anger to complete horror.

Anne turned over on the ground and pushed herself up. She looked at Herman, but said nothing. Tears cascaded down her face.

"Then if he ain't my daddy, you ain't my mama! Whatever blood between us is bad blood. I purge myself of you! I never want to see you again! I hope you rot in hell!"

Frank gasped for air. He had heard enough, yet he waited to hear what else would be revealed, but that was all. He could see the look of devastation etched across Anne's face. He heard the intensity of hate with each revelation that escaped Eula Mae's mouth, and he felt the enormous sense of powerlessness that brewed deep within Herman Wilcox's spirit.

As he cried softly, he wanted to run from behind the tree and grab Anne. He wanted to console her, but instead, he turned around and walked away from the house he'd grown up in, never again to return.

On that night, Franklin Coles Wilcox vowed he would never trust another living soul. He never saw Anne alive again; never had the chance to tell her how much she meant to him, how much he loved her more than anyone else in the whole world. One year later, he stared at a closed casket, and felt a piece of his soul depart from his body in search of his sister's lifeless spirit.

1962

Ida watched Frank intently. She wanted him to know how much pain his absence had caused the entire family. She wanted him to show some sign of emotion that he cared, but he never said a word. He just sat beside her in a daze, lost in his own pain.

"She your mama, Frank, Jr."

"Unfortunately."

"What do yuh mean 'unfortunately'?" His coldness astonished her.

"We can't pick our parents, can we?" He threw the remaining corn back into the burlap sap he'd taken them out of moments before.

"I don't know much, but I know she favors you over all of us," Ida said, looking Frank directly in the eyes.

"Just bad blood, that's all. Gon' take a lot of time to heal these wounds and Mama and me can accept that. It's more than just forgiving and forgetting 'tween us," he said.

"How much longer will you allow yuh own mama tuh suffer?"

"As long as it takes." Frank put the pot of corn down onto the front porch.

"Yuh never know how much time on Earth a person got left, Frank, Jr."

"Yeah, I could die tonight." He laughed but there was no joy in the sound.

Ida picked up the towel and wiped her neck. She was sweating profusely. Frank had a window unit air conditioner, a luxury few in the Low Country enjoyed. She wanted more than anything to ask him to turn it on, so that she could go inside and relax. Then she remembered Frank paid double for the holidays. Besides, she really needed the money. It was worth it for now to sweat a little. She was used to the heat in the Low Country, but she liked it about as much as she liked the snakes that slithered through the garden.

As the sun descended, out in the distance the silhouette of a man appeared. Ida turned to yell after Frank who had walked into the house. "You 'specting someone this heah evenin'?"

"Only the usual. Don't no one come on my property unannounced. He got this far, he's invited by me sho' 'nough." Frank walked out onto the porch and placed his hand over the top of his eyes to block the glaring rays from the sun.

"Who dat, I wonder? He walking all jolly like he carrying good news."

"Ah, I see 'im. That's my boy. I'm schooling him. See, his peoples got into some trouble with the Klan and I helped them out. Turned out, they didn't need my help. They were all crazy! Klan doesn't mess with them either. That youngin' needed some real tough love. He was cutting school and running around with them Habersham fools. I had to rein him in before it was too late."

Ida stared at the stranger approaching. He did not look familiar to her. He was small in the distance but became larger the closer he came. Much younger than her brother Frank, the guy in front of her wore blue denim overalls and beat up brogan boots. The sleeves to his plaid shirt were rolled up neatly to his enormous biceps. When he was within fifty feet of the front porch, he stopped and took out a handkerchief to wipe his brow. Then he simply stood there on the long dirt road looking toward the house.

"Come on you fool boy, she ain't gone hurt you," Frank yelled to him.

"He scared of me?" Ida said in shock. "I ain't gon' hurt him. Besides, you said he was fool crazy! What I want with 'im?"

"Hush your mouth, young gal. Don't you ever say a word of what I spoke to you about him. That's that boy's personal business. I don't want none of these country bumpkins repeating what I told you or that'll be your tail," he warned Ida, with a stern look on his face.

"Yes, sir."

Ida was embarrassed. She knew too well that Frank wouldn't hesitate to take a belt to her. She looked down at the fresh basket of green peas waiting to be shelled and kept looking down until the young man stood directly in front of her.

"What's happenin', young mullet," Frank teased.

"Nothing. Mama said you wanted me to drop by for supper," the boy said as he smiled and tried to see the face of the young girl that sat next to his mentor.

"She shy. Don't pay her no mind. This my youngest sister..."

But, before Frank could finish the sentence, the young man said, "Ida Mae Wilcox. I know."

SEVEN

1953

There were plenty of rules in the Low Country, all of them unwritten but just as vital as anything in a law book. Rules existed with respect to the color lines in the South although Jim Crow was on his way out, he was dying a slow and painful death. Ida was familiar with the basic rules that her father had taught her, although her mother was the one person she witnessed break each rule more than once.

Rule number one: Never look a white person in the eyes when talking to them.

Rule number two: Cross to the other side of the road when a white person approaches and there is not enough room to pass without stepping into the way of oncoming traffic.

Rule number three: Always address white people by sir, ma'am, mister, or missus. Never call them by their first name.

Rule number four: White people were never to be questioned about their actions, no matter how wrong they appeared, they were always right.

Rule number five: Rules and laws in the South were applied differently towards negros. This too was not to be questioned.

Going into Ridgeland to shop on Saturdays was always an adventure; one that Ida felt she could do without. For one, without an automobile, it was a long walk from where they lived. Second, there was no such thing as local public transportation, which meant whatever one purchased had to be carried home. Often a trip to Ridgeland took the entire day. And finally, there were no public restrooms, which meant negros had to use the bathroom before leaving home, and hold their water until they returned. It was that or the bushes.

Eula Mae and Ida walked down Highway 17, now a lesser driven service road since the new highway, Interstate 95, was being built along the southern seaboard. They walked with a pace that was almost a trot, with Eula Mae constantly telling Ida to walk faster. Within an hour they approached the end of the service road which marked a remaining distance of exactly one mile.

Retail stores were located on both sides of the town square. The oldest grocery store, Piggly Wiggly, sat adjacent to the square in a location that everyone could see. The newest store, IGA, was a few blocks down the street on the other side of the square. The local Five and Dime sat next to Piggly Wiggly, and the local barbers were next door. There were a handful of smaller stores, yet they had a reputation for mistreating negros. In addition to the ill treatment negros received in these stores, they were often cheated out of their money, and consistent with rule number four, they could never dispute white merchants as to any discrepancy.

Larger stores like Montgomery Ward and Sears and Roebuck were in Beaufort, thirty miles away, or Savannah, which required an automobile to get to. Ida's clothing and shoes were either purchased from these stores' catalogs, or from the big discount houses that had recently opened in Walterboro, the next major city in between Ridgeland and Beaufort. Household items like cleansers and linens were generally purchased from the Five and Dime.

It was the largest store in Ridgeland, and it attracted the most people since it had a lunch counter that served easy to prepare foods such as grilled cheese sandwiches, hot dogs, hamburgers, milkshakes, French fries, coffee, sodas, and desserts. This made it Ridgeland's first public hangout other than the two diners that were open until seven p.m. each day. For negros, neither were establishments that welcomed them with open arms. In fact, they were confined to a restricted area in the back of the store.

Eula Mae walked down the street with Ida in tow, looking into the faces of everyone she passed. There were a few hisses and sneers from persons as they passed by. One man even commented, "Watch it, gal," as he walked by. Eula Mae never parted her lips and just kept her head high.

As a family of three approached them, it was clear that there was not enough space on the sidewalk and that, consistent with rule number two, Eula Mae and Ida would have to step down from the sidewalk and cross over to the other side of the street if necessary. However,on this day it was particularly crowded and there were persons strolling down the sidewalk on both sides of the street. Often Ida saw a Negro family step off the curb into the street and await passage by a white family before proceeding. She prayed her mother would do the same.

As the family neared, Eula Mae grabbed Ida by the hand and pulled her body in front of her. Then, walking on the edge of the sidewalk, they proceeded to pass by. The male, obviously the father, stopped dead in his tracks and refused to move, blocking both Ida and Eula Mae. Ida stopped walking and felt her mother's nudge. She looked over her shoulder.

"Go on, chile. Say excuse me and the gentleman will let you pass."

"Excuse me, suh," Ida said quietly. The tall white man behaved as if he did not hear the young girl.

"She says excuse me," Eula Mae voiced a little louder, clutching a black snakeskin pocket book, looking the man directly in his face.

"Well, ah'll be damned. This darkie thanks she gon' walk right past and push us clear off our sidewalk," he said indignantly.

"There is enough space for us to pass if you move behind your wife and kids like I just did," Eula Mae said impatiently.

"For what? Yuh step off the sidewalk entirely like you s'posed to," he warned.

"I don't think so. You see this heah chile, she just as important as yo' chile. She wearing her Sunday best, not her play clothes like your gal. I don't want her to mess up these heah black patent leather shoes I just bought by walking in the grass or stepping out into the road," Eula Mae explained.

"Look, darkie, I don't give a hoot what she wearing. The law says yuh gotta move." He was now yelling, his face beet red.

"What law? Some law I ain't know about? We got a right to walk on the same side of the street with you!"

"You know darn well the laws of the South if yuh lives here, gal." The man balled his fists and prepared to strike.

"I don't care about you or the so-called law! Now be a kind boy and move over." Eula Mae slowly reached down into her purse.

Ida began to breathe heavily. She knew her mother had just broken every rule. Here she was out in the open challenging a white man that did not look like he cared one way or the other what became of the two of them. Scared speechless, Ida stepped over to the side and was about to raise her foot and place it on the grass. Just then, Eula Mae snatched her back.

"Stand still, I say!" she warned.

The white man stood there shaking his head, not sure what to do. He had never been confronted so boldly before. His wife, a tall pale blonde woman, grabbed him by the arms and pleaded with him to leave the matter alone and move on. She then looked at Eula Mae with caution in her eyes.

"We don't want no trouble, gal. My husband will step over just this one time be it your gal is so dressed up today," she said.

Eula Mae never acknowledged the wife. Instead, she kept both eyes on the tall figure standing in front of her. They stared at each other like two tom cats with enough evil in their eyes to set the sidewalk ablaze. When the man saw the color of Eula Mae's eyes, and realized she meant business, he stumbled backwards.

"Yuh somethang evil. I'm not gon' fool wid'cha today since my wife is begging me not tuh. But I won't forget. Yuh best pray I never set eyes on the likes of yuh again, gal," he threatened.

"I don't believe in prayer," Eula Mae stated as he moved over and she and Ida walked by.

Ida wanted to turn around and look at the family they had just passed by, disobeying the crossing rules. Instead, she held onto her mother's strong, rough and calloused hands. She could see other people watching and whispering to themselves. She knew they were the subject of those conversations.

"Don't pay them no more never mind," Eula Mae said, as the onlookers stared into their faces. "It's just hard for them to deal with change. That's all."

"You ain't scared, Mama? People get flogged for this and some even get lynched. You called that white man a boy!" Ida said, her voice trembling.

"Hush ya fool mouth! I heard myself. I ain't afraid of nobody in these heah parts. I can handle myself. That man not fool enough to mess wid me. He best go on with his family if he wants to live," she said as she looked back and chuckled.

The remainder of the day almost went by without further incident. They went to Piggly Wiggly and IGA, since

Eula Mae said the meats were fresher there. Finally, they ventured into the Five and Dime. When she was finished making her purchases, she motioned to Ida to head over to the lunch counter.

"You feel like having one of those thick shakes?" she asked, grinning mischievously.

"I'm too scared. I won't be able to hold my water that long. Last time I peed my pants when I was with Daddy," Ida confessed.

"If ya water starts running, I know a place you can use the bathroom. Real nice woman," her mother said.

"Oh, really?" Ida exclaimed. "Yeah, I want a chocolate shake then, Mama!"

It took a few minutes to get the waitress to acknowledge them so Eula Mae began tapping on the counter lightly at first and then heavier and with a steady pace. The waitress, as well as the other patrons, both Negro and white, began to stare.

"My little girl would sho' love a chocolate shake. We been heah all day and we still got to walk home," she said.

"Be with yuh in a minute, gal," the waitress answered.

Eula Mae kept tapping, although it was lighter; it sounded as if she were attempting to play the tune, 'Dixie' on the counter top. The waitress turned around again.

"What kind of shake yuh gal want?" she asked rudely.

"Ask huh," Eula Mae said, continuing to tap.

"Whatcha want, gal?"

"A chocolate shake, please," Ida answered.

When Eula Mae saw the waitress grab a metal cup and begin to scoop ice cream from the freezer, she stopped playing her tune and watched every movement the young girl made, never letting her eyes off of her until the milk-shake was completely done.

"Where's the cherry?" she asked, alert to any slight.

"S'cuse, me?" the waitress asked as she stood directly in front of Eula Mae.

"I asks where's the cherry that ya put in every shake? Run out? Forget? Which one is it?"

"I didn't know she wanted one," the waitress replied.

"That's cuz yuh didn't ask. Now can my daughter please have what I paid for?" Eula Mae said rudely.

The waitress walked over to the back counter and took a glossy red cherry from the jar. Holding it with a large spoon, she quickly placed the cherry on top of the shake that Ida had already begun to devour.

Ida looked up slowly and locked eyes with the young girl who looked angry enough to knock the tall glass out of her hands. Slowly, Ida smiled and said thank you. The waitress's eyes softened and she walked away.

Later....

It was close to dusk when they walked home. Ida knew that they would have to trot once again to make it down the lonely service road before darkness fell. She looked at her mother, who seemed more at ease now than on the walk into town. Seeing the streets were almost empty, Ida began to relax.

Although she was watching where she walked, she continued to glance up now and then at the strong face of her mother and wonder what she was thinking so hard about.

"You aw'right, Mama?" she asked finally, unnerved by the long silence.

"Un huh. I be fine. Ain't got a care in the world. Thinking about getting supper done now and some other things," Eula Mae responded.

"Like what?"

"Grown folks business. What are you thanking, Missy?" Eula Mae asked.

"About you and how pretty yuh are," Ida said.

"Is that right? Well, I sho' thanks yuh, Miss Ida."

"You quite welcome!" Ida exclaimed, mocking her mother's voice.

They walked toward the service road laughing all the way. As they approached the bend leading to where Highway 17 connected with Main Street, there was a group of young men standing on the corner holding dogs on long repe leashes. This time, instead of placing Ida in front of her, Eula Mae grabbed Ida's hand and pulled her behind her. Ida began to slow up; she was afraid of any kind of dog and her mother knew it.

"Keep still, Ida Mae. Don't twitch and shake or those dogs will know yuh scared and try to harm yuh. If they sense fear, they react. If they don't sense nothing, they'll sniff yuh and then move on," Eula Mae explained.

They were five feet from the three young men and their dogs when Eula Mae began to walk faster. Once again, she walked toward the edge of the sidewalk and the street. This time she did not look into the faces of the onlookers, but kept her head straight, focusing on the service road ahead of them.

The young men in their overalls and white tee shirts saw the two approaching and stopped talking. They stared at Eula Mae and Ida and watched as Eula Mae walked closer to the edge of the sidewalk. Two of the boys were standing on the grass and one was standing with his dog on the side-walk, yet there was still enough space for a single person to pass if necessary.

Eula Mae walked by without acknowledging the group. Ida, focusing on the prints in her mother's dress, dared not look up at the boys and tried not to look at the brown German Shepherd that stood on the sidewalk with its owner. As she passed the young man, she heard him make a hissing sound; Ida clinched her teeth together and tried to hurry along. Just as they had cleared the group, the young man standing on the sidewalk said something that was inaudible, but obviously a reference to the two of them.

Eula Mae slowed, but did not turn around. The boys were heckling - something about being afraid of dogs. Eula Mae never got the gist of their conversation, but knew it was not friendly. Then she heard one of the boys say that it would be nice to see niggers run. Eula Mae stopped dead in her tracks. By this time, Ida was standing on her left closer to the houses that bordered the street. Eula Mae stared ahead and then slowly looked back at the boys.

"Whatcha looking at, darkie? Ain't no one talking to you," one of them said.

Eula Mae kept looking, now directly at the young man she had passed a moment before. Although he was not the one talking, she kept her eyes focused on him. He seemed to be the leader.

"Whatcha lookin' at?" the young man holding the German Shepherd asked.

A suspicious look was on her face. "Mmm. I don't know," she finally replied.

"Go on, girl. Don't try to sass us. You see us standing here with these dogs ready to bite your nigga behinds." He was holding a black dog that appeared rather old.

"Sorry, gentleman. No one is getting bit tonight," Eula Mae said.

"Says who?" all three asked in chorus.

"Says me," Eula Mae replied, pushing Ida back on the grass, whispering something into her ear, and walking toward the crowd.

"This some bold nigra. She coming ta'wards us with three dogs in hand. Fellas, I says we teach this gal a lesson," said the owner of the German Shepherd.

Eula Mae and the young man stood face to face. The dog growled, low and deep in its throat. The other gentleman moved in closer. The one who had not spoken directly to Eula Mae now did the talking.

"Gal, go on home and there won't be no trouble." Then he looked at his comrades. "I don't want no part of no trouble, y'all. She's trying to start somethang that she can't finish. I say we let her go on her way..."

"I say we do not," the owner of the German Shepherd interjected.

"It ain't worth it. I know the likes of her. She's one of those crazy geechies. Let it be or you'll be sorry," the speaker warned.

"That's a smart young man," Eula Mae said as she backed away from the young man with the German Shepherd.

The black dog started barking sounds to which the other dogs joined in.

"I have never been afraid of dogs," she warned them.

"Maybe it's 'cause you ain't run into the right one. Them muts you darkies keep ain't no real dogs. That's what you used to. Not around here though. No sir. We got real dogs." The black dog's owner jerked the dog's collar as if he intended to undo the leash.

Eula Mae peeked down the street. Ida was long gone. As planned, she had distracted the young men long enough for Ida to run into one of the houses. She knew exactly which one and she knew what was about to happen.

"You best git on now," the young man with the German Shepherd said.

"Just remember, I ain't 'fraid of no dog," Eula Mae said before turning around and heading in the direction of where Ida had gone for safety.

She took two steps before she felt something grab the hem of her dress and rip a piece of fabric. She turned around abruptly to discover the black dog, still on a leash, only now a more extended length, barking ferociously at her. Eula Mae reached toward the dog's face trying to avoid his teeth. She reached for him three times before she was successful. Holding him just below the jawbone, she tightened her grip until the dog whimpered.

"Turn him aloose you witch! Turn him aloose or all these dogs will eat you alive."

"Yeah, but this dog will die with me," Eula Mae warned as she struggled to keep the dog still.

"Turn him aloose, you fool geechie. I say turn him aloose," the rational teen spoke again. Then he said to his other friend, "Don't let the leash go! She's got a hold of his throat and she plans to choke him. Don't do nothing to excite her."

The owner of the dog kept yanking the chain to no avail. Eula Mae had the dog almost standing on his two hind legs gasping for air. As the young men pleaded with her to release the dog, and the dog began to lose all strength, she loosened her grip, let one hand go and punched the animal straight in the face. He yelped and collapsed, falling to the ground.

The three boys stood frozen looking at Eula Mae standing over the dog. None of them said anything for a few minutes. Eula Mae, on the other hand, started to smile as she watched to make sure the dog was still unconscious. She became aware of the heat from the sidewalk and the birds squawking overhead, as though everything had come to a standstill.

"Serves yuh right. I told yuh I won't 'fraid of no dogs! Now do yuh understand?" she teased.

The owner of the dog opened his mouth but no sound came forth. Tears streamed down his face, and then finally he cried, "Shep! This crazy geechie killed Shep!"

The other two boys turned and looked directly at their friend, still holding onto their own dog's leashes. Shep's owner walked slowly toward his dog with his arms outstretched. He kneeled down and touched his beloved pet. The dog remained still. Eula Mae had turned around and proceeded down the dark street.

The boys crowded around the dog without uttering a word. Shep's owner knelt down and hugged the dog, continuing to cry. Just then, the owner of the German Shepherd spoke to the one teen that earlier had advised them to leave Eula Mae alone.

"Yuh know that crazy nigra?" he asked.

"I know of her. She got a reputation for being pure evil. You see them blue eyes? She some kind of darkie witch. I told you all to leave her be. Now look! Shep may be dead or close to dying." Then he turned toward Shep's owner as he held Shep and said, "Come on, Jimmy, let's get him to the house. My dad may be able to revive him."

Jimmy lifted Shep from the ground as the two others held their own dogs and followed. The owner of the German Shepherd stood up and looked down the street for Eula Mae. He saw her enter into the yard of the sixth or seventh house from the corner. Then he saw a porch light come on, the screen door open, and Eula Mae disappear.

"I saw where she went. We coming back here!" he said, gritting his teeth.

"Hold on, Charlie!" the attempted mediator began. "Let's take Jimmy here and take care of Shep. You know he's old now and might not make it. That dog is all Jiimmy has."

Around eleven o'clock that same night, Charlie, Jimmy and four adult males returned to the location of the earlier incident. Charlie pointed to the house at the end of Main Street that Eula Mae had entered hours before.

"Y'all stay back. This is grown folks' business. We gonna handle that darkie and the nigger lover that let her into her house," one of the men told the boys.

"How you know a white person let her in?" Jimmy asked.

"I don't. All I saw was the door open and the wench walked in," Charlie replied.

"Only white folks live on Main Street. All I can think of is some darkie maid let her in. If that be the case, we gone put a whip to that monkey right here in the front yard," one of the men whispered to Jimmy and Charlie.

"Come on, fellas. Let's git this over with!" another man yelled to the group.

Hedges that were tall and thick bordered the front yard of the targeted house. The men opened the gate and walked inside. Before they approached the front steps, they stopped for a moment and each man looked carefully around the yard. Two men remained close to the front gate, while the other two approached the steps leading to the wide front porch. They noticed that the yard was well maintained, and the house was freshly painted in a soft pastel color. This was obviously the home of a white family.

There were large windows on both sides of the wooden double front doors. Above the door was a stained glass window with a sun design. There was a spindle railing around the front porch with baskets of flowers neatly hanging from it. A metal glider was to the right of the front door and three matching chairs were on the opposite side. The metal mailbox posted to the front of the house bore the numbers "179."

"You know who lives here?" one of the men asked another, as he opened the screen door.

"Hell no and I don't care. Whosoever it is gonna pay for knocking poor Shep out cold like that."

"Sure hope y'all know what we're getting into. Don't want no trouble from the likes of some of these yankies that's been moving in lately," another man added.

"Yankies need to go back north. This may be the old South and it's gonna remain the old South if I have anything to say about it."

As one of the men reached up to knock, the porch light came on. It startled them. Then the front door opened. The men could not see the person standing in the doorway so they stepped backward into the light.

"Who's there?" the diehard Confederate called out. "We got business with a darkie that came here earlier tonight."

The woman behind the door stepped forward and then unlocked the screened door, stepped out onto the porch, and stood barefoot before the two men.

"Problem, gentlemen?" she asked.

The Confederate stood speechless, while his comrades looked to him for leadership and direction. "Stand down, y'all!" he yelled to the men in the yard. "Put yer weapons away and stand down!"

"What the Sam Hill?" asked one of the other men standing in the yard.

"Come on, Blake, let's go. We ain't got no business here."

As the men quickly backed off the porch and walked toward the gate, Blake turned around and looked back at the small framed woman again. She was a ghastly figure wearing all black with a necklace of skeletal bones around her neck that appeared to glow in the dark. She could not have weighed more than one-hundred pounds and was no more than five feet tall. Her black hair hung down past her waistline and shined like the coat of a black bear. She never said another word, nor moved, while the men exited the front yard. A small smile played at the corners of her mouth but they never saw it, so busy were they with their retreat.

When all four men were safely off the property, Charlie, who had been guarding the gate, said, "What happened? You see the darkie with the blue eyes? You beat her? Wow, that was too quick."

"Hush ya fool mouth, boy, and get back in the truck," the Confederate ordered. "We done here."

The Confederate climbed into the front seat of the old Ford pickup truck and removed a small can from the glove compartment. He climbed back out of the truck, walked around to the back, and kneeled down in front of the license plate.

He sprayed the contents of the can onto the plate.

"What's the matter? What's that you spraying?" one of the men yelled from the back.

"Protection."

"Protection from what? What's going on, Gus? You acting strange. First we back down from a half-white nigra woman, and now yer telling us we need protection?"

Hearing the commotion, Blake walked to the back of the truck and saw what Gus was doing. He looked at the other two men and the boys sitting in the bed of the truck and suddenly had the feeling he had bitten off way more than he wanted to chew.

"Y'all wanna tell me what I done gone and got myself into?" He looked back at the small woman still standing on the front porch.

"This is just some strange superstition, that's all. Gus really into that mess. He thinks he has looked into the eyes of a Devil worshiper. According to some fool geechie myth, you gotta cross out any identifiers to yer property when you see one, or they'll put a curse on everything you own. If that woman don't curse us, this here truck will for sure be cursed, at least in Gus's mind," the man explained, laughing.

Gus heard their conversation and hissed, "Shush! Stop yer foolish talk! Yer standing here in front of that woman's house talking foolishness. I say we get the hell out of Dodge before she decides what she gonna do with us."

Charlie stood up. "Y'all saying that was a woman standing up on that front porch? I couldn't see good. What color was her eyes?"

Gus put the top back on the can of spray paint and whispered, "She didn't have any!"

EIGHT

1976

Ida stood crying in the doorway, hands cradling her cheeks, tears streaming from her eyes. She could not believe who was standing in front of her. They'd known each other since childhood but never would Ida have expected them to meet up again in the likes of a noisy, smoke-filled juke joint.

"Lordy be!" she exclaimed. "I'm lost for words this heah evening. Chile, is yuh crazy? Walzing in heah alone. Who brung yuh way out heah?"

"What makes you think someone had to bring me?" the woman answered.

"Cuz yuh ain't just walk down these dark roads some ten miles from yuh house and waltz in heah on foot."

"Maybe. The Lord sho' works in mysterious ways!" The woman laughed.

"So tell me, what's this? An exorcism? You come to pray the Devil out of me?" Ida asked.

"Well, if Mohammed can't come to the mountain...." she replied.

"I knew it! You picked a fine day to come and try to convert folk. Folks in heah almost drunk enough to try anything until tomorrah when they hangovers wear off," Ida said.

"I only have to convert one, remember. It's like the game of dominos. One equals all the rest eventually."

"Do you ever stop? You still say your way is better? Look at all you been through! Yuh standing heah all dressed up to proclaim what? That we sinners? Well, missy, that we already know." Ida laughed and dropped her arms down by her sides, as she stood face to face with the surprise guest.

"The Good Book says we all fall short of the glory of God. Nobody's perfect. All have sinned and that's for sho'."

"And you standing right heah in a juke joint committing a big sin! Why? Why tonight? Why the urgency?" Ida started to panic. "You had one of those dreams again? Oh, Lawd, is my time shawt? Am I 'bout to be called Home?"

"Hush ya mouth, girl. You shall live and not die. I'm here to celebrate the living. Look where the Lord has brought us from. Isn't it wonderful? You are celebrating three decades on this earth, so I thought it was way high time I come to celebrate with you." she declared.

"I just don't believe it. A church woman in a house of ill repute. That's sho' nough funny. Wait till Timmy see you! I know he won't believe it either. He gone think it's the moonshine." Then she whispered, "We drinking private stock tonight. "

"Christ lives in me. I can go where I please, "the woman countered.

"That true, but please tell me who was your escort?" Ida walked further into the foyer and peered out into the parking lot.

"I got a local to bring me this far. I didn't know y'all had moved. I may not party with y'all, but I keep track of the local nightlife, especially everything you two get into."

"Well, I know Timmy came past to see yuh and I thought I remembered him saying that you said you gon' try to make it past the party tonight. Well, I sho' didn't believe 'em. I swear befo' God, I never thought I would see you in a place like this."

"Like what? You run these kinds of establishments so you tell me, what kind of place is this?" the woman asked.

"The kind yuh don't get caught dead in unattached."

"Is that so? I never thought I would hear such foolishness coming from the likes of you! You claim to be a modern woman, Ida Tilley. You smoke Kool cigarettes and tell yourself, you've come a long way, baby! No one in the Low Country is more independent-minded than you. I, on the other hand, was forced into independence as a widow. Or have you forgotten? Both of my masters are dead."

"Modern or not, you still s'posed to have someone escort you into these kinds of establishments," Ida warned.

"Someone did. You just could not see him," the woman replied.

"Oh really. Who? Some ghost?"

"The friendly ghost." She continued laughing while looking around the small entryway.

"Well, friendly or otherwise, you definitely a brave soul! I just never thought you would come see me heah," Ida said.

"Ida Mae, you only turn thirty once. It was big enough for me to take my house coat off, fry my hair, powder my nose, put on stockings, and catch a ride up the road to see. I know for sure it was worth it all just to see the look in your eyes."

"Well, you the biggest surprise I ever had. I sho' won't forget this. Yuh really come out heah just to see me?" Ida looked puzzled.

"Yes, Miss Ida, 'cause I know you would do the same for me," the woman teased.

"Oh no! I ain't stepping foot into one of them churches! I ain't care what's going on. I come as far as the front steps. Whatever I got tuh say tuh you I can just yell into the foyer at yuh. No way! Miss Ida not coming into no church. I don't care who in there tuh see."

"Church has little to do with a particular place, Ida Mae. Real church has to do with your heart. Real church means loving someone so much that you are willing to go to the ends of the earth to find them."

"That's if they lost. I ain't lost and yuh know it! I am just not on the road yuh travelin', that's all. I love dancin', whiskey, moonshine, and juke joints, and I ain't about to give them up so that I can fit in with churchfolks," Ida said.

"Nobody's asked you to give up anything. Come as you are…"

"Shut yo mouf! Now you done come all this way to just stand heah, or were yuh planning on coming in to see how us sinners live?" Ida asked.

"I'm definitely coming in. Nothing is going to stop me now that I have been warned that real women are not supposed to go out at night unattached," she whispered into Ida Mae's ear.

Ida grabbed both of the woman's hands and lifted them up to her mouth, tenderly kissing each. She was still in shock and knew Timmy would have a similar reaction. Getting one last look at the beautiful tall woman standing before her, Ida slowly turned around and pulled the woman behind her, using her body to block everyone's view.

She had taken only a few steps before some of the patrons noticed that she was not alone. Another few minutes and some found themselves staring at the slender woman dressed in red, wearing a hat with a long feather adornment. Her shoes were the scarlet color of her dress and hat. She looked as if she were going some place far more sophisticated than the small juke joint that sat hidden just west of the Beaufort County line.

Timmy by now could see the red dress and shoes, but not the face of the woman Ida marched before him. He started to laugh.

"Well, Lawdy, I do declare, if it ain't Miss Ruth!" he screamed.

Ruth Garrett walked around Ida laughing at the look on Timmy's face. She had never been in a juke joint but often heard wild stories about them. She looked at Ida who still looked as if she was in shock.

"Old Man, look at your woman! Still in shock. I told you I was coming. As a good Christian woman, I cannot tell a lie."

"That you did, Ruthie. That ya did," Timmy said. "Now, what can I get you to drink?" He motioned to the patrons that sat at the bar to vacate their seats so that Ruth and Ida could sit down. "I reckon we could find somethin' widout no alcohol."

Several people stared at the sight before them. Most of them knew of Ruth Garrett, had heard her name several times, and had heard of her sorrows. They could not believe that someone so well known for serving the Lord was standing amongst them.

Ida saw the way some were staring.

"Is y'all fools? Staring at my cousin like yuh crazy! She ain't the law! Some of y'all act like you seent a ghost! Go'ne now. Go'ne 'bout yuh business. Enjoy yuhselves. This here is mah birthday party, and Ruthie here is my honored guest." She bowed grandly and turned back to the beautiful woman in the red dress.

Timmy poured Ruth some apple cider and handed her a dixie cup. Ruth raised the cup up to her mouth.

"Watch it, old man. Don't play with me and spike my drink. I may be saved, but I ain't a fool, ya hear? Y'all don't want me to pour oil on this joint. It will be a church before long."

"Stop it, crazy gal! Don't prophesy no foolishness on us! We happy the way we is. Besides, what better entertainment can people in these back woods get? They need a little lifting. Nothing much else to do besides lay up and have babies," Ida said.

"That depends on who you ask," Ruth replied.

"What else you got to do at night, Ruthie, besides hold those prayer meetings at yuh house and drive those kids of yearn crazy?" Ida asked.

Timmy interrupted. "Now, sista. You two act as if yuh happy to see each other, okay? Y'all can fuss tomorrow. Let's just enjoy Tilley's birthday tonight."

II.

They grew up together in Coosawhatchie, watching the small town shrink from being a major port in the state to almost nothing. Everything had moved on and what was left was a ghost town. Few people lived there and most were of the same family. Both said one day they would leave the Low Country for good when they grew up, but destiny kept both of them tied to Jasper County.

Ruth was older than Ida by five years and had been married twice by the time Ida turned thirty. Ida always adored her and thought Ruth would become someone famous because of her beauty and the way she spoke proper English. In fact, while Ruth had the same accent of most southerners, she was able to sound as if she'd never lived in the South when she needed to. Ida loved her ability to fit in anywhere she went by adjusting her mannerisms and changing her tone. Though they were different on the outside, Ruth was actually Ida's soul mate, representing Ida's alter ego, for what Ruth would not dare do, Ida did fearlessly.

She looked Ruth up and down before she spoke again.

"My gal, what dat yuh wearing? Red? Red for wild women I hears. Mama always said red is the sign of a free woman. One that's not afraid to say she love pleasure as much as a man." Ida laughed.

"Hush up. Don't start. I bought this dress in New York after the funeral. Felt I needed something bold since the Devil had taken everything from me except my children. When they let me out of that place, I decided I was going to live life on my own terms. I don't care what these fool geechies think about me either. I'm going live a little," Ruth said.

"Now how dat gon' affect your other man?" Ida questioned.

"I didn't say I was going to sin, I said I was going to live. That's what He came for...so that we could have abundant life and not live tied down to anything and nobody," Ruth explained.

"I'll say! Maybe all of us need to go away for awhile and come back. Mama was right. Maybe I should have tasted real freedom when I had the chance, hey?"

"Eula Mae is wise, but she's wrong about a lot of things. You are never free unless you serve the Lord. Salvation frees not just the soul, but the troubled mind," Ruth said.

"I ain't know, cuz. The only bondage I got is from Sheriff Bryant, who was heah earlier tonight. He won't leave us be. Comes 'round near every night. Dropped by tonight sayin' he was looking for Edgar Carter. He know that fool man don't come 'round here."

"Ooh," Ruth sighed.

"Ooh what? I hate the way yuh say that, Ruth. I know something is wrong. What happened yuh ain't saying?" Ida asked.

"Nothing. Just let it be. I don't know what Bryant wants, but I know Edgar Carter is bad news. I am so glad Mary got away from that man, I tell you. He doesn't mean her any good. The Lord never meant for her to marry someone that evil. Pure evil. Edgar can be like the Devil himself."

"That Edgar sold his soul to the Devil a long time ago," Ida agreed.

"Sho' 'nough," Ruth said, slipping back into the familiar dialect. "He ain't saved. Comes to church every Sunday though. I swear that man is drunk every time I see him. Mumbling words and chanting, calls himself speaking in tongues. That man doesn't have the Holy Spirit. He got a spirit, but it ain't holy. I tell you that!"

They moved to a small table in the corner and gossiped about local townsfolk. The two women were the queens of gossip, Ida very bold with her assertions and Ruth the more observant one. What Ida accepted when she heard something from someone else's lips, Ruth insisted seeing with her own eyes. Ida used to say Ruth could sense trouble, either with the dreams that had folks thinking she was clairvoyant, or with the other gift that few understood.

Timmy left the bar after midnight and came and sat down next to them, pulling up a chair and spinning it around to straddle it. He loved to see Ida so happy. Loved to see her relax. Tonight was her night. He had planned it that way. He could control mostly everything except Sherriff Bryant, an enemy they always had to be on the lookout for. But at that moment, Timmy did not care whether Charles Bryant returned that night. He had a chance to witness something rare: Ida at total peace.

"Ah, Miss Ruthie, you gonna dance?" he asked when he could get a word in.

"No, man. Stop your foolishness. Now I've come this far, but I bet you won't catch me dancing and spinning around with the likes of these heathens," Ruth answered.

"Then what you gon' do for fun? I hear yuh telling Ida about your new lifestyle. Yuh all dressed up wid just enough make up on so's no one notice yuh got it on. Ruthie, tell us what you up to? You got you another gentleman caller?"

"Hush up, boy! I'm not interested in another man dying on me. I plan to live my life as a widow totally serving the Lord and looking after the things of my Savior. Besides, the apostle Paul said widows were to remain single if they could. I'm gonna take his advice and walk the remainder of this life's journey alone. My kids will be happy to know that," Ruth said.

"Them kids needs a daddy," Timmy interjected.

"They got one. I mean two. We had good years together as a two-parent family. I can handle the rest. They act a fool and I'll just send them to you. That's what family is for. As for me, no sir. No man is coming back into my life and taking control of my household unless the Lord says so. And right now, he isn't saying a word."

"You sho'?" Timmy asked, all the while stroking Ruth's fingers as she sat next to him.

"Brother, I am positive."

"Leave it be, Timmy. I know my cousin and when she done spoke her piece that's it. She don't need to be tied down tuh another man no way," Ida said.

"That's how you feel, Ida? Like you tied down to me?" He looked at his wife, surprised at her assessment of marriage.

"Don't you go there. Yuh know what I mean, man. I'm tied tuh you cuz I wanna be. No other reason. When Ruthie finds someone she wants tuh be tied down to, I know she gon' change her mind."

"I'm just checking widya, Tilley. Making sure yuh ain't feel like I'm suffocating yuh or nothing," he said slowly.

"If yuh was, I ain't afraid tuh let yuh know and let yuh know real quick," Ida countered.

"My Tilley is telling the truth. She don't hold her tongue to no one. That's why I love yuh. That's why," Timmy smiled at the two women.

As the morning crawled forward, many of the attendees began their exit. Several reached out to shake Ruth's hand. Some even came by and kissed her on the cheek. Timmy watched each one of them carefully. He knew by now that some were just a little inebriated and probably should not be trusted to drive home at this time of night, but he was too tired to lecture them. He had spent so much time making Ida's gathering a success that all he wanted to do was lock up the club and go home.

As the last person walked up to them, Timmy took one more glance around his establishment.

"All right, Ronald. You can call it quits. All the booze gone too," he yelled over to his brother.

"Help me with these heah chairs and tables. I want to put the tables up against the wall so that I can sweep up in the morning. I ain't gonna try to lift a broom tonight," he yawned.

"I can come first thing in the morning. You sleep in late, baby," Ida said.

"Ah, that ain't necessary. Sho' kind of you though," Timmy answered, then he turned to Ruth. "Ronald gonna run yuh home, yuh hear?"

"He already told me. Thank you kindly. I am so glad I came out tonight. Love to see the two of you all in love and being kind to each other," Ruth said as she reached up and removed her hat.

Ida walked over to the bar and started throwing the empty cups, left by the patrons, into the trashcan.

Ruth got up and looked around. Then she walked over and whispered to Ida, "You hear something?"

"What? I ain't hear a thing. What sort of thang yuh hear? Outside? Or in heah?" Ida asked.

"Somewhere close," Ruth said.

"Oh, Lawd, Ruthie. Where? How close? Did yuh actually hear something or are yuh just foretelling again? Has it already happened or is it going tuh happen later this morning?" Ida questioned.

"Ooh. It happened all right. Maybe a few minutes ago and my hearing was delayed. It already happened though. I can feel it," Ruth commented.

"What now, sista? Something happens everytime I see yuh. Why stuff wait till I'm around?" Ida wondered.

Ruth kept looking around. Slowly she walked over to the small doorway and proceeded into the foyer. Then she walked out of the front door. The air quality was rather humid, causing her to perspire through her new clothing. She raised her arms and sniffed. Her dressed reeked of cigarette smoke. She smiled.

Someone in the distance called her name. Ruth walked toward the parking lot. It was empty with the exception of the two cars that belonged to Timmy and Ronald. She walked past the concrete pavement toward the open field. She heard it again.

Suddenly she turned around and headed around to the back of the club. With the exception of the night flies, the night seemed at total peace. Ruth was no longer afraid. She knew by now that something out of the ordinary had happened and that is what drove her to Timmy and Ida's juke joint on the other side of town. It had to all be a part of her destiny, which was the only reason she kept walking straight ahead into the blackness.

NINE

1975

Ida stood in the kitchen packing foods to take on her bi-weekly journey. It had been six months now and without fail, she made the trip alone every time. Townsfolk stayed away from folks they believed were crazy, particularly those locked away in mental institutions.

She glanced at Timetheous as he sat in front of their brand new television set and imagined what her life would be like if she lost him. Would she too find herself alone in a mental institution, unable to speak, unable to accept the fact that her world had fallen apart? She could not bear to think about it much longer.

She remembered Ruth's reaction when James died in December 1967.

"Ruthie, I just know ya gon' be all right! Ya gone have chirren one day. It ain't over for ya, yuh hear? I may not do much praying, but I know that everything always works out in the end. I just want to see yuh smile again."

Ruth sat on the couch with her feet on the coffee table, humming a tune. She had been there since the funeral which had put her often complicated husband into the ground. Ida was alongside her the entire time.

"What was James doing on those tracks?" she asked for the fiftieth time, praying Ruth would one day answer her.

"I don't know. It was his time. I do know that. Just seems time was running out for him," Ruth said slowly.

"What? Ruthie, that don't make much sense! How could yuh tell time was running out?"

"I slept with the man, remember? We may not have seen eye to eye on some things, but over the years, James and I had gotten close. He helped me through one of the toughest losses I have had to endure."

"Losing that child hurt you badly, huh?" Ida asked.

"Yes, Lord. I will always have a void in my life where she was. I miss her so. It was James who waited on me hand and toe during my grief. I never knew he had such compassion in him. But he did. He showed that to all the children. Just as he was changing and we all could see it, something started to happen that showed me that he was leaving, never to come back again. What I did not know at the time was that we had so little time left."

"Tomorrah ain't promised tuh none of us."

"Which is why it's so important to say 'if it be God's will'. We never know when He will call us home, so we best live right. Seek the Lord while He is yet to be found. No greater word than that."

Ida ignored Ruth. At this particular time in her life, she did not want to hear a lecture on serving the Lord. She closed her eyes and tried to meditate on something more positive, but she could not. Her cousin was in enormous pain and there was nothing anyone could do to help.

"So James accepted God before he pass?" Ida whispered to Ruth without opening her eyes.

"Sure did. I could not marry or live with a man that was not saved! James loved the Lord. He was just the jealous type. I don't know why he never felt he could trust me. Always thought I was going to up and leave him at any moment."

"He had reason tuh think that. Everyone loves yuh, sista. People admire yuh wherever yuh go, even white folks." She paused and opened her eyes. "Ruthie, how many times yuh had tuh deal wid the Klan?"

"What kind of foolish question is that, sistah? My life was destroyed by the Klan, or don't you remember? I certainly won't soon forget. Maybe they finally feel sorry for me, killing the biggest threat to them in my family." Ruth stood and walked toward the front door.

"I'm sorry! I ain't forgot our past wid 'em. Have they bothered yuh since?"

Ruth turned around and stared at Ida. "Let's just say as life went on, I acquired some collateral I never knew I had."

"Collateral! That's why Frank say Klan never mess wid 'em. I always thought he was talking foolishness. Yuh got some too?"

"Sistah, let's just say I stumbled onto some one night and the Klan has never looked my way again." She paused then continued, "They tried to mess with James one night. Did I tell you? We were out on highway 17 in Pokey when a truck ran up on us with bright headlights. Of course, James pulled off the shoulder and waited for it to pass, but the truck just stayed behind us. It would not move, I tell ya. We sat in that truck for half an hour, praying, until finally the driver's side door opened. When the light came on, I could see three men inside. I don't know if any more were hiding on the back. Well, two men got out and walked toward us. James looked at me and we held hands in prayer. They walked up and started questioning us about being out so late. James looked up and when he did, one of the men flashed a flashlight in his face. He then told James not to look at him and that's when I looked up and noticed the man had on a white hood!"

"No! Ruthie, say it ain't so! Klan was on the prowl and they spotted you two driving down the road, yuh say?" Ida stood and walked over to her cousin.

"Sure did. Well, after a few minutes, they weren't on the prowl anymore! No sir. The Lord turned that thing completely around! While one man held the flashlight in James' face, the other stood on the passenger side watching me. I kept my head down in prayer until something told me to look at the man standing next to me. So I did. I looked straight into his eyes and guess what?"

"What?"

"I knew him!"

"No!" Ida was astonished. "Ruthie, you could see who it was under that hood and they let y'all live?"

"Remember what I said about collateral? Well, that fella looked back into my eyes and must have remembered where he knew me from. He turned the flashlight off and stepped away from the truck! I went in for the kill at that point and started speaking in tongues! At first the fella on the driver's side did not notice the commotion, but James noticed I was getting louder so he nervously looked in my direction, despite that flashlight in his face. When he looked, the other guy shined his light on me. I just sat there looking at his friend on the other side, talking to my Lord and savior."

"Then what happened?"

"The guy ignored us, and told the man on James' side that he did not know what I was saying. But, he knew all too well because we had met somewhere in his sordid past. Instead of telling his comrade the truth, that man did what I expected him to do: He lied! He told the other guy that I worked for his family! Can you imagine the look on James' face? He knew my father would never allow me to work for a white family. James told me later that he thought the man had mistaken me for his family's maid. I just laughed. I never told my husband why that man lied like that. As far as I was concerned, that liar saved our lives that night. The man turned the flashlight off and told us to go home and never mention what happened."

"Did James ask yuh had yuh seent that man before?" Ida asked.

"No. He thought it was all a misunderstanding on the Klan's part. I knew otherwise. That man was no fool. He knew if he told on me he would have to tell on himself! He kept his mouth shut that night and I am sure he continued to keep his mouth shut!" Ruth exclaimed.

"Come on, sistah, tell me what happened that first time yuh laid eyes on this Klansman?"

"Baby, I cannot. If I tell you, I will have to kill you!" She laughed. "No, seriously, I made a promise to someone else that I would never breathe a word to another living soul about what happened that night. It will go with me to my grave and if I tell it that would make my going into the grave all the quicker."

Staring out the window in deep thought, Ruth was no longer smiling.

1975

Ida walked up to the entrance of the hospital. She loved the manicured lawns, and especially the flowers that edged the sidewalks. It was the inside of those buildings that she hated. The doors to each building were opened to entrants but locked to those exiting. It was a way to keep the patients inside and to prevent them from sneaking off the grounds, getting injured, or hurting someone else.

Ida could not envision Ruth living in a place like this. Ruth, the epitome of gentleness, who could she hurt? She was the type of person that followed the rules and did exactly what she was told.

The large gray steel doors swung open and Ida walked in. There were ten patients seated in wheelchairs who looked like they wanted to make a break for the outdoors. Initially, Ida thought those patients were confined to those chairs because of a physical disability, but later discovered they were secured by a seat belt to prevent unnecessary injuries. She avoided their eyes, because she hated the pathetic looks on their faces. If she could get away with it, she would hold those steel doors open and let them all roam throughout the grounds unattended.

Ruth's room was on the other side of the corridor at the end of the hall. She had been moved three times and now had a private room. Ida wondered how her cousin could afford such luxury and special attention. She was relieved that Ruth was in a safe environment, but felt the best place for her to recover was at home with family.

Ida pushed the door open. A small black and white television blasted throughout the room at an uncomfortable decibel. She looked around the sterile room and saw Ruth, covered by white pressed sheets, staring straight at the television screen with no emotion at all on her face. Ida walked over to the chair next to the window and pulled it closer to the bed. As she placed the aluminum containers on the mobile arm, she noticed Ruth looking straight at her.

"Well, hi!" she yelled. In all of her previous visits, Ruth had never looked at her.

Ruth looked at Ida, her outfit, and finally the food in front of her.

"Cat still got your tongue, old gal!" Ida laughed.

Ruth closed her eyes and starting humming.

"Well, God in Heaven!" Ida grabbed her cheeks and stared. "The dead has risen!"

Ruth continued humming while Ida busied herself making a fuss over the bed linens. She lifted the top blanket and tugged at the flat white cotton sheet underneath, pulling the ends until they hung over the bed and then, walking to all four sides, she tucked the sheet neatly underneath the mattress. Next, she picked up the fluffy pink knit blanket draped over the edge of the bed, folded it and placed it horizontally along the foot of the bed. When she was done, she addressed her cousin again.

"Sistah, your chirren been heah? They miss yuh badly. It seem everyday folk show up at your house wanting to know when yuh coming home. I don't think they really know yuh heah and all." Ida's voice faded as Ruth opened her eyes.

She said nothing, but reached out and grabbed Ida's small hands. Lifting them to her face, she kissed each one, and, without fail, started to hum again.

"Oh, Ruthie!" Ida cried. "We miss yuh and we want yuh home. What happened ain't right. Life is not fair, but folk love yuh and know yuh can make it through this."

Then she asked, "What they say wrong wid yuh?"

"Crazy!"

"Crazy? What you talking, sistah? Yuh ain't crazy! Yuh been hit by a truck so getting back on yuh feet is gonna take awhile! What is wrong with these hospital quacks? I have known yuh forever and yuh don't have a crazy bone inside of yuh!" Ida lamented.

"Schizophrenic." The word caught Ida by surprise.

"Skit-so who? What that yuh talking?"

"That's what they say," Ruth whispered.

"Well, they don't know what they talking about! Yuh not skit-so whatever the hell they say!"

"Delusional, with multiple personalities, and depressed too," Ruth continued.

"Stop yuh foolishness! I don't understand everything yuh saying. Yes, you are depressed. That's what the loss of a loved one causes. But delusional? I ain't buying that one. You have a firm grip on yuh reality. That's why yuh stopped talking. What else yuh got tuh say? The air was knocked right out of yuh with all that's happened. I don't know why no one else seems tuh understand. Some things knock yuh flat on yuh back, and getting up takes such a long time. Funny thing is, sometimes when yuh get up, yuh still not the same as yuh were before the fall."

"I'll never be the same again, Ida." Ruth leaned toward the food in front of her. "Your cooking is still the same," she beamed.

"But you will go on. Yuh will survive this, sweetie. Yuh come home and yuh go on wid the wonderful life left in front of yuh," Ida reassured her.

"Yeah, I am coming home soon. I just have to get this medication out of me. It makes me drowsy and unable to walk. I need to go home whole, not dependent on anyone. I won't be a burden to my family," Ruth said with certainty.

"Ruthie, yuh helped so many others. It is time fo' yuh tuh let others help yuh!"

"They are. I can feel the help of everyone from this here bed. So many folk have passed through to shake my hand, it warms my heart. I may not have spoken to them but I remember every last one of them. " She scooped a big spoonful of potato salad onto the plastic plate. Inwardly she commented that as usual, Ida had overcooked the potatoes to mush.

"Oh, sistah, I can't wait fo' yuh tuh get back up and come home. Yuh make all of our lives easier. Them women that come over all the time seem so lost. I seent one of them girls in Piggly Wiggly, and she looked like she was walking in circles trying tuh find something nobody knows. I tried tuh help huh, but she kept talking tuh huhself and walking isle by isle looking fo' God knows what."

"You're talking 'bout Gloria Tisdale?" Ruth looked up after she bit into a piece of cold fried chicken.

"How yuh keep track o' all dem names? Folks come all time o' day and night fo' yuh to put that cooking grease on their heads and pray. Now they lost. Maybe it won't so good that yuh always around. They got tuh depending on yuh fo' everything. Folks so desperate, they won't even let yuh sleep."

"They just need to know God. I help them through the process, but it's never a wrong time to pray. Some folk just want to ask for prayer and then be about their merry way, but I don't allow that. When they ask me for prayer, I hold them right there so they can hear the words trickle off my tongue. One day they will feel like they can say the same things to God and he will respond."

"I ain't know, Ruthie. Them folks seem lost widout yuh. Last month, there were about twenty-five women hanging around in yuh yard, talking about they were forming a prayer circle tuh make the Devil release yuh from his grip! Child, I run them fools away from there! Sent them packing and told them not tuh come back or they gon' deal wid me. They chanting and stirring up mess, upsetting yuh chirren." Ida reached down into her nap sack and pulled out a bowl of banana pudding.

"Ooh, my children are used to that by now. They know the power of prayer. They are not afraid, no sir!" Ruth said, as she hungrily cleaned every bit of food from her plate.

"Well, I ain't care! Whatever devil that's messing with yuh not in yuh yard, he right here in this room talking tuh yuh mind telling yuh that yuh crazy."

"I never said I was crazy, Ida. I said that's what the doctors around here say! That's a different thing. If I accept their report, I will be here the rest of my life! I can't do that and I won't. The God I serve is able to deliver me through this and, believe me, I got some help on the inside of these hospital walls looking out for me. It won't be long now."

"So yuh coming home soon, Ruthie?" Ida asked with excitement.

"Won't be long now, Ida Mae. Not long at all, I say."

As the aroma of the banana pudding reached her nostrils, Ruth Harrison Garrett, sniffed and smiled.

1976

Ida took her shoes off and felt the cold concrete floor. It was the coolest spot in the room that night and a spot she could not enjoy unless she freed herself from the black patent leather shoes that held her painfully bound.

She walked into the doorway and looked out into the parking lot. "Ruthie, where ya be?" she yelled.

There was no sound. She walked back into the foyer and headed to the bathroom that sat just inside of the entry way. This was the first club they'd owned that had a public bathroom inside. Prior to that, patrons used the wooden outhouse in the back. Timmy was so proud to have a real bathroom built that the sign on the front of the building read, "public restrooms," as a bragging right that they had finally made it.

"Timmy," Ida yelled down the hall. "Timmy, come quick."

Timmy and Ronald ran toward her. She had a suspicious look on her face.

"What's a matter, Tilly?" Timmy shouted. "What's all the yelling about? Where's Ruthie?"

"I ain't know! She walked outta da door and into the night. What in God's name is going on?" Ida squealed.

"Calm down. We gon' find huh. She ain't gone far. Ruthie known tuh walk off and y'all knows it. She walking somewhere in huh own world. Let's git huh befo' the Klan do," Ronald said.

"Why would she just run off? She knew yuh were giving huh a ride," Ida asked.

"Yeah. Ida Mae, that cousin of yearn is strange. Yuh know she got them problems," Timmy stated, tapping a finger to his temple.

"Hush yuh foolishness, Timmy. This ain't got nothing tuh do with no problems. Ruthie was in huh right mind tonight. Had yuh been through all she been through, yuh would have lost yuh mind too!" she cried. "Now hush up and find my cousin!"

Timmy and Ida headed out to the parking lot while Ronald headed toward the side of the building and then around back.

He walked slowly and reached into the right side of his belt buckle to release his hand revolver. Given the culture of juke joints, he never knew when he was going to have to use his gun to defend himself from an unruly patron. The police were notoriously slow to respond to calls for help.

Slowly he pulled the revolver from its holster and held the gun out in front of himself. He sensed fear, but something told him that Ruth was still alive. He headed toward the back of the building, and then stopped. There was no sign of movement. He turned back and faced the back door. Something moved, he turned around and then he heard it again.

He turned back to face the cornfields in front of him. "Ruthie?" he whispered.

There was no response. Then he heard a sound. Someone was moaning. Ronald's hands begin to shake.

About five-hundred feet from the club, near the cornfields that bordered the property, he could see a bright color near the ground. Walking on tiptoes, he crept closer. Then he recognized the form.

"Oh, dear God."

"Ooh. Oooh. Ooooh," the figure continued to moan.

As reality struck him, Ronald found his tongue. "Miss Ruth? You all right? We all worried sick about yuh." And then he noticed she was not alone. "Who that yuh holding, baby?"

She was sitting on the ground, in the thick of the stalks, legs straight out in front of her, rocking back and forth. Her eyes were closed; one hand was clasped around a man's head, and the other was placed at the center of his chest. His body was sprawled out on the ground, his eyes were closed, and his arms lay limp by his sides.

Ronald came closer. He could see clearly now. His eyes focused on the man Ruth sat holding. He slipped the revolver back into the holster and knelt down beside her.

"Hang on, Miss Ruth. I'm going to get help!"

He ran around the building and into the parking lot. "Timetheous!" he shouted. "Timetheous!"

Just then Timmy and Ida ran across the parking lot.

"We got ourselves a problem."

"Yuh find huh?" Ida was out of breath.

"And then some," Ronald said.

"Where is she? Where my Ruthie at?" she cried.

"She's all right, Ida Mae." He paused, "She done found something though."

"What do yuh mean, she found something? What out heah in dese heah woods but possums and snakes?" Ida asked.

"Naw, not that. She done found a body," he added, his eyes widening dramatically.

"A what?" Timmy and Ida screamed in unison.

"You heard me. A body. I ain't sure who it is or what happened to him. Miss Ruth sitting on the ground singing tuh the poor fella. I was too 'fraid tuh get a closer look." He shivered.

"That's all we needs, Tilley! Someone done collapsed in the back of the joint?" Timmy threw his arms into the air.

Ida ran toward the cornfields. Barefoot, sharp objects pierced her feet, but she kept running, barely feeling the pain. She had to get a glimpse of Ruthie for herself.

"Ruthie," she whispered when she spotted the red dress. "Ruthie. I'm heah, sista. I'm heah."

Ruth did not look away from the man whose head she was stroking. Ida arrived just in time to witness her cousin putting a small piece of fabric inside of her bosom.

"Oh, Lawd!"

Ida recognized him. In total shock, she stared for a few seconds, then turned and yelled to Timmy and Ronald, who were approaching a few feet behind her.

When the two men were within inches of the scene, Ida whispered, "This is all we need now. We gon' get shut down fo' sho.'"

TEN

1974

"I'm going to make your life a living hell."

Ida never forgot those words. She never forgot the person who said them to her either. She hated him with all her heart. She hated him for the things she'd allowed him to do to her all those years ago.

She vowed back then she would one day get revenge, but as the years drifted by, she came to believe in the old saying that what goes around, comes around. He would soon be confronted by the very demons he created and they would destroy him. All she had to do was wait for him to self-destruct.

But now, it appeared he held all the power. It was rumored he made poor folk buy their freedoms and bootleggers trade alcohol and money as payment for his silence. It was even said he forced young girls to perform oral sex when he caught them out past curfew in places they had no business being in. He even used young men to do his dirty work in exchange for jail time.

Folks knew about his illegal activities, but dared not complain. He carried a brass shield and that made him God in the Low Country. Yet he never knew how many enemies he had. He only knew, when it came to Ida Mae Tilley, he was at the top of her list.

Ever since she'd met him, Ida had started having bouts of depression. There were days when she could not get out of bed. Days when she thought more highly of suicide than the wonderful man she'd married. Days when all she could think of was taking a gun and putting it to her enemy's skull and pulling the trigger. She thought if she could kill him it would ease her own pain.

She was wrong. There was nothing anyone could do to ease the feelings of hatred that flooded her mind when she woke up each morning, and were the last thoughts she remembered before she drifted off to sleep each night.

There was once a time when depression was a foreign concept to her. A time when all she did was smile about the wonderful life she lived. It was a great life and nothing seemed to be able to penetrate her happiness. Nothing.

She never estimated the power of the Devil incarnate himself.

1965

Timmy and Ida walked hand in hand that hot sunny afternoon. The wedding was a few months away and everything was going just as Eula Mae planned. The two love birds simply found other things to do since they were spectators at their own event. Timetheous worked two jobs to build the home they would share. Although with his busy schedule they saw each other less and less, Ida held onto the knowledge that soon they would live together as man and wife.

"So you gon' quit afterwards, huh?" she asked.

"After what, Ida Mae?"

"After we gets married and the house built."

"What that got to do with nothing? I like my jobs and I am keeping both of them. I bring home good money and we can save some of it so I can go into business for mahself one day. I told yuh I want tuh get a liquor license and open a night club like they got in Savannah." Timmy stopped at one of the benches to sit down.

"This Coosawhatchie, Timmy. These folks don't care about fancy places. They just want some place tuh get drunk. Besides, they already got The Shanty. It's packed on weekends. It's someplace everyone goes to."

"Everyone who? You talking 'bout them youngins? What about the older crowd around heah that have to go to Beaufort or Savannah tuh find a nice place?"

"They still not going tuh hang around heah, even if you build a club." Ida sat down and pulled out the lollipop he'd bought her earlier that night at the state fair.

"It's about choice, Ida Mae. I want folks tuh have a choice. I guarantee yuh, folks gon' choose my place most of the time."

"Well, that's in the future. I say we get the house done, have some chirren, and then when they in school, yuh can talk about opening yuh club."

"You sho' have become bossy these days. Sound like yuh mama. She always telling men what tuh do and now yuh doing the same. When did we talk about having chirren now? I thought yuh wanted tuh wait in case yuh got one of those good cleaning jobs on Hilton Head?" Timmy walked away and turned his back to her.

"I told yuh, I ain't cleaning no one's house! I told yuh that before. Now that might be what all us do around here tuh survive; I ain't got no problems wid folks trying tuh feed they family, that's just not us. I have a job, can make extra money working fo' Frank, and my daddy done give yuh and I money for this heah house. What else we need?"

"We need mo'. I'm not living off Herman's money. I make the money fo' mah family. We need tuh work tuh build something better fo' our chirren, Ida. Yuh gone thank me later. Yuh can have all the babies yuh want then."

"I ain't waiting until I am old tuh have chirren,Timmy! If yuh want any, yuh better get them while the getting is good."

"There yuh go again. Yuh want everything now, Ida Mae. Well, this time yuh gon' have to wait. Wait until we have something tuh call our own. This house might not be finished when we get married. My family will still be working on some parts of it. That means we need tuh take it slow and hold off on having babies until later."

"Huh! I got yuh later! Yuh best hope I want to have chirren then. Okay?" She marched in front of him, waiving the lollipop. "Yuh gon' mess around heah and get no chirren because I have locked up shop."

Their disagreements escalated after that day. Rumors run rampant in small towns and they found themselves caught smack dab in the middle of the mill. As Timmy became more engrossed in his job, folks said he was cheating on Ida with a new girl in town. This one was hard for Ida Mae to ignore.

The culprit's name was Jesse Richards. She was a year or two older than Ida and had a reputation for being promiscuous. She was the kind of girl Eula Mae repeatedly warned Ida about. In fact, she told Ida Mae that this type of woman could not be trusted around her own stepfather.

Timmy never denied knowing Jesse. In fact, he said they were friends and that she often hung around his day job in Hardeeville. He claimed he did not find her attractive, nor had he ever been out in public with her. Townsfolk, on the other hand, said otherwise.

Rumor had it, Jesse was pregnant.

Ida was working when she found out, but apparently everyone in town knew about it, yet, Timmy said nothing. Ida drove to his job in Hardeeville.

Timmy, surprised to see her, took her over to the diner for lunch, and explained that it was all speculation. He said he did not tell her because he did did not want to spread gossip. He calmly spoke about the rumors until, to he and Ida's surprise, the subject of their conversation walked into the restaurant.

Timmy did not introduce them. Instead, he nodded to Jesse as she sat down at the lunch counter. He avoided

Ida's stares and kept looking around the room, cool as a cucumber.

Ida needed no further explanation. In a matter of seconds, she convicted Timetheous Tilley of lying and cheating. Actions always speak louder than words, and his actions proved he was somehow involved with this Jesse character. She could never forgive him. Three weeks later and still uncertain, Ida called off the wedding.

"What I tell ya? You a fool! I told you not to marry so young. I told you that you needed to live a little. Now look at ya?" Eula Mae stood on the front porch and screamed at her daughter.

"Look at what? If he was going to cheat, he was going to cheat regardless of whether I waited a few more years to marry him," Ida cried.

"Ya think! I told you to get to know other folks, not to surround yourself with one man! You put all ya hopes into Timmy. He could do no wrong. You should have kept your hindparts in Jersey with your uncle. You had a chance of working and going to college. Now, you out of school with a job as a clerk and spent all your savings on building a house with that fool. Now what you gonna do?" Eula Mae walked back and forth past her weeping daughter.

"We don't know if he did anything wrong, I just can't trust him. Don't go around saying he cheated with Jesse Richards 'cause we don't know. I don't even know if he ever cheated on me. I just know he changed, wanted to be in Savannah all the time. He claim none of these women mean a thing to him."

"Ida, you got a lot to learn! Sex never means anything to a man! He probably told you all the women he slept with don't mean nothing to him either. You better be glad he wanted to marry you or you could be in that same boat."

Eula Mae grabbed Ida's chin and forced her to look directly into her eyes. "If I were you, I would go straight to the horse's mouth for the answer. Men lie, but a woman scorned is dying to tell somebody the truth!" She walked into the house and stood facing Ida behind the screened door.

"Get your crying out now. You got to stand strong against this thing. It's the only way you will ever keep a man!"

1967

As she turned around, he forcibly stuck his long slimy tongue in her mouth. Ida sighed, and his hands were underneath her skirt. It all happened too fast.

An attractive smooth talking young man answered the door, said he was Jesse's older brother, and a student at Morehouse College. The entire family was from Atlanta, but moved to Jasper County when their mother died. He said he was visiting for the weekend.

He told Ida that the rumors about his sister's pregnancy were true. According to her, she and Timmy had been together for a few months before the surprise. She also told him that she knew Timmy was engaged to some other girl. The sex meant nothing to her; they were simply fooling around. It was never supposed to go this far.

Ida could not contain herself. She cried on his shoulder. He said she was beautiful. Said any man would be grateful to have her as his wife. He said a lot of things before convincing her to sit back down. He went into the kitchen to get Ida a cold glass of iced tea. She sipped and cried. He handed her tissues and massaged her curly locks.

"You must be Indian," he said as he held her face in his hands. "You are so beautiful."

Ida was frozen. This was not what she wanted. It was, though, just what she needed to feel like a desirable woman again. She let him kiss her gently because it felt good. He whispered in her ears and then softly bit her earlobes. She smiled and she forgot. He rose from the small couch they sat on and reached out for her. She arose and they held each other. This time, his hands were everywhere. Ida wanted to back away, she wanted to turn around and run out of that house, but she could not. She did not have the strength, and she did not have the energy to fight the urges she felt inside. They walked hand in hand toward the bedroom.

There are some things a woman just knows. No one has to confirm it. She just knows.

Ida knew. A month after the encounter, she knew she had more problems than she'd had before with the rumors that circulated about Jesse Richard's baby. Now she had a secret of her own. She forced herself to rise each morning, knowing she would have to tell someone before it was too late.

Savannah had places for this. Places where women could hide the truth. No one would ever find out. She could move back to Jersey, go to school, and then return if she wanted to. A clean slate. That is what she needed now. That is what she planned to have. Jasper County would become a distant memory.

She planned everything in advance. Not even Eula Mae would ever know. Then again she thought the less people that found out, the better. The only person that needed to know was outraged when she told him.

It seemed choking her made him feel good. He slapped her too. Held her down, slapped her across the face, and then took his strong arms and tried to choke the life out of her. He almost succeeded, but Ida fought back. She kicked and screamed, twisted her body and gave it her best shot. This was not a day that she was prepared to die.

"Get rid of it!" he threatened. "If you don't get rid of it, I will. I will cut that crumbsnatcher right out of your womb with my pocket knife!"

Ida laid in the mud gasping for air. The pain around her neck intensified as if his hands remained around her tiny throat. She dared not look at him as he stood above her, staring her down. With tears drenching her small face, she cried in shock. He was not the man she'd met before. The sensitive, caring man who said she was so beautiful. The one who said any man would be privileged to have her as his wife. Well, not him. He wanted absolutely nothing to do with her.

"You think you gon' destroy my future? I told you I was in college studying to be a doctor. You think I am foolish enough to give up everything because your black tail got pregnant? You Low Country trash disgust me!" he ranted.

He walked away, but suddenly turned and headed back in her direction. Before she could catch her breath, he grabbed her by the throat and hoisted her into the air.

"I can't trust you! We need to go to that clinic now! I need to know that this nightmare is really over. This has plagued my mind for two weeks. It ends tonight for the both of us!"

Ida struggled to get away. She tried to wrap her tiny fingers around his. When she could not, she pounded her fists into his chest, to no avail. She tried to look into his eyes and beg for mercy, but she saw no sign of emotion as he held her tighter than before. Ida wrestled harder. Then she remembered the switchblade in her pocket.

With one swift thrust, she stabbed him in the face. He never saw it coming. He screamed, released her, and grabbed the knife. Ida did not know where it landed. She prayed she missed every vital organ. Stumbling to the earth, she ran with all her might.

She ran through the woods, straight to her father's house. He was the only one who knew her dilemma. He said he would pay for the procedure. She trusted him and thought he would never tell another living soul.

Ida landed on the wooden beam stairs and collapsed. As she lay on her back, she panted for air. Realizing no one could hear the faint sounds coming from her, she used her feet to pound on top of the floorboards. The back door opened. It was a man, but not the one she sought at that moment.

"Where my daddy at?" She turned over on her stomach as her insides collapsed.

His face was filled with horror. He was the last person on earth that she wanted to see. The only person who could never discover the truth.

"What's wrong wid yuh, Ida Mae!" The sight of her lying on the back porch, drenched in mud, immediately got his attention.

"Leave it be. Ahm fine. It look worse than it feel," she said through labored breaths.

He walked toward her and reached down to lift her frail frame from the porch.

"No! No!" she screamed. "Don't you touch me! Leave me be, Timmy! G'wan now, ya hear?"

"Don't let your pride kill you, Ida! You needs help. You can barely breathe. I am heah now! I ain't care that we over. I ain't care about none of what happened. You need somebody to help you and I am the only one standing around." Tears strolled down his face. "Now, either you gonna let me, or I can run and get help from God knows who. Maybe the law."

"Oh, Lawd! It can't get no worse! What are you doing heah? You not s'posed to be heah!" Just then, the sharp pains in her abdomen intensified. "God in Heaven, I can't take this!" She let out a wail that reached the heavens.

Before she could raise another objection, she felt herself being lifted in his arms. He carried her through the back door into the kitchen. She did not resist; she had no strength to do so. He put her down in a chair and slowly removed her clothing. Then he went to get a basin to wash her face. When he returned, Ida was slouched over in the chair.

"Lordy be! Ida Mae, you need mo' help than I know how to give. Tell me what to do! I won't stand heah watching you die!"

Ida struggled to look up. She was out of answers. She was out of hope. At that moment, death was the better option.

"Come on, Wilcox! Say somethang! Don't do this to me!" Timmy pleaded.

Ida kept her face buried in her chest to avoid his screams. There was too much emotion coming from the likes of him. At that moment, she hated Timmy Tilley and every man that he represented. He was the one she ultimately blamed for her problems. If he had only been ready to get married instead of running the streets with Jesse Richards, none of this would have happened.

"Ya got your own problems, Timmy. Just leave it be!" she managed to get out as she pulled herself up straighter in the chair, determined to regain some dignity and control.

"What problems I got? I told you I ain't father no chirren with Jesse! That girl pregnant by one of them Habersham boys I used to hang with. I promised her I would protect her. I promised her I would not tell another living soul!"

Ida was dizzy. She had to lie down. She waved her hands at him, "I just needs to lie down."

"You can't lie down in all this mud. Let me at least wash off your arms and legs," he begged.

Reluctantly, she agreed. The pain had subsided, but the news that escaped from Timmy's mouth caused more pain in her head than she could deal with at that moment.

Timmy took the dishcloth from the kitchen counter and used it to wash off the mud, now caking and hardening like cement. Her body was limp as he gently lifted her motionless limbs and scrubbed them. When he finished, he carried her into the bedroom. Ida fell instantly sleep.

When she awoke hours later, Eula Mae and Herman were standing over her. Her worst fears had come true. She looked at them for a split second before she closed her eyes and turned away.

"Ida Mae. I've been where you are now. I don't know why you never told me. I figured it out on my own. I felt so bad for you to have to experience the same shame I had all those years ago. Child, I know that guilt can kill a person. I just didn't know how to approach you." Eula Mae stroked Ida's arms as she spoke.

"Mae, I told you I would not tell your secret. Your mama came to me a few days ago and she told me. I never let on that I knew. It wasn't until we saw you that I told her the truth. She's the only person I trust with my life and, since she already knew, I told her before something bad happened to my little angel." Herman Wilcox sat next to Ida crying.

Ida opened her eyes and looked at her parents. "This is not Timmy's baby. This is the baby of the Devil himself! Timmy never dishonored me. I guess he really loved me, cuz he was always willing to wait. Then I hear today that he's not the father of Jesse's baby either. What am I gonna do? I have to get rid of this demon seed!" she cried.

"Child, you a day late and a dollar short!" Eula Mae smiled. "I think you already starting to lose the baby. It might take a few days, but I think so. I called a friend and she come and say the baby's heart is really weak and she don't thank this child gone live much longer." She reached for her daughter's face, and went on, "See, Ida Mae, the Lord works in mysterious ways. It is not your time to have a child."

Ida looked around the room in astonishment. For three months, she'd cried herself to sleep. For three months, she'd hung her head in shame. Now the worst part was coming to an end. She was free, or would be soon. She thought she would feel relieved, but she was wrong. Her agony had only just begun.

As Timetheous Tilley sat next to the bed, Ida could feel his eyes as they pierced her skin. Her shame was too heavy for her to look back. He never asked who the child's father was, and she never told him. He said it did not matter. Said he loved her still. Those were the words she longed to hear. Maybe now they could get married and move into the house that Timmy'd continued building long after they broke up. She never understood what he was doing with Herman that day, and neither of them ever said a word about it.

The demons from her past never left. Long after she and Timmy moved into their home and started their lives together, they returned. She had not thought of him in several years. There was a time when he only chased her in her dreams. Chased her straight into Timmy's arms and then shot them both through the heart with one bullet. It was a scene that haunted Ida every night when she closed her eyes and every morning when she awoke.

One day, like all nightmares, this one vanished somewhere into the confines of her subconscious. Then reality set in. That following year, Ida stood face to face with the Devil, and he did what her dream foretold her years before: He chased her, setting traps to one day catch her and destroy her life, once and for all.

ELEVEN

1970

Fire is a vicious thief. It comes in quick, usually in the night, and destroys everything in its path. It sometimes leaves no evidence of its origin, and has no mercy on its victims.

Timmy and Ida stood and watched as their club burned to the ground. They arrived on the scene minutes before the roof caved in. Attached to their home, both structures were barely recognizable. It was where all their hard-earned money went. It was the bulk of their dreams.

Ida never wanted to be a club owner. Something about it seemed out of character for respectable folk, but Timmy convinced her that the club he opened would be unlike anything in the Low Country. He kept his word.

In the beginning, it seemed their hardest challenge was obtaining a liquor license. They tried several times and each time, their request was denied. They both knew it was customary to deny licenses to blacks so that alcohol could not be sold on the premises. Alcohol is what produced a solid profit, and everyone, including the Ku Klux Klan, knew that.

After six rejections in a two-year period, Timmy gave up and considered taking a second job for extra income. He thought about his dream of opening a club in Savannah. The one Ida shot down every time he mentioned it. Yet, here he was with no club in either city and the denied license was evidence that there was not much else that could be done.

The Klan controlled Jasper County, the courts, and City Hall. Every license and permit had to be approved by those offices. Liquor licenses were authorized by one individual, and he had more control over county affairs than anyone else.

"Ahm never selling out tuh the Klan," Timmy declared as he lay next to Ida, rubbing her swollen belly.

"I don't know, man! Seems the only way us black folk can git anything around heah is tuh dance with the Devil himself. Problem is, them devils come in all colors. Can't trust the white folks, and can't trust the blacks. Everybody out fo' somethang. They all want a piece of the pie," Ida lamented. "We'll never make a red cent if we gotta pay them tuh open the club, keep the club open, and fo' a license just tuh sell alcohol. How we gone make money? How they expect us tuh live?"

"Ain't know," he said. "There has tuh be another way. Maybe since we trying tuh come through the front do', we need tuh try going 'round the back."

"There ain't no way 'round the Klan. They the only way into this business. Black folks don't have that kind of power down at City Hall, never had and never will. The minute we get any type of business license, we have tuh look over our shoulders everywhere we go. A black businessman or woman is never safe around heah." She rolled over on her side, and continued, "You talk to them Habersham boys about The Shanty? They got a liquor license. How they get one?" She looked up into his eyes.

"No telling. Them fools may have held the clerk at gun point! Ain't nobody fool enough to mess wid 'em and they know it."

"You ask them fo' help?" She reached up and grabbed his chin.

"First place I started. Went to Derwin, since he the oldest. He said 50%. I knew that won't gon' work so I just walked off, got in my truck and got out o' there. That man is kin tuh the Devil, that's fo' sho'." He kissed her softly on the lips.

Ida thought for a moment and then sat up with excitement. "What about Frank?"

"What about him? I told him about the club before he left town, but he's gone so much now, I never see him. Thought things would change once Reverend Brown died, but he went into overdrive, working all over the place."

"Frank is never too busy fo' me." A sly grin crept across her face.

1971

He only owned one suit, purchased to impress Ida on their wedding day. That was a long time ago. Now, years later, the suit had a snug fit and desperately needed a few inches let out of the waistline. He had to stop drinking. It was taking a toll on his body.

Timmy reached into the wardrobe and pulled out the suit. Then he walked over to the dresser, opened the top drawer, took out a pair of navy blue socks, a tie, handkerchief, and an undershirt. This was a special occasion. If everything went well, he would be the second black owner of a juke joint in Jasper County. That, in and of itself, was a major accomplishment. Certainly worth putting on the tight-fitting suit and shining his shoes to a high polish.

He got dressed with a sense of urgency. After he put his shiny shoes on, he stood looking in the mirror. It was now or never to live his dreams. This had to work because he had no idea how he would handle another rejection.

He walked into the living room, and to his surprise, Frank Wilcox was standing on the front porch.

"I ain't hear yuh drive up!" he exclaimed.

"They never do," Frank teased, opening the screened door. "Y'all fool geechies always leave your doors open and act like no body crazy enough to walk in on you."

"Well, we good folks. We just believe anyone come around heah been invited. Got no beef wid dese folks. Just want tuh live peaceably among 'em. You know me and Tilley welcome the whole town." He reached out and shook Frank's hand warmly.

"Well, that's why you can't get the liquor license. You don't pose a threat to the very people you're inviting into your house." Frank walked over to the fireplace and examined the dusty pictures on the mantel.

"Ah, Frank. Yuh know I don't understand as much about business as you. Ahm just trying tuh run a small juke joint tuh ease the folk's around heah burdens. You would think everyone would see it as a good thang."

"No good deed goes unpunished." Frank laughed. "Let's get out of here, young mullet. Where's Ida Mae?"

"She out on the town, I s'pose. Doctor told her tuh take it easy, but she don't listen. She already had two miscarriages. This one last the longest. She near seven months. Guess that mean I can put together a crib now." They walked down the steps side by side.

"Nothing can slow Ida down. God knew that before this baby ever came. You two just hold on. Everything is gonna be all right. We get this license, you open the club, have that baby, and probably have plenty more babies after that. I'm proud of you."

When they arrived at City Hall, Frank pulled his car directly into a front parking lot. It was known throughout town that only whites parked in the front lots. Blacks parked on the side of the building or in the back and had to walk around the building to the front entrance.

Timmy looked at his mentor. Something about power was etched across his face. "Just tell me what to do," he said as he exited the vehicle.

"Nothing. That's what you do. Nothing. You've been down here before. Every one of them hicks knows what you want. They just don't want to give it to you." Frank stepped on the sidewalk and proceeded toward the steps of City Hall.

"I know you know what tuh do tuh make it happen. Me and Tilley so grateful yuh took time out tuh come back and help us." He practically walked behind Frank up the steps.

"I had some unfinished business down here anyway. I can kill two birds with one stone." He smiled at Timmy and then led him down the long hallway to the office that delivered the six prior rejections.

The clerk recognized the tall distinquished Negro as soon as he walked in. Dressed in a three piece pin-striped blue suit, Frank Wilcox was no stranger to that office. He had been there on several occasions, and each time he had come, his visit had been brief but successful.

He motioned to Timmy to take a seat and then walked directly over to the long wooden counter behind which the clerk stood, and took a small piece of paper, wrote down instructions, and handed the paper back to the clerk.

"Sir, you have tuh take a number," she said as she handed the customer standing in front of her a form to complete.

"Just tell Peters Mistah Wilcox is here." He never looked directly at her.

"You have tuh take a number!" Her voice escalated. "Besides, I don't know if we can help yuh anyway. Just take a number and we can find out." She noticed how smartly he was dressed and decided to lower her voice.

Frank told the customer in front of him to step aside. "Just give him the note. He'll take care of it." He could see the fear in her eyes as she held the piece of paper tightly in her hand.

"He's not to be disturbed," she mumbled and then proceeded to open the folded piece of paper to read the contents.

"Miss, please don't do that. Private business between Mr. Peters and Mr. Wilcox." He reached up and grabbed the paper. "For his eyes only." He winked at her and refolded the note.

She looked at the other customers who stood watching the unusual scene play out. She then looked directly at Frank, spun around, and headed toward the back office. She returned within a few seconds.

"He said give him a few minutes and he will see yuh."

Frank and Timmy waited for about a half hour before another clerk walked over and interrupted their conversation.

"Excuse me, gentlemen, you all may have to come back tomarah. We are quite busy." Frank's back was to the woman. He turned around.

His presence startled her. "Frank Wilcox, I did not know that was you! Does Mr. Peters know you're here?"

"He does." Frank gave her a warm smile.

"It's good to see you. You don't come around anymore. We heard you moved on." She looked at Timmy while she spoke.

Timmy recognized the woman. She had been a thorn in his side each time he requested a license. She was the one who delivered the blows of each rejection. She had a nasty way of giving bad news that sent chills down his spine.

"Oh, so you two know each other?" She continued to beam.

"Guess we do. This is my family, if you must know, Kathryn. How's Sam?" Frank watched her suspiciously.

"Oh, well, I'm sorry. This gentleman comes in here all the time. I didn't know you two was related." Then she looked directly at Timmy, "Next time let me know who you are."

"So it's who you know?" Timmy blurted out.

Frank gave him a stern look. "He's just giving you a hard time. I hear he's had more rejections than you've had marriage proposals." He laughed out loud.

"Frank Wilcox, you better behave yourself! I am sorry for the trouble in the past. Seems your relative was lacking information on the form that was necessary to receive the type of license he was after, that's all. Nothing that could not be fixed, had I known who he was." She tried to seem reassuring.

"No sweat, Katie. It's all water under the bridge now. I'm sure he'll have that license in a few more minutes. Peter's taking care of it. I'm sure next time, you'll assist him to the best you know how." He walked past her to the counter.

She nervously looked at Timmy and mouthed the words, "I'm sorry."

Timmy smiled and nodded his head. He knew that she too was just a pawn in this office, with no real authority for getting anything done.

Chadwick Peters controlled City Hall. He was Ridgeland's comptroller by day, and the Grand Wizard of the local Klan by night. He made no qualms about the fact that he hated blacks and refused to do business with any of them. Said the only thing a darkie could do for him was wipe the dust off his shoes.

He abused his authority by denying every license request that came before him. If he could not find a way to deny the request, he simply held onto the paperwork for an inordinate amount of time until the challenged victim was either too tired to continue fighting, or had given up all together. Should the message not resonate as clear, he resorted to his nightly activities to further explain his point.

He was married to Lula Peters, a woman that seemed just as confused about being a white woman in the Low County as she was about the lifestyle of her infamous husband. They had three children; one child had disappeared years before, causing one of the greatest stirs in and around Jasper County.

The clerk opened the hatch on the counter and Frank walked through to the back office. When he reached the door, he turned around and surveyed the people standing or sitting in the outer office. He looked at Kathryn Hawkins and then opened the door and walked inside.

Five minutes later, he walked out of the office holding a manila envelope. He was smiling.

1972

Ida knocked on the front door. A few months ago, this would have never been an option, but just like the two previous times, she never made it to full term. She vowed she would never experience this kind of pain again.

A woman opened the door and stepped out onto the front porch. "Who yuh heah tuh see?" she asked.

"Ah come tuh see the root doctor," Ida said just above a whisper.

"What?" The woman hollered, "Nobody in their fool mind refer to Miss Beulah as the root doctor, yuh know?"

"That's what she is. You know who I mean. What other reason would I come heah?" Ida stood back frowning.

"Well, it's Halloween. Folks want all kind of stuff."

Ida put her hands on her small hips. "Well, honey, this ain't no trick and being here ain't a treat! Is Miss Beulah heah or what? I called first and she told me tuh come. The sooner we can get this over with, the better."

"All right, all right. Just checking. I tell you, folks coming all times of the day and night around this time of the year. Folk that would not be caught dead come here in the middle of the night. You'd be surprised." Her tirade was suddenly interrupted.

"Mind your own business, Edna. I told you that before. Miz Tilley did not come to talk to you about foolishness. She has an urgent need." Beulah Chaney herself suddenly stood framed in the screened door.

Ida never thought the two of them would meet for the reason she had come. She remembered Beulah more than anyone else in the Low Country. She had that kind of reputation. Eula Mae called her a very nice person, but Ida could find few that agreed with that assertion. Most folks said she was evil, and warned that doing business with her would cause a curse that could not be reversed.

But Ida felt she had no other choice.

The latest miscarriage had occurred just shy of eight months. After enduring thirty-six hours of cramping, Ida suffered a violent and painful miscarriage, losing the baby her body now ached to hold.

Everyone told her to give it another try, besides, she was still a young woman yet in her twenties. But to Ida, that meant very little. She wanted a child, had wanted one since she was fifteen years old, and to this day, had not carried one to full term. It was just something she dreamed of doing before she left the earth.

"What can I do for you, Miss Ida Mae Wilcox Tilley." Beulah sat down in the parlor looking at Ida.

"I want tuh get my tubes tied. Can't go tuh a hospital. I would need Timmy's consent. The less he knows, the better. I can't see him go through another loss. I don't know if I'll get pregnant again, so I gotta do something."

Beulah looked at Ida and sat up on the sofa. "You sound like all the other desperate young mothers that come here to rid themselves of a child or to have one. I think I understand what you are saying. But..." She stopped mid sentence.

"But what? I know what I want, Miss Beulah. I just can't see mahself going through this again. It's too painful."

"Right now it is. Let me give you some advice. I want you to think on it and then come back in a week with your decision."

Ida looked at her suspiciously. "I thought you said you would do it."

"No. I said you could come. That's different. I offered you the invitation because I suspected what your issues were." Beulah stood up.

"What that got tuh do wid nothing? I come tuh you fo' help and yuh turn me away. I ain't like these other folks, I can pay whatever yuh want. Just give me some herbs I can take tuh close my womb for good," she demanded.

Buelah chuckled. "You think that's all I do?"

"I ain't care what else you do! Folks say you can make this thing stop. Then stop it, I say." Ida started to cry, big tears rolling down her brown cheeks.

"Ida Mae, I do everything on a case-by-case basis. I'm not in it for the money. You've been listening to too many rumors about me. I can send you to fifty places for drugs that induce menopause, but is that really what you want? I see a young, bitter woman who thinks she knows what she is asking for. Babies come in their own time. When God has a time for you to be a mother, you shall be one."

"Yuh startin' tuh sound like my cousin Ruth. She say the same thing. I thought yuh were a root doctor. Ain't that how yuh make all this money?" Ida waved her hand around the well-furnished room and turned to leave.

"My money, Miss Ida, is my business. I earned it, like you do, by hard work. Any money I took from these hicks was well deserved, not that it's any of your business."

"I knew it was a bad idea tuh come heah askin fo' yuh help! You bad they say. What kinda curse you gon' put on me now?" Ida opened the door.

Buelah reached over and placed her hand on Ida's. She felt the young woman trembling, whether from fear or rage she wasn't certain.

"Ida Mae, your womb is already cursed! I didn't curse it and neither did God. You did that to yourself the first time you held a seed. Only you can reverse those words you said to yourself. Once you do, you'll have a child but it's your decision. You can take the drugs to stop another pregnancy and never conceive, or you can wait on your time."

"What I do in the meantime? I can't bear another pregnancy. I just can't do it!"

"And you won't have to, I assure you. In the meantime, you must enjoy life. Your husband and family need you more right now." Beulah smiled at her.

"I'm so tired of the promises, Miss Beulah. I don't mean no disrespect. I'm tired and I hurt so bad inside I want tuh die. That last baby was 'most full term. A beautiful little girl." She turned around again to depart.

"She had a rare heart disease. She would have died at the age of three months tops." Beulah did not want to tell Ida this, but felt she had to ease the woman's guilt.

"How you know that?" Ida put her hands over her face. "How you know? That's what they said at the hospital. Said something was wrong with her heart. I never told another soul."

"I knew when I felt your stomach in the Piggly Wiggly that day. I knew the child would not live. I knew that just as I stand here with my hand on your abdomen now telling you that there is strong seed left inside of you. It will be many years, but you will have more than one child before you leave this Earth." She grabbed Ida by the shoulders and held her tight. "Can you hold on a little while longer?"

"I just ain't know. I'm scared of another miscarriage. My poor husband can't take it, I tell ya. He put all his hopes into each child and still nothing. Nothing to show for all the love we have for each other. Nothing."

"Now that's not true. There's plenty evidence of the love you both have. Hang onto that love for now. Run those clubs and enjoy life. One day you will look up and see yourself with a baby in your arms." Beulah kissed her on the cheek, tasting the salty tears.

Ida walked out the front door and then turned back to face Beulah. "Can I give you anything for your time?"

"Like what? Just watch yourself, Ida. Secrets have a way of killing us. Those demons you're battling have not given up. You have a lot of turmoil inside that you need to work on. Do the work now and live your life. Remember this: Nothing is what it seems. Just when it seems like it's all over, it's really just about to begin."

TWELVE

1974

"Where we going?" Ida looked out of the car window at the beautiful weeping willows that lined both sides of the highway.

"That's fo' me tuh know, and you tuh find out!" He had a wide grin on his face.

He had told her to put on her best clothes that night, said they were going out on the town. It had been such a long time. Ever since the fire had destroyed everything they owned, they'd stayed to themselves, rarely going out of the house.

It had been two years. Two years of misery. Two years of regret. Two years wanting to forget about the whole thing. It was time to start over, but neither of them knew how.

Since that awful night, they'd moved in with Herman Wilcox on the other side of town. He owned a medium sized six-room house with a huge wraparound front porch. It had the usual crawl space underneath, visible from the outside, supported by stacked cinderblocks on each corner. The three steps leading up to the front porch on both the front and side of the house were made of concrete, enclosed by brick borders.

Ida wanted to rebuild their house immediately, but both Herman and Timmy argued against it. According to them, they could save money by living with Herman and focus on purchasing land for a new club. With a liquor license, the club was expected to automatically generate the income needed to rebuild.

Herman convinced Ida that Timmy's plan was a good idea.

"That husband of yours is a true businessman. He won't stop until he sees his vision, I tell you. Not until he sees his vision." He stood over the stove in the kitchen frying chicken.

"That's what I'm afraid of. The vision gone, Daddy. When is mah husband gonna see that? Owning a club is just not a good idea. Yeah, we got the license, but look at what we lost because of it." She sat at the kitchen table reading a newspaper.

"Losing that club and your home had nothing to do with Frank getting you the license, Ida Mae. No one from around here would mess with Frank like that."

"Oh no? There are some folks that really hate the ground Frank walk on! He got too many enemies to name." She put the newspaper down on the table.

"Ida Mae, no one is that crazy. Frank got enemies like everyone of us in town, but few black people have the power over folks like Frank. I'm too scared to ask him how he got that power. Seemed one day he was robbing stores and the next he was owning them. Now he traveling to God knows where all the time. Told me he owns a house in Savannah and one in New York. Right in the center of Harlem. Ya don't say!" He turned around and placed a bowl of crispy fried chicken in the center of the table.

"I know he ain't doing nothing that's against the law. Frank is too smart fo' that. He just can't protect us while he's away. The club was burned down while he was off in Europe of all places. Those people knew Frank was not going tuh fly back tuh South Carolina for a small juke joint owned by me and Timmy. Had they touched anything on Frank's property, he would have returned and stormed the town!" She opened the cabinet, took out dinner plates, and began setting the table. "There would have been hell ta pay fo sho'!"

"Don't think because he did not come, he don't care. Don't think he's not going to pay those fools back. Frank got a way about handling revenge. He knows when to strike against his enemies. That's what they hate so much about him." He set bowls of white rice and green peas on the table to flank the chicken.

"I ask Frank about them enemies one day a long time ago. He told me he had some kind of collateral that protected him. I asked what, but he never told me. I sho' would like to know now! I need some of that fo' myself."

Herman burst out laughing. "Frank got all kinds of collateral. Now we ain't never been close until a few years ago. We had words one day and next thing I knew, he was coming around every night to check in on me. That's when Barbara was living with me. Maybe he knew she was crazy." He laughed even harder.

"I'm glad he did! That woman put root on you and tried to take yuh outta heah!"

They sat down and ate dinner. As usual, Timmy was away working on his prized project: Timbuktu, the club on the other side of the world.

1970

"You sure you want to know?"

"Ah'm sho.' Whatever you gon' tell me, will set me free. Set my heart free."

"I think you already know. Why did you ask me to get involved?"

"Because Ah knew yuh were da only one Ah could trust. Ah got fifteen stores because of you. Anythang yuh tell me meant fo' me tuh know." The old man stared at Frank with enormous passion in his deep-set eyes.

"Yeah, seems Peters can't keep his hands off of anything his son touches. It's like he only craves his son's pickings.

Charlie took advantage of her, you know that. Then she fell into a deeper cave by taking up with his father. He was supposed to be consoling her. Said she was like a daughter to him. I don't know many men that sleep with their daughters. Chad is one low down bastard, if you ask me."

"No daughter o' mine is gon' ever be a Peters! That's fo' darn sure."

"I hear you! Pure vile. That's what the entire Klan is. Vile."

"Look a heah, Ah never had no use fo' the Klan. Mah daddy was college educated when we opened our first store and filling station. He would turn over in his grave if Ah joined such a lifeless group of individuals." He placed his gnarled hands on Frank's shoulders and said, "You'll take care o' them girls won't cha?"

"That's something you don't have to ask me to do. Those girls mean as much to me as my blood sister. They can count on me for anything."

"Yuh took care of the paperwork, Ah asked yuh to?"

"I did. Everything's completed and filed away. Your lawyers will know what to do should anything happen to you."

"Somethangs gon' happen, Frankie. The only thing we don't know is when." He laid back down, exhausted.

They had more in common than anyone in the Low Country ever knew. An unlikely friendship, the old Caucasian man took Frank under his wings when he was a skinny fourteen-year-old. In a period of twenty years, Frank had become the best employee Hawk's ever had, expanding one modest country store into a chain of fifteen stores across the southern seaboard.

Wallace Hawkins never let him forget it. He entrusted Frank with practically everything he owned, and before he left the earth, he publically proclaimed that Frank Wilcox was the only real son he ever had.

1975

"Tilley, come git me."

"Where you at? Timmy, where you been fo' three days. I've been sick tuh mah soul wid worry! Who took yuh?" Ida was furious but relieved to hear his voice.

"Don't worry. I'll tell yuh later. I'm outside the Ridgeland jailhouse."

"What? What in God's name is going on, man?"

"Calm down, Tilley. Just come git me and fast befo' they change their minds and won't let me leave." Timmy hung up the telephone.

Ida ran into the living room and screamed. She had been on the couch for two days, unable to move, worried that the Klan had taken Timmy, worried that he would never come home.

Neighbors had gone door to door inquiring of his disappearance, but no one seemed to know anything. Even domestic workers tried to coax their Caucasian employers into revealing whether they knew of his disappearance. Everyone seemed in shock and utterly clueless.

Ida believed the Klan was to blame. Timmy had no known enemies in town. He had a reputation for being a good man that helped everyone, gave to everyone, and could be trusted by everyone. No one would harm him if they knew who he was. She was sure of that.

When she could not reach Frank for help, she contacted one of Timmy's brothers. At midnight the following night, all three Tilley men stood on the front porch and promised they would locate Timmy before the sun went down on the next day. By the hatred in their eyes, Ida knew they would deliver on that promise.

Before the sun set on that Monday night, Timmy called. Seemed the brothers pressure on just about every business owner in Ridgeland sent a message to the police chief to release anyone with a last name of Tilley. The chief ordered the new sheriff in town to do so immediately.

Ronald drove Ida into town. He was on his way from Savannah when he heard the news that his brother was safe and sound in jail.

When she saw him, Timmy was wearing his classic wide grin on his face. "Lordy be, Ida Mae. I knew something was wrong. They threw me out of jail today. Said they didn't care where I went. I asked about a trial and they told me there wouldn't be one!" He jumped into the back seat of the car.

"What? You all right? Why did they put you in jail anyhow?" She turned to face him.

"Said we was open beyond curfew."

"Curfew? They ain't got no curfew around heah! What that yuh talking?" Ida looked at Ronald.

"New sheriff in town. He enforce a made-up curfew on all juke joints. Can't be open pass two in the morning." Timmy wiped his forehead and chuckled.

"Yeah. That some fool mess the white man come up with. He just trying to slow us down. He know good and well that juke joints don't start filling up until midnight. Now what kind of sense that make?" She handed him a handkerchief.

"None at all, baby. Funny thing is, the new sheriff not a white man." He waited for her reaction.

"No joke? Ridgeland got a black sheriff? Timmy you done lost yuh mind!"

"Y'all didn't know?"

"No!" they both yelled in unison.

He laughed. "I heard it on the radio in Savannah. How come y'all ain't know?" He asked the question fully aware that most local folks only kept abreast of their immediate family and job concerns.

"Where he come from? He must not be from around heah, having a curfew and all," Timmy stated.

"Atlanta. I heard he was a deputy sheriff in Dekalb County before coming down here."

"What? Why would he want to come to this hick town?" Ida rolled the window down to feel the cool breeze outside. This day was wearing her out.

"Power. He ain't have no power in that big town. They won't let 'im. They got to deal with the aftermath of King's killin'. They ain't about to give no black man power to get revenge." Ronald turned the car into the driveway.

"So he choose heah? What kinda power can he get among these white folks and their white sheets? They don't ride at night in Atlanta no mo,' but they sho' ride around heah. That man is fool to think he gone get power heah." Ida stepped out of the vehicle. "What his name?" She walked around the car and grabbed Timmy's hands.

"Bryant. Charles Bryant, I think," Ronald answered knowingly.

A sharp pain riveted through Ida's body. The name was unfamiliar, but her insides sent a chilling message that the appointment of Jasper County's first black sheriff was not a blessing, at least not for Ida Mae Wilcox Tilley.

1976

The sign on the outer door read, "Closed until further notice."

Before Timmy could bring the car to a complete stop, Ida swung the door open and ran toward the club's front entrance.

"Hold on, Ida Mae!" he yelled from the window.

She reached the door, read the entire notice, and then within seconds, collapsed on the ground.

"Tilley. What's wrong wid yuh?" Timmy ran to her, kneeled down, and lifted her head into his lap.

Ida lay on the concrete in a semi conscious state, eyes partially opened, but body as stiff as a board. She blamed herself for the notice posted on the club's door. One look at Timmy would force her to disclose just how much she actually knew about the entire situation.

Why had he returned? Why now? She heard his family had no connections to the Low Country. In fact, they moved away only a few years after their arrival. To everyone's knowledge, they had no other relatives in the area. She honestly thought she'd never see him again.

But she was wrong. One day out of the blue, she saw him. The monster in her nightmares had a new name: Charles Bryant.

With the exception of his police uniform, nothing about his countenance had changed. His eyes still held enough hatred to fill an ocean, and when he spotted Ida Mae, it was clear that his memory was a tall as his height. He would never forget their past, and he would make sure that neither did she.

He followed her into the parking lot of the Five and Dime store one day. Ida heard him gaining on her heels, but she ignored him.

"Black trash," he hissed. "I know you see me."

Ida put the key into the car door and opened the door. He grabbed the door from behind her.

"Don't try to act as if you don't hear me. You know who I am, right? I can throw your hindparts in jail if I wanted to. Hell, I just might do it for the fun of it."

Ida sat down in the car and stared up into his face. "And what would you say the charge was?" she asked.

"Assault with a deadly weapon." He stroked the crooked scar on his face.

Ida turned and looked straight ahead. When he stopped speaking, she put the key into the ignition and started the engine. He held onto the door and watched her every move.

"Ignoring me won't make me leave you alone. I owe you something and I never renege on a promise to pay someone back, ya hear?" He tipped his cowboy hat politely, mocking her, and slammed the car door.

Ida never said a word. She held onto the steering wheel and tried to sum up a prayer to protect her from the monster outside of the car, but there was nothing much she could say. She had only talked to God as a child, and when she did not get what she wanted from him, she gave up on her small belief that he might exist, and stopped talking to him all together. What could she say now that he would listen to?

Alone in a world of fear, Ida felt no one could save her. He could do anything he wanted to her. Though she may have deserved something for the knife wounds that were still evident on his face, her husband, Timetheous, was purely innocent.

She had to protect him if no one else. She would not allow the nightmare to come true, even if it meant striking a deal with the Devil himself.

1972

Long before they arrived, she stood watching him. He claimed he had forgotten the past, and forgiven all the people in it, but she doubted every word that came out of his mouth.

He returned to Jasper County for something and every road led to revenge.

She stood watching him in the parking lot that hot sunny day. She saw the way he whispered something into that poor woman's ear, yes, she saw the fear in woman's eyes.

Even from a distance, the observer knew he was up to no good. There was no one close enough to stop him, and no one he would allow to get close enough to him in the first place. No one but the one person he trusted the most.

The puzzle's many pieces had not yet been connected, but the handwriting on the wall was crystal clear. She walked down the street knowing that she would have to take action to end his reign of terror once and for all.

1974

"Well, well, well. We meet again."

"Unfortunately, and it's still not a pleasure."

"What are you doing around here?"

"I could ask you the same thing."

"That's obvious. I'm the sheriff of Jasper County. That's why I'm here. Now you? You were the thorn in my side in Georgia. I hope this is a coincidence."

"No. Devils travel in similar circles." The man handed the sheriff his driver's license and registration card. "Just git this over with, will you?"

"I see you know the drill. Never dawn on you to obey traffic laws, I bet."

"Yeah right. When the law don't obey the laws, why should I?" He took his dark shades off and stared at the sheriff.

"Because you don't want to find your butt behind bars."

"I'm trembling in my boots! Look a heah, write the ticket so I can be on my way." He leaned out of the car window.

"You'll sit your butt right there until I finish with you." Sheriff Bryant examined the license. "Says here you live around here."

"Surprise, surprise!" Edgar Carter said, mocking the television character Gomer Pyle.

"Well, I'll be damned. Let me warn you, don't give me no problems this time. I couldn't get you in Atlanta, but I sure can get you here. I am the boss, or haven't you heard?"

"Dem white boys in sheets got yuh thinking so? You a bigger fool than I thought." He put his shades back on and turned the ignition switch.

"How's your wife?" he laughed.

Sheriff Bryant grabbed the billy club secured to his waist, and brought it to Edgar Carter's throat. "You watch yourself, Carter. I got the law on my side. You on my turf now!"

"Is that a fact?" Edgar never flinched. "You ever hear of Carterville?" he asked.

The statement caught the sheriff off guard. "What? All I need to know is Jasper County. You driving on my roads now. I don't care where this Carterville is located, because in this county I could break your sorry neck and get away with it!" He looked around the interior of the car for a weapon, hoping to find some reason to arrest the man.

Edgar Carter raised his arm and swatted the club away like an annoying fly. "Carterville is in Jasper County and right now, you in Carterville."

"Then I own it too." Sheriff Bryant held both ends of the club in his hands watching Edgar carefully. After a few minutes, he took the license and registration card from his pocket and handed them back to Carter.

"You think so? Maybe you should go home and ask your wife. I'm sho' she could tell you where it begins and ends." He let out a hearty laugh as his vehicle spun off into the distance.

Charles Bryant stood on the side of the two lane highway boiling with anger. He had moved to Jasper County for a chance to shine. A chance to prove that he could lead an entire police force. Nothing could get in his way now, including the arrogant

Mr. Carter.

Edgar Carter was a distraction and one that he could not afford to have around. It had been decades ago in Atlanta, but Carter had proven that he was a worthy opponent that was somehow above the law. Charles Bryant had to find a way to control him in Jasper County, because he knew as long as Edgar Roland Carter was within one-hundred feet of him, he would never again rise to prominence.

1979

"Somebody set us up, man!" Claude Habersham yelled as he put his shotguns back into the wooden case.

"Oh yeah, if that's true, we got some killing to take care of." His father, Nate Habersham, proclaimed.

"I done told ya'll we was being framed by that good for nothing, Uncle Tom down in the Sheriff's department." Claude's younger brother, Jerry, chimed in.

"You trust your source?" His father's eyes pierced right through his younger son.

"Daddy, she 'bout as good as dey come. It was almost like coming straight from the horses' mouf." A smirked was etched across Jerry's face.

"How you know dis woman? You trust just about anyone smile good in yer face! She could be a set up too." Claude, demanding the attention from his father, yelled.

"I been seeing her fo' a while. She real good people, in fact, she from that herd of Pickney's, you know we ain't ever had a problem with dem boys." Jerry shot back.

"I say we wait. I think it's time he got a good taste of our kind before we go doing something to him. He's protected by the Klan now. I'm gonna see that by the time I finish with his butt, the Klan will beg me to allow them to kill him for me." Nate yelled.

"I agree, Pops. Junior kind of sweet on this woman. He trust too easily. He ain't her type. I wonder why she acting all sweet on him. Somethang ain't right about this." He rolled his eyes at his younger brother.

"You jealous. No woman with that kind of class would want you, that's for darn sure." Claude chuckled.

Nathaniel Habersham continued watching the discourse between two of his sons. He could kill the Sheriff now, but torture was a more enticing option. Besides, it just might be an opportunity to kill two birds with one stone. That option, he liked even more.

II

Ruth Fields Harrison Garrett
"Mother Ruth"

ONE

1975

Ruth washed clothes on the back porch that entire hot, humid summer day. First, the white sheets from the bedrooms; next, the lighter pieces of clothing, towels, and, finally, the darker clothing which included much of her husband's overalls he wore to work each day. After four hours of rubbing, wringing, and lifting water-laden clothing and linens, she was exhausted; yet, she enjoyed the time alone.

Their one-story white clapboard house with green shutters on the windows had a screened back porch that could be seen from the left side of their octagon-shaped yard. Her husband, Augustus Garrett, used it as a storage area, but when they could finally afford a washing machine from Montgomery Ward in Walterboro, Ruth insisted that it be placed on the back porch, so that a water hose could be connected to the newly installed faucet in the kitchen sink.

All the extra money from Augustus's job at the local steel plant went to remodel their five-room home so that an extra bedroom could be added. The addition was needed to accommodate their growing daughters who could no longer share a bedroom with their brothers. However, when the renovations started, Ruth decided it was time to become a modern family and install an indoor bathroom with all the trimmings: running water, a commode, and a cast iron claw-foot bathtub. Upon completion, the new bathroom became her favorite attraction, for it was the one place she could run and hide from the cares of the world. In fact, it was the only room in the entire house that had its own door that could be locked from the inside. To Ruth, its privacy was her own taste of paradise.

Surrounded by piles of wet and dry laundry, she manually fed individual pieces of clothing through the metal ringer affixed to the top of the washer, while the remaining clothes soaked in the opened bottom cabinet below the ringer. Methodically, with one hand she fed an item between two rolling pins and with the other, caught the fabric on the other side and placed it inside the wicker laundry basket on the floor. She had washed four loads of clothes, and when the basket was full, walked outside and hung them on the long wire clothesline suspended between two enormous oak trees whose roots rippled across the yard. Just opposite the trees were twenty neatly carved rows of whatever crops her family planted that season.

She was having a familiar moment; one in which something inside whispered that something bad had or was about to happen. She barely paid attention to the clothespins that she pulled from the hand-sewn burlap bag. Although the sky appeared clear, a feeling somewhere deep inside her suggested a storm was brewing. Something was destined to happen that not even her foretelling could predict, nor her prayers would be able to stop.

Ruth fought against the demons in her mind, besides, she reminded herself that it was Saturday, her favorite day of the week. The children were away with relatives and Augustus was at work. Although she had a ton of chores to do around the house, she looked forward to Saturdays. It was the day she prepared everything in anticipation of the weekly Sunday church services. Never knowing how long her family would be in service from one week to the other, Ruth prepared Sunday's dinner on Saturday night so they could eat the minute they got home.

So tonight, like all the others over the years, she would boil neck bones for the collard greens, potatoes for the potato salad, and eggs to make the deviled eggs. Earlier that morning she'd chased a chicken 'round and 'round the chicken coop, broke its neck, plucked it clean, scraped out the insides, and placed the remains in a large pot of water to stew. She kneaded a lump of dough and placed it in an aluminum baking pan on the counter to bring to life her famous self-rising yeast rolls.

Returning to the back porch, Ruth walked up the steps, opened the screened door, and stood just a few inches inside. She forgot to sit the laundry basket in its usual spot, but instead, held onto it and turned in a complete circle. She sniffed repeatedly, wondering if the bad feelings brewing within her were somehow connected to the weather. She could tell a lot just from the smells emanating in the air. These smells were familiar, yet strange, which limited her immediate ability to understand their warning.

Ruth sniffed again, putting her nose in the air like a bloodhound, and then set the laundry basket down, reached into the front panel of the washcabinet and pulled the lever to turn the machine off. A small mountain of overalls lay piled next to her, but she did not bother washing them. Instead, she disconnected the black rubber hose and pulled the machine toward the screened door, opened it, and placed the hose down into the yard allowing the dirty wash water to escape onto the ground below.

"The postman always rings twice," she mumbled as she looked up into the crystal blue sky and walked out to the front yard.

She stopped to admire her garden. This year she'd planted hydrangeas, star jasmine, tulips, and perennials. A kaleidoscope of bright colors made her smile. She almost forgot what was plaguing her until the awful feeling of dread returned. She swiftly dismissed all negativity, knelt down into the flowerbed, and picked up two mason jars filled with rooting plants and water. She stood up, walked past her front porch in the direction of the long winding road that lead to the other houses on the family plot, and hummed softly. Just then a familiar sound pierced through the skies.

Sounds played a major role in Ruth's predictions. Since her sixteenth birthday, she had been able to predict tragic events, using sounds like an oweje board indicator. She was never wrong. Sensing she recognized a catastrophic prediction, she stood still, eyes focused on the skies above.

A train approached from the distance.

Ruth looked around the yard and shook her head. She hated the rattling sounds from the wooden tracks as metal wheels spun across them. Hated them so much that each time she heard them, she stood still, bracing herself, until the entire assembly of freight cars had completely passed by.

She memorized the daily train schedule: the eight a.m., eleven a.m., two p.m., and seven p.m. trains. The fifth and final freight train passed by every night around ten-thirty. Passenger trains had long been re-routed to the metal tracks on the other side of Highway 17, near the newly expanded train station in Yemasee.

All of a sudden, a light went off in her head. Ruth could not recall hearing the eleven a.m. nor the two p.m. trains. It was now well after four in the afternoon. She ran towards the back yard, stopped, and stood dazed staring into the woods in fornt of her.

The tracks directly behind the house formed a short cut for just about everyone in town. Less locomotive traffic brought about more foot traffic. Folks walked the tracks all times of the day and night, except on this particular day. It had been unusually quiet. Why?

Their home was conveniently located along side a narrow barge built over the Coosawhatchie River. Augustus arrived home a half hour earlier if he walked alongside those tracks. It was a peaceful scenic view with one major interruption: the sound of an oncoming train.

Déjà vu.

Ruth felt warm and prickly all over. She started to panic as surges of heat pulsated down her long expresso-colored fingertips. The sounds drew near. She held onto the Mason jars and looked up into the sky. Its clear blue expanse had now become a misty gray. Even the Earth behaved as if it were bracing itself for impending danger. Ruth ran towards the noise that filled the air.

Like exploding firecrackers, sounds burst through the sky, followed by faint cries or screams from an unknown source. Ruth started to run, but stopped just as a thunderous sound shot through the trees, as if headed in her direction. And then the earth started to tremble.

Running towards the sounds, Ruth glanced at her wrist watch. It was a quarter to five. The plant where Augustus worked shut down at 4:30 every Saturday. There was no need to worry. History, no matter how brutal, would never repeat itself.

"Get it together, girl!" she chastised herself as she turned to walk toward the house.

She took two steps forward as she noticed another heated battle between wood and metal.

Déjà vu.

The noise intensified, as the wooden beams of the bridge struggled to hold the metal of the train. With each move, the ground shook harder. Ruth turned and ran toward the tracks, yet, the pressure from the oncoming train crippled every stride she took. With all her might, she broke into a swift sprint, lifted her arms above her head, and released the jars, pouring warm water onto her face.

Louder. Louder. As she ran faster and faster, she gripped the sides of her face to shield her ears. It was no use; she could not block out the horrific sound.

Out of breath, Ruth knew she could run no further. There she stood in the middle of the woods, panting uncontrollably as she clutched her chest. Something invisible pulled her body further into the woods. She wanted to resist, but gravity shifted her position, causing her to move forward, and then, without warning, collapse onto the ground.

Déjà vu.

She lay in the same spot as before and smelled the remnants from the tears she'd shed all those years ago. Once again, the ground eagerly soaked up her sorrows.

And then there was total silence.

The brakes from the train braced gravity to come to a complete stop. Ruth looked up and let out a sharp, contralto sound, rich with deep intensity. This was not the sound of a woman in sorrow; this was the sound of a woman angered by circumstances beyond her control.

She pounded her fists repeatedly against the ground. When she could no longer strike the earth for causing continuous suffering, she screamed even louder, reaching yet an even higher octave than before. Tears rolled down her cheeks while liquid soaked the lower part of her dress. She struggled to block the sound coming from the train and that of her own voice.

Sorrow, no matter how distant, was a familiar place. Somewhere in the back of her mind, the pages of her past re-opened and fought to reclaim her life. Ruth was forced into a dance with the grim reaper as it sought to choke the last bit of life out of her.

She willingly gave in.

Later.....

Peter Washington sat on his front porch in a rocking chair. Though he did not hear the sounds from the train, he heard a sound that convinced him that someone was in trouble. He immediately stopped rocking, stood up, and looked around. He heard her screams floating in the wind.

"Pearlie, come quick! Somethang done happ'n tuh Ruth!" he yelled, as he opened the screened door.

Ben Porter's house faced Peter and Pearlie's. When he heard the sound of Ruth's voice pierced his conscience, he leaped off the wooden porch steps and ran toward her cries. Seeing Ben, Peter joined him. Pearlie, bolting out of the screended door in time to get a glimpse of her husband, ran barefoot, lagging some distance behind.

As each ran with a steady pace of urgency, soft drops of rain began to fall. They could see their cousin's neatly manicured yard just ahead, sitting proud and pretty just past the crops that lined the road. Once they turned the final corner, they split up and ran in opposite directions. Peter headed toward the back yard, while Pearlie and Ben headed toward the front.

Running into the woods, Peter broke off bits of tree branches that swung into his view. He had run about one-hundred kilometers when he was forced to leap high over a wooden log that blocked his path. He landed safely and ran a short distance before he stopped dead in his tracks.

Ben and Pearlie caught up with him. From the expression on his face, they knew he had found her. Pearlie followed her husband's stare directly to the object of his astonishment. She opened her mouth to scream, but released no sound. In shock, she walked past both men and stared ahead.

Covered by wet earth, Ruth was barely recognizable. She lay prostrate on the ground, hands over her ears, and face buried beneath the mud. A tree branch partially covered her limbs, its leaves draped over her body as a piece of fabric. What little of her once pastel dress not ruined by mud, clung to her legs but bunched high enough to reveal her panties underneath.

Peter was the first to find his voice and speak. He walked over to her and whispered softly, "Ruthie, what's the matter, baby?"

She did not answer.

He thought she was unconscious, until he removed the dirt covering her face. That's when she started to hum. Her eyes remained closed as she lifted her head out of the soft mud, sat up, and rocked back and forth. She was wearing one house slipper while the other lay partially hidden under the gold and brown leaves that covered the earth.

Pearlie walked over and touched her shoulder. "Hey, dere gal. It's all right. Da Lawd is in control. It's all right now."

Ruth continued to hum.

With a gentle touch, Pearlie stroked Ruth's back in what she hoped was a calming circular motion. Then she got up, placed both hands underneath Ruth's armpits, and tried to lift her distraught sister-in-law to her feet. It was no use. Ruth's tiny body was limp dead weight.

Pearlie looked at the two men in front of her.

"Pete, y'all got tuh lift Sista Ruth. I don't thank she wants tuh go back tuh da house. We got tuh git her out o' dis heah mud," she said.

"Ben, you grab her on one side and Ah'll get de ahda," Peter said.

Ruth held her hands to her ears and ignored them. The two men stood next to her for a moment and then reached out and lifted her from the ground. When she became limp again, Ben, the taller of the two, hoisted her small frame into the air and carried her over his shoulder like a sack of potatoes. She never uttered a sound.

Pearlie and Peter led the way up the stairs to the front porch and opened the screened door.

"Where's Gustus?" Peter asked as Ben put Ruth down onto the living room couch.

Ruth started screaming. Gripping her abdominal area, she laid back and screamed at the top of her lungs. The three spectators stared in disbelief, yet she never opened her eyes.

"Ruthie, you got tuh tell us what ails ya!" Pearlie walked over and sat next to her.

Ben and Peter surveyed the room. The house was spotless with the exception of the sofa, now covered with mud and leaves.

Ben closed the front door. He looked at Ruth. "Where's yuh husband? Yuh chirren? Do yuh know?" he pleaded, trying to get her to respond.

She did not acknowledge their presence as she screamed one complete note of music for more than fifteen minutes.

Pearlie leaned over, grabbed Ruth by the shoulders and gently shook her. "Oh, Lawd, Ruthie! Stop all dat fuss and tell us what's wrong so dat we can help yuh! Are yuh hurting, Sista? Do we need tuh call a doctor?"

After a while, none of the onlookers said a word. Ruth screamed until her voice became hoarse, no longer able to effectuate an audible sound. Within minutes, she resumed humming. Then, suddenly, she stopped. Pearlie let go of her shoulders, grabbed her frail hands and rubbed them gently together. Ruth sat unresponsive as total silence filled the small room.

They sat for what seemed like an eternity. No one spoke or looked at the others. They all existed only in their own worlds. Then they heard the sound of an approaching automobile. Ben leaned over from the recliner he sat in and pulled the curtains back. He did not recognize the pickup truck that hurriedly sped into the front yard. He looked at Peter, who looked at his wife, who in turn looked at Ruth. Her eyes were still closed.

The royal blue pickup truck slowed directly in front of the front door before coming to a stop. Two men sat in the front carriage and two rode on the back of the truck. Ben opened the door and stepped onto the porch. He had never seen the likes of any of the men before. Peering intently at the strangers, he stood next to the front steps and leaned against a wooden column. The driver turned the engine off.

"Evenin'," the men yelled in unison.

"Evenin'," Ben replied suspiciously. "Y'all seen Augustus?"

The two men seated inside the truck looked straight ahead into the back yard. The two on the back arose and jumped to the ground.

"You some kin tuh Gus?" one of them asked as he put his hand into his pocket and pulled out a bag of chewing tobacco.

Ben stepped down onto the stair below. He watched the two men carefully.

"Gus my cousin. Who you be?"

"We work wid 'em," one of the men replied.

"He ain't heah and his family needs to find 'em. Seems Cousin Ruth done gone off again. She real bad this time."

The men did not say a word. The two standing in the yard looked at the two seated in the truck. Both men dropped their heads.

"Y'all wanna tell me what's going on?" Ben said, breaking their silence.

Finally, the driver blurted out, "We got some real bad news."

"What?" Ben asked.

"Train hit Augustus a couple of hours ago. Nothing left. Poor soul. Train came out of the blue and struck him as he crossed the bridge. He was walking alone. The rest of us was some distance behind," the man explained.

Ben stumbled backwards. He looked at the man chewing tobacco as Pearlie bolted out of the screen door.

"What dat ya say?" she screamed. "What happened tuh mah brotha?"

"Ah'm so sorry, ma'am. Ah really am. Ah hate tuh be da bearer of bad news. It's just we ain't seent wut happened, but we heard da train come tuh a stop and we run on tuh see wut was ahead. Augustus must have crossed dem tracks near da river. Train finally come tuh a stop some hundred feet down da road. Ah'm so sorry."

Pearlie looked at Ben, opened her mouth wide, but before she could let out a scream, she fainted. Peter, who exited while the gentleman provided the details, knelt beside his wife, lifted her head into his lap, and tried to revive her lifeless body. The strangers stood still.

"Dat his wife?" The man seated on the passenger side asked.

"Naw," a few of them replied.

"She in da house." Peter looked up and said, "She found out some sort o' way. She sense things. She been screaming goin' on a li'l over two hours now."

None of her former audience knew that Ruth was listening to the conversation outside. She heard all the details. It was all too familiar. She started to hum. When the three re-entered the house, she sat still in a catatonic state of total silence.

Ben could tell when he walked back into the house that Ruth had heard everything that was said. Then again, it was evident to him that she already knew before those gentlemen arrived. He looked at her with tears in his eyes. No words came to mind. No words spilled out that could somehow soothe her pain. Tears fell down his face as he grabbed his forehead and sobbed.

Ruth closed her eyes and made a faint humming sound. After a few minutes, she stopped, opened her eyes, looked at the two men standing over her, and dropped her head to her chest. She never said a word. In fact, from that point forward, she never uttered another sound.

Not after Ben and Peter placed an unconscious Pearlie beside her on the couch, nor as Pearlie grabbed her and screamed in agony over her brother's death. Not even when, hours later, she listened as family members broke the devastating news to her children, she said nothing.

In the middle of chaos, Ruth did not move from where she sat. Her children sought her comfort, but she kept her eyes closed.

Later as the hours passed and daylight faded into night, Ruth remained seated in the same soiled clothing in which she had hugged the earth so tightly. Her Aunt Bea arrived, carried her into the bathroom, bathed her, put her in bed, and turned the lights out. She did not assist, nor did she raise one objection.

She never said one word. Not during the ensuing days that led to the home going of her dearly beloved, Augustus Garrett. Not one month later as the local doctor arrived to examine her, and seeing no change in appearance, recommended that the family commit her to a mental institution.

Still, she said nothing.

Not one comment, cry, scream or objection. Not then and not on the morning her father arrived to take her to the hospital in Beaufort County. She said nothing.

Not for days, weeks, or months after she heard the news that tore her life apart. Ruth Fields Harrison Garrett never said one word.

TWO

1941-1953

Ruth, the fourth of seven children, was born into a typical size southern home in the Low Country of South Carolina. By the time she entered the world on a blustery, cold December night, her mother had already, single-handedly, given birth to three children. Rosetta Fields despised midwives, demanding that her younger sister, Beatrice, remain seated outside on the front porch in the event of a real emergency, but, according to her, children came out on their own. Additional hands were only needed to snip the umbilical cord and stitch any possible wounds. The rest, she said, was left to nature.

The owners of a produce farm in Poketaligo, Ruth's father, Frank Fields, was a farmer and also worked at the Coosawhatchie train station as a Pullman Porter. A well liked gentleman and highly respected by blacks and whites, he once boasted of never having a run in with the Klu Klux Klan, something few blacks could ever testify. Rosetta "Rose" Fields was all together different. She was a chestnut brown petite woman from Hampton, South Carolina, who stood no more than four feet eleven inches tall. She first met Frank, a towering muscular dark brown man, at the local feed store when she was fourteen and married him before her fifteenth birthday. He was a twenty year old widow whose first wife died during childbirth. They moved to

Poketaligo, built an impressive sized farm, and sold their crops to the local merchants in town.

Rosetta worked much of the farm with her own hands. Even when her family came to help out, they were not allowed to touch the cash producing crops. They had to be taken care of solely by her. In the shadows of Madame C.J. Walker, by the time she turned twenty-one, Rosetta Fields had brokered "agreements" to sell produce, hair products, and clothing to over thirty establishments throughout the Deep South. She later graduated from a prestigious colored school in Savannah, Georgia, and managed to finish college before the birth of her seventh child.

Townsfolk called Rosetta Fields one uppity woman. "Stuck up," they often said. She ignored their comments and spent most of her time schooling her seven children. She boasted that Ruth was special and would probably attend Bennett College in Alabama.

"There is no time for you to speak and act like a geechie. God has plans for you to become a remarkable woman," She would admonish her daughter.

By the time Ruth was twelve, she was sent to Atlanta to live with Aunt Bea and attend a school for colored girls that was famous in elite circles of black America before integration hit the South.

Rosetta warned her to stand a certain way when in public, look people directly into their eyes when addressing them, and to listen very carefully. Bad behavior, she threatened, would be met with the greatest embarrassment of them all: a visit from Rosetta herself.

1954

On a sunny day in June, Ruth's life changed forever. While the day began with its usual splendor, by its ending, Rosetta Fields had been captured and, by sunset, still had yet to be found.

Frank knew she had gone into Hardeeville to deliver produce to four of her customers. When he stopped by one of the grocers and was told Rosetta had not arrived, he simply shrugged his shoulders, thanked the merchant, and drove off to work. He suspected she was tied up with one of her customers in Ridgeland, and never gave the matter a second thought.

When he arrived home later that night, he discovered his children in the kitchen, hovering over the stove, clumsily preparing their own dinner. Since they'd married, Rosetta had only missed dinner once, and that was during Ruth's birth. She prepared breakfast and dinner for her family each day regardless of her hectic schedule. At that point, he knew something was very wrong.

"Where ya mama?" he asked.

The stair-step children, barely taller than the table they stood next to, looked

suspiciously at each other. "She ain't come home yet," one of them replied.

"She has not come home yet," he corrected, not thinking of the insignificance of the grammar used at that moment. What mattered most was that his wife had not returned and no one had heard from her.

He ate supper with his children nestled around him and waited. He did not want to put them to bed without Rosetta first telling a bedtime story; a tradition in their home that was never broken. Even without knowing her whereabouts, everything had to appear normal. At least to the seven young people who stood watching his every move that evening.

By nine o'clock, Frank grew weary. He started a bedtime story, but kept peeking outside whenever he heard a noise. The minutes marched by like hours and as each second passed, he suspected something tragic had happened to his wife.

He telephoned Beatrice and then summoned relatives. Word spread fast and within minutes, a small crowd of concerned neighbors huddled in the yard. Frank came onto the front porch, thanked each of them, and told them of his suspicions. He openly admitted that he suspected Rosetta had been taken against her will and possibly harmed, even dead. He vowed he would find her captors, even if it was the last thing he ever did on God's green earth.

Before he leaving, he returned inside, knelt on his knees in front of his children and prayed. Ruth's eyes were partially open as she watched her father's facial gestures carefully. They were two of a kind, and like him, she too suspected that something awful had happened to her mother. Their eyes locked for a moment. Frank arose, kissed each one of them and walked out onto the front porch and joined the thirty or so men headed toward Hardeeville, armed with handcrafted shotguns.

Sometime in the wee hours of the early morning, the small band of brothers returned with Rosetta. Draped in her husband's overcoat, her stockings were torn and her legs saturated in dried blood that cascaded down into her shoes. There were fresh bruises on her face and deep scratches on her arms.

Frank Fields hurried past the small crowd in the front room and headed directly into their bedroom at the end of the hall. He placed his wife's badly bruised body on the bed and closed the curtains that hung over the doorway. It was silent for a while. After the visitors departed, Rosetta's screams could be heard non-stop until the first sign of daybreak.

She spent eight weeks in bed, with no visitors, not even her own children. Aunt Bea carried wash basins filled with urine and clean and dirty water throughout the day, but there were no appearances made by the victim herself. Bea kept the children preoccupied during the day, or busily working in the fields. She had each one of them firmly distracted, with the exception of Ruth.

Ruth obeyed her aunt, but kept one eye on what she was doing, and the other in the direction of her mother's bedroom. If Rosetta made a move, she would be the first to know. Frank watched carefully. He feared the moment an opportunity presented itself, Ruth would head into that room. He played inference for several weeks, but knew he could not fool his very wise daughter. She knew he was hiding something awful.

For three months, seven children eagerly listened as they heard soft footsteps tap back and forth across the wooden floor boards. Yet they saw no sign of the woman who mysteriously disappeared and returned in the early morning. There were no signs of the woman they once called Mother. The woman who nurtured them and cared for their every need. She had deserted them. The mother who told jokes all day long while she hustled back and forth between the farm and the city to conduct business was gone without a trace.

If things had been normal, Rosetta would have awakened early in the morning, gone to the chicken coop for eggs, boil or fry them, cook ham or bacon, boil a fresh pot of rice for the day, and bake corn bread or fresh rolls, depending on her mood. Regardless of how she felt, she always rose before dawn and meticulously prepared a hot breakfast for her family. Her cooking was the first smell that confronted their nostrils each day. In their tiny lifetimes, mornings were defined by their mother's show of affection. First breakfast, then prayer, and then Rosetta would tell a story to enlighten their hearts. It was a reason to get up each morning with a smile on their faces.

Just before fall settled in that year, Rosetta, wrapped in a pink robe and wearing wool socks, marched out of her bedroom, right past her entire family and walked out onto the front porch where she sat on the glider for the remainder of the day. When her children surrounded her, she shooed them away and signaled to Bea to remove them from her presence.

No one would utter the obvious: something had forever changed the woman they cherished. Her physical appearance changed drastically due to a considerable amount of weight loss; her eyes now sat back in her head, and her skin appeared sallow, barely clinging to her frail bone structure. Her countenance changed too. Once known for her beautiful eyes that sparkled when she smiled, they now held a blank stare that no one dared look into for long periods of time.

She stayed on the front porch and lost all interest in her crops and the businesses she'd created. Aunt Bea, whose husband died before Ruth was born, hung around to manage the smaller affairs of the business and to take care of the younger children. When it became obvious that things would never be the same again, Frank asked her to move in.

Ruth chose not to return to school that following year. At fifteen, she went to work as a housekeeper on Hilton Head Island. The mother she once knew would have never allowed such a thing. Yet the woman she saw everyday never spoke or looked in her direction. It was as if they'd never met. She prayed their lives would someday return to normal.

1956

Rosetta sat dozing in the back yard in one of the wrought iron chairs Frank had welded together a few years before. Her children were nestled inside while her oldest daughter, Edna, read a bedtime story to them. Aunt Bea lingered over the kitchen sink cleaning the remains of a possum that Frank killed earlier that day. On the surface, everything appeared peaceful.

Later that night, Ruth escorted her younger siblings into the bedroom and put them in bed. She slept on a palette on the floor when Edna, who was married by then, spent the night. After the younger ones dozed off, she joined Edna, James, and John in the living room.

They awoke to sounds of what seemed like a heated dispute. Across the room, Aunt Bea sat resting in a chair, while she held the daily newspaper. They walked past her into the kitchen where they could hear their parents voices clearly.

They heard Rosetta as she threatened to leave South Carolina and take the children with her. Frank objected, but she ranted on about feeling as if she were living in a hell hole, traped in a prison in which she could not escape.

It was silent for a few minutes. Finally, they heard the word they dreaded most: divorce. Then, suddenly, the remaining words spoken became inaudible to the listeners on the other side of the door.

For a while, they stood near the door, trembling, and waiting for more. But nothing came. It was quiet. Then without advance notice, another argument erupted. The words were muffled but intense. Just when it seemed the conversation was over, their parents' voices escalated again. The eavesdroppers feared they would get caught so they sprinted past Aunt Bea, and headed into their bedrooms.

Like wornout boxers too exhausted to throw another punch, Frank and Rosetta Fields stared tiredly at each other. There was nothing left to say. Rosetta had spoken the last word. She made it clear that she wanted out of the marriage to Frank and away from the children she gave birth to. Her words shocked Frank, but they rolled off of Rosetta's tongue as if she had given them much rehearsal.

Unable to hold back the tears, Frank allowed a few to cascade down his stern face. Rosetta just turned and walked toward the screened door, opened it and walked down the steps into the back yard. He begged her to come back, but she whispered she needed time to clear her head.

The argument was nothing new. In fact, the subject had reared its ugly head several nights a week ever since Rosetta'd recovered. Frank could not remember the way they started, but he knew the way they ended rather well. It was clear that things would never be the same.

She no longer looked at him with admiration in her eyes, nor did she allow him to physically touch her. She warned him to keep his distance, and Frank eagerly complied.

Devastated by her rejection of him, he was a firm believer that time healed all wounds.

1954

Rosetta refused to elaborate on the details of the event that changed their lives forever. Like a well designed vault, she let nothing escape from her lips as to her captives or the activities she was subjected to before being thrown off the back of a pickup truck into the woods. That much Frank knew about. How she got to those woods and who had hurt her would remain a secret. That secret left Frank Fields with an enormous amount of anger bottled up inside that he did not know how to deal with.

He needed someone to hate; someone to point a finger at and blame for the destruction of his family. His children were motherless and he was left without the loving wife he'd once known. For twenty-five years they had carved out thirty minutes of each day to sit on the back porch and discuss future plans for themselves and their offspring. There was nothing they did not talk openly about and no secrets existed between them.

The unknown incident pierced his mind like a nagging instrument caught somewhere between his flesh and his insides. It held him captive and refused to release him. Every day since it happened he wondered if there was something else he should have done to protect her. Was it right to allow her to remain so free spirited all those years, roaming around town selling things to folks who did not believe Negros had a right to make a living for themselves? The very folks who smiled at them during daylight hours, but stalked them in white sheets during the night.

1956

Frank Fields walked outside to use the outhouse, returned inside to wash up, then changed into his pajamas, and sat dazed, while he ate the cold dinner Aunt Bea prepared hours before. Finally he walked into the bedroom and lay across the bed. Sleep did not come easy and within a few hours, he was awakened by an unfamiliar sound.

He reached for Rosetta's warm body, and upon discovering her not there, startled, he sprang up and searched the entire house. She was no where to be found. Angry, he opened the back door and peered out into the pitch black night.

He called her name several times, but she never answered. He stood frozen, unable to move, unable to explore the unknown. He turned the porch light on and looked around. The light from the barn shone brightly on the very chair Rosetta had sat in earlier. Still, there was no sign of her.

Frank called out again and again until he was exhausted, but there was no response. He turned around, ran into the bedroom, put on his shoes, pulled a rifle from the gun chest, and headed to the back yard. As he opened the screened door, he stepped down onto the wooden plank steps and peered into the darkness. Suspended midway in the air, less than fifty feet from her beloved wrought iron chairs, was a scene that would haunt Frank Fields for the next twenty-five years.

THREE

1956

Beatrice "Bea" Gladney cried a river that fateful early winter morning. After Frank woke her from a deep slumber, she ran out onto the back porch and stared at her sister's lifeless body. Frozen and unable to move, she cried out in agony and collapsed. When she recovered, she watched in horror as Frank took Rosetta's body down from the tree that seemed to hold it in suspended animation, covered her with a cotton sheet and placed her remains in the back of his pickup truck. He did not bother calling the police, for there was only one direction he was headed.

Like exhausted distance runners, the two of them sat on the glider on the front porch not saying a word to one another. When daybreak struck, Frank took his sister-in-law by the hand and escorted her over to the truck where they each took one last look at Rosetta. An enormous cloud of peace engulfed the two of them, confirming that her soul was finally free. Bea looked at Frank and motioned to him to take the body to the undertakers. She would handle the children alone. She knew he was too distraught to look into their precious eyes and tell them they would never see their mother alive again.

Bea watched as Frank drove toward the service road. She held onto the sturdy wooden pole that held the front porch for strength. When she heard rustling inside, she prepared herself for what she would say to the angels on the other side of the front door. She prayed for strength, and then prayed Rosetta's soul had gone to heaven. She was praying when one of the children opened the screened door. She knew then, it was time to do the unthinkable.

Based on their nonchalant reaction, Bea suspected her nieces and nephews barely understood what she had said to them. Unable to convince them or soften the blow to their ears, she started crying and said her sister, their mother, was finally resting with the Lord. At that moment reality set in and, without warning, tears dripped from their eyes like a perculator releasing fresh coffee.

The chorus of sobbing lasted for hours until Frank returned later that day. As he walked in the front door, he instantly leaned forward so that his children could take comfort in his large muscular arms. Bea, relieved the anchor had returned, stood sobbing silently.

Ruth had matured since the incident that tore their lives apart almost fifteen months ago. News of her mother's death was something she expected to hear every morning when she arose. Once confirmed, the fifteen-year-old long tall bronzed Sally looked around the room and appeared relieved. Then she walked back into her parent's bedroom and lay across the bed. She could smell Rosetta's favorite perfume, ***Chantilly***, as soon as she walked in.

For the entire next week, with the house swarming with visitors who came to pay their respect to her family, Ruth barely ate a morsel. Her mind was on her mother, her best friend. Someone committed an awful sin; someone had taken away her greatest inspiration and no amount of words of consolation could ease her pain.

Rosetta's remains were brought back to her uncle Sam's house who lived up the road. He had the largest home on the family property so the body was placed in his front parlor for viewing, such was the custom of the day. Ruth pulled a chair up to the white metal casket and sat beside it. Oftentimes she stared into her mother's lifeless face and, each time she did, she lost her composure and ran outside onto the front porch sobbing uncontrollably.

On the morning of the funeral, she dressed in the lavender princess-bodice dress Aunt Bea purchased for she and her sisters, took her all weather coat out of the front closet, and left the house without telling a soul, enroute to Sam's. Realizing that the casket was probably closed and the entire house asleep, she sat on the glider on the front porch and hummed her favorite songs. She remained there for what seemed like an eternity, clutching her Bible, full of rage. Grief had saturated her mind; and now anger was paying her a visit.

Hours later, the front screened door opened and there stood Samuel White dressed in a black suit, white shirt, and pencil thin black tie. He noticed Ruth, smiled, and walked over to the glider and sat beside her. She kept her chin buried in her chest while she stared at the wooden floor beams that formed the front porch. He placed his arms around her shoulders.

"It's aw'right to cry. That's the only way we can truly say goodbye. Your mama is going to miss you. You were her favorite. You remind me of her sitting here with that Bible in ya arms."

"What happens next? Are we gonna bury Mama in the backyard?" she asked.

"No. No, child," he laughed. "They gon' come git her shortly and take her to the church. We all gon' walk down there so we can celebrate ya mama's life. After that, we says our final goodbyes at the gravesite in the back of St. Paul's Baptist Church. That's where most of our people's be."

"She won't be afraid all by herself?"

"Chile, your mama is with Jesus. He just took her back. She was tired and looked more to dying these past few months than living. It hurts me to bury my niece today. But I know if she is away from us in the body, then her soul is with da Lord."

"Why y'all won't tell us what really happened?" She looked up and stared defiantly into his deep set, moist brown eyes.

"Only the Lord knows 'zactly what really happened, Ruth. All everyone else doin' is speculating on what they thinks happened. None of us knows for sho'." He started to rock back and forth. His black leather shoes had received a flawless military shine.

"But Aunt Bea said Mama slipped away to Heaven. Then I heard Daddy on the back porch with some people and they said the Klan hurt Mama. Which one is true?" Her eyes pleaded with him for answers.

"Baby, I don't know. Sometimes I think she may have been helped to her death, sometimes I think she just slipped away on her own. None of us were there. Don't trouble ya little mind with grown folks business right now. You just focus on growing up, getting married, and having kids of ya own that you can raise good like ya mama raised you."

Ruth was still angry. Angry at her family for refusing to tell her how her mother left the earth, or who was to blame so that she would have a holding cell for the hate she felt on the inside. Gone was the greatest person in her life and someone was responsible. She vowed she would get to the truth before she left this earth.

Two men with stoic faces, dressed in black suits and black shirts, exited a long hearse, greeted Sam and Ruth, and then proceeded into the house. They knew their business and went about it without undue conversation. Ruth sat trembling as large puddles of water flowed down her face.

"We'll understand it better by and by," was all Sam White could muster out of his mouth as he too shed a tear.

A few hours later, Ruth joined her family at the processional outside of the church. Edna handed her a handkerchief and two pieces of saltwater taffy candy. As she placed them in her purse, she felt the stares of her father's eyes. He had not looked directly into Ruth's eyes since that fateful night. Ruth returned the stare while she stood frozen in her tracks.

On this hazy, overcast day, Frank Fields seemed smaller in stature. A well-built, muscular specimen, standing over six feet tall, his skin defied time, leaving no trace of his actual age. As he stood with a host of friends and family, something about him had changed. For on this day, his normal youthful look of a well-conditioned boxer in his twenties was traded in for a much older, broken man filled with rage. Ruth could see and sense his anger, in fact she believed they were battling the same nagging feelings inside.

"You stand next to me," he whispered in her ear as his seven children stood outside of the church with the rest of Rosetta's immediate family members. Aunt Bea stood on the other side of him.

Ruth looked down at the dirt paveway that lead to the front steps. She avoided the stares of onlookers and even the words of condolences as everyone packed into the freshly painted white clapboard edifice.

A few minutes later, Edna poked her in the back, and caused Ruth to turn around and stare straight into her face. She was holding their mother's favorite Bible. Ruth trembled at the sight of it. Frank, noticing her reaction, put his arm around Ruth's shoulders, and turned her small frail body around to face the doors of the church. He did not acknowledge Edna or his other children standing quietly behind him.

As they entered the building, Ruth saw the opened casket in front of her and for the first time noticed the color of the dress her mother wore. It seemed every woman in the family wore matching lavender dresses, yet Rosetta's dress appeared more striking than everyone else's. Maybe it was the iridescent stones that covered the front bodice, making it look more like an evening gown. Ruth stared at her mother's face, and then looked up at her father. He stared ahead at his beloved wife. She clutched his hands tighter.

The church was packed well beyond capacity. People were nestled tightly together in the aisles on the side of the pews, in the foyer and vestibule, and even in the choir loft behind the altar. Ruth could feel their stares following her as she passed by.

They sat down on the front pew amid dozens of flower arrangements. There was a large photo of Rosetta displayed on an easel to their left. Ruth recalled it was the portrait of her mother in her wedding gown that Frank painted a few years after their tenth wedding anniversary.

To Ruth, the two women did not resemble each other. The woman in the portrait, displaying a wide happy smile, looked like the Rosetta Fields the whole town remembered; someone full of life, laughter, and warmth. In contrast, the woman lying in the casket, though eyes closed and mouth sewn shut, possessed a harshness that was cold and uninviting. It was if they were attending the home-going of a stranger.

Ruth pulled out her handkerchief as the obituary was read by someone from the funeral home. With a strange expression on her face, she stared at the ghastly figure who read the pages of her mother's life. Although she had been away in school for some years now, she did not recognize the woman who stood before them and wondered how she had acquired the information she now recalled. The audience laughed and cried as they listened to stories about the Rosetta White Fields that the entire Jasper County population admired. Ruth sat still and rolled her eyes.

She managed to keep her composure through three hymns, including *By and By* and *Jesus Keep Me Near the Cross*. She even hummed a little after Edna's loud outburst that startled everyone in the room, including their father. Slowly, she turned around to survey her other comrades. Her brothers James and John appeared bored by the festivities while her younger siblings, Caroline, Joseph, and Thomas leaned against the other and wept silently.

When it was time for the family to speak, Frank Fields did not move, but Aunt Bea rose, adjusted her lavender A-line dress, lifted the front of her feathered hat so that she could see the audience, and approached the podium. Grief stricken, she broke down crying twice during her speech. She told them that Rosetta was more than a sister, she was a mother figure as well. Finally, she stopped speaking and stood, weakened by grief, looking out into the audience. Ruth clutched her father's hands tighter, yet he looked straight ahead at the now closed casket.

The final viewing started from the back of the church. The last row proceeded to the casket in the front, turned around and headed over to Frank or Rosetta's siblings to say how sorry they were for their loss. Ruth just sat there, playing with her father's tie. Whenever Frank stood to greet someone, she would fidget in her purse as if she were looking for something. She never looked at the passersby.

When it was time to view the body, Ruth felt her father's tenseness as he held her hand and pulled her up out of her seat to face the casket. She immediately looked away. She could not bear to see her mother lying in a casket, all alone, going someplace she had never been before. Ruth let go of her father's hand as weakness overtook her every step. Frank stood behind his children and stared at the spray of roses and gladioli that once draped the top of the closed casket.

The children huddled together in a semicircle and cried. Edna placed a silk handkerchief in her mother's cold hands. She believed every proper woman carried a clean pressed hankie at all times. Ruth held onto James for dear life, but he barely looked at his mother. When they turned to leave, Frank walked past them and stood before his wife's body. He slowly bent down and kissed her on the cheek, whispered something into her ear, and then let out a piercing wail. The sound was so unnerving that it caught everyone in the room off guard.

His cries sent chills down Ruth's spine. She jumped up from her seat, bolted into the aisle, ran down the steps, and trotted toward the street in front of her. She was beside herself. Panting, she ran down Highway 17 in the direction of their home. She turned onto the family property and headed toward the back where they lived. When she arrived, frantically she ran up the front porch steps, turned around, and ran down them into the yard, before she headed around back. It seemed she was looking for someone. Anyone to tell her it was all a dream.

"Who?" she cried. "Who did this to her? Why? God, tell me why!"

She fell to the ground, reached for her Sunday hat, and tossed it away. She laid there for what must have been hours before getting up. When she did, she noticed all of the wrought iron chairs her father had made were missing. Suddenly she was herself again and could no longer cry. All she wanted at that moment was to die...anything to be next to the woman she'd spent her whole life adoring.

She raced up the back porch steps, banged open the screened door, and walked around the porch. Then she opened the back door and marched right into the kitchen. She forgot the hat she left behind. The house smelled like her mother's cooking. Sighing heavily, she ran from room to room.

She cried out in agonizing pain.

"Mama! Say something, Mama! Tell me that everything is gonna be all right! Tell me you didn't leave me here all by myself with no future in these heah woods? Tell me, Mama. Tell me who hurt you and I will see to it that they are brought to justice! Just tell me who. I can't eat; I can't rest at night and I can't think about school anymore. I need to know that you are at peace...and that won't happen unless you tell me!" She screamed at the top of her lungs.

Physcially and emothionally exhausted, she walked into the living room, sat in Rosetta's favorite rocking chair, and fell asleep. In her dream, she was sitting on the front porch rocking back and forth in the same glider her mother spent the last months of her life on. Standing out in the yard, feet buried by the high grass, stood Rosetta, wearing the smile that made her famous and well loved. She was wearing the lavender gown Ruth admired earlier at the church. They smiled at each other and then Rosetta spoke.

"Ruth, finish your schooling, ya hear?"

"Yes, ma'am. One day I will go back. Just not right now, Mama. I need to know that Daddy is all right first," Ruth said.

"Your daddy will be fine. I could not stand to see his heart broken like that. He will be all right, you just trust me." Rosetta looked around the yard as if to say one final goodbye.

"What about you? Who did this to you?" Ruth stood trembling.

"Evil people and my own self hate. I don't know if I wanted to live any longer."

"But why?" Ruth held onto the banister rails.

"Fear. That's all, Ruth. Folk fear a strong woman. You remember that. That doesn't mean you have to live your life weak and docile, but there is a time to know your place," her mother advised. "There's something to be said for hiding your light beneath a bushel sometimes."

"But why you? You were kind and generous to everybody." Ruth started to cry. "Was it the Klan that hurt you?"

"Ruthie, baby, don't trouble yourself with who or why. Just know that I am in a better place and I am sure my children are going to be fine. I would not have left you if I did not know that each of you were going to be all right without me."

"So you wanted to die?" Ruth was perplexed.

"I wanted to be free! I could not handle the rage I held inside for the men who hurt me. I could not handle the pain in your father's eyes when he looked at me."

"But they hurt you, Mama! They deserve to be punished!" Ruth screamed.

"Ruthie, you needed one parent. If I told Frank who did this to me, he would have gone on a killing spree. I know that man. I could not live with that guilt in my heart." She walked closer and stared into Ruth's eyes.

"It's just not fair! They hurt you and we can't do anything! I can't live like this, Mama."

"Ruthie, you must." She reached up and grabbed Ruth's tender hands. "You must do something for me. Take care of your father, but also take care of your brothers and sisters for me. Y'all should always stay together. Whatever you do, I want you to finish school. Make sure Caroline gets an education too. Above all else, live your life without hate. Love your enemies and become the awesome woman God intended you to become."

As Rosetta released her hands, Ruth noticed she was not wearing the solitaire diamond she often wore on the middle finger of her left hand.

"Mama, please don't go!" Ruth struggled to pull her mother closer.

"Ruthie, I have to. I am at peace. You hold onto that. I am with the Lord and everything is beautiful. Tell your sisters and brothers not to spend time at that gravesite because I am not there. I am right here with each of you." Rosetta stepped away from the porch and walked out into the yard.

"How? How are you right here with us?" Ruth called after her.

"I am in your heart, baby. Safe and sound. Always there for you. Just trust in the Lord and never stray away from His will for your life." Her voice trailed off into the wind as she disappeared down the road.

Ruth woke up. She felt different. Gone were the smells of Rosetta's sweet potato pie. She looked around and then started to hum her mother's favorite spiritual, *Nearer my God to Thee.* The words comforted her soul and, for the first time since everything happened, she smiled.

She was peacefully rocking in the chair when she notice a stack of papers that poked out from underneath the rocker near the front window. Ruth walked over and picked them up. A typewritten sheet of paper caught her attention first.

It resembled Ruth's school registration papers, but a closer look revealed the contents pertained to another matter. Every line referenced Rosetta, including her maiden and marital names, home address, spouse's name, and occupation. A physical description was listed too.

Ruth glanced at every line, but understood very little of its meaning. As reality set in, her eyes began to tear afresh. Too many phrases to comprehend, however, one stood out in particular: Cause of Death--Self-Inflicted Suffocation. On the next line, there was a phrase she studied while away in school. She read it out loud.

"Death by Suicide."

FOUR

1961

Ruth sat in the last pew of the small chapel in the woods and hummed loudly. Her sounds were slightly off key and noticeable to just about everyone in the room. She could not carry a tune, so instead of offending others, she simply hummed the notes to each and every song, each and every time she came to church.

At nineteen, she was strikingly beautiful. Poised and tenaciously neat, her espresso chocolate complexion radiated in the sunlight. She stood approximately five-foot six inches tall and had extremely thick black hair which hung in a mass to the middle of her waist. A few years back, one could always spot Ruth because when she wore her hair out it cascaded down her body like an expensive piece of drapery. She had a definite air of distinction about her back then, but things changed.

After becoming Mrs. James Harrison, she no longer wore her hair down, replacing the free style with a more conservative small bun centered in the back of her head. There were no signs that make-up touched her face. But this was not everything that was different. At one time, she was considered one of the best-dressed women in the Low Country because whatever color or style of outfit she adorned her small frame in matched from head to toe.

Folks loved to see her family parade across town on Sundays, for it was truly a production. After Rosetta died, Ruth took center stage and impressed everyone with her impeccable taste for fashion. Using expensive fabrics she purchased from a Savannah textile shop, Ruth designed dresses that looked like costumes fit for a performance on Broadway. Yet her signature piece became the elbow length gloves that matched every dress she wore. Folks marveled when she walked by, some out of jealousy, but most out of admiration. She was a sight to behold; a very real African princess in the the Low Country.

Many said she would eventually move away to a place that accommodated her sense of style and everything she learned while away in school. No one ever expected her to stay, even after Rosetta died. To them, Ruth was a young woman with a future that could only be realized far away from Jasper County and the Deep South all together.

It was her passion for sewing that kept her in the Low Country long enough to fall in love and get married. She could design clothing for men and women that looked better than anything on a store rack. When it came to women's dresses, her hems were shorter and her bodices lower. She loved making evening gowns and with the extra money she made working on Hilton Head Island, she designed satin and silk gowns and showcased them in the back of Ms. Janie Crosby's store during the spring and summer months for women who expected to marry soon. Pretty soon, talk spread and women of all races from as far as Charleston and Macon, Georgia headed to Jasper County to order one of Ruth's designer dresses.

Her designs were daring and made bold statements about women in America. Admiring designer Co-Co Chanel, Ruth designed dress slacks that became the talk of the town. She even sported dress shorts that were above the thighs. To make a point that her shorts were versatile and could be worn anywhere, Ruth wandered into a cotton field one day, wearing a cut off tee shirt and a pair of shorts that highlighted her muscular legs. Everyone watched as the foreman asked her to remove the shorts or either leave the premises. The crowd waited in anticipation while Ruth, laughing devishly, took out a pair of overalls, and without removing the shorts first, put them on right in the front of the man who chastised her. No one could keep a straight face.

That was the Ruth everyone knew and loved, but that was the old Ruth. Post marital Ruth was quite different. More humbled and reserved, the new Ruth's clothing was a far cry from sexy or daring. Plain and simple, she no longer strutted through town in a new outfit every week. Gone were elbow length gloves, and gone were the fancy low cut dresses and high heel shoes. In fact, gone also was the bold and talkative free spirit every one knew as Ruth Fields.

She was now Ruth Harrison, married woman. Remembering her mother's advice in the dream, she had to respect her place as a wife, and she dared not cross the line. Her light stayed well hidden.

1957

They met on a Saturday as Ruth was walking down the street towards Ridgeland's courthouse square. One look and James Harrison dropped what he was doing and followed Ruth four miles back to the Field's property. He tried to get her attention, but she paid him no mind. When all else failed, he collapsed on the ground as if he suffered a heat stroke. Ruth, believing the stranger needed medical attention, walked over to his limp body, knelt down and reached for his arm to feel for a pulse. She stood rather quickly, carefully removed several of the Bobbie pins that secured her hat, and placed her sweaty hat over the stranger's face.

"The dead don't need to see. That's why you cover the face," she muttered.

James Harrison rolled over onto the sidewalk laughing uncontrollably. Ruth just stood watching. When he finally stopped laughing, he picked up her hat and stood up to hand it back to her.

"Fool man! You should be ashamed of yourself rolling around in the grass like that. Now go on and leave me be," she said.

"I can't do that, ma'am."

"Why not?"

"Because I have found everything I ever wanted in life all wrapped up in this tiny package," he beamed.

Athough he was rather attractive, medium build, golden brown skin and wide, seductive black eyes, James Harrison was a charmer by nature. Ruth had yet to learn that charming is what someone does and not who they are. She would soon find out.

Frank Fields was not as gullible as his young daughter and possessed a keen sense of discernment. He knew a bad apple when he saw one. When he met James, he knew the Devil had stepped clearly into his house and it would be hard to get him to leave empty handed. He avoided conversations with the young gentleman caller but kept a watchful eye on his interactions with his family. It became clear to him that James Harrison would do anything in his power to take Ruth away from her family.

Frank tried to talk to Ruth about his concerns, but that proved to be virtually impossible. When she was not at work or in school, James was right by her side. He came over and stayed until her curfew almost every night of the week. He even took to dropping by unannounced. One day, Frank finally addressed him.

He spotted James' car driving up in the drive way and yelled out, "She ain't heah." He never turned and looked at him.

"Evenin', Mr. Fields," James said.

"Uh huh."

"Ruth 'round the way?" he inquired.

"Ya see huh?" Frank snapped.

"Ah, no sir. I just wondered when she would be back home," the young man replied.

"Then say that! You asked me if Ruth was here, not when she was coming back. So I take it you knew she was not home, but you were just checking to see if she told you the truth."

"Not exactly."

"But damn close, I believe." Frank turned to face James.

"Sir, I just figured she'd made it back by this hour."

"When she makes it back, I'm sure those nappy heads out in that field will let you know," Frank said.

"They not spies, sir!" James smiled.

"Damn near close. Every time Ruthie come back, you're here within five minutes. How do you know when she's home? We don't have a telephone! Listen, it's not good for a man to track a woman like that. Let her have some space. What are you afraid will happen?" he asked.

"Nothing, sir. I just like to be around Ruth. She real special to me. I want to marry her and take care of her," James said slowly.

"Ruthie knows how to take care of herself. She makes her own money, and cares for this house like her mother used ta."

"Yes sir. I sees what she been doing. Um not trying to take her away from y'all." Then, he smiled and asked, "Can we share?"

"Share what? She's not a piece of chattel, James. I've been watching you. You're not too sure of yourself. I bet you think if you give Ruthie some space, she'll run off with some other young man. But you're wrong, Ruthie is not that fickle. She's loyal and she's devoted to her family. You understand me?"

"I do." He walked closer to Frank. "So I guess no time better than the present. Can I have her hand in marriage?"

"That's a question you have to ask my daughter. It doesn't matter one way or the other with me!" Frank opened the front screened door and walked into the house.

1961

Her father's suspicions about James Harrison were right; things aren't always what they seem.

James was the type of man that folks said had a jealous eye. To him, Ruth was his property and only he could look at her. If he spotted someone else looking in her direction, a confrontation followed. Whether he was right or wrong, he picked so many arguments that men started crossing the street whenever they saw Ruth coming their way. Eventually, Ruth stopped going out so much.

She devoted herself to James and tried to make their home a haven of rest for him everyday when he came home from work. At first he talked of nothing more than how well his wife dressed. Said she had the prettiest clothes around. That was in the beginning. After they married, the comments changed. He also had problems with her working outside of the home, and he said it embarrassed him.

Ruth desperately tried to make him happy. She stopped sewing as often, just handling a few small orders for special occasions. She let many of her clients outside of Jasper County go. Occasionally she would make an item for customers during the day when James was at work and have one of her siblings make the delivery.

That did not stop his complaints. If he was not complaining about her work activities, he complained about how she dressed when she left the house. Of course, her dress was never an issue when she was in the house catering solely to him.

"You look so worldly. Don't look like a saint to me. You s'posed to be a holy woman of God. Look at you. Dressed like you going to a juke joint. You ain't in New York. Where ya going dressed like that?"

"I like the way I look. I made this dress with my own two hands. What's the matter with it? You say it's too short, I make it longer. You say it's too long, I make it shorter. What do ya want, old man?" Ruth pleaded with him.

"I want my woman to look like she taken."

"And? How does a taken woman look?"

"Covered up," he mumbled.

"Stop ya foolishness, James. I am not showing anything extra that is not supposed to be seen. I look respectable and you know it," she countered.

"Don't tell me how you look. You can't dress like these other women 'round heah! You too pretty," he blurted out.

"What? Too pretty? Oh, James, you oughta hush ya mouth!"

It was always something her husband chose to nitpick about. Ruth often ignored him and simply complied with his many requests, but things grew worse.

Frank Fields was suspicious too.

"Ruthie, just watch yourself," he warned her one day. "Everyone around here knows that boy got a jealous mean streak. His own mama told me about it at the wedding. She said you are all he talks about night and day."

"What's wrong with that, Daddy? A Man s'posed to be crazy 'bout his wife."

"It's not normal, I tell ya. Men are not supposed to act like that. James acts like he'll die if you walk out of his sight. Oh, it might seem cute, but it's not funny, and it will only fester with time. Mark my words," he said.

"Daddy, I can control James. Just give me some time," she pleaded.

"Time won't change a fool! You tell me if he ever lays a hand on you. That's going to be his behind, for damn sure!" His voice was an octave higher than when he spoke moments before.

"Come on, Daddy. You don't think James fool enough to hit me, do you?"

"Ruthie, that boy used to have them nappy headed brats checking on you night and day. He drove up one day looking for you. Ever since that day, I don't trust him. I didn't want to hurt your feelings or interfere with your life, but I used to pray that you would see that he was not the one for you." He looked at her with sadness. "I think he knew what I was thinking too."

"Daddy, how did he know? You told him how you felt about him being so crazy about me?"

"Didn't have to. I told him that his behavior was not normal and when I did, he kicked it into high gear, taking you on all those trips, buying you all those fancy dresses and hats. Whoever witnessed so much foolishness?" he ranted.

"Daddy, it's called courting." Ruth laughed out loud.

"Then tell me something? Are you still courting? Have you been on any trips lately? How many times since you two married has James come over, picked up your brothers and sisters and took them out like he used to? That's funny; I have not seen him around here at all. And how come he never takes those brats over there with y'all?"

"He says those kids are bad," she answered.

"That's an excuse for he doesn't want them telling you anything about his fool behind. He loves keeping you in the dark. He doesn't want you to see him around his family, because then you would know the truth."

"I know the truth, Daddy. James is just crazy about me. He won't go too far. I won't let him, I promise." She leaned over and kissed her father on the forehead.

"Promise all you want, Ruthie! The proof is in the pudding." Then he grabbed her by the hands and turned her toward him. "Tell me this? Where is your sparkling fingernail polish? Where are your beautiful gloves? Hats? The shiny lipgloss that you're so famous for? You were one of the best looking women in this town before you met him."

"Daddy, before I came over today I was working around the house doing some work for the locals. What do I need to dress up for?" she asked.

"What were you dressing up for before? The Ruthie I know who not be caught dead outside looking like you look today. You might as well put on a burlap sack the way that dress swallows you up!" he yelled.

"Daddy, stop your foolishness! Do I look that bad?" she queried, her feelings hurt by his criticism.

"Not bad, Ruthie. Just different. Different in a not so good kind of way." His voice trailed off into the wind. *I want my old Ruthie back*, he thought.

1962

She loved church and everysince she was a young girl, Ruth looked forward to going. From where she lived, there were three churches within a one mile distance. She attended all of them. She loved to hear folk sing spirituals, even loved the words, *Go down Jordan...Nearer my Lord to thee*...and her all time favorite, *Jesus, Keep me near the cross.* She sang in the morning when she awoke; she sang while doing housework, cooking, working in the garden, going to the bathroom, and wherever she went, she sang a song.

Ruth was fascinated with the Southern church and could not wait to hear the morning testimonies, her favorite part of the service. Folks would thank God for just about everything that happened that week and in between their stories, someone would sing a song. She carried a tambourine in preparation for the event. She would find a rhythm, beat against the tambourine with one hand and dance in a trot like formation to whatever song was being sung. Fast or slow, Ruth stood up and joined in.

"Giving honor to God who is the head of my life, to Jesus Christ, his son," someone would start. Ruth got excited.

"All those who know the words of prayer, pray my strength in the Lord." Ruth always stood up toward the end. She knew another song would follow.

James sat next to her, stared ahead and made all sorts of grunting noises. Ruth knew she would hear about it when they got home.

"Where it say dat in the Bible?" he inquired as soon as they walked into house.

"Right in Psalms 100. The Bible says we are to praise him in the dance. See, there's nothing wrong with dancing. It just depends on what you're dancing to," she smiled.

"Well, you ain't dancing to nothing. Not gon' see my wife in public shaking while other men lust over ya body," he said.

"Oh, hush up, James. Nobody lusting over me but you," she teased.

"You be surprised! Ruthie, men likes a woman with a shape you can shake a stick at."

"Old man, hush up, I say. You always talking foolishness." She was determined to keep the conversation in a joking spirit.

"Um talkin' what I know." Then, he continued, "Ah don't want to hurt one of these fools for looking at my wife like she dere property."

"Property! I may be married, but I am still a free woman! I'm nobody's property. I know my place around here and I respect it. It doesn't matter what other men think."

James Harrison remained suspicious. In church, he behaved as a bodyguard, standing whenever Ruth stood and remaining next to her until she sat back down. It was a sight to see, Ruth, eyes closed tightly, dancing and spinning around, sometimes falling down in a trancelike state, and James standing next to her, emotionless. He never clapped his hands, never held the hymn book, and never took his eyes off of his wife.

He eventually tried to put a stop to the church services all together, but he lost that fight. Defeated, he resorted to fear tactics.

"Look at ya, Ruth. Your hair out all the time. You shine your lips like you going to town everyday, even when you out in the yard and even when you out in the fields. Who ya trying to impress?"

"No one. I am not trying to impress anyone but myself. My lips stay ashy. I told you. I am not about to walk around with ashy lips, all cracked and sore," she said.

"That's what Vaseline is for! You wear it at night and put a little on during the day. You don't need anything else is what my sistahs say. And, what's the matter with your hair? It hurt to be tied back behind ya ears?"

"What's wrong with my hair now, James? You used to always love my hair…"

"It's a distraction, woman! A big one! How many times must I tell ya tuh stop causing men to lust over ya. I see how they look at you. Even white men stare at ya. Whatcha thank gone happ'n next? They coming afta me tuh take you."

"What? I never heard such foolishness. White men around here don't mess with me! I must be too funny looking for them, huh ?" She laughed.

"Shoot. Ya think? You the right color and the right size. A small figured woman like you all they dreams of," he said.

"Well let them keep dreaming. That's all they gon' do," Ruth yelled as she walked to their bedroom.

"Was they dreaming when they took ya' mama?" he mumbled.

Ruth was down the hall, but she heard the words that came out of her husband's mouth as clearly as if she were standing right next to him. She boiled with anger.

"Leave my mother out of this, James! Don't talk about what you don't know. You weren't here then." She tried to control the rage that rose from deep within her.

"Don't matter. Talk all over town. Folks know. They won't admit it, but they know. The geechies in Pokie may not want to admit it. They let their guard down. That's how they took her the first time. The second time, well, blame ya' daddy!" he boasted.

"What does my father have to do with this?" She ran toward him. "You keep Frank Fields name out of your mouth, James!"

"I speaks the truth, Ruthie! Not trying to hurt ya' feelings. Your daddy should have never left his wife outside in the dark alone." He had gone too far, but it was too late.

"So is that what they are saying, James Harrison? My daddy is responsible for my mother's death? You sound like some of these other fools around here. It's always a different story and no one knows the truth except my mother and whoever was with her when she died." Ruth fought back the tears.

"Anyway, ya daddy should have been outside. The woman had already been whupped by the Klan earlier. What was she doing outside alone in the middle of the night? He was supposed to protect her."

"He did protect her! I was there that night, or don't you remember since you seem to have been a fly on the wall, mister!"

"Ruth, you were a child. You were sleep when everything went down." He turned and walked into the kitchen. "And so was ya daddy!"

"James Harrison, you have crossed the line and you know it! Now, I can just pack my bags and let you stay right here in Goosecreek. Maybe my daddy needs protecting. Maybe I need to go back home."

James ran back into the living room. He hurried over to where Ruth stood, and grabbed her hands. "Ruth, I am so sorry! I meant no disrespect towards yuh people. Yuh mama was a good woman. Everyone says so. Ya daddy a good man." He paused and smiled. "I know he's jealous of you loving me, but that's understandable. If I had a daughter as beautiful as you, I would be jealous too of any man that tries to get next to huh." His eyes pleaded for forgiveness.

Ruth stared at her husband. He had given her a way out if she was ready to take it. She pulled herself free.

"He's not jealous of you. Maybe he sees you for the man you really are behind that mask! I accept your apology this time, but you need to repent and turn from your wicked ways. I don't want to hear no more foolishness about me or my parents. You better thank the Lord Almighty that I'm a woman of God. If I wasn't, I would pack my bags and never speak to you again!" She turned to walk away, but added,

"You just give me one more reason, and I promise you'll never see me again."

Ruth was a woman of her word and James Harrison knew it. He said many things about her family during their marriage, but he never spoke of Frank and Rosetta Fields again. He kept what he knew and his opinion about it, to himself.

FIVE

1957

Frank Fields' roots were deep in Coosawhatchie, a town that reminded the Fields family of tragedy. It was rumored that their grandfather, Thomas "Tommie" Fields, who had no formal education, taught his entire family how to read using newspapers he recovered from the passengers on the trains he serviced. Pretty soon, the whole neighborhood took part in Tommie's lessons. Then one day, word got out. Like a whiff of smoke, he disappeared; in fact, his body was never found.

The Fields family lived on a two-hundred acre piece of property of which each heir received ten acres after reaching adulthood. Frank's father,Thomas Fields, the oldest son, lived there for a while before one day moving his family into Ridgeland, the county seat. Frank and his sister were never told why the family moved away because back then children did not involve themselves in grown folks' business. After his father's death, he and his sister, Mae Alice, left Ridgeland and moved to Beaufort. They frequented the property in Coosawhatchie to visit family, but nothing was said to them about their entitlement to the land.

Frank inquired about his acreage once he married Rosetta. Jake, Tom's brother and the oldest heir at the time, told him that Tom sold his rights to him before he moved to Ridgeland. Frank offered to buy a few acres to cultivate for a produce farm, but Jake refused, contending that there were no available plots. Any remaining lots, he added, were already promised to heirs living in New York who were close to retirement and soon to return.

Something about the way his uncle carefully explained the situation convinced Frank that he was lying. Yet, without his father to set the record straight, no one in the family would speak against Jake, so in the end, Frank purchased sixteen acres of land down the road in Poketaligo.

Thirteen years later, the truth came out. Apparently, Jake and Tom had a longstanding dispute over a red bone woman whom they both dated. Jake dated her first, and apparently she dropped him for another man: Tom. Tom had no idea of the woman's past and eventually asked her hand in marriage. Once word reached Jake, he insisted that his brother end the relationship, but he refused. After a series of brutal fights, the family took sides.

Jake's side prevailed and had Tom and his family outsted from the property. Jake divided the remaining land any way he wanted. That's how Tom ended up in Ridgeland; that's how Frank ended up without a plot of land.

1957

It had to be the coldest winter morning ever that February when Frank Fields arose, put on his Sunday suit and hat, and left the house en route to Ridgeland. He did not tell anyone where he was going. When Ruth woke up two hours later, she discovered he'd made a fresh fire in the fireplace, baked biscuits, boiled rice, fried up some smoked sausages, and quietly left the house. She went out into the backyard to look for him, but he was nowhere to be found.

He'd caught a ride into Ridgeland and waited outside of the office of Harlan Boone, the only lawyer in town that represented Negros. When Mr. Boone arrived, he opened the front door and let Frank inside. Frank explained his understanding of the heirs' rights. Boone agreed to check the courthouse records for evidence. At that point, Frank knew that was not the right plan of action. The courthouse did not hold the answers.

Boone's suggestion would take years to sort out. Frank's family, like many in the Low Country, had been kicked off of Hilton Head Island for the same reason. No documentation was available to prove they rightfully owned the land they occupied. Frank knew enough about South Carolina law to understand that an heir's rights could be challenged by any other living heir. There was one ray of hope.

Jake was dead.

He was killed during a fight in a juke joint months before his youngest son was born. Since heir's rights were granted by the oldest living relative on the land, that family member could unilaterally grant another member access to the land without getting anyone else's permission.

Frank did not know who the oldest living relative was, and dared not take a chance on starting a feud all these years later, but time was running out. He wanted to move into a new house on his inherited land before the next school year began.

On his walk back from town, he decided to ask for his birthright. From the service road he noticed two large wooden houses, one which sat at an angle from the highway, and the other, a white clapboard structure, that faced Highway 17. Next to the second house stood three young men huddled near the porch steps, playing a game of dice.

Frank took his jacket off. If they let him, he would teach them a few of his old tricks. Things he learned in the streets before he married Rosetta.

Four games of dice, four major victories. Just enough time for Frank to learn everything he needed to know about the families that currently occupied the land. Interestingly enough, he discovered forty acres remained unoccupied and even uncommitted to other heirs. In fact, no family member had ever occupied either plot of land.

Blame it on superstition.

It was believed that both plots were cursed. One plot was just off the highway, right next to a local merchant who owned a store with a small filling station. It was feared this land was cursed a long time ago when the Klan lynched an innocent young boy there. The second plot bordered the Coosawhatchie River. That presented another problem.

Townsfolk believed that hags and witches travelled throughout the land seeking whom they could devour. One of the entry ways that such spirits used was water. Some folks believed that anything next to water was susceptible to being possessed by the spirits of the dead. It was a popular belief that the Coosawhatchie River was home to a host of spirits that refused to die. The land surrounding it was believed to be cursed too. To fight those spirits, a church was erected in the 1800's, and after being destroyed in a fire at the turn of the century, a second edifice was built.

Frank knew exactly which piece of property he wanted to start his new life.

The oldest living heir was his great Aunt Jesse. She was Tom's youngest brother's wife. Twenty-five years her senior, Jesse married Henry Fields when she was thirteen. He had long been dead by the time Jake and Tom started feuding. Because she was a young woman with small children, the family allowed Jesse to remain on the property, despite her remarrying to a person who had no relation to the Fields family. That is how much she was highly respected and revered.

Frank remembered her. She was the kind of person one never forgot. When he and his sister visited as children, they loved to talk to Jesse because she was, to their young innocent minds, the encyclopedia on sex. Any question perceived as taboo, she answered in explicit detail. She even had toys for demonstrations. Frank remembered she referred to one such toy as "a woman's revenge." A huge smile lit up his face.

Jesse lived in the center of the property in a house that was made of cinderblock. There was a wooden back porch and two wood sheds in the back. The house, a large structure, looked nothing like it did all those years before. Now it resembled an old shack, with no electricity or running water, in desperate need of repair.

As dirt flew into his face, Frank stopped in the front of the house and stared at the chickens running around. He could see old automobile parts underneath the house, more than likely owned by Jesse's twelve sons. They were another reason no one was bold enough to force her off the land. Seven were by Henry. Folks called them seven bad seeds. They had reputations all their own.

Frank climbed the narrow steps to the front porch as the floorboards squeaked loudly. He glanced at the front door and noticed there was no screen door to keep the flies out. The door was painted white, but so dirty it looked like a spotted animal. The handle was dark metal. He said a quick prayer and knocked.

It had been years, but Jesse Fields White Hamilton recognized his face even as he stood in the afternoon sunlight.

"Ah, good Lord! Dat Tom's son! Ah know it ain't so!" She beamed with excitement. "Frank, dat you?"

"Yes ma'am. How ya d-d-doing?" he stuttered. He was embarrassed that he had not visited her in over twenty years. "I know it's been quite some time since I passed through. I did not mean any disrespect. I been meaning to get by here, but you know how it is with a family and all."

"Yes, Ah sho' do. You come on in and sit down. Got some rice and peas on da stove. You welcome to it. Ah even got some jelly cake if ya' likes," Jesse said.

She was considered red bone, with silky black hair that hung down her back. The years and good cooking had taken their toll, for she carried more than two hundred pounds on her five foot frame.

"Thank ya kindly. I better get back on up the road to my children. You know their mother passed away last year, so it's just me and her sister, Bea, taking care of the house these days." He looked around to see if she was alone, then said, "It would be nice to leave them in a place I know kinfolk can keep a watch on them after I pass."

"Frank, you gots family right heah. Never understood why all y'all move away from ya family like dat. Where your sista? Ah wouldn't know huh if she came up and bit me on da cheek, ah tell ya." She laughed.

"Me either. She's been in Chicago with that yankee husband of hers. She writes every once in a while, even said she was coming to Setta's funeral, but she never showed."

"Oh, you poor soul! How y'all managing widout huh? That woman was a fierce machine. She put everyone in dey place. Bet she ran you rugged, huh?"

"No, ma'am. Rosetta was the best thing that ever happened to me. Yes, Lord. We have seven children and I swear, no one could ever take her place."

"Frank, a man like you don't need tah be alone. You need tah think about marrying sometime again, huh?"

"No, ma'am. Been married twice. Now that Setta's gone, I'm satisfied. It makes me no never mind if I ever have another woman in my life."

"Yeah! Mmmhum. Yah say dat now. Ah been married three times, and if old John out dere die, Um going to marry a fourth!" She slapped her knee and hollered, "Everyone need somebody warm in da bed at night. Git my drift?"

"Yes, ma'am, I do." Frank knew he had to change the subject quick.

"Well, I better get home," he said as he rose from the wooden chair he had sat in at the kitchen table.

"Okay, Frank. It was so good to see yah again. Don't yah wait so long to come visit again!" She rose and headed toward the front door. "Yah ever gone move back heah wid us?"

"Would love too." She had miraculously opened the door he'd been afraid to ask about. "Just thinking about living on that family land next to the Coosawhatchie River."

Then, he turned and faced her. "What do you think about that?"

"Swampland! Why y'all want dat swamp land? Dere iz other land near Highway 17 dat ain't nobody touched. Yah want dat?" she asked.

"Nah. Got little ones. I don't want 'em running in that street, getting killed by some fool drunk. These youngbloods don't need cars the way they drive around here."

"Ah say! So yah think y'all safer near da swamps? Cursed land. Den yah gots tuh deal wid da hollering coming out o' Second AB on Sundays! If yah wanna battle dem demons, yah can have it." She walked out onto the front porch. "When yah thinking of moving back?"

"Just as soon as I can get Roger and his boys to build me a house. Hopefully, they can be finished before the weather turns," he explained.

"Come on, den. We'll be glad tah have yah." Standing barefoot, she grabbed Frank and gave him a hearty hug. "May stop some o' dis foolishness going on wid dese heah youngins. Come on, Ah say! The sooner da betta."

By October, Frank moved his family back to his father's land. With the help of his cousins, he built quite a large house on his ten acre lot. He even fixed up Jesse's house some. Yet, his home stood out as the most beautiful creation on the entire plot. There were four bedrooms in the back and one large parlor and bedroom which opened to the wrap around porch that surrounded the entire structure. He made sure that every bedroom had its own door. He thought of the privacy Rosetta so desperately needed after the attack. He wished over and over again that she had lived to see this beautiful house and live in it with him.

Every design was based on Rosetta's wishes and desires for their dream home. They one they planned to build once their children were older. The one she never lived to see. The house with the beautiful gardens and the wrought iron furniture neatly displayed under an Oak Tree out in the yard. That was the dream.

Yet, as reality slowly settled in, Frank Fields knew that he would never enjoy this house with his beloved wife, and the thought of having wrought iron chairs sickened him all the more. Instead, he surrounded his haven with a large garden, over populated by a field of flowers that reminded him of the beauty and love he had once known.

1958

South Carolina dark nights: Pitch black and filled with buzzing mosquitoes and stinging night flies. Scary to some, yet craved by others. Between the night time cool breeze and the sounds of mother nature, the Coosawhatchie River was Ruth's baptismal pool.

Although she was familiar with nearly every Low Country tale about ghosts and evil spirits, that did not stop her from dropping a fishing pole into the river every weekend. In fact, she enjoyed every stretch of land her father owned. On weekdays, she spent most of her evenings sitting down by the water relaxing. She had finally found her solace, a place to heal her heart and restore inner peace.

Dusk had fallen. Ruth sat underneath a large oak tree with her eyes closed, humming to herself. All of a sudden, she heard an unusual noise. She opened her eyes and looked in the direction of the church several yards in the distance. Then there was another sound.

Alarmed, she rose to her feet and collected her blanket, picnic basket filled with her spoils, the fishing rod, and any bait that remained in the small metal bucket. She took fifty steps before the sounds became fully audible.

Someone was in deep trouble. Ruth, shaken, stopped walking and started to pray. As she passed the small church in front of her, she spotted several men huddled around a dark colored pick up truck. With diminished vision in the night, she counted five or six in number, before she hid on the side of the building, and placed her belongings down on the ground. A distraught woman was screaming.

The men, too engrossed in what they were doing, never noticed Ruth had invaded their space. As blood curling screams continued coming from their direction, Ruth, ducking beneath the bushes, stood up just in time to see a tall, slender man jump down from the back of the truck. She covered her mouth in horror as he adjusted his belt buckle; his zipper remained undone. Fear crept all around her. The man, fixated on what he was doing, mumbled something.

"Shut up, ya darkie," another man spat. He had dark colored hair and was standing next to the truck, wearing a white tee shirt that exposed his protruding gut. "That's how y'all like it I hear."

The woman screamed louder as another rman hoisted himself onto the back of the truck, the springs squeaking under his weight.

"Gal, if you don't hush up, I'm gonna give it to yah in da rear, split ya wide open," one of the men said.

"Hurry up, Hank. We ain't got all night. Hurry befo' she pass out. I want her to see my lily white face banging the hell out of her," he said to his comrade, who could not be seen from where Ruth stood.

Ruth bent over and picked up a large stick, figuring out her next move. With nowhere to run, she knew she was that woman's only chance of leaving the scene alive.

"Jesus, are you with me?" She picked up a medium sized rock in her other hand. With all her might, she tossed the rock into the air and with every bit of strength in her one-hundred pound frame, swung the wood against the rock in the direction of the truck.

The rock came down, smashing against the hood of the truck.

"What in Sam Hill was that?" the man who'd jumped down moments before yelled. Ruddy looking, a massive brute, he held his belt slightly below his buttocks exposing his private parts, which continued to hold its excitement.

Two more men jumped onto the back of the truck. Within minutes, the woman's screams had been muffled.

Ruth swung again. The rock hit the dark-haired man upside his head.

"Ouch! Damn it! What is going on? Hank, you throw somethin' at me?"

"Hell naw, Mike! I'm standing here wiping my jimmy off! What the hell ya' talking 'bout?"

Ruth gathered several rocks and held batting practice, using the men in front of her as targets. Some of the rocks pelted against the truck while others hit the intended targets. Then they spotted her.

"Hold on guys, I think we got us a visitor," the first man said, now standing up on the bed of the truck, staring in Ruth's direction. "If'n it's a woman, we got some more rounds to do. If it's a man, hell, we gonna make him do the same thang and then we gonna shoot his black arse."

Ruth backed away and leaned against the building. The men, now holding flash lights, approached her.

"Well, what have we got heah?" they said almost in unison.

"Hold up boys, we got company and she look real fresh," Hank yelled to the remaining men on the back of the truck. "Give the wench a break, or shoot her if she moves."

The two men on the back of the truck jumped down and headed over to join the others. Ruth looked straight ahead at the first group approaching her. Then she started speaking, but addressed no one in particular.

"What the hell? What is she saying?" The bald headed man turned to Mike.

"Hell if I know, Bob!" Mike replied.

Ruth stood still, stick bat still in her right hand, eyes glaring at the strangers in a trancelike state.

"Girlie, what's 'at you ranting 'bout?" he asked.

Ruth kept speaking in tongues, her eyes seemingly looking at them but unfocused, staring straight ahead. A minute later, the men seemed to be hypnotized. Hank stretched his arms out toward her. Ruth continued to stare ahead and then she looked directly into his sullen blue-grey eyes. She held his gaze for several minutes.

Hank staggered and fell backwards. The other men nervously reached out to break his fall.

One of the men who had joined the others last, stared at his now helpless comrade. Then he looked at Ruth. "Wait one minute! Hold on boys, let's git the hell out of heah! I done heard of this mess befo'. This ain't no ordinary geechie, this is some kinda witch!"

"Oh, hush up ya' foolishness!" Bob dismissed what was being said. "Grab her arms and give her the same we just gave her sister. I bet she'll speak English then." He laughed but the sound was hollow and not convincing.

"Hell naw! She don't look familiar. Don't know if I ever seent her around these here parts. Maybe she a Yankee witch." They all started to retreat.

Ruth's voice became louder, her eyes wider. Her whole body vibrated like a musical instrument.

Just then daggers of lightning slashed through the clouds. The men jumped at the sound. Ruth, now staring directly at the man named Bob, continued speaking. She seemed unmoved by the lightening striking around her. In fact, she seemed to welcome it. When the men noticed her reaction, they looked up as lightning struck around their feet, lighting up the entire sky. Even the inside of the church was visible to the naked eye. The men backed away, reluctant to take their eyes off the strange woman.

Ruth never let up, even as she heard the woman on the back of the truck jump down and sprint away into the woods. As thunder joined in the lightning symphony at an unbearable decibel, the men turned and ran in the direction of the truck. The lightning intensified. Thunder roared as winds picked up speeds that caused branches on the trees above to bend and touch the ground. The sky lit up as in the middle of the day. The men turned and looked back at Ruth. She was still leaning on the building and looking up into the sky. They turned to escape. If she could call down lightning, what else could she do? They did not want to find out.

As they ran, one by one they stopped in their tracks. Whatever vision in front of them must have been more ghastly than what was behind them.

Ruth knelt down when she heard their screams and closed her eyes. She heard their feet scurrying about in different directions. Their cries grew more intense. She kept her eyes closed and waited until the thunder stopped. Small streaks of lightning continued. When silence returned to the night skies, Ruth slowly opened her eyes, got up from the ground, and walked around the building.

Standing on the hood of a truck was a petite woman of no more than five feet in height, wearing a long dark hooded robe. Resembling the Statue of Liberty, she stood barefoot; in one hand she held a wooden cane, and in the other, a flaming torch.

Ruth walked closer to the truck, stopped, and looked at the woman. Her face was raised to the sky while she spoke directly to Mother Nature. When she lowered the torch, the lightning subsided and the entire sky was calm again. Ruth walked closer to where she stood and their eyes met. The woman removed the hood that concealed her identity.

Trying to ignore the intensity of the woman's glare, Ruth adjusted her focus and walked toward the back of the truck. A cat jumped off the bed startling Ruth who then noticed the woman watching her every move.

"You all right?"

Terrified, Ruth remained calm. "Yes, ma'am."

"You best get back to Frank and them kids. They'll be looking for you in no time flat."

"Yes, ma'am," Ruth mumbled and pointed toward the back of the truck. "She still back there?"

"No. I'll take care of her. You did good. Just keep moving and don't say a word about what you just saw."

"No, ma'am. I won't say a word. Is she going to be all right?"

"She is. You make haste. I'll take good care of her."

"What about those evil men?" She turned to leave.

A vicious smile crept across the woman's pale face. "I doubt they'll say anything to another living soul!" She placed the hood back over her head and jumped into the front seat of the truck.

The truck sped off toward the river. Keeping her promise to the strange woman that night, Ruth never told another soul.

SIX

1962

No seed. No grand. That is how Ruth used to describe her life. After five years of marriage and no pregnancies, she knew something was wrong. James said it was her fault, said she praised the Lord too hard and gave so little attention to him that his sperm could not get through. All blocked up by the Holy Ghost.

It was definitely not for lack of trying. They made love almost every night and every month they received a visit from Proud Mary which meant the stork would not be visiting them in a few months like it had visited others in the neighborhood.

Everyone around them had children by then. After a while folks felt sorry for Ruth for they knew she longed to carry a child of her own. Her barren state became so commonplace, that folks began to drop a child off for a night, then a week, and it just continued. Some were more responsible than others and did not take advantage of an already bad situation, but Ruth did not mind being used. She never questioned anyone and never judged a soul. She just loved the children dropped in her lap.

Townsfolk started calling her Mother Ruth because, at twenty-one years old, she had a unique way of handling children. She could hold a crying baby and in seconds, the child would stop crying, on its way to a deep sleep. News of her calming abilities spread and even white families on the other side of the railroad tracks brought their colicky and often fussy babies to visit her.

She loved all of the children equally, but she grew especially attached to two of them. One was the son of a white woman who lived in Ridgeland. She came to Ruth in the wee hours of the night, claiming her husband threatened to kill the boy. Ruth told her she did not need the details of the entire story and, after calming the woman, took the bright-eyed, brunette little boy into one of the bedrooms and laid him down. The woman did not mention the father of the child, but Ruth was smart enough to know that it was not the husband who now wanted to end the child's life.

Ramona Rose Brown was the daughter of one of Rosetta's close friends. She was the first child that Ruth babysat that was not one of her younger siblings. Folks said Ramona had a bad heart. In actuality, she was born with a hole in her heart. When one of the local merchants saw the child, she immediately recommended that Ramona's mother to contact Ruth. It was a match made in Heaven.

Ruth said Ramona was an angel because when she looked into her piercing light grayish-green eyes, it seemed she was looking directly into the sky. With curly sandy brown hair, Ramona was smaller than an average three-year-old, yet her hair was almost longer than her petite body. When she spoke, a smile automatically graced her face and the words that came forth sounded like those of a wise old soul.

"Ruthie, who dat baby ya holding?" Pearlie asked Ruth one day.

"Ooh. What's that child's name? I can't rightly recall. She's married to that Reverend from Savannah. Her people's the Staples or some such. I don't think she's from around this way." Ruth never divulged the exact information of the parents.

"Who? What Reverend? Not that crazy man, huh?"

"I don't know what you're talking about, Pearlie Garrett. Everyone is crazy according to you," Ruth uttered.

"No, not everyone. Where some of these youngins come from?" Pearlie shot back.

"What difference does it make, Pearlie? Babies need love just like the rest of us. Doesn't matter who gives it to them," Ruth insisted.

"That ain't right, Ruthie. Some of these folk just using you to babysit their chirren. That's a shame."

"Ah, hush now! I don't care what the situation is. I have a place in my heart for everyone of them."

"Every bastard child ya mean, Sistah." Then she turned to Benjamin. "I swear befo' God that child look more black every day. Even his olive skin is getting browner."

"Oh, stop your foolishness, Pearlie Mae. That's just the sun changing his hair and skin. Mind your business, please!" Ruth said.

Now at peace, Ruth understood that her time for conceiving a human being would eventually come. It was all in God's hands. For now, she had the best of both worlds in the four children that lived with her and the other three that went home every night.

They traveled with her everywhere she went. As she walked into town, she piled them inside of the red wagon that she'd had since she was a little girl. The children held onto each other, and if there was an infant in the wagon, one of the older children held it on their lap.

Humming the entire five-mile journey, Ruth stopped to rest on the side of the service road. She placed a blanket on the ground and sat the children underneath a tree. Then she handed out pieces of apple and crackers while they each played together. Often times, they never made it into town on foot for some passerby would spot Ruth with her wagon of kids and offer them a ride.

One hot summer day, a dusty blue Ford pickup truck slowed near where Ruth and the children were walking. The driver pulled off the shoulder and motioned for them to get inside. Something about the vehicle alarmed Ruth. She adjusted the straw hat she wore, looked at the ground, and then turned to look in the opposite direction toward Coosawhatchie. The driver exited the truck.

"Afternoon, Miss Ruth. It's Hank Gray. Can I give you a lift?"

"Ooh. Hank, Jr., ya say. You sure grew up fast! I didn't recognize you in that big pickup truck. Is that ya daddy's?" She noticed how much he had grown up over the years, well over the average height of a teenager with blonde hair and and a full moustache.

"Yes, ma'am. He gave it tuh me when I turned sixteen," he said with obvious pride.

"Ooh. I see. We're not going far. Just slightly into town," Ruth said with caution. "We fine."

"Don't matter, Miss Ruth. I'll make sho' y'all get there safely. My father would want me tuh."

"Okay. If you say so," Ruth said, as she turned to survey the children. "Let me put these kids in the back of the truck."

"Don't ya bother yourself. I can get them for ya."

Ruth remained apprehensive. Hank Gray was innocent, but his gandfather, Henry, was the Devil incarnate. Had the bad seed been passed down? He was a known Klansman that boasted about putting negros in their place. Some even were put in the ground. Ruth stared at the truck and then remembered why it bothered her. It was too late to turn down the offer now.

Hank put the children in the back of the truck and secured the wagon with rope. Ruth prayed she had not placed their precious lives in jeopardy.

"Going shopping?" he asked.

"Nope. Just going for a walk. That's all."

"Well, you sho' walks a lot! I see ya nearly every day!" He paused, began to tap on the steering wheel, and stared straight at Ruth. "I need to ask ya something."

"Go on, baby." Ruth removed her hat, revealing a set of intense brown eyes.

"How old are yah, Miss Ruth?"

"Not too much older than you, Hank. I just probably seem older."

"I find that hard tuh believe! You seem so mature and polished. Older than most." He looked out of the front window and continued. "You know mah wife, Samantha, she wants kids real bad."

"I suppose all young folks want children, son. Nothin' new 'bout that."

"She wants one bad. Real bad. Just nothing happ'nin," he explained.

"I know how you feel. I'm dealing with the same thing."

He looked totally surprised. "So these here youngins ain't yours?"

"No. I'm just caring for them while their parents are off working," she lied.

"You take care of five babies that ain't yer own?"

"Well, sometimes I take care of more than that," she admitted.

"Miss Ruth, I am honored tuh know yah. I never knew you had no children of yer own." Then he added just above a whisper, "Makes my question kinda stupid now."

"Hank, there's no such thing as a stupid question. Go on, son." She looked back at the children.

"Well, ah..ah..ah was going to ask you to come lay hands on my wife so she could have a baby, but seeing you ain't got none either, what good's that gonna do?"

Ruth looked out of the window. "Might just do some good for the both of us."

"I don't understand."

"Maybe she and I just need to come together in agreement before the Lord." She looked over at him. "You are a believer in God, son, right?"

"Yes, Miss Ruth. Been in and outa church my whole life. My wife too." He seemed to relax and started to smile.

"Well, then you both are entitled to the promises of God. The Bible says where two or three are gathered together in

His name, He will be in the midst of them. Maybe Miss Samantha and I just need to get together and petition God for what we want regarding having children from our wombs."

Hank looked doubtful. "So you really think God gonna come around if the two of you barren women get together and talk to Him?" he asked doubtfully.

Ruth burst out laughing. "Shucks no! I don't know. I only know that prayer changes things."

"I dunno. I tried everythang. Even stuff from folks we afraid of," he said.

"Like who? Who are you afraid of?" Ruth asked.

"Some of these Devil worshippers."

"Boy, hush ya foolishness! The Devil can't stop what God has already commanded! Whatever God promised to his children must come to pass. I don't care how long it takes. He promised me I would have children one day. That's why I am not worried."

"Well, I don't know if he promised Samantha the same. I just done give up. She's sad all the time and won't go out o' the house. I can't take much more. I didn't take those vows to put up with this type of crap."

"She will be fine, ya hear me? You both are going to be just fine," Ruth assured him.

The remainder of the drive into town was peaceful. Neither said a word until they arrived at town square. There was a small crowd of people walking up and down the streets. Hank pulled the truck over to the curb on the right hand side. He put the gear into park and looked at Ruth again.

"This as far as I can take you. I'm going ta turn on Byrd Street and head on to the feed supply store."

"That is fine, chile. Those children will get restless before long anyways," Ruth said, as she grabbed the door handle.

"One mo' thing, Miss Ruth. Can I ask you another question?"

"Go on, son. Get it out," she said.

"You believe in hags?"

"What's that ya say? Hags?"

"Yeah. They say people can put hags on a person and bad things happen. I think somebody put a hag on my whole family for all the trouble my folks caused the coloreds," he said slowly.

"Hush now. That's just superstition. I don't believe that mess! I believe in Jesus Christ. Can't no hag compete with him, I tell ya that!" Ruth smiled.

"You thank so, Miss Ruth?"

"Chile, I don't think....I know." She opened the door of the truck. "Besides, your grandfather is going to pay for his own sins, either here on Earth or wherever his soul ends up."

"We all know where that's gonna be, Miss Ruth. Ain't no changing that man."

"Well, maybe he will see the light on his deathbed."

Hank jumped down from the truck cab and headed around to the back to retrieve the children. He unlatched the handle, pulled out the red wagon, then he lifted each child high into the air before placing them on the grass next to the side walk. Ruth placed the blanket on the wagon and put the children back ontop.

As soon as Hank secured the back door, his eyes widened, then he ducked behind the truck. Ruth turned and looked at him suspiciously.

"Chile, you all right?" she asked.

"Uh huh. I'll be fine in a minute. Just give me a few seconds," he whispered.

"Who ya hiding from down there?" She looked up and down the street at the passersby. Then she spotted something odd.

Directly across the street, a petite woman sat primly on a park bench. Despite the enormous heat, she was dressed in black with a black scarf that covered most of her hair. Her dark shades prevented others from seeing where she was looking, but it was obvious to Ruth that her eyes were focused on Hank Gray.

"Don't pay her any attention." Ruth turned and looked down at Hank. "She is just fooling with you, child. Go on and get back in that truck and go on about your business."

Hank practically crawled on his knees back to the driver's side of the truck, jumped in and turned on the ignition. Placing the gear in reverse, he backed away from Ruth and the children. He then turned the truck around and proceeded in the opposite direction from where he had intended to go.

Ruth pulled the wagon up the street. She kept her eyes on the woman. Then she noticed the sign posted above the woman's head: Whites Only. Ruth proceeded across the street.

"You ought to be ashamed of yourself," she yelled. "You know that boy doesn't know a thing about the sins of his father. You should leave him be."

The woman ignored her, all the while following the truck with her eyes as it sped off down the street. She held a red parasol in her left hand, while her right hand rested on her lap. A smile crept across her face as she looked at Ruth standing before her in the blazing sun.

"I'm not afraid of you giving me the evil eye!" Ruth yelled. "And don't think about cursing none of my children."

"You don't have any children, Miss Ruth," she finally spoke.

"Any child God sends to me is mine. At least for the moment!"

"Your time for birthing babies has not come to pass. Just be patient, Ruth. I don't think you'll carry a child this season."

"Now, who are you? You can't stop any blessing God gives me."

"You're right. I can only tell you what I know for sure. This is not your season, but a delayed promise is not a denial."

"And you know this because of what? I didn't think you and God were on speaking terms," Ruth snapped.

"Some things a woman just knows." She removed the shades so that Ruth could see her beautiful onyx eyes.

"Stop faking that you practicing evil, Beulah. I know you full of crap most of the time."

"Watch yourself, Ruth, you are no match for me." Then she turned to the children. " My, oh my, that's a beautiful angel sitting right there. What's your name?"

"Ramona," the child proffered as she stared at the woman's long, shiny black hair.

"Ramona!" Beulah said, "You look like your name should be Rose."

"It is. It's Ramona Rose, ma'am." The child grabbed Ruth's hand.

"Well, Ramona, you are one beautiful blessing. I can now say I have met an angel in the flesh." Beulah smiled, took out some coins and held them out to the children.

Ruth watched the children's interaction with the stranger. She did not object to the gifts, because she understood the generosity of the giver. Beulah Chaney had everyone fooled, but Ruth knew the heart of the woman most of the town feared. Yet to the contrary, Beulah was more friend than foe and they would all learn that as the years went by.

On the way home that day, Ruth pondered Beulah's comment about Ramona's name. According to Ramona's mother, her name was originally Rose but she changed it two weeks after the baby was born. Rose then became Ramona's middle name. A fact not too many people were privy too.

SEVEN

October 1964

The church was packed. Ruth sat on the front row holding Ramona tightly. It was a sad day. Reverend Brown was a beacon of hope in the Low Country. His church, Chapel in the Woods, was the first church in Jasper County to have an overflow section, located in the choir stand.

Sunday mornings would usher in folks from as far as Savannah. Most, under the age of thirty, were not raised in the church, did not understand its traditions, but fell in love with Pastor Roy's deliverance of street gospel. He said God's people sat on untapped potential. Said whatever someone said had a 99% possibility of coming true, if only the person believed it would. The tongue, he professed, was the strongest weapon against the Devil and the Klan.

"You are more than a conqueror!" he proclaimed to the congregation. "You need to walk in the authority of Christ and let no man tell you what you can and can not accomplish! I tell you, the sky is the limit for all of God's children."

Ruth admired the teachings of Pastor Brown and could not wait each week to hear his uplifting sermons. He believed nothing was required to obtain salvation but a request. Once that request was made, a person had the power of God wrapped around them immediately. That's it.

Unlike the other churches in the rotation, new members of Chapel in the Woods gained immediate membership privileges. No year-long internships to complete or chaperones watching over them and a majority vote to be accepted. In fact, Roy Brown opposed public confessions, for he believed when it came to demonstrative proof that someone loved God, one could find out by simply looking at the relationships that individual had with others. A person's heart, he often scolded his congregation, changed from love and not embarrassment.

"If folk spent more time getting the beam out of their own eye, we would not have to deal with all the problems in the church. Stop pointing fingers at other folk. We all have skeletons in the closet that if we don't ask God to kick out, they will jump out and overtake our entire life!"

He introduced an entire new belief system to folks in the Low Country. One in which a person took full responsibility for his salvation. It was a process, he told them. A Christian needed to focus on the very actions of God found in the Bible and learn to live a holy life. That change would not come overnight. To those who said a person had to be perfect in order to live a holy life, he laughed and said once a person reached perfection in life, God would grant them the ultimate prize: Death.

"None of us are perfect," he preached. "We all got some repenting to do whether we like it or not. Myself included. If you sin, repent. Do it at home or do it here. There is no need to come before the church and ask to be reinstated. Once you become a member of this sanctuary, you will remain a member until you depart this area or this life. Your choice."

Pastor Roy's sermons focused on unconditional love and the Christian walk. He had an understanding of the issues young folk faced. That is why so many of that age group loved the ground he walke on. It was a new way of thinking and believing and it was the start of the transformation of religious beliefs in the South.

1962

"Hello, there. Anybody told you they love you today?" He sat behind a large mahogany desk looking at the woman standing at the door.

His question caught her by surprise. "That's a good question. Most of the people that have told me they loved me turned around and broke my heart," Ruth answered.

"Well, they say we only hurt the ones we love." Pastor Roy smiled and offered her a seat in his office.

"I wasn't prepared to meet you. Heard so many things about you, I thought I would drop by and make an introduction," she said, still standing and trembling.

"Why are you nervous, daughter? You're in God's house. There is nothing to be nervous of here. I promise you we won't ever hurt you or make you feel unwanted."

"Well, I'm not a member, Pastor Roy. I know you have to be a member to seek help from the other churches in town. We attend Second AB. Moved away with my husband and since we've been married, he has not liked one church home we've found. Now he's complaining about all the churches around here," she tried to explain.

"Well, tell him to come by and talk to me. I would be happy to share my perspective on things with him." He leaned forward. "But you're here now. That means you need something too."

Ruth noticed his green eyes and thought of Ramona. "Well, I'm..." She hesitated.

"Ruth Harrison, right? I should know the woman who keeps my child." He smiled.

"So, you knew who I was when I walked by your office?"

"Guilty! Ramona described your gloves and told me to look out for you one day because God was going to send you to this church."

"You got to be kidding? That girl is something else. Anointed, I declare! She was born with God's word in her mouth." Ruth felt a sense of comfort all around her.

"That she was! You have done some great things with her too," declared the preacher.

"Well, it's the Lord's doing." Ruth laughed.

"Yes, it is. We are merely vessels!"

"Well, I wanted to ask you something because James, my husband, says what I'm doing is wrong."

"And what does your heart tell you? I don't have to know what you're doing, I'm more concerned about how you feel about what you are doing." He walked over to where she was now sitting and sat down in the chair next to her.

"I feel so good about it. I mean, ever since my mother died, strange things have happened to me. I can't explain them. I see visions, have dreams, sometimes I think I can tell the future. Othertimes, I don't see a thing, but a feeling comes over me that tells me something bad is going to happen. Don't seem like I can do anything to stop whatever it is from happening either."

"Well, you are anointed with something special. I must admit, I've heard the rumors. Folks say you have healing powers and can intercede in prayer better than anyone in the Low Country. The call on your life is becoming quite popular, Ruth. I think you know that the enemy will try to destroy everything God has poured down into your spirit. He will try to turn what is meant for God's glory into something evil for the Devil's. You must continue to fast and pray that the Lord protects the anointing over your life. Satan is after your praise. He's after the praises of others as they bless God for what He has allowed through you. Whatever you do, Ruth, never let the enemy steal your praise," Pastor Roy told her.

"Amen." She nodded her head in agreement with the Pastor's words.

"Is your husband challenging this anointing?"

"James challenges everything. Everything I did was wrong when we first married. He hated the way I dressed, wore my hair, you name it, especially the way I praised the

Lord during morning devotion. He thought that was a sin too."

"Sometimes us men folk don't understand the call that God places on the women in our lives. I suspect your husband thought you had something special too. That's why he married you. It excited him in the beginning, but the enemy tried to turn it around so that every time James saw what he loved so much about you, he also saw what he hated. That's a trick the enemy uses to bring strife into our homes and destroy God's first established institution, which is holy matrimony."

"I'm sure you're right. James was so jealous I almost left him a few years ago. Then he changed, started getting into what I was doing with those children, and became so involved, he could not let it go." Ruth smiled as she described her husband's passion for the children in their care.

She continued, "Now he's upset about the women that huddle around my kitchen to pray. He says we need the direction of a pastor to hold church in our home."

"Is that so? The Bible says we are all ministers. That means each of us has a responsibility to help others have a better understanding and relationship with Christ. I don't see anything wrong with praying in your home. You must understand that anything you do for God will eventually blossom into something bigger than you expected."

"You are so right about that! I never saw this coming. I mean, I just wanted to serve God and his people. Now folks coming from miles around to pray and sing praises unto the Lord. Before you and Miz Mary came, there was no where for them to go unless it was to a Sunday service. Now we have a choice and with all the activities around here, I'm sure folks can take advantage of them."

"Ruth, your talent makes room for you. It does not matter how many Bible studies are going on in town. If God told you to have one, have one. Let it grow and become what God meant for it to become. That's how you accomplish what he intended for you. Just keep praying." He grabbed her hands and led her into prayer.

Ruth sighed heavily as the anointing filled the room.

1963

Her pulse was always on the children. Throughout the school year, she had a house full of children living with her. During the summers, Ruth and James held an overnight camp for children ages four to twelve. During that time, they graciously gave up their bedroom and made pallets on the floors of the other bedrooms to hold six to seven children per room, while the remaining children slept in the living room. The adult volunteers sometimes slept on the back porch.

Her structured summer program became known as Mother Ruth's Developmental Camp, and without any advertising, news spread from miles around. By its second year, Ruth had to caution parents that the camp was limited to thirty students who enrolled on a first-come first-served basis.

In its third year, thirty-three children registered, but forty showed up on the first day. It caught them all by surprise.

Ruth, James, and Pearlie Garrett stood in the back yard as children crowded along the back porch steps waiting to get into their already overcrowded small house.

"What's the weather like for the next two weeks?" James asked Pearlie as they stood watching the chaos.

"What? How am I supposed tuh know dat?" Pearlie was frustrated that Ruth would even consider accommodating all of these children. Surely she would send some of them away.

"Mah wife knows. She know everythang. Ask huh."

"Why don't you ask ask huh?" Pearlie pushed James forward toward where Ruth stood at the bottom of the stairs.

"Cuz I ain't tryin' to know." He looked about the yard. "Just put them out heah!" he yelled to Ruth.

She turned and looked at them. "Great God, man. You and I were thinking the same thing."

"Oh, Lord," he whispered. "That's why I ain't wanna know."

"It could work, huh, Pearlie?" Ruth asked smiling brightly.

"Heck no, sistah! How y'all gon' watch all dese chirren in da night?" she asked.

"Tent, sister! That's a real camp!" Ruth was overjoyed. "There's enough space to put up tents. We'll hold classes by the river. We can still do much of what we been doing these past years. It just might work." She slapped her hands in excitement.

"You done gone cracky, Ruthie! Just where are we gon' git tents tuh put up 'round heah?" Pearlie asked, looking at James suspiciously.

"I'll ask Pastor Roy. He uses big tents during revival."

"Chapel in the Woods probably borrowed those tents. They don't belong tuh them," James interjected.

"And how do you know?" Ruth watched the children becoming restless.

"Where Colored folk get money to buy them tents?" he inquired.

"What? James, let's not worry about those things. If God sent this many children to us, we have to find someplace for all of them to stay," she pleaded with him.

"What about snakes?" he asked.

"What? What about them? This is South Carolina. Snakes are everywhere," Ruth shouted, becoming frustrated with all his objections.

"Yuh don't want no mess with dese here folks about one of these crumbsnatchers being bit by a snake."

"Burn some sulfur then! James, you know how to keep the snakes away. These children are not scared of snakes. Those that are can stay in the house."

Ruth turned her attention back to the children. "Anybody here scared of sleeping outside in a tent?" she hollered, knowing their response before she said it.

When townsfolk saw what Ruth had done to accommodate all of the children, they banded together and hosted a picnic to coincide with the closing ceremonies. All four churches made donations and prepared food for days leading up to the actual event. Yet it was Pastor Roy Brown who was most active during the entire two weeks. Ruth loved having him around. He not only taught classes and worked to get the tents up each evening, he also donated the church's van for the three field trips that were planned. He even suggested taking the children to Singleton Beach, still segregated, to enjoy the outdoors. It was a welcome relief to the entire staff.

At the closing ceremonies, Pastor Roy surprised Ruth by honoring her efforts with an official Key to the city. On the following Sunday, he presented all of the staff with plaques of appreciation and by the time the service were over, he honored Ruth again with a plaque that would hang in each vestibule of all four churches declaring that Ruth Fields Harrison was the official Mother of Jasper County.

Spring 1964

"Good evening," Ruth called out as she opened the screened door.

"Good evening," she heard a voice ring out from a back room.

Eula Mae Wilcox walked out and stood smiling. "Whatcha standing like dat fo'? Cat got ya tongue?" she hollered.

"No. Just catching my breath. Been walking all day," she panted.

"Doing what, crazy chile?" Eula Mae turned and headed back into the kitchen. "Come on in heah and get something to drink."

"Thank you, ma'am." Ruth hurriedly followed.

"You doing all right? Where's Ida Mae? I did not see her with Frank at service this week."

"What kind of service? Frank who? Ya talkin' bout my son? Frank going to church now?" Eula Mae spun around and looked at Ruth. She was in the process of straightening her shoulder length hair. One side lay down on her neck shining brightly, while the other side was held together tightly in an afro puff awaiting the heat that would loosen its natural curl.

"Yes, ma'am. Frank's been going to Chapel in the Woods since they opened. He never asked you to come along?"

"No. Great Scott, no! Frank know I don't do church. What difference does another one coming to town make? They all alike?" She opened the refrigerator and pulled out a pitcher of Cherry Kool Aid.

"No, ma'am. I really believe Pastor Roy is different. I think cousin Frank would agree too. That's where all the young folks hang out around here. Right in that church. There are a lot of things for Ida Mae to do." Ruth looked around the room.

"Yeah, I doubt that. All she want to do is run up to Piggly Wiggly and spy on that boy she like. She think I don't know."

Ruth suspected the conversation was about to turn to Ida and Timmy's relationship, so she quickly changed the subject. "Well, Aunt Eula Mae, we're all going down to Hilton Head tomorrow to the beach. Going as a church family, a community of saints. Anyone can come."

"They gon' have church out on Hilton Head?" Eula Mae seemed puzzled. "Outside on the water? Sound crazy. Who's bright idea was that?"

"No, ma'am. We're not having church, just a fun day for everyone. The whole town and anyone that wants to join us."

"And who paying for this? That crazy preacher know dese folks don't have no kind of money to be all out at Singleton Beach." She shook her head and handed Ruth a warm cookie from the stove.

"It's free. Pastor Roy doesn't charge for anything. We raised money all year to celebrate his anniversary. This is what his wife wanted to do," Ruth tried to explain.

"His wife? What she got to do with nothing?"

"She's over the Pastor's Anniversary committee. She planned a week full of stuff to celebrate Pastor Roy's twentieth anniversary. I hear he started preaching right here in Jasper County."

"Oh, I hear ya talking. That fool boy that used to stand on the corner by the grocery stores shaking everyone's hands like he was begging for money." Eula Mae started to laugh. "I thought he would never come back. Whole town said he was a little cracky."

"Really? Well, he returned to town a while back, after pastoring in Savannah. Folks say he had a large congregation, but he said the Lord told them to move here and start a church. I'm so glad he did. I know his preaching changed James attitude about church all together." Ruth boasted.

"How so?" Eula Mae sat down at the kitchen table interested in what her niece had to say, but very doubtful that it was true.

"Well, James didn't like any church we went to, so I started going to Chapel in the Woods on Sunday evenings. Eventually, anxious to see where I was going, he tagged along. One day he admitted Pastor Roy was different. When Frank asked James to do some work for the men's ministry and he agreed, it shocked me."

She watched her aunt carefully and then continued.

"Then he started saying he was doing more and more for Pastor Roy. Next thing I knew, James was hooked. He started reading his Bible and even attended Bible Study on Thursday nights. I could never drag James to a Bible study, let alone get him to read the Bible on his own. But Pastor Roy did. Bless God, he did. " Ruth clapped her hands in joy.

"Well, Ruthie, you seem awfully happy about this church. Don't let them brainwash you. Church folk good for doing that!"

Ruth kept quiet. Moments later, Ida Mae walked up the back porch steps. "Ruthie, that you?" she yelled inside.

Ruth jumped up from the table, kissed her aunt on the cheek and said, "I'm inviting the both of you. Think about it, please."

"I can tell ya now, I ain't coming. Don't care to spend my time with the likes of churchfolk. Don't matter how much yuh say they changed. It may have changed James, but I still ain't seen Frank come around in years. What kinda change is happening to him that he still hating me for Anne's death, huh?" She stood in front of the stove, back facing Ruth and Ida, as tears fell down her cheeks.

Fall 1964

It was time for the family to approach the casket. Ruth sat still and ushered Ramona up to join her brother Micah, their mother, and Roy's parents in the front of the auditorium. Ramona slowly joined hands with Micah and stood in front of the casket. Mrs. Brown took her daughter's hand and while holding it, bent over and kissed her husband one last time. Micah was next. He looked at his father and turned away. There were no tears but pain was etched across his youthful caramel-tone face. The parents did the same, speaking to their son's remains and looking proudly at him lying in the coffin on his way to glory. The last person to approach the casket before it was closed was Ramona.

She looked at peace. It was difficult to tell that she was grieving. There was actually a smile that spread across her face. She bent over and stood staring at her father. Then she whispered something to him.

Ruth could not hear what the child said from where she sat, but for some reason she was able to read Ramona's lips. Shocked, she covered her mouth with her white handkerchief, and started to cry.

EIGHT

Spring 1965

Ruth contemplated cancelling the summer camp she and James had hosted in their backyard for four years. She thought Pastor Roy's presence was too big a loss to replace. Both she and Ramona were grieving and she expected the other children were as well. James said it was a good idea but Ruth suspected he just said that because he wanted to have his wife all to himself for a change. He probably used Pastor Roy's departure as an excuse.

She struggled with her decision. Maybe everyone was right; Pastor Roy had worked himself to death and she was next. They could not save everyone. For two weeks, she prayed and fasted, looking for a sign, and then, miraculously, one came and it was clear as the blue skies above.

Mary Brown knocked on the door.

"Oh, Lord. How ya holding up?" she asked the pastor's widow.

"Well, sometimes I want to lay down and not wake up. Other times, I want to live forever. Just feel like we started something that God is not finished with."

Mary walked on into the living room. Immaculately groomed, styled in a white hat, hair swooped to the side in a bun, she wore a turquoise cashmere sweater, pearls, and a matching pencil-thin tweed skirt. The white pumps on her large feet were accessorized with a clip of colorful rhinestones.

"Well, I never questioned God's timing until now. Just seem like Pastor Roy had so much vision left inside of him. So many things he wanted to get done." Ruth, fussed with her uncombed hair, pulled her terrycloth robe tighter, and sat down in the recliner next to the fireplace. She was suddenly selfconscious about her appearance in the company of the fashionable Mary Brown.

"I think the same thing sometimes. Then it seems like I have a dream and there he is smiling at me. He's teaching me to ride a bike in the dream. At first he is holding the handlebars and then he whispers into my ear and lets go. I struggle to balance the bike at first, then I look back at him, smiling and all, and I get the courage to ride the bike on my own." She removed her white wrist-length gloves.

Ruth sat listening silently, then said, "Sure is a beautiful hat. You always knew how to pick them."

Mary sat down on the couch. "Learned that from the queen herself! There was not a hat made that your mother could not command attention wearing. She had impeccable taste in fashion. I see the fruit didn't fall far from the tree."

"Oh hush. I am no match for the likes of you two. You can set the town ablaze the way you dress. I'm trying to think if I have ever seen you with a hair out of place." Ruth laughed.

"That's because I know when you coming. Catch me by surprise and you might end up having nightmares." Mary was laughing too for the first time since her husband died.

"How are the kids?" Ruth finally asked.

"Bad and grown. I tell you, Micah thinks he's getting revenge on God. He has it in his head that ministry work killed his father. The same work he has loathed since he was fourteen. Now he finally has a reason to run from God's house." She shook her head. "I believe he was waiting for one all along."

"He's just acting out."

"Well, he deserves an award. I just don't like it when he brings that mess around Ramona. She's a child. Everything about her daddy was perfect. I keep telling him I don't want no foolishness in the house. We still serve the Lord. But I don't know about that wayward son of mine." She leaned her head back on the couch and closed her eyes.

"Mona say anything about camp this year?" Ruth sat rocking in the chair as Mary rested.

"Oh, hush! That's all she talks about. She says she's going to be a team leader this year. Is that so? That girl gets all these ideas in her head. I keep telling her to slow that imagination of hers down."

"She can't. She's into everything. And smart! I never seen a child with an anointing like that, I tell ya." Ruth threw her hands up into the air. "She's going to wear us out."

Mary lifted her head and stared hard at Ruth. "So you think you're going to hold summer camp this year? Who will help out from the church?"

"Bless God, that's all I've been thinking about. I don't want to do it. I'll tell you the truth. Just too many memories. You know how crazy some of these folks are. The only reliable person was Pastor Roy. I don't want to start something that I can't finish in the tradition the Lord has set already."

"No need to worry. This is my first day knowing that ministry was still in my bones. God sent me here. I already talked to Frank and he'll help out. So will some of the missionaries. Everyone feels this is what Pastor wants. You know when Pastor Roy wanted anything, he would pray until he got the people to move in the same direction." Mary stood up.

"Yes, Lord! That man knew how to motivate these dry bones in this here land. He had everyone doing something. Even my husband, James."

Mary put her gloves back on. "Then, Ruth, why don't we join forces and come together. We women have the power to get anything done. Is that not what Rosetta taught us?"

"That's what both she and Pastor Roy taught us. And I think from the sound of those dreams you've been having, he's still trying to teach you a thing or two about following God's call on your life." Ruth stood also.

"Well, that settles it, little sister! I'll do the closing ceremonies and the rest of the church will assist with the children and the field trips." She started to leave. "That should make Miss Rose and her father very, very happy. "

"Oh, Big Sis, I got a feeling, it's gonna make all of us feel so much better. Yes, Lord. The song is right. *And we'll understand it better by and by.*" She walked over and put her arms around Mary Brown and instantly they both received the strength they so desperately needed.

Summer 1965

"There's that awesome woman of God." Ramona Rose stood in the doorway waving wildly at Ruth. She was getting taller, yet still thin enough to appear younger than the six years she had managed to survive on Earth by then. A small oval face, pudgy nose and tiny pink lips, her eyes captivated whatever audience was graced by her presence.

Yet after her father died, Ruth noticed immediately that there was something different about her. She had aged a lifetime by the time she arrived for camp. It was if she were living the life of someone else. Someone much older, more mature to the goings on in the world. To Ruth, she spoke like a world traveler; definitely not a child growing up in the Low Country.

On the second morning of camp, Ruth arose to discover the children already dressed, seated in the living room, deep in prayer. She asked what was going on, and then she heard a small voice leading the group. It was Ramona. She was kneeling underneath the kitchen table. Her voice was low and she was praying that God would cover Ruth with His love and bless every part of her house. Then she prayed that God would cover every person in the camp and their families with love too.

Ruth stood in shock. She kept her eyes on Ramona as tears cascaded down her cheeks. When Ramona eventually opened her eyes, she looked around and then caught Ruth's stare. As their eyes locked and held each other in a momentary trance, Ruth could sense that she was no longer looking into the eyes of a child, but into the eyes of some force with an anointing far more powerful than a child could ever possess.

Each day of camp was filled with Bible games, reading, music lessons and field trips as far away as Charlestown. By the end of the day, James helped Ruth prepare dinner, and Ramona and the two other six-year-olds set the table for supper. After prayer, everyone feasted and then shared in the chore of doing the dishes before nightly service. The evening ended with Ruth, in memory of her own mother, sitting in the center of a circle, animating a story right out of the Bible. She concluded by anointing every child's head with olive oil and declaring God's blood protection over their lives before they were whisked off by James to bed.

One night, Ramona asked to say the closing prayer. Ruth never objecting, nodded her head and immediately Ramona knelt down beside her and started to pray. Within seconds, she began to speak in other tongues. All of the children opened their eyes and stared at her in astonishment before turning to look at both Ruth and James. Ruth could feel the stairs of the tiny angels assembled in her presence, but did not open her eyes. James squeezed her hand gently as he too gawked at the child speaking in, what appeared to him, a foreign language.

Ramona continued to chant. After a few minutes, she opened her eyes, revealing a blank stare as if the words spoken came from someone else. She then walked around the semi-circle and laid hands on all of the children, who seemed afraid of her. As she passed each one, some backed away, while others stared at the floor and allowed her to touch them gently.

Next, she approached Ruth, who kept her eyes closed the entire time, yet could feel Ramona's tiny hands on her abdomen.

"In the name of Jesus, I anoint your womb. You shall conceive and bring forth the number of man. Your children shall bless you richly," she whispered.

Ruth staggered and then collapsed. James stepped forward to prevent her fall. He looked at Ramona who avoided his glare. Forcibly he moved the small child out of his way and swiftly grabbed Ruth and carried her over to the couch.

"Y'all chirren go'n' to bed now," he said. "You too, Missy."

The children in silence went into the back rooms. Ramona did not move.

"I said make haste, little woman!" he shouted.

Ramona stared at Ruth. Then she looked at James. There were tears in her eyes. James walked over to her and grabbed her tiny arms to physically escort her in the direction of the bedrooms. When he touched her he realized she was burning hot all over.

"Baby, what?" He was astonished.

Ruth opened her eyes and looked at the two of them. "Turn her aloose, baby." she interupted. "Ramona, come here to me."

Ramona looked at Ruth and ran into her arms. Ruth could feel the heat pulsating through her tender skin.

"You got a fever?" she asked.

"No, ma'am."

"You burning all over. Want to take a cool bath?"

"No, ma'am. I'm fine. I'll go to bed now. Nighty night." The child hurried off to bed.

That night Ruth was restless. She checked on Ramona every hour. While she paced the kitchen floor that entire night, she thought of the years she had spent with Ramona. Pastor Roy had been dead for over a year now, yet Ramona seemed to have supernaturally received a call to the ministry. It was unheard of and she knew no one would believe her. As she struggled to keep her eyes open, each time she drifted off, she could hear Ramona's voice.

"Everything is gonna be all right. Don't you worry. God has called you for great things, Mama Ruth."

"The Lord has someone else for you. Your time for babies gon' come then."

"Sometimes people just here for a short while. It doesn't take long to do God's will."

"Mama Ruth, you are a prayer warrior. This whole town gon' need your prayers one day soon."

"That strange woman is not evil, Mama Ruth. She's just scared. God's got something for y'all to do together."

"Mama Ruth, your home is holy ground. God is gonna use it for people to speak directly to Him."

"I wish I could be with you forever, but my work is almost done."

"You're not barren. Your home is gonna be filled with children. Yours and theirs. God directs them to you."

"Mama Ruth, when you get to glory, you will have lived a long time. God knows that you will always honor His word and He is going to bless you with long life."

And then finally, she heard the words that broke her heart. "Promise me you won't grieve for me when I am no longer here with you on Earth."

Winter 1965

In the fall, Ramona started school so Ruth saw less and less of the child who kept her daily in amazement. Just before Christmas, she received word that Ramona was seriously ill. Immediately, she traveled to visit her.

James complained about the drive, but he drove Ruth every time she mentioned she needed to see Ramona. Ruth knew that he cared about Ramona almost as much as she did. So each time they visited, they drove in complete silence, neither saying a word. The first time, James stayed in the car but told Ruth to give Ramona his love. He said he could not look at her in such a weakened condition. Ruth went in alone.

Ramona was asleep on the couch. Ruth just sat nearby and watched her. When she awoke, she looked at Ruth, but did not speak. She just played in Ruth's hair. Her appearance was difficult for Ruth to handle. Her skin was pale, and she weighed less than fifty pounds. Her eyes were different too. With dark circles around them, they appeared weak and sunken. She was too frail to walk and had to be spoon fed liquids for her body could no longer digest solid foods.

"What do the doctors say?" she finally got the courage to ask.

"They say her heart is bad again and without a transplant or a miracle, she won't make it."

Ruth sat down in the chair and looked around. "I don't understand. One minute she's fine, and now..."

"We just can't believe what we see. I still believe Rose is going to get up, walk, and outlive all of us." She smiled as she grabbed Ruth's hand.

"We just have to keep faith in the Lord's will," Ruth said.

Ruth visited Ramona six more times. Each time, her condition was unchanged. Then one early morning in February 1966, the telephone rang. It was Ramona. She sounded as if she had never taken ill. She told Ruth that on the following Saturday, she was having a birthday party. She did not want presents, just their presence, she said. To Ruth, it was like old times. She promised her that she and James would be there with jelly cakes in hand. As Ruth hung up the phone, she recalled an important fact: Ramona was born on Valentine's day, which was two weeks away. She would not give this miraculous recovery further thought in fear of jinxing it by questioning the healing power of God out aloud.

On that frigid February Saturday afternoon,, Mary Brown's yard was packed with children of all ages. Dressed in winter coats, hats, scarves, and woolen gloves, many of them had attended Ruth's summer camp. Others were from Ramona's new school. There was even a clown. Ruth stood in the driveway admiring everything. James, who never went to parties, had a big smile on his face. He looked at Ruth with tears in the corners of his eyes. Ruth walked over and put her hand on the back of his neck, looked into his eyes and smiled. She knew that out of all the children, he loved Ramona the most.

They were both shocked when Ramona walked down the back porch steps. She was strikingly beautiful. She wore a long winter white wool dress coat with matching daisy print winter accessories. Once inside, she revealed a white taffeta dress also adorned in daisies, with a matching jacket that had three-quarter length sleeves. In the tradition of her mentor and friend, Ramona wore elbow length white gloves.

Ruth was beside herself. There was no evidence that the child in front of her had ever been sick. Her caramel-colored skin had regained its glowing complexion, her eyes, though slightly sunken, were no longer ringed by dark circles, and her once limp legs stood strong as she walked with the authority of heaven toward her guests. It was the miracle Ruth and Mary prayed they would see.

During the party, Ruth and James spent a few minutes with Ramona reminiscing over the times they'd shared together over the past four years. James hugged her repeatedly and Ruth watched quietly as Ramona handed a small bag to James and then put her index finger over her lips. Ruth behaved as if she had not noticed.

As forty or so children stood around the few adults singing happy birthday, Ramona walked up to the two-tiered yellow frosted cake, turned around to look for Ruth, and when she found her winked before blowing out all seven candles. A warm sensation traveled down Ruth's spine.

The party ended as the sun set, dropping below the horizon. Most of the children from Ramona's first grade class had already departed. Removing her hat and gloves, Ramona sat at the kitchen table chatting endlessly with a group of like-aged girls. When their parents arrived to retrieve them, Ruth made sure she got a moment to speak to Ramona alone.

"You sure are beautiful," she said an hour later as Ramona stood before the mirror and combed her hair. "Wow, a seven-year-old. Someone is getting old. Well, I don't see you much but I know you like school. Your mama told me that all of your teachers say you are really smart! You keep up the good work, ya' hear?"

Ramona looked at Ruth. In the few minutes they stood alone in the room, her countenance had changed. Her broad smile was golden and her eyes possessed an angelic glow. She dropped the hair brush and ran over to hug Ruth.

"Ah, child. You feel so good! I love you so much and I pray the good Lord blesses me with a child just like you," she whispered.

"I am your little sister and I shall remain your sister in Christ your entire life," Ramona said.

Ruth stood back and looked the innocent child in the eyes. Something was different.

"I did good, didn't I, Mama Ruth?" She stood with her chest puffed out, mimicking the way Ruth sometimes posed.

"You did great!" Ruth replied.

"And my father in Heaven is pleased! I have finished my course, I have fought the good fight of faith!" she stated emphatically.

As tears drenched her cheeks, Ruth could not think of anything else to say. Slowly, she turned around and walked to the door. Then she turned back and blew the child she loved with all of her heart a kiss. Ramona was already kneeling in prayer. Ruth smiled and walked out.

The next few days were filled with restless nights. Word came that Ramona was again under constant care, unable to speak much, weakened by the disease that would rob her of a full lifetime. On February 13th, Ruth could not sleep. Tomorrow she would visit Ramona and sing an official happy birthday. Yet that night, she tossed and turned so much that she finally got up and put on a silk robe and walked out into the living room. Finally falling asleep on the sofa, a silhouette appeared before her dressed in a white gown, standing in a field of daises. Before the image became clear, Ruth knew who it was. No longer a child, the young woman stood with a group of people who all looked vaguely familiar.

Ruth struggled to see their faces. Then she noticed the man standing next to Ramona. He was wearing a tan suit, black shirt, and a paisley print ascot. He was smiling, and as she suspected, the chain around his neck held a sparkling diamond cross.

Saturday. Valentine's Day. Ruth woke up but could not move. All she could do was hum. She managed to partially stand and then fell backward onto the bed. She remained there for hours until she heard someone banging on the front door. She rose, walked into the living room, and suddenly remembered the words she had seen Ramona whisper into her father's ears as he lay in a casket two years ago:

"I'll see you soon."

NINE

Spring 1966

In a lot of ways, the death of a loved one sets us free. That's what happened to Ruth Fields Harrison. Immediately following Ramona's death, the once caring, devoted wife and caretaker of the unwanted seemed completely aloof and less concerned with those around her. It was as if she desired nothing more than to reclaim the freedom she had once possessed.

It was a calculated move. First, she changed toward her once overbearing husband, demanding he release her from the chains of jealousy that kept her locked inside of the four walls of their home. She served notice that he could no longer control her actions or the amount of time she spent worshiping the Lord. In fact, there were Sundays when she left the house without James all together.

"You don't have to go," she yelled at him as she walked into the kitchen.

"What do you mean? You're my wife."

"Yes, James, I am your wife. Not your child, not your servant, your wife. Now the Bible I read says I am to be a helpmate. Funny thing is, I can't be a help anything because of your insane jealousy. So no, you don't have to go. In fact, I'm giving you a pass today. Stay home. You don't like church anyway. Just stay home. Get acquainted with the kitchen you refuse to go into. Dinner is already made, but anything else you want, you need to fix it for yourself."

His jaw dropped. Never had he heard such harsh words erupt from Ruth's mouth.

Like her mother, Ruth now spent much of her days sitting on the front porch, reclining in the glider, humming a tune no one recognized. That left seventeen children with little or no direction. Gone were the hours she spent home-schooling, teaching everything from mathematics, spelling, and geography, to the Bible. These days, she washed them, practically all together in a large tin basin outside on the back porch, helped them get dressed, fed them breakfast, and allowed them to play outside in the back yard until noon time, when she re-emerged from the glider for lunch. After they ate, she hurridly put them down on pallets for a long nap. By the time they woke up, they continued playing indoors until James arrived.

She never asked him to take on a secondary role with the children, but he did. Seeing all the pain she was in, James came home in the evenings from work and helped Ruth prepare dinner. Then he lounged in his room, or sat outside on the back porch, while the remaining seven children that lived with them studied in the living room. By eight o'clock, Ruth had all of the children in bed asleep.

She held her tongue until she was ready for everyone to know what she was thinking.

"James, I feel so empty inside. Seems my whole insides are hollow. Nothing excites me anymore. I don't want to die, but I'm struggling with the concept of living if you know what I mean." Her hair was hanging down but there was no lustre in her curls as before. Her beautiful brown skin was sallow and her eyes swollen.

"Just tell me what to do, Ruthie. You a good woman and I know we losing you. Just don't go without giving me a chance to make it better fo' yuh."

"That's just it. I don't know what to do. I only know I can't live like this any longer. I need to do the things I love doing. I love these children, but you were right; folks just taking advantage of our situation. I wanted children, but like my mother, I wanted a life outside of my home too." Her sad eyes looked straight into his.

"You're not happy. I know that. I thought the children made you happy." He grabbed her long fingers and held them.

"They do. But they are not my life. I will always love them, but I know God wants me to do more."

"Maybe that's why we don't have any children ourselves. Maybe God wants you to do your thing now. I just hope I'm a part of the mission you think he's sending you on." Tears surrounded his eyelids.

"It's not you, James. I made the decision to marry you. Under all your thick skin and craziness, you are a good man. You want to do the right thing, all the time. It's just we can't go on like this. I can't stand being in this house some days, but I stay inside because of all the fussing you do when I leave. You're going to have to share me with others."

He started to cry. "I don't have a problem sharing you, Ruthie, I'm just afraid of losing you. I thought if you didn't get any attention, you would be safe and I could make sure no one ever took you away from me."

"Oh, James." She stroked his cheek. "God gave us to each other. We are still young and the Lord has so much life for us to enjoy. You knew how much I loved church when you met me. I'll never understand why you tried to take that away from me."

"Ruthie, I'm just a man who saw something I never expected to have and I keep fighting to keep it." He wiped his eyes.

"But I'm not your property! I know times are changing and some women don't even want to get married any longer and put up with this type of possessiveness, but I love being married. I love taking care of this house and my man, but you need to understand that I love other things as well. It's those things that Ramona taught me that I needed to go back to."

"I miss her too. Out of all those children, she had my heart the first day. How can you not be angry at God just a little bit for taking her away from us?"

"James, God does not make mistakes. We all wanted her, and believed that she would live, but God said otherwise. I don't understand it, but I accept it now. I know that she fulfilled her purpose on this earth. Sometimes when I'm sad, I think about poor Mary. That woman lost her husband and her daughter. I can't imagine that kind of pain." She leaned back and, for the first time in months, allowed James to console her.

"Whatever you want to do, Ruthie, I may not like it, but you can do it. I'll be by your side."

"You mean that, man?" She turned and looked at him, smiling. He could see the sparkle already returning to her eyes.

Summer 1966

Ruth walked to every house, knocked on the front door, and if no one answered, sat right in the front yard until someone came home. All of the children were with her.

"Hey, Mable!" she yelled across the yard. "You recognize these two beautiful little girls?"

"Yeah, Ruth. They mine." Mable was planting seeds in her garden.

"Then act like it," Ruth yelled as she walked toward her.

"What do you mean? I know they safe and sound wid you." Mable stopped and wiped her hands on the dingy white apron that draped her shoulder.

"But God blessed you with them. Now I don't mind caring for these angels, but that's my temporary occupation. You have left these girls on me for weeks at a time. You tell me you're going to a club and I don't see nor hear from you for days. This stops right now." They stood face to face.

"Okay, Ruth. What's the matter wid yuh? Yuh acting strange! You love kids and dem kids call on you night and day. I can't take your place. I think they want to come live wid yuh." Mable looked over at her daughters.

"Well, sorry, they can't. They live with you. You are their mother. I don't know their daddies, but it's not my James. We love you, but these here kids are your responsibility. Do you understand me?" She put her hands on her tiny hips.

"So you mad at me, Ruthie? That's why you brung dese chirren over here?"

"No, Mable, I forgive you. You are probably doing the best you can most days, it's the other days that make me mad. Now here you are in the garden, working the fields, trying to take care of your family. That's what you're supposed to do, but you can't leave your children on us for days at a time anymore."

"They school age now, Ruthie. I guess I can put them in school. You got'em so smart, I wonder which grade dey in?" Mable, big busted, oval shaped face and practically bald, always admired Ruth and would do anything she said.

"They can come over when you need me to babysit. They can even come over when you have to work and the school house is closed, but if you want them to spend the night, we have to charge you."

"Say what?"

"You heard me. We are charging for overnight guests in our house." Ruth stood laughing at the woman's look of shock.

"Serious, Ruth?"

"Serious, Mable. If you leave them with us, it's two dollars a head."

"What?" Mable's daughters were standing behind Ruth looking at her.

"That's for the night. If they stay during the day, you have to pick them up by five o' clock and send a change of clothes, including church clothes on Wednesday and Thursday. I will no longer clothe your children unless I feel like it." Ruth turned, winked at the girls, and walked over to hug their mother.

She made several trips that day and when the evening came, the entire town knew that Ruth meant what she said. She would no longer be taken advantage of.

Over the next few weeks, the new Ruth slowly emerged from her cocoon and it was evident that she and James had become a united front. She handled the day care, and James handled many of the chores and care of the seven children during the night. On the weekends, he worked out in the yard with the children while Ruth ran errands, alone.

James noticed the difference his intervention was making, but He wasn't the only one who noticed.

"Who is that beautiful woman?"

Ruth drove up in the yard, parked the car, and stood leaning on the driver side door. Her hair was pressed and cascading down her back. With a slight touch of face powder and blossoming orange lipstick, she wore an orange dress that hung just above her knees with two rows of ruffles around the edges. The sleeves were midlength, accompanied by elbow length red gloves. And finally, the leather multi-colored pumps gave her at least four more inches of height.

"I have not seen you look like this in years! Where ya headed?" Frank Fields stood on the front porch admiring his daughter.

"To see you, old man." She casually tossed her long hair.

"Oh, don't do that! You remind me of your mama. She could swing her hair and strut her stuff like no other. Stop it I said." He walked down the steps and embraced her in spite of his fussing.

"Well, I learned from the best. You know they say the fruit don't fall far from the tree," she teased.

"So what has you so happy? You look wonderful! I sure have missed you." He stood smiling.

"I missed you too. It's been a long time. The front lawn looks so good. Man, I wish I had your green thumb. I came by to get some advice and to bring you some of my cooking. I know you miss it." She laughed.

Frank took the food out of the car and they went up the stairs. The house smelled like cinnamon. He was baking a cinnamon-apple pound cake from his wife's old box of recipes.

"Daddy, what are you up to?" Ruth removed her gloves and placed them in the matching pocketbook she carried.

"Oh, nothing much. Just making something for the Deacon Board, that's all. We have our monthly meeting tonight." He opened the oven and looked inside.

"You can give them something else. Maybe some store-bought cookies. I'll pay you for those cakes. Lawd, they smell good." She fanned herself.

"You look good, Ruth. Real good. Like the young lady I once knew." He closed the oven and turned to face her.

"I am the lady you once knew. Things are changing for the better."

"How so? You got rid of James?" He pulled out a wooden chair and sat at the kitchen table. There was a colorful plastic table cloth, a napkin holder, toothpick holder, and salt and pepper shakers at the center of the table, all neatly aligned.

"No. I traded him in for a better model." She laughed. "Running pretty good now." She sat down opposite her father.

"You think it's going to last? You must have threatened him with divorce papers or something."

"No. Just talked to him one day and he changed. I can't believe it, but I prayed for years for the freedom he now realizes I have a right to."

"Is he still sitting underneath you at church?" Frank got up, walked over to the refrigerator, opened it, and pulled out a pitcher of fresh-squeezed lemonade.

"He goes sometimes. Sometimes he stays home. I don't know what he does and I don't care." She laughed. "Seems he's reading the Bible more and more, though. I thank God for that."

"The Bible? Ruthie, how long has this been going on? Did he see you leave the house today?" He poured two glasses of lemonade and handed one to her.

"He picked out the dress!" She sipped and laughed again.

"No! Aw shucks, Ruthie! You're starting something now. I pray the good Lawd it lasts."

"Okay, Daddy, enough on James. I need to get the twins and Ben in school." She added sugar to her lemonade.

"Ruthie, I know I put a lot of sugar in that lemonade. I forgot how sweet you like it."

"Yes, Lawd! I love me some sweet lemonade." Stirring the syrupy lemonade, Ruth displayed the new diamond ring her husband had given her after Ramona's funeral.

"Okay, I see that rock on your hand. That ring is too big to wear around here! Somebody gon' knock you in the head fo' it."

"Be quiet, Daddy, and tell me how to get these children enrolled in school!"

"You talking to the wrong Frank, honey. You know that." He got up and walked over to the telephone, dialed, and immediately started talking without an introduction.

"Ruth need birth certificates to get the kids in school. Okay," he held the telephone receiver out to her. "Give him the exact names and he'll take care of it."

The birth certificates arrived a week later.

The next fall, Ruth strolled into Thomas Haywood Academy, an all white private school, with Benjamin in tow. She stood in line with the other parents, ignoring the looks directed her way, and when she reached the front desk, she handed the papers over to the administrator. One quick glance and Benjamin was declared a first grader, no questions asked. Within minutes, her worries were over as Benjamin was whisked away into a world he had never known: Whites only.

She enrolled the twins in school as well. The birth certificates listed them as being six years old. Ruth knew that was probably impossible but enrolled them anyway. They had been literally dropped on their door step three years ago, barely walking. Their size was somewhat hefty so she and James assumed they were around one or two years old, but they never knew for sure.

Just who their mother was remained a mystery. They did not look like anyone either Ruth or James knew. The color of dark red clay, they had piercing black eyes and sandy brown hair. Their names were unknown as well, but after James saw one of his favorite actresses, Lauren Becall, on Hilton Head Island one summer, he renamed the babies. They had only called them Buddy and Li'l Babe, but they became Laurence and Lauren, or Larry and Lori for short.

Everyone in town knew Ruth and James were not the biological parents, that was obvious, but no one ever said a word.

1967

"Ooh, can I get that, Mama Ruth?" The blonde hair, blue-eyed child with olive skin begged. He was seated in the carrier of a shopping cart at the Piggly Wiggly grocery store.

"May I have that, Ben." She looked down at him. "And what did I tell you about being anxious?" she asked.

"That God said be anxious for nothing!" he shouted as customers walked about the store.

She could feel their eyes on them, but never gave uneasy onlookers the time of day. She knew what they were thinking and hated to spoil their imaginations.

Ruth walked up to the cashier and paid for the groceries. Benjamin was looking around while holding a sour apple Charm's lollipop with one hand. He never noticed the man on the other side of the room staring at him.

Ruth walked out of the store and then turned around. She was wearing a wide brim hat so few could see exactly where her eyes were focused. With a quick glance, she noticed five or six people that looked suspicious. Still, she never spotted him.

1963

Ruth picked up the cross she'd buried in the front yard years ago. It was protection for the children. In all of her years of caring for other people's children, none were ever harmed on her property. Not even a bee sting. She gave the credit to the cross and the spirit it represented.

She was sitting on the last step when she saw a woman approach her yard. It was an unfamiliar face. Ruth stood up and waved.

"Hey there." Her usual opener. "What can I do you for?" She waited for the woman to get closer.

"You Mother Ruth?" The woman seemed puzzled.

"Bless God, I hope so. I've been answering to it since I was a child," Ruth answered with a laugh.

"You so young? I thought you'd be older." The woman looked over at the garden.

"No, honey. Age is nothing but a number. I'm as young or as old as I feel and sometimes, whew, I feel old, I tell ya." Ruth started up the stairs. "Come on in out of the hot sun and sit on the porch. I'll get you some cold tea."

"Thank you, ma'am." The young girl sat down on the glider. She had to be no more than nineteen or twenty years old, dark-skinned with a short cropped hairdo that looked like it needed the relief of a straightening comb. Her hips had yet to materialize, but her breasts were large and full.

"Everybody talks about yuh. Dey say if ah need prayer, come tuh you." She looked up at Ruth who stood in front of her.

"Chile, don't pay these folks no never mind. You need prayer, you talk to the Lord." Ruth sat down next to her.

"Ah don't thank he listening anymore. Least ways not to me."

"He's always listening, girl. Always ready to hear his children talk to him even about the smallest things in life. Things we don't think are important, mean a lot to God." She grabbed the young girl's hands.

"Ah been bad, Mother Ruth. Done some thangs ah ain't proud of."

"There is nothing you can't ask God to forgive you for, but first I have to ask you, have you accepted him into your heart?"

"Long time ago. Usta go tuh church every Sunday. Ma used tuh read the Word tuh us every night. Papa was a drunk. Den Ma stopped going tuh church all together. Drinking finally claimed da both of 'em. Us youngins raised our own selves. Ah'm da eldest." She was crying now.

"And what is your God-given name?" Ruth pulled her close.

"Pauline. Pauline Marie Davis. Pretty name fo' un ugly person."

"Beauty is in the eyes of the beholder. You are a child of God. That's why your mama gave you such a beautiful and powerful name. Your name should be in lights." Ruth held her and hummed into her ears.

"Mother Ruth, I wanna feel dat way again. Like somebody love me." She looked into Ruth's face.

"Somebody does, me and Jesus, and baby, once you join in, that's enough. If God is for you, He's more than the whole world against you."

They sat on the glider talking for hours. Before Pauline left that day, she accepted Jesus Christ as her personal savior. Ruth taught her how to pray. It was not clear if they would see each other again. Until the next day.

Pauline was the first in what later became known as The Prayer Circle. Humble beginnings, a group of women congregated in Ruth's kitchen and prayed after weekly Bible Study. After a while, the women started coming by during the day while their children where in school. They sat around the kitchen table while Ruth cooked one of her tasty meals. Then someone would start praying.

Two years later, there was an average of twenty-five women that assembled in Ruth's kitchen for prayer. Overcrowded in a blazing hot small kitchen, Ruth thought it was just too much.

"I have an idea," she said, fanning herself wildly. "Y'all see that oak tree out in the yard? It needs a lot of love. Why don't we go outside, sip on tea and lemonade, hold hands around that tree, and pray to our God."

She had no idea that a ministry was unfolding right before her eyes.

1966

"Oh, great God! What have y'all done!" Ruth stood behind the screened door yelling at the top of her lungs.

"Come on in here! You gone too far now. We have no choice." She opened the screened door to let them inside.

"She took sick, Mother Ruth. Been down fo' days. Made me promise I'd bring huh tah you!"

A young girl cried as four women carried the frail older woman inside Ruth's house.

"Girl, are you a fool? What kind of sense does that make? I'm not a doctor! This woman needs to be in a hospital. A spirit of death is all around her."

Just then, four more women opened the front door and gathered around the woman now lying on the couch.

"Ma Ruth, I tell 'em don't do it, but dey won't listen. Dey say she die if she don't come here." Pauline did the talking.

"Great God. Sometime I think you gals don't have the sense God gave you, bringing a white woman into my house. Not just any white woman, the wife of the Klan devil himself. What kind of spirit you think we dealing with?" She sat near the woman with her hands on her head.

"Mother Ruth, God is on our side." A tiny woman emerged from the back of the crowd. "I felt I was being led to bring her here. The evil in her home is sho' 'nough gonna kill her."

"Well, let's see, Molly. What do you suggest we do?" Ruth was agitated. The woman lying before her was pale and had a faint pulse. Her time was near.

"What we know best," Molly answered. "Pray."

Sixteen women prayed non-stop until the fever left Ms. Lula Peters' frail body. Molly and five other women stayed on through the night until the next morning. Ruth did not turn the porch lights on. She wanted no more visitors. No one could know who was in her house. No one could know what they were doing.

They agreed that by ten o'clock the following day, or twelve hours from when they began praying, they would take Mrs. Peters to the hospital. If her condition worsened or she died during the night, they would take her immediately, yet by five a.m., her pulse had become stronger. Ruth knew what was going on.

"Bless God. The spirit of death has passed by our sister. Now we must continue praying like we agreed," she said to the tired women.

"So she gonna be okay?" Pauline asked.

"That, I do not know. I believe that the spirit of God has healed her. I believe a miracle has come and I receive God's word. That's about all I can do." Ruth dipped a handkerchief into the tipid water, wrung it out, and laid it back on the woman's forehead.

Around nine-thirty, Lula Peters opened her eyes. They were bright blue. With the exception of a thin waistline, she was covered with wrinkles, yet her hair had remained long, thick, and black, with only a faint sprinkle of gray.

She tried to smile and then looked up into Ruth's eyes.

"Mother Ruth." Her voice was weak. "Thank you, Mother Ruth. Thank all of you." She closed her eyes and drifted back into a light sleep.

The women stopped praying at ten o'clock that morning. Then Ruth offered them communion and they began dancing and singing praises for Ms. Peters' healing. It would not be the last time Ruth Fields Harrison would be summoned to lay hands on her.

1967

"Witnesses say the train was at fault," Frank said, trying to console the woman.

"Yeah. What's that suppose to mean? He was a Colored man. That train company will never give us one dime for our loss," James' mother declared as she stood in the parlor.

"I believe they will. I believe God will turn this thing around," Frank said. Then he walked out of the room. "Ruthie, baby. You ready? We have to do this. No matter the pain. It's time to say goodbye." He laid his head back against the wall next to the portrait of he and Rosetta.

Ruth walked down the steps appearing smaller than usual. She wore a navy blue dress and a double strand of white pearls. On top of her head was a colorful piece, so big no one knew if it was a hat or some other contraption she had invented. Her black patent leather shoes laced in the front. Of course, she wore elbow length off-white gloves.

At the funeral, she placed the wedding ring James had given to her in the casket on the same finger that held his gold band. She knew how much he loved that ring. Bragged so much about it, she thought he would appreciate having it when he got to heaven.

The children were in attendance, all seven of them. Benjamin took James' death the hardest. Besides, James was the only father he had known in his few years of existence. He sat behind Ruth, softly, rhythmically, kicking the back of the pew. He was wearing one of James' ties and he adjusted it every few minutes.

The twins were resting on both sides of Edna, while the four older children sat across in the pew on the other side.

They had all come to pay their respects and say goodbye to a man that had devoted himself to them. He would be missed.

When she got home that evening, Ruth went into the bedroom and collapsed across the bed. She did not know what to think or how to feel. She had suffered a great loss, but something inside her gave her hope for the future. She kicked her shoes off and started to cry.

Around midnight, she awoke to a practically empty house. Edna and her husband, Sam, had taken the little children and only two of the older children were in their rooms. Ruth walked into each room, put things away, and moved on to the next one.

Then she remembered what happened earlier that day.

As she walked out of the church with her father, she caught a glimpse of a woman dressed almost like her, but in black. The woman's dress hung on the ground. Ruth busied herself paying attention to the mourners before she looked back in the woman's direction. As expected, the woman had disappeared.

That's when she saw it. A satin bag, the kind used by a bride to carry face powder and other essentials during a wedding ceremony. This particular one was placed on the edge of the banister at the front entrance to the church. Ruth kept watching it. After a few minutes, she excused herself and walked over to retrieve the small bag. Instead of opening it, she placed it in her purse, took out a piece of peppermint, and headed toward the cemetery.

Two years later, on her wedding day, she finally opened the bag.

TEN

1965

He was all she ever talked about. In fact, he was all any of them talked about: Augustus "Duke" Garrett, the pride and joy of his entire family and the youngest legend of the Low Country. Maybe he received so much attention because he was a long-awaited blessing to his parents. By the time he entered the world, his mother, Hattie Mae Garrett, had prayed for nine long years that the Lord above would bless her womb with a male child. To her, that made him extra special.

Folks say he was always smart. Nothing white folks could teach him. He had read more books by his twelfth birthday than most people read their entire lives. He was ahead of his time and too quick minded for the slow life of the Deep South. So no one was surprised when he left for college at the age of sixteen, and subsequently joined the United States Air Force. Neither were they surprised when they heard stories that he was training to be a fighter pilot; nor, when they saw pictures of him standing in front of the first plane he ever flew. No one gave it a second thought, because when it came to the "Duke," a name that seemed to fit him more than any other, the sky was the limit to what he could achieve.

He was the youngest in the family, but to Pearlie Mae, his closest sibling, he was her big brother, in spite of their four year age difference. When their father suffered a stroke, Augustus took over work in the fields, dropped out of school, and became the man of the house. Handling it all in stride, there was no crop he could not grow, and no animal he could not control.

Hattie Mae vowed her son's life would not begin and end in the Low Country. So working as a domestic maid, she saved enough money to see one of her lifelong dreams come true. August became the first person in his entire family to to reach that level; in fact, he used to say there were two things he would accomplish before he left the earth: A college degree and flying airplanes.

Overjoyed and filled with excitement, the whole town pitched in to send him off in high fashion to Tuskegee Institute in Alabama. Weeks before his departure, rumors surfaced that members of the Klan were determined on capturing him, destroying everyone's dreams. Townsfolk banned together and promised Hattie Mae that Duke would arrive at the train station in Yemasee safe and sound, and they kept their word.

Five years later, with Hattie Mae on her deathbead, they summoned for his return. Doctors had given her a few hours to live, but her faith refused to give up. In agony, leaning over the bed holding a worn out black leather Bible in her hands, she raised her weak arms towards the window and begged God to allow her to lay eyes on her baby boy once more before she transitioned to Glory.

Over the next three days, she drifted in and out of consciousness, holding on to her last hope to see her son. When there was nothing left to be done, and Augustus had yet to arrive, the small community joined forces, suspended work in the fields, and went into their houses and prayed.

Pearlie ran to Ruth's house and collapsed at the front door.

"Ruthie!" she screamed. "Tell God he can't take my mama widout huh seeing 'im!"

Ruth ran to the front and stood behind the screened door. "Pearlie, is that you?" She could hear weeping beneath where she stood.

Slowly, she tried to pry the door open, but Pearlie's body obstructed her efforts. "Pearlie Mae, hold on, I'm here." She ran through the house, out the back door, and around to where Pearlie lay sobbing uncontrollably.

"Pearlie, get up! What are you carrying on about? " Ruth knelt down and tried to lift her off the porch floor.

"Mama 'bout dead and Duke ain't ever come," she managed to say before continuing to cry.

"Oh, chile. Your mama shall live longer than today."

Pearlie looked up. "What, Ruthie? How you know that?" She tried to get up.

Ruth sat there crying and smiling at the same time. "I felt the spirit of God when I left the room this morning. She's just resting."

"But she so weak," Pearlie cried.

"Weak is not dead." Ruth put her arms around Pearlie and lifted her up.

"You must not focus on what you see with your eyes, but focus on what you know in your heart. Duke is coming to see his mama, you take my word for it." They sat down together on the glider, Pearlie leaning on Ruth's shoulder.

"Where is he, Ruthie? We wrote and called all the numbers he gave us. No one seen 'im for months! For all we know, he could be hurt somewhere all by hisself."

"He's all right. You just run home and get ready. I know the Lord will keep every promise he made to Hattie Mae. She wants to see her son. That's what's going to happen." Arm in arm, they walked down the steps into the front yard.

As Pearlie Garrett walked back into her mother's home, Augustus was the first person she laid eyes on.

1968

Pearlie talked non-stop the entire week. She cleaned five houses, including her own. Everything had to be perfect for his arrival. Everyone had to be on their best behavior and nothing out of the ordinary was to occur. Peter tried to assist her with cooking and cleaning, but she would not allow it. No one knew what Duke liked better than she. He would be home in a few hours. Ruth had said so.

She borrowed linens for the kitchen from Ruth. The place setting was exquisite. They would eat in the dining room that nobody ever sat in. This was such the occasion. The family's hopes and dreams had returned home. Pearlie skipped all the way down the road.

"Hey dere, Ruthie Girl!" she yelled at the top of her lungs. "Ruthie!" she screamed as she got closer. She could see the curtain in the front window slowly open.

"Who dat? Y'all playing? Y'all know I'm a coming today of all days. Yes, siree! Today is da day. Duke coming home! Open up and let me in," she ranted.

The front door opened and Pearlie saw Ruth standing in the doorway. She was smiling.

"What dat big smile on yo' face fo', sistah? You never been that excited tuh see me!"

Hair draped in tight curls, Ruth was wearing a house-coat. She tried to contain the smile on her face.

"Pearlie Washington. Why are you doing all that yelling? Everyone around here knows your brother is returning home today. You have been yelling it to the world ever since you found out."

"Mah soul is filled wid so much joy! What did you expect? I got one brother and he is the best thing dat ever happened tuh me."

"And, baby, we are all so happy for you, Hattie Mae, and the others. This is the Lord's doing and it is simply marvelous!" Ruth unlatched the screened door to let Pearlie inside.

"Oh, what smell so good? Ruthie what you up to?" Pearlie walked into the kitchen and started removing pieces of aluminum foil that covered the dishes.

"Well, of course I cooked something for him too. I only met him once, but y'all keep saying he's particular so I want to make sure he has enough to eat with all the folks you invited."

"Girl, I invited da whole town. Everyone I could think of." Pearlie beamed.

"Yes. And you announced it at every church you went to."

"Couldn't help myself." Pearlie pulled a piece of crispy hot, fried chicken out of a bowl. "Mmm. Ah shucks now! Once Gus get your cooking, he won't want to leave heah! I think we better hide this stuff until tomorrow."

"Stop ya foolishness, Pearlie! If I trust you with this food that boy will never taste it." She walked over and took the bowl of chicken out of Pearlie's hands. "Why do you think my cooking is going to get his attention? All them good cooks in your family."

"He tasted our food his entire life. Your food is gonna knock his socks off. I just knows it. He won't know what hit 'im."

"Stop playing matchmaker, Pearlie! When God gets ready to bless me with another husband, he will. I am perfectly okay with these children I take care of. They need me more than anything. My focus is on their wellbeing."

"And, sistah, my focus is on yours!"' Pearlie laughed and sat down at the kitchen table to eat a meal that she knew would steal her brother's heart.

It had been a long time since Ruth had felt like going out on the town. James had been gone for over a nine months now and she was resigned to the life of a single parent. At times she was lonely, yet she reminded herself God had some promises he intended to fulfill in her life. Besides, she still had not conceived a child. That was one promise she knew the Lord would fulfill before she met Him in the sky.

She prayed that her second marriage would be different from the first. Much different. At this stage in her life, she needed someone who was comfortable with her way of life and her independent nature. There were the children, but there was also the woman she missed being. She had sacrificed her way of life to please James. She would never do that again.

At twenty-six, Ruth wanted a man with a sense of purpose, who was comfortable in his own skin and knew how to enjoy life. She would no longer stay locked up in the house afraid that other men would see her and lust after her. The woman she was now wanted to enjoy life.

All she ever heard about Augustus "Duke" Garrett was that he was the greatest catch in the Low Country. The most eligible bachelor, but he had never taken a wife. Highly intelligent, he joined the segregated Air Force and after awhile was commanded to teach even the white officers how to fly planes. According to Pearlie, he was a decorated war hero who never settled down. The world was his canvas, and he planned to explore every inch of it.

Stories about the Duke's heroism fascinated Ruth. His life reminded her of all the dreams she'd had as a child about leaving the Low Country. In her future, she saw herself traveling on an airplane. She had even written the vision down in her hope diary. One day it would come true.

She had no idea just how soon.

May 1968

"It would be an honor if you escorted me to the train station."

"Really. Duke Garrett, what am I going to do at the train station?" Fully dressed, Ruth stood in the front door. She was in the process of removing the pink foam rollers from her hair.

"See your man off!" He laughed. He had to be about six-feet-three-inches tall. Tenaciously neat, his clothes appeared to be painted onto his soft Hershey chocolate bar skin. His coal black hair made him appear to be the twin brother of singer Nat King Cole, or so he was often told by smitten women.

"So, now you're my man, huh? You've spent less than three months home and you calling yourself my man," she teased.

"What would you like me to call myself? I've been bit by the love bug." He put his fist up to his mouth, covering a set of sparkling white teeth, and laughed uncontrollably.

"Duke. Now, you know you are crazy. I'll come to the station because you asked me, not because you think you are my man." She was determined not to be any man's property.

"So, Miz Harrison, what do I have to do to become your man?"

"If you have to ask, you are not ready, Duke." She pulled on a black cashmere sweater.

"I'm asking because I'm a gentleman. I need to know exactly what you want from me at all times. I heard that's what a good man does." He walked down the steps and then turned back and looked up at Ruth.

"And where did you learn that?"

"The Bible." He opened the passenger door. "Sit in the front. You know a whole bunch of folks gonna try to pile in this car to see me off."

"Oh, Lord. I'm glad you came to get me first. Where's Pearlie? I know she's coming. Her heart is broken about you leaving," Ruth said.

"I don't understand it. I'm a pilot. My family knows I work for Uncle Sam. They know I can't stay forever, yet every time I come home, they get like this. Pearlie cried all night. Ruined the party," he said.

"She just loves her big brother and hates to see you go again."

He laughed. "She's my older sister, Ruth."

"Come again?" Ruth watched him as he walked around the car.

He folded his tall frame inside. "Pearlie Mae has me by four years. She's called me her big brother since I could remember though."

"Oh, so you might be too young to hang with me?" Ruth laughed as he carefully steered the car out of the driveway.

He had a smirk on his face. "Wisdom is more important than age, right?"

"You tell me. Everyone here says you're a real hero. You had to be smart to get where you are."

"And what about to you? I heard you were one hell of a woman. Smart, beautiful, festive, and loving. What do you think?" he asked.

"You're just a nice young man to me. I have not had the pleasure of witnessing all this greatness I hear about," she winked at him. "Yet."

"Well, let me be the first to say that from this day forward, all of my best years will be devoted to you, Miz Ruth." He blew her a kiss.

Ruth Harrison would discover that Duke Garrett meant exactly what he said.

1970

A silence fell over the room. No one said a word. Something was wrong. Something was terribly wrong.

The baby's face was pale and there were no signs of life in his tiny limbs. Augustus walked over to the midwife who placed his still son in his arms. He looked at Ruth who appeared unconscious.

"What's…going…on?" She struggled with each word.

"Just rest, baby." Tears fell down his dark face etching tracks of pain.

"Why's Elijah so quiet?" She struggled to open her swollen eyes.

Augustus could not get the words out. He stood there trembling all over.

"Elijah," Ruth whispered. "Elijah Francis Garrett. You still sleeping?"

Everyone in the room was startled. Moments of silence.

"Bring him to me, Gus." She kept her eyes closed but held out her arms.

Augustus stood several feet away. Hattie Mae wrapped the still-born infant in the blanket.

Ruth opened her eyes. "Why y'all so quiet?" Then she saw Gus standing on the other side of the room. "What's wrong with you? Bring that chile to me," she demanded.

"Ruthie, I'm sorry. He's not moving," he sobbed.

"That's because he's sleep, Gus. Bring him to me! Let me talk some sense into him."

Augustus finally got the courage to take the stiff body over to Ruth. He knew how much she wanted this child and how much pain she had suffered to deliver him. He could not take all of her hopes away. Slowly, he handed her the baby.

Ruth pulled the blanket back and looked at her son. "Oh, Elijah. You got to greet everyone, you're scaring them. Just say hi and you can go back to sleep, you little mullet." She kissed him on the forehead. Everyone in the room was crying.

When the child still did not move, Ruth held him up in front of her and said, "God always keeps his promises. He said my second would be called Elijah. This is him. I know it. And he shall live and not die."

No one said a word as the minutes stretched by. Ruth kept her eyes firmly fixed toward the heavens. Then they heard him, loud and clear.

"See, y'all? This one's a jokester. He barely kicked in my womb. Just laying around, lazy. Gus, we are going to have a time to get this little one walking. I told you he was supposed to be Isaiah's twin. Then he up and arrive ten months later." She brought the baby down in front of her so that the witnesses could see as her son finally opened his eyes.

Augustus knelt beside her and cried. He placed his hands around Elijah and felt the pulse of life sweep through the tiny infant's body. He was too weak to say another word.

1972

"You wanna hold the baby?"

"Almost afraid to, Ruthie."

"Why is that? You are going to be a wonderful mother one day. You mark my words."

"I don't know 'bout that. I had one child and I thank my womb closed up. Maybe it's punishment fuh mah sins?" Ida stared at the baby squirming on Ruth's lap.

"We all have sinned and come short of the glory, Ida Mae. What makes you think God is singling you out by closing your womb?" Ruth put the pacifier in the infant's mouth.

"Sometimes I think dat's what happ'ning tuh me. I don't know if I can stand another miscarriage. If the good Lawd is counting, this makes fo.' Too much heartache for anyone to stand. Don't know how much longer Timmy will stay."

"Hush up now! That man loves the ground you walk on. He married you for better or for worse. Well, this period in your lives, and trust me, it's just a season, is the worst you will ever have to endure." She turned the baby over on her stomach and started rocking.

"You thank so? We been through a lot. Having everything yuh worked for burnt to the ground is hard. We lost so much and just getting the money to rebuild. I ain't know why Timmy even want to. I say we just give up this liquor business." Ida walked over to where Ruth sat to pat the dozing baby.

"Get out or stay in, y'all need to find yourselves in church!"

"Dat won't stop bad thangs from happening, Ruthie. It didn't stop the train from hitting James and y'all was in one church or the other almost every day," Ida protested.

"It's not the place, Ida Mae, it's what's in your heart. This is all about a relationship with God. You're too focused on the people attending church. You know they are not perfect. Don't let the saints keep you from getting your blessing."

"Wut the Lawd gonna bless us for? We sinners. We sell moonshine and promote bad living, let y'all Bible thumpers tell it." Ida backed away and walked toward the steps.

"Oh, Ida Mae Tilley. God loves you! He loves you in spite of how you feel about Him. But He's a God of free will and election so you must choose this day whom you will serve." Ruth started smiling.

"I chose to serve God a long time ago. It was different when Pastor Roy came. But then lookaheah, he dropped dead in the pulpit. Wut dem no good saints do? Dey run his wife out o' town. This after dat po' woman's child die befo' she get good and grown."

"That's a different matter all together..." Ruth started to say, but Ida interrupted.

"No, it's not! I believe in God and all, I just don't believe in da mean God preached at none o' dese churches."

"What does that have to do with God blessing you and Timmy with a seed?" Ruth stood up with the baby in her arms.

"Dat's wut I wants to know. Wut does us going tuh church have to do with nothing? Long as we believe in God."

"When are you going to allow Him to be your Lord and your master, Ida? I hear you calling Him 'Savior', but that's only when you need something from Him. He wants to be the Savior and the ruler over your life. That requires some sort of sacrifice, honey."

"Well, if dat sacrifice mean going tuh church, we may not neva' have no chirren." Ida stood next to Ruth and played with the baby's hair.

"You can't barter with God. It's not this for that, Ida Mae. I'm suggesting that you all start somewhere. There is no word going forward in your home. That's what worries me."

"We be fine, Ruthie. We love each other and we good to so many folks." She held her arms open so that Ruth could place the baby in them. "She light as a feather," she cooed.

"And quiet as a mouse. This child makes no noise. Then again, the whole house is spinning out of control. Every child in there thinks the baby belongs to him or her. They want to hold her all day. That's why she just sleeps all day. Man, I'll be glad when Gus retires. He says it will be soon. I'll believe it when I see it." Ruth placed a blanket on her daughter.

"Ruthie, how you deal with raising nine children and Gus gone all da time?"

"Through God's help, Ida Mae. No other way. It's rough. All the children the Lord placed in my life have been blessings. They each do their share of work around the house. I don't worry about much. Never had to." She smiled.

"I'll say! We don't know how yuh keep doing it. Timmy say you got some kind of strength. I agree." She held the baby's head carefully.

"It's from the Lord, I tell ya! I finally told Gus that he had to do better. That man is gone all the time. He's been promising to leave Camp Lejuene for four years. I see he's taking his sweet time honoring that promise." She looked out into the yard at her garden.

"Ruthie, you ever think you would have three children of yuh own? I mean, you had none with James. Was it something wrong with 'im?" Ida kept looking at the baby as she sucked on the bottle.

"What?" She turned to face Ida.

"Was something wrong wid James? Is dat why y'all ain't have no chirren?"

"Lord only knows. Could have been. Bottom line, I don't think it was my time. That's what I keep saying to you and

Timmy. When your season comes, nothing and nobody can stop what God is about to do in your life. Mark my words."

Ida smiled at her cousin. "Ruthie, why yuh give dis beautiful girl a boy name?"

"What?" She bursed out laughing. "The name Jonah can used for a girl or a boy. It was the last name given to me so I used it." Ruth came over toward Ida and sat back down.

"Given to yuh? Who give it tuh yuh?" Ida seemed puzzled.

"The Lord sent me three names after James died. The same number of babies Ramona said I would have. I never told a soul. Soon as I started having babies, I knew what names to call them. Gus just laughed. He said Jonah was a boy's name too. Then he saw how much this baby sleeps all the time. He says to me, "Ruthie, I think Jonah thinks she's still inside of that whale!"

They both burst out laughing. Baby Jonah opened her eyes and looked around as if she understood everything that was said.

ELEVEN

1976

One had reached adulthood, the twins were sixteen, and Benjamin had just become a teenager. In total, she was a full time mother to ten children. Over the years, many had come and gone, but the last seven were around when her entire world fell apart. Four witnessed the burial of two fathers; three experienced the greatest loss of their lives, the death of a natural parent. Nothing would ever be the same.

Only the older children were allowed to make the trip to the hospital in Beaufort. Week after week, Frank Fields drove them there, but he did not get out of the car. Said he did not want to see her until her smiling face came back through the double steel doors she'd walked into months before.

Laurence, Lauren, and Benjamin were brave souls. They spent at least three hours staring at a woman in a catatonic state every week. She was the only mother they knew so none of them complained. They just prayed she would return one day soon.

"She looks like she's a vegetable," Laurence said to Benjamin as they walked to the bathroom down the hall from Ruth's room.

"I wonder does she even know we're here? I mean, there is no life in her eyes. Seems as if she looking at something that can't none of us see." Benjamin sipped water from the fountain, splashing it everywhere.

"I can't believe any of this! First Daddy J and now Gus. He seemed like Ma's last hope to find somebody to love." Laurence looked up and down the hall.

"Man, maybe it was meant for us to be alone. I mean, our parents gave us to Ma Ruth and now she's gone. Who gonna take care of us now?" Benjamin leaned against the wall outside of the bathrooms.

"Hell, I'm almost grown. When I graduate next year, I'm getting the hell outta here! Ma Ruth got us so far ahead in our studies, maybe she knew this would happen and wanted to make sure we could take care of ourselves."

"It's just not fair! Once we got used to having a family again, Gus died. Now Ma really ain't here. I can't take it if she goes too." He beat his fists against the wall. "It's one thing if she was buried in a grave, it's another seeing your Ma lying in a bed like a vegetable, not knowing her own children." Benjamin walked into the bathroom.

Laurence stayed in the hall waiting for his younger brother. That's what they were. Regardless of who gave birth to them, their parents said they were blood brothers and sisters. They were to always take good care of one another, with or without their parents being around.

He and Lauren had been with Ruth the longest. Jacob, their oldest brother, was twenty-one and had run off with some woman that was part of a religion that did not believe in Jesus Christ. Ruth said one day he would return to the fold, but until then, they were to pray for him and his girlfriend as if they believed in the same savior she taught all of her children to believe in.

Laurence was not sure what he believed. They had spent their entire lives in church. Day in and day out, they'd witnessed a mother who arose every morning and by the time they got up, she was right next to her bed or the couch, on her knees. If she was not praying, she was sitting next to the back door in the kitchen reading her Bible.

There were scriptures posted throughout the walls of the house. They had to memorize them all. When Frank allowed them to retrieve their belongings after she was hospitalized, Laurence suggested they remove the scriptures, but Lauren would not hear of it. She said Ruth would never recognize her house without them. He doubted she would ever return. If she did, would she be the same fun-loving spirit the whole town admired?

As his anger raged, Benjamin walked over and put his hand on his brother's shoulder.

"You gitting tall, man." Laurence tried to fight the tears.

"Almost tall as you. Maybe my daddy was tall," Benjamin said.

"I doubt it!" He laughed. "Your daddy is a white boy. He ain't tall, trust me."

"What does that have to do with his height?"

"You see any really tall white men around here? The average Klan artist living in these parts is just shy of six feet." They turned and walked back in the direction of her room. "They short and small minded too." His lips twisted into a sneer.

"You're sick. What is a Klan artist?" Benjamin asked.

"Someone practicing how to be a member of the Klan. They don't graduate until they lynch a nigga."

"Where did you get that from? I never heard that."

"You wouldn't. Not at Thomas Haywood Academy." Laurence jumped high into the air as if he were shooting an imaginary basketball into a basket.

"Don't remind me. I usta beg to go to school with y'all. Why Ma put me in that school with all the white kids?"

"Because you're white. If she put you in the black school, you would have been in trouble with the white folks in town. She had to keep you there until integration was here," his older brother tried to explain.

"That's so stupid. I don't understand any of it." Ben looked at him.

"You don't have to so much. You're not black. We have to understand it because if we don't we could get killed. For a long time, there were places you and I couldn't go together, or we had to appear as if we were not brothers. You remember that?"

"Yeah. It was stupid. We couldn't talk but we could play together in public when we were younger. That's why I love Ma Ruth so much. She never said to me I was white until I asked how come I couldn't go to school with you guys. I forgot what she said. I knew it was hard for her." They turned the corner and walked into the room.

Lauren, Laurence's twin, the picture of a flawless woman, silky toasted skin, small bust, and a pencil thin waistline, was blessed with long legs and feet born to wear spiked high heels. She sat on the side of the bed massaging Ruth's hands. Sounds from the television blared from across the room.

"Why is that thing so loud?" Laurence asked.

"That's the way they keep it I suppose." She did not look up at her brothers.

"Why? She ain't hard of hearing," he screamed over the sound.

"She isn't..."

"Shut up! You know what I mean. Let's go man. I am tired of this." He walked over to the night stand and picked up a card.

"Where are all the people Mama helped over the years? I come here every week and how many folks have we seen? Two? Not more than you can count on one hand." He placed the card back on the stand.

"Maybe they come during the week?" Benjamin added.

"Maybe they don't come at all! That's how much all her good Christian work has paid off. Where are all those cats that came to our house every year for camp? You see any of 'em?" He turned and faced his sister.

"Larry, everybody knows she's sick. She needs her rest. Visitors don't mean a thing if she is still in a coma," she said.

"Coma! What planet are you on? That is no coma our mother is trapped in. She's tired and if God won't let her die, she checked out any way." He leaned over and looked closely at Ruth.

"Grandpa said it's something like a coma," Benjamin interjected.

"What does he know? He scared to get out of the car. She's not going to bite him." He kept watching his mother for a sign of life.

"She might. Once she find out he had her committed to an insane asylum."

"Asylum! What does my young brother know about an asylum?" he teased Benjamin. "That's a mighty fancy word, brother."

"We're here every week. Kids at school say she's here. Everyone knows it. Ain't no need to deny it. The world thinks Mama Ruth is cracky." He laughed.

"That's not funny and you know it, Ben! Mama Ruth is just tired. She will rise from this bed any minute now and if she caught you speaking evil like that she would spank your behind!" Lauren scolded him.

Laurence finally focused on his two siblings. "What would the two of you do if Ma just woke up and started talking this very minute?"

"Run!" Benjamin yelled.

"Scream halleluhah!" Lauren added.

"Well, that's not going to happen. I say we get out of here now."

"How do you know?" Lauren picked up her purse and stood to leave.

"Some things, dear sis, you just know." He grabbed her hand. "Go on. I done give up praying."

"That's blasphemy, Larry and you know it. We must never stop praying for everyone, including our enemies." She bowed her head.

"Well, you go on. I'm tired of praying to a God who ain't listening." He snatched his hand away.

Benjamin looked over his shoulder at Laurence as he exited the room. "That boy is angry. Real angry. Mama Ruth spoiled him. She's to blame." He looked over at his mother. "You gotta come back before that fool boy lose his mind, I say."

Lauren spoke softly in prayer.

"Father, we come as humble as we know how. Forgive us for our sins. Father we know we are not perfect and that we fall short of your glory, but we love you, Lord. We trust you to honor your word to us as we try to honor ours to you. Lord, you sent us this woman of God and we stand here today knowing that your healing hand is upon her. Lord, give her rest and keep her mind fixed on you so that she might have perfect peace. When you are finished working out things in her life, dear Father, we ask that you send her back to us. Bless my brothers and sisters. Bless my grandpa Frank, grandpa David, and Grandma Hattie Mae. Bless everyone in this hospital. Give the nurses all the help they need to serve their patients. Bless the doctors and everyone that works here. Bless all the visitors and Lord, send some people to visit my mother. Let her know that she is dearly missed. In Jesus name, we pray, Amen."

One by one, she and Benjamin planted wet kisses upon their mother's dry cheeks. Laurence just stood in the door way shaking his head.

1977

"How old is grandpa Frank? Better yet, how old is his girlfriend? She don't seem as old as he be."

"Watch yourself. She does not seem as old as he does," she corrected him.

"All right, all right. Who knew our grandpa was courting someone? All of a sudden, you're home ten minutes and he announces he's tying the knot." Benjamin played with the perfumes on her dresser.

"Probably was a secret. I think he met her at Chapel in the Woods. She's from Savannah you know. Daddy told me her only child died a few years back. Edna met her a long time ago, maybe she introduced Daddy to her." Ruth put her earrings on.

"You think he'll be happy now? He said he was never marrying again. Why can't she just stay his girlfriend?" He looked at her in the mirror.

"Well, Master Ben, when you love someone, you want to spend the rest of your life with them. So you get married. That's what your grandfather is doing. He's lonely in that big old house by himself all these years. He claims he liked it that way, but I don't think he's being honest. I think he was lonely all the time." She turned and reached for her shoes.

"Are you lonely, Mama?"

"I reckon so. We all get lonely sometimes." She secured the straps of both shoes and stood facing him.

"You not wearing a hat to the wedding?" He stood admiring her.

"Not today. Sometimes I like to shake things up. I suppose everyone in town is still trying to see what I look like. Do I look crazy?" She laughed.

"You were never crazy. Grandpa said you were in a coma." He grabbed her hand.

"Great God! Is that what they called it? Oh well, I guess I just needed some rest. I was probably more tired than I thought I was." She kissed him on the forehead.

"I'm so glad you're back with us, Ma Ruth. We missed you. We visited you every week and we prayed, well, Lauren prayed, but I listened," he whispered.

"That's okay. You're going to get comfortable hearing your own voice petitioning God one of these days. It takes some time. Lauren has had more practice. That's all."

"One day those women showed up and they prayed at the oak tree. When we got home from school, they were still praying and chanting, and speaking in tongues. Lauren dropped her books on the couch and went outside to join them!" He became excited with the telling of the story.

"Oh, God! That child is something else. Well, she only did what she knew how to do. The Bible says '*where two or three are gathered in My name, there will I be in the midst thereof.*' There's power in prayer, my dear. Real power that most saints never tap into." Holding hands and strolling slowly, they walked out of the room.

1974

Ruth sprang from the bed. She looked back at Augustus sleeping peacefully. Someone was coming to pay them a visit. An unexpected guest.

She walked out of the bedroom down the hall toward the living room, humming all the way. There was no need for alarm. Someone needed her help.

Sitting in the chaise next to the front door, she pulled the curtains back and looked out into the night. The porch light was off. She reached up and turned it on. The person would be there within the hour. She laid her head back against the chair and prayed.

"Hallelujah! Glory hallelujah! God, I bless your holy name!" she whispered. *"Dear Lord, whomever is coming, let my spirit connect with theirs to receive the Word that you have for them. Let the words of my mouth and the meditations of my heart be acceptable in thy sight, oh Lord, my strength and my redeemer."* She stopped praying.

She heard a noise outside. The stranger was almost there. Ruth dared not look out to the window. That might alarm her guest. She stood behind the front door and waited.

There was a thud. No knock on the door, just a loud thud. She listened for another sign. Nothing. The person was not moving. Ruth opened the door and stood in the entranceway between both doors. She turned off the light and looked down.

A woman's body was stretched out near the steps. Ruth opened the screened door and walked onto the porch. As she stood peering down at the woman, her face did not look familiar. Dressed in a rather nice wool overcoat, she wore no stockings and her loafers were badly scuffed. Ruth knelt down beside her.

She pulled the woman's hair back so that she could get a better look at her face. "Oh, great God! Ohh! Dear God! Wait a minute! You just hold on." She ran back into the house to summon her husband.

Gus heard footsteps and immediately said her name. "Ruthie, baby, what is it?" He put his feet on the floor and searched for his warm slippers normally placed directly below where he slept every night. For some reason, they were not there.

"Ohh, come quick, Gus. I need you badly." She ran into the room wearing his slippers.

"What is it, baby? What's wrong?" He leaned over and reached underneath the bed to retrieve his shot gun.

"Gus, Mary Carter is out there on the porch. She's unconscious. I just need you to lift her inside, okay?" She hated guns and he knew it.

"What? Where did she come from this time of night? What is going on?" He scurried about the room, putting on his robe and an old pair of shoes.

"I don't know. She looks bad, though. That Edgar probably gone off and hurt her. I've been feeling like she was in danger ever since I met him." They hurried toward the front porch.

Gus picked Mary up and brought her inside. "Open Jacob's door so we can put her down on his bed. Larry and Ben not here."

Ruth opened the door and then ran into the kitchen to get a basin of water to clean Mary's wounds. Then it hit her and suddenly Ruth's abdomen felt like it was on fire. She bent over in agony.

"Ooh, dear God, what has this woman been through?" she cried out.

Gus walked around the corner and saw her slouched over. "Baby!" He ran to her. "What's wrong?" He helped her to a chair.

"I can feel her pain. Someone kicked her in the stomach several times. She was beaten really badly." She kept her arms around her waist while she sat down.

"Maybe we should call an ambulance. I don't like the sound of this." He headed toward the back.

"Where are you going, baby?" Ruth yelled out.

"To get my gun!" he shouted.

"Oh no, man! Don't give the Devil what he wants! Edgar Carter is a fool! He's pure evil. I knew it the first time I laid hands on him." She tried to get up.

"Yeah, I got something for his behind when he comes here looking for her. He comes over here, he gon' get a whuppin from a real man!" He returned with his shotgun in his hand.

"You know I don't want guns in my house with my children, right?" She walked to the bedroom where Mary was resting. "God already got everything taken care of. He doesn't need your help, man."

"Sure, you right. God gave me the sense to protect my family and anyone that's invited on our property. Now, I respect everything you saying, baby, but I'm not about to let some fool come up in here and harm us. You hear me?" He stood in the doorway.

"Loud and clear, Gus. Now stop all that fuss before you wake up these kids." She wiped Mary's forehead with the wet cloth she'd soaked in Epsom's salt. Just then she heard voices outside.

"Gus!" she screamed, and ran to the door.

Ruth stood behind the screened door. She could see the bright lights from the automobile. She knew who it was. She would let Gus handle it. Edgar Carter was crazy, but something told her Gus was an equal or better match. She stood listening.

"Yeah, she's here," she heard Gus saying. "What you want, Edgar? This is not the time or the place to show up demanding that I send your wife back home so you can beat the crap out of her again."

"Man, she my wife! My property. You ain't got no business coming 'tween a man and his wife," Edgar shouted.

"Look a here, Edgar. At three in the morning, I don't care about her being your wife! You may be the king of your house, but you ain't nothing here but an uninvited trespasser. Now go on home. Your wife is in there fighting for her life. Either she gon' stay here with us, or I'm calling the sheriff."

"Sheriff! You can call who ya want to. I ain't scared of no one. None of y'all gonna come 'tween business I gots wid my own wife."

Edgar came two steps closer to the front porch. Augustus stood at the edge of the steps with the shotgun pointed directly at the intruder.

"Edgar, I killed folks for a living in the Air Force. You might scare the life out of all these folks around here, but I'm not listening to what you're saying. You standing here on my property, talking about going into my house, and taking your wife out of there to go home with you. Now either you lost your mind or you a bigger fool than I thought you were. If I pull this trigger, no law in the country is going to find me responsible. You are trespassing and I am telling you now to get back in your car, go home, and sleep off all that liquor. If your wife comes back, it's her decision and not yours, and by God I pray she has a little more sense than that."

"You ain't right, Garrett. I can't take ya tonight, but ya never gonna be safe. You must not know who I is! I'ma remembah this night. You mark mah words!" he threatened Gus as he backed away and opened the car door.

"Yeah. I'm already pissing in my pants. Now go on and get the hell off my property." Gus cocked the shotgun.

Ruth stood in the foyer with her hand over her mouth. She knew Gus meant what he said. She also knew Edgar was crazy enough to return for Mary. She turned, walked over to the telephone, dialed a familiar number, and waited.

1977

"This is Rosa Lee. She's from Wilmington, North Carolina. Moved out to Savannah to join Pastor Roy's church when he first started preaching." Frank kept watching Ruth.

"Oh, yeah! Well, it's nice to meet you." Ruth stood up and walked over to the banister.

"Nice to meet you, sister. I heard so much about you from Pastor Roy. You are the woman who started that Prayer Circle I hear so much about. We started one in Savannah. Maybe one day we can all come together and join forces. I sure would like that." Rosa Lee walked up the steps and hugged Ruth warmly.

Ruth had cooked a huge meal. The children placed everything in the backyard on the picnic tables. There were lots of things to celebrate and lots of things to be thankful for. She had been home for months now, back in the flow of her life much like before her 'sickness'.

The house felt different without him. Augustus' spirit had such an incredible presence that he could be felt throughout every room. It was hard to imagine a life in which he was no longer around, strong and protective. Maybe that's how Mary Brown felt when Pastor Roy died. It was probably the same when Frank lost Rosetta. Now Ruth truly understood their pain.

Nothing anyone said could ease the sharp arrows that pierced her heart more than one hundred times a day reminding her that he was gone. The thought of being with anyone else was devastating, for Ruth believed that no one could replace her soul mate, not now, not ever. She could never live long enough to separate her heart from his grasp and that, she knew for sure.

She was glad her father finally decided to remarry. It would be good for him. He had been single for more than two decades. Yet, he always assured her that he loved the life he had. Memories with Rosetta were enough to last him a lifetime he said.

Lots of folks crowded around. There were balloons and paper decorations throughout the backyard. On the back porch, Ruth took out the wooden ice cream maker, poured in rock salt, and made homemade ice cream twice that day. She let the children do the churning. It kept them busy and preoccupied. When they finished there, there were games and lots of crafts to be made. It reminded her of summer camp, which seemed like a lifetime ago.

Frank and Rosa talked incessantly to all the guests. Everyone in town wanted to get a peek of the woman that finally stole his heart. Even Aunt Jesse and her husband sat out in the yard laughing, joking, and eating boiled crabs.

On the surface, everything was okay. Ruth looked like she was truly enjoying herself. What no one knew was, at times, she was unsure where she was and what she was doing. The feelings of confusion came and went like the trains each day. She also saw people out in the yard, but as she approached them to say hello, they seemed to disappear.

She walked into her bedroom and sat down.

"Father, I receive this healing. I walk in it and I trust that you will restore what was lost." She held onto the bed post and started to cry. *"These children need me to be strong for them. I've been gone too long. Thank you, father, for by your stripes, I am healed. I am whole. My mind is complete and I'll never lose my senses again. In Jesus name, I pray. In Jesus name, I believe."*

She sat there until she heard movement in the house and knew that her absence had been noted. Taking off her straw hat, she untied the bow that held her thick long hair together, but before she could pick up the brush, she heard footsteps approaching.

"Who is it?" she called out.

"It's Larry, Mom." He suddenly stood in the doorway. "Just checking on you. Told everybody you're tired, been up all night cooking and cleaning. They understand. You can rest a little longer."

"No, sir. I better be about my guests. It would be rude to have everybody come to spread love to me and my family and I'm nowhere to be found." She smiled at him.

"They understand." He walked into the room.

"Understand what? I doubt anyone will ever understand where I've been, not even myself."

"Are you afraid it will come back?" He sat on the bed next to her.

"No. Faith can't operate with fear. My faith tells me that I am healed of this demonic disorder. You hear me?" Tears formed in her eyes.

"I hear you, Ma. You just need to tell us when you get scared, when you need more medication. If there is anything we can do to help, you got to tell us." He laid his head on her shoulder.

"Larry, what about school? You graduate in a few months. What's next? The world is big place and we didn't work this hard for you to just stay here."

He looked up at her. "I can't leave you like this?"

"Oh, great God! You always had a spirit of protection on you. Boy, I'll be fine. In fact, I'm better than fine. It may take a while, but God keeps his promises. He said I am healed, and bless God, I am healed." She kissed him on the forehead.

"I don't know. I just don't feel good about leaving now. Been looking at schools in Charlestown so I can be close."

"Oh no! I did that when my mother took ill and I never left this town. If it were not for Gus, I would have never seen all the places I dreamed about. You remember? She put her hand on his chin. "Listen to me, son, God has everything in control. We're going to be fine without you and Lori. Y'all go on and become something great. Live like Gus and James taught you, without fear."

A tear rolled down his face. "Why'd they have to die, Mommy?"

"What ya talking? You think I know? No, Mother Ruth doesn't know everything. I just act like I understand, but I don't. I just know that God never makes a mistake. Gus, he was wise beyond his years. That man was a walking encyclopedia. I think he did more by the time he was thirty years old than most folk around here will do in two lifetimes. God gave him to us. You hear me? That's how much he loved us." She stood up. "I would not trade any of you for nine lifetimes, that's for sho'."

Larry started to laugh. "Sure, Mommy. That's for sure!"

"Don't you correct me, Laurence Michael Harrison Garrett. I am your mother!"

She walked out of the room to rejoin her guests, smiling with pride.

TWELVE

December 1975

The nocturnal ultra florescent lights blinded her. Residents were not allowed to sleep in the dark, so as a safety precaution, everything had to be exposed to unnecessary brightness.

Ruth had no idea where she was or exactly how long she had been there until it became crystal clear. Ammonia-filled sterile rooms, steel beds, over-bleached cotton sheets, black and white tile flooring, and men and women walking about in long white starchy pressed coats.

She remembered being examined. Remembered a scope being placed in her mouth, flashes in her eyes, and fingers in places she never thought another human being would touch.

Then there were the dark rooms, tightness about her head, and constant jolts of electricity that riveted through her body until she was reduced to a state of total numbness.

She tried to speak. In fact, she thought she made sounds, but no one could hear them. In her world, she never stopped talking, never stopped feeling, never stopped living. In her world.

Yet in reality, she was trapped in a world where not even the screams at the top of her lungs could be heard. Desperate to break free, she soon discovered there was no salvation, and even her truth was fragmented. She suspected that she was married with children, lived on a farm, flew airplanes and planted gardens.

The place she now resided was an extended motel of some sort. She had come for rest and relaxation. Three people sat next to her bed all day as protectors to ensure that her body received the rest it so desperately needed.

Yet, evil lurked throughout, and even the folks in the white coats were suspect. They fed her too much and sometimes yelled at her, but one of them was different. She only came during the night, sat down on the bed, and combed Ruth's thick, long hair. She also told lots of stories which Ruth enjoyed. But lately, she was nowhere to be found.

As darkness resumed its position of authority over the atmosphere, someone entered the room.

"Never thought you'd see me here again, did you?" The nice one had returned. "Too much medication. I'll change it so you'll feel more alive." She scribbled on the pages of the chart that hung at the foot of the bed.

Days later, a nurse noticed a painful expression on Ruth's face.

"What's wrong, Miz Garrett?" she asked.

Ruth stared straight ahead. "I'm in a lot of pain."

"You shouldn't feel anything, definitely not pain." She said as she examined the chart.

When the doctor walked in, Ruth reached up and grabbed his hand. He flinched at her touch.

"May I help you?" He was startled. Middle aged, his wire-rim glasses hung at the end of his shiny red nose. With small brown eyes, his head was covered in hair as white as snow; there were traces on his face of where a beard had once formed.

"I need something for the pain," she said just above a whisper.

"Oh, my stars! You're coming back around. Where does it hurt?" he asked.

"Everywhere." Ruth looked at him directly.

"Well, that can't be. The medication should keep you heavily sedated and out of pain." He flipped through the pages in the chart. "Nope. Don't see anything that explains where all this pain is coming from."

"Please help me, doctor," she pleaded.

"Miz Garrett, you have a disorder that makes you think certain things are happening to you, but they are not. It's all in your mind," he said.

"The pain is real. You must give me something or call my father and tell him to come quickly," she demanded.

"Miz Garrett, that won't be necessary. Let me try to sit you up in this bed and see if that makes you feel better." He adjusted the bed.

She continued to moan. "When can I go home?"

"Well, that won't be for some time now. You are still a very sick lady. I'm glad you're talking, but it's too early to send you home in your condition." He stood watching her adjust her body repeatedly, then, turned around and walked out of the room, shaking his head.

Though she struggled to decipher fact from fiction, Ruth held onto what her guardian angel predicted, and two weeks later, she rolled around laughing on the cotton sheets of her own bed, in a place she still affectionately knew as home.

February 1976

"Hello?"

"Go see your daughter," the voice on the other end of the telephone commanded.

"Who is this? What daughter yuh talkin' 'bout?" he shouted.

"The one you put away." He then heard the dial tone.

Frank Fields ran into the other room, turned the television off, put his shoes on, and headed out the front door. He was outraged. Something was wrong with Ruth.

He drove up the driveway and honked. The front door cracked open but no one came out onto the porch.

"Timmy!" he yelled. "Where's Ida? I need her to come with me to the hospital in Beaufort. Something may have happened to Ruth."

Timmy slowly opened the screened door and stepped outside. "She coming. We seent ya drive up. We knew something was wrong. Ruth call you?"

"How is she gonna call? She hasn't talked to a soul in months." Frank opened the car door.

Timmy ran down the steps. "I hear she's been talking for two weeks. That's what Tilley say."

"Say what? No one told me a thing. " Frank was angry.

"Man, we thought you know'd about it. You up dere every week. How come you ain't know she back in huh right mind?" Timmy stood next to the car.

"I take the children to see her but I don't go inside. Just can't see my baby like that," Frank admitted.

"Well, them chirren should have told you. Dey mama talking. Say she coming home soon, yeah?"

"This is the first I hear. I want nothing better than to take her out of there. Y'all know Ruth has no business in that hospital." He was more upset now than when he'd first arrived.

"Ida Mae, don't wait till Christmas tuh come on out heah! Frank gotta go. Come on now!" Timmy yelled into the house.

"I'm coming right quick." Ida appeared at the front door. "Frank, let me get my shoes on, okay?"

"Go on, Ida Mae. She's going to be fine. Just fine." He looked at Timmy with worry etched across his face.

"You need me to go?" Timmy asked.

"I'm not sure. Somebody called to the house and said I needed to come see about her. I don't know who it was." He gripped the steering wheel tightly.

Ida Mae ran down the stairs. "Uncle Frank, you want me drive?" She kissed Timmy and approached the car.

"Oh no. I'm okay. Nothing will stop me from getting to my daughter. Everything better be all right when we get there. You mark my words." He put the car in reverse and backed out of the driveway.

January 1976

"I hear you've come back to life," the nurse whispered into Ruth's ear.

Ruth blinked and tried to adjust her eyes away from the blinding light.

"They won't let me leave. Say I have some kind of disorder that they need to work on. Then they tell me that I'm making up stories about being in pain. That I'm lying about them taking me into that cold steel room, covering my eyes and doing things to me that have me stone out of my mind."

"Electric shock," the nurse said.

"What? Shock? What kinda shock they need to treat this disorder?"

"It's a type of treatment, Ruth. They use them all the time. They say it is painless. But I wouldn't know. I've never witnessed the actual procedure before."

"What's wrong with me? Tell me. You came here to keep me safe, right? I've been asking for you but they say they don't have any colored nurses on staff, that you must be an orderly or a nurses' assistant. I tell them that I know a real nurse when I see one." Her voice trailed. "Unless you're in my head too."

"No, Ruth. I'm real. I don't work here. I work in Savannah." She smiled.

"Then how you get in here at night like this?" Ruth put her hand over her eyes to block the glare.

"I have my ways." She laughed.

"I'm too weak to pry now, but you gotta help me get outta here. I can't take anymore of this. God says I'm healed and they say I'm crazy. What is wrong with me?"

"You have a condition called Schizophrenia." She spoke slowly.

"What? Come on. That sounds demonic." Ruth put her hands on her chest.

"It's a condition that troubles the mind. No one understands it. It causes you to have multiple personalities at times, other times, you become quite afraid, so afraid that they fear you can hurt yourself or others." She pulled the side bars down and sat on the bed next to Ruth.

"How long does it last?" Ruth asked.

"A lifetime. There's no cure. We can just treat the symptoms, but you might struggle with it every day. Do you see things too?" she asked.

"Like what?" Ruth knew exactly what the nurse meant.

"I don't know. They say most schizophrenics suffer with hallucinations."

"So you mean my visions are hallucinations? I can't believe that. I can touch a person and tell if they are going to die. Feel spirits all around folk, even the spirit of death. That's this disorder?" Ruth shook her head.

"They don't know. I say you have a gift. The same one I have. I say you're only crazy if you think you are. I know for certain we can fight this."

"We," Ruth laughed.

"Yes, sistah, you may have thought you had seen the last of me, but here I am again!" She stood laughing.

"Ramona said you and I were meant to be together. Like we are kindred souls." Ruth smiled.

"I wouldn't go that far."

They talked strategy the rest of the night. The next morning, Beulah Chaney telephoned Frank.

1968

"Why are your eyes closed?" He kept looking straight ahead at the open skies.

"I want to experience this without fear. This is exciting, but it's scary all together." She beamed.

"Are you going to let me teach you how to work the controls?" Augustus glanced over in her direction.

"Man, you must be crazy. Not on the first date." She laughed.

"First date! Woman, I've been courting you for six months, though you won't admit it. The post office knows you by name now, huh."

"Sally Waters knew me by name before that, but now I'm coming to receive packages at least once a week. How do you keep up?" She opened her eyes and looked at the control panel.

"I wouldn't have to if you just say you'll be my wife," he teased.

"I'll think about it, Gus. I need to talk to the children. I wanted you to spend more time with them before we start a new life together."

"I know, Ruthie. It's hard with me living in North Carolina. I want y'all to come there. We need to be together. I want you with me everywhere I go."

"Augustus, I have more help with them kids in Jasper County than at Camp Lejuene, and you know it."

"But there you have something you can't find no where else," he teased.

"And what, pray tell, is that?"

"Is it not obvious? Me, and I'm more help than anyone you can find in the world, let alone Jasper County."

At seven-thousand feet in the air, he proposed. When the plane landed and she was sure they would live, Ruth Fields Harrison agreed to add another name to her own: Garrett.

On her fortieth birthday, she dropped the others, and a half a century later, Garrett would be the only last name she took to her grave.

1974

"Remember when you kept telling me that Dr. Martin Luther King, Jr's time was short? How did you know that?"

"It's a long story that not even I can explain. I probably would not have known if Mary had not invited me to hear Shirley Chisolm speak before she ran for Congress a few years later. You see, Dr. King was there and after Mary prayed, the Holy Spirit led me to lay hands on him," Ruth explained.

"And he let you?" Augustus asked.

"Well, I asked him politely and he was so gracious. He said it would be his honor to have a woman of God lay hands on him. So I did." Ruth looked down. "That's when I felt the spirit of death all over him. I knew then his time was coming soon. Still to this day, I regret ever touching him."

"It's a gift, Ruthie. A very special gift. You can't change who you are and you shouldn't want to. You are a divine woman of God." He smiled.

"And you are a man after God's own heart, ya hear me Augustus?" She leaned on his shoulder.

He kissed her forehead. "Ruth, if you felt that spirit on me, would you tell me?"

She jumped up. "Augustus Dexter Garrett, what that ya talking? Don't put that into the atmosphere. I've already been a widow once."

"I'm just asking," he paused, "what would you do? Would you tell me?"

"No. The authority of life and death lies in the power of the tongue. I would never say it. Instead, I would believe God that the prayers of the righteous would be able to stop it from happening." She gripped her chest.

"Calm down, baby. I'm not trying to alarm you. It's just something I always wanted to ask you. Just something I thought of after you told me about James' death."

Ruth sat back down. "I didn't find out about his death until about thirty minutes before it happened. I could not get to him to warn him. Seemed I just knew something terrible was going to happen that day."

She took a few deep breaths then continued. "It was all in slow motion. There was no vision or dream that came while I was asleep. No. I was wide awake. It seemed the minute it was revealed to me, I tried to get up, get dressed, and head over to the station, but everything came against me. No matter how hard I tried, I could not get there.

"I went to get Ida. Ran toward her land, but something dragged me toward the river. I don't even remember coming that way. Something pulled and pulled until I had no strength to go any further. Then I fell and, with no strength left in my bones, I lay on the ground." She started to cry as the memories pressed down upon her.

"I heard the train. I mean, I felt that train pick his body up and split it wide open. I saw the fear in his eyes as if he were standing right in front of me. I never want to feel that way again. It's like an out-of-body experience. I just knew I had been hit too."

"Did you think he suspected anything was going to happen to him?" Augustus walked over and hugged her.

"He was acting strangely. They say folk know. I used to say I thought James knew. He was no longer the man I'd married. He became someone else." She pulled away, "But it was for the better."

Augustus and Ruth had been in Naples, Italy for a week. The year before, they visited Paris and a few months ago, they'd traveled to London for the weekend. Even the children had their share of travels, riding buses, trains, and automobiles.

Ruth lay on the bed with a puzzled look on her face. Clairvoyance came to visit her sometime after her mother's death. A week later, the visions started. A few months after that, Ruth discovered she possessed a gift far more comprehensive than visions and images of what was or had occurred; it was the gift she always wanted to return to its giver.

THIRTEEN

1976

New York, New York: Fast cars, Broadway, cotton clubs, jazz music, and the Harlem Renaissance. The Garretts celebrated their honeymoon there and because they had so much fun, they returned every year for their anniversary. It became their Heaven on Earth for the seven years that he was in her world. In the eighth year, Ruth packed up her children and boarded a Greyhound bus for Manhattan, Augustus' favorite city on the planet.

Like a member of royalty, Ruth, neck arched in motion, dressed in a purple linen dress with matching jacket and shoes, strutted down the street, slow enough to sache and fast enough to not look like a tourist. It was a Saturday; the streets were not as crowded as they were on the weekdays while thousands of folk rushed off to jobs that did not exist in the Deep South.

"I found the dress!" Lauren, standing on the opposite side of a narrow alley in the garment district, waved at her mother.

"Lori, how many times have you told me that during this trip? You don't expect me to purchase every cute dress you lay eyes on, do you?" Ruth walked over to where her daughter stood peeking into the window of the clothing store.

"Mommy, say we can go inside, please?"

"Why not? This is not the South. I don't need to check whether we can come in." She laughed. "I'm just joking. You would think Jasper County knew it was 1976 and not 1936."

"Bicentennial! Can we get something to eat?" Benjamin, bored out of his mind, added. " I'm hungry,"

"Oh, shut up! You ate earlier." Lori walked into the store, a bell tinkling to announce their presence.

"No, ma'am. Don't start that foolishness out here in public. You all better act like you have home training, talking to one another like that. Where do you think you are?" Ruth scolded them.

"How come Larry got to stay at Aunt Sadie's, but we had to be dragged down here?" Ben whined.

"Ah, hush up, boy. Nobody dragged you anywhere. Larry stayed back to watch Jonah. She's too young for these city streets." Ruth held her two youngest son's hands.

"But I'm missing The Jetsons! All we doing is running after Lori who wants everything she sees. She bought a dress yesterday," he continued.

"Ben, this is a big time for her. She'll be off to college soon and you are going to miss her terribly, mark my words."

"That's Daddy's word, Mommy. You can't say it like him," he teased her.

"I can't do a lot of things like him." Ruth looked up into the sky as an airplane flew over their heads.

The next day she went shopping alone. It was time for her to visit some of Gus's favorite stores. She enjoyed a slice of cheesecake from Junior's in Brooklyn and then perused through stores to get ideas for the new fashion statement she wanted to adorn.

She spotted a dress on the previous day while watching all of the excitement Lauren displayed over everything she laid eyes on. That night, as she lay trying to overlook the obvious feelings of loneliness, Ruth could not get that particular dress out of her mind.

She returned to the store and stood looking in the glass at her reflection. At thirty-four, she had aged very little.

Other than a few gray strands, nothing about her physical appearance confirmed that she had mothered ten children. Nothing revealed she had lost two husbands.

"May I help you?" The store clerk spotted Ruth sorting through a carousel of blouses.

"I saw a dress yesterday and I wanted to try it on?" Ruth held a blouse in front of her.

"Well, the dresses are over there in the back." She seemed slightly agitated.

Ruth never looked up. She sensed the woman's eyes as they surveyed her body. A smile crept across her face.

"Are you waiting on me?" she finally asked the clerk.

"Just waiting to see if I can help you further." The young woman came closer.

"No. I need some blouses too. I've already decided about the dress." Ruth finally looked at her.

"Well, which dress do you want me to put in the fitting room?"

"The one on the far right hand side." Ruth pointed at the dress.

"What color do you want to try it on in?" The clerk waited for additional instructions.

"Are you suggesting it comes in more than one color?" Ruth stopped admiring the blouses and walked over to where the woman stood next to the dresses.

"It does. It comes in red too."

"Oh." She turned back to the blouses. "I've changed my mind then."

"You don't want it?" The clerk was now perplexed. What was this woman up to?

"I don't want the black one," Ruth said as she grabbed three colorful blouses. "I'll take the dress in red."

1972

She had her share of visitations from evil spirits. They lurked about, but she knew she was protected by the blood of Jesus. They could never win. Not even when Christians invited their presence into their lives willingly.

That's how Ruth felt the first time she met Edgar Roland Carter. She would have the same opinion for a long time.

"Why, if it isn't Sister Ruth!" Mary Brown leaned against the fender of a fancy car.

"Oh, God! Mary, where have you been? You look amazing, like you around twenty-five, not a day over!" They hugged.

"Oh, shucks! Add about twenty years to that!" She laughed. "God has smiled on me. I see he has smiled on you too." She looked at the two boys standing next to Ruth.

"Yes, Lord! I have nine children now. These little ones come from my womb, ya hear me?" She rubbed her stomach.

"Well, we knew it was all a matter of time! God always keeps his promises."

"Can't anything be closer to the truth. I tell you." She addressed the boys, "Isaiah and Elijah, say hello to Pastor Mary Brown, will you?" They looked up and waved their fingers.

"How you do?" she smiled sweetly.

"Pastor who?" A burly man, dressed in a three piece suit, sporting a wooden cane, walked towards the two women.

"That's what they used to call me, you remember Edgar?" Mary reached out to grab his thick, masculine, ruddy hand.

"I do. But your name is now Carter, baby, and you should let everyone know 'bout that." He kissed her on the cheek. "I'm the second coming!" He shouted with his signature hearty laugh.

"This here is Mother Ruth. A woman totally on fire for the Lord." Mary backed up so Ruth could shake his hand.

The temperature was ninety degrees on that day, yet Edgar's hand was cold as ice. Ruth immediately dropped her head towards the ground. "How you do?" she said.

"Well, sure is nice to meet another saint on fire for the Lord." He smiled cautiously. "Where you from?"

"Jasper County." She stared into the distance.

Suspicious crept into the corners of his large, black eyes. "I see Jasper County is a well populated place."

Ruth's attention was diverted to the warm spirit that walked up behind her. She turned around and smiled with all her might. "Well, well. Here comes my king?" She glowed.

"You know I can't stand being without you." Augustus leaned over and kissed her on the cheek.

"Especially when I sent those two princes in the store to remind you that we were standing out here waiting." She winked.

"How could I forget?" He noticed the couple standing in front of Ruth. "Have we met?" He looked from one to the other, then added, "I'm Augustus Garrett, Ruth's husband. You must be?"

"Edgar and Mary Carter."

"Okay." Augustus recognized Mary from pictures around the house. "It's a pleasure to meet you both. Y'all still living in Savannah?"

"No. We live near Beaufort County now. Not too far from Jasper," Mary said.

"Well, we just moved back from North Carolina. Had a house built near the Tullifinney River," Augustus said. "Y'all drop by when you in town. Everyone knows where Ma Ruth lives." He smiled at his wife.

They shook hands and Edgar opened the car door to let Mary get inside.

As the car sped by, Augustus noticed the look on his wife's face. "Come on, Ruthie. Stop it, I say." He grabbed her hand.

"What in God's name is Mary Brown doing married to that man?" She shook her head.

"Ah, you know there is nothing better than a good woman. He may have changed from whatever you knew or heard about him." They turned to walk in the opposite direction.

"That's just it. I never met him before this day. I recognized the last night just by the way he proudly declared it to me. According to gossip, his family comes from somewhere straight out of hell." She covered her mouth. "Y'all didn't hear that, babies."

Augustus laughed as they reached the car parked on the other side of Piggly Wiggly.

"Don't laugh. I should know better letting something upset me like that." She put the boys in the back seat.

"I just wonder how she could go from that angel Pastor Roy to that man. Something just doesn't seem right, I tell ya, Gus, something is not right about that picture at all!" She stared out of the car window.

1973

Ruth stopped hanging clothes on the clothesline as she watched the red pick up truck approach her house from the long driveway. A young man, blonde, medium build, with soft brown eyes, exited the car and ran up the front porch steps. She did not move.

"Who's there?" she yelled from the side of the house.

"Charlie Peters, ma'am." He stood next to the banister and upon seeing her in the yard, walked in her direction.

It had been years, but Ruth recognized his face as soon as he walked toward her. They had met before. It was not a formal meeting, but she would never forget as long as she lived. She knew he would not either.

He was visibly shaken. "I'm lookin' fo' Miss Ruth." He was out of breath.

Then it came to her. "What can I do ya for, son?" That was all the kindness she could muster toward him.

"My Ma's real sick. They told me to come git you and you'll know what to do."

"Where is she?" Ruth looked suspicious.

"She's back at the house, asleep. Wouldn't go to the doctors widout seeing ya first."

"I'll be there shortly. I know you want me to come this minute, but I have children in the house," she lied. "I'll come within the hour."

"Thank you, Miss Ruth. My ma said you the best dere is. She trust only you." He turned and ran back to his truck.

Ruth tried to remain calm. Forgetting the load of wet clothes in the wicker basket on the ground, she ran into the house and picked up the old black dial telephone.

"Pearlie Mae. Ruth here. Gather up some folk to pray. Lula Peters summoned me to that evil house of hers. I need the saints to pray and for you to accompany me." She spoke quickly into the receiver.

Pearlie was ready when she got to the house. Peter answered the door.

"Ruthie. You sho' this is a good idea?" he said with caution. "I mean, Chadwick Peters is da head of da Klan snake."

"I'm sorry, Pete. I should have asked you if it was all right for Pearlie to go." She wiped her brow. "The Lord gave me her name. I don't know why. Gus is in Virginia at the Quartermaster Center on Fort Lee. In the house are all his numbers if you … something happens and you need to call him."

"What dat, Ruthie? You think somethin' gonna happen?" Pearlie entered the living room, an anxious look on her face.

"No, chile, I'm not saying that. I don't have time to track that husband of mine down. He could be any number of places." She turned and faced Peter. "Just in case, ya hear me?"

"Loud and clear. Lord, let your will be done. In Jesus name." He kissed Pearlie on the lips. "You mind Ruth. She know what she doing. I trust her and you know I trust you."

"All right, baby." They headed outdoors.

The front yard to the Peters' house looked like an official gathering was taking place. Crowded with over one-hundred people, mostly men, some held shotguns in their hands as if they were preparing for battle. Ruth and Pearlie approached from the side of the house, and slowly walked toward the front porch.

"Y'all ain't got no business heah!" A dirty-blonde haired woman who could have easily passed for a man, shouted as they reached the steps.

Neither said a word.

"What you darkies want? Ain't no cleaning going on today! Y'all just turn around and go on back where ya come from." Another man, dirty and saturated in sweat, wearing thick black-framed glasses stepped out of the front door.

Ruth stopped directly in front of three men who resembled members of a militia. Pearlie held her hand and looked straight ahead. Ruth looked at the one who appeared to be the leader of the pack.

"Charlie come for me. I am an invited guest of Lula Peters," she said defiantly.

"Lula Peters! This darn nigra calling yo' mammie Lula!" one of them shouted into the house.

Charlie Peters appeared in the front door and quickly came running down the front steps toward them. He shoved the men out of the way that blocked their entrance.

"Come on, Miss Ruth. She's waitin' for ya."

The enormous pale blue house with a wrap-around porch was completely dark on the inside. All of the shutters on the windows remained closed. Ruth remembered when Dirk Peters had asked her father if she could clean their house. It was the first and only time she heard Frank Fields speak to a white person with such disrespect. She doubted the request was ever repeated.

The bedroom they were shown to was an enormous room, cavernous and cluttered in spite of its size. Decorated in a shiny wallpaper of pastel blue, there were rustic pictures of the Confederacy hanging on each wall. Several feet away from the bed sat two little girls, dressed in overalls, each with long blonde pig tails, playing quietly with paper dolls.

Lula Peters lay in a large mahogany four-poster bed. Her wrinkled skin seemed dry, her eyes hollow. There were large dark circles beneath them and her once thick black hair had thinned down and barely covered her pale scalp. She tried to speak as Ruth and Pearlie walked into the room.

"Miss Ruth," she said just above a whisper.

"No, Miss Lula, don't speak. Save every breath you get." Ruth walked over to the bed and rubbed her hands. Pearlie stood on the other side of the bed, near the large windows, watching.

"I have something I've been wanting to give you," she said, as she looked into Ruth's eyes.

"What is it, sweetie? You don't have to give me anything." Ruth smiled down on the frail woman.

As she struggled to speak, she pointed a bony finger toward the chest of drawers in the corner next to where Pearlie stood eyeing Charlie suspiciously. "Top drawer."

Ruth looked at Pearlie and motioned for her to open the top drawer. Pearlie did not move. She looked at Ruth in horror.

Ruth snapped her fingers to get Charlie's attention. She pointed to the chest. "She wants something out of it."

He had not paid attention to their conversation. He opened the top drawer and hollered to his mother. "What is it, Ma?"

"Black box," she whispered as she held on to Ruth's hands.

Charlie walked over and handed Ruth a black velvet jewelry case, the kind used by fancy jewelers to protect expensive necklaces.

Ruth looked at Lula before she opened the box. Tears formed in the corners of the old lady's eyes. She struggled to speak, but no sound emanated from her lips. Instead, she mouthed the words, "I'm so sorry."

Her grip on Ruth's hand loosened. Her eyes closed.

Ruth looked over at Pearlie and Charlie and then opened the box. Inside there were two necklaces nestled on top of an old black and white photograph. On top of the necklaces was an old, elbow length, white satin glove, now yellowing, possibly from Lula's wedding. Something caused Ruth to pick up the glove. She then noticed a diamond solitaire had been placed inside of the glove.

For several minutes, Ruth looked at Lula and felt the spirit that breathed life into this woman for more than seventy years quickly fly away. Charlie stood frozen, tears running down his cheeks.

"She was wantin' you to have her jew'rey, is that it? And here I thought she wanted somethin' else." Charlie watched Ruth as she carefully surveyed the contents of the box.

"Charlie, listen to me." She hesitated, then said, "Your mother is no longer with us." She turned to face him.

"What? What's 'at ya saying, Miss Ruth? She's gone on to glory?" He was trembling.

Ruth got up from the bed, closed the jewelry box, and handed it to Charlie. "I have what I came for." She held the folded glove up to show him.

"Uh uh, no, Miss Ruth. I wants you ta take that entire box like my mama said. She was determined and made me promise. Take it all, fo' whatever it's worth. She wanted you ta have it and that's that." He looked at his mother as her face softened and radiated rays of total happiness.

Ruth looked at Pearlie and signaled to leave. As she walked away from the bed, she put her hand on Charlie's shoulder. "Your mother lived a good life. She's finally at peace. You can take consolation in that."

"Miss Ruth," he looked up, "Mah daddy don't know yer heah so best if y'all go out the back way. Avoid the mob and him when he gits back." He addressed the girls still seated on the sofa, "Y'all show these fine ladies where I wants 'em ta go." The girls jumped to their feet and led the way.

September 1976

Ruth stared at the wardrobe. It was now or never. She pulled out the red dress. It had been hanging there for months since her return from New York City. Now that Jacob was back in her life, he constantly reminded her that she needed to experience the finer things in life. Tonight was an occasion that called for the silky red dress.

She opened the top drawer of the dresser and removed the satin bag that once contained the names of her three children. After Jonah was born, she placed the piece of paper with the names written on it inside of her bible and used the bag for the pieces of fine jewelry Augustus purchased over the years.

Ruth pulled out a necklace, a pair of earrings, and two fourteen-carat gold rings. There were ten gold rings in total, one for each year of marriage and three for the children she bore. Augustus marked every milestone with an expensive piece of jewelry. Pieces that she wondered where, if ever, she would get the chance to display.

Tonight she wanted to reveal a side of her few knew. The side that she'd only shown one man and he was no longer around to appreciate it. Tears cascaded down her cheeks. "This one's for you, baby."

Ruth put the red dress on, smoothed it down over her hips, and took the hat box from the top of the wardrobe, opened it, and took out the red hat. Then she went to the front closet where she kept her Sunday-best clothing, removed a pair of red patent-leather shoes, and smiled.

As she covered her face and neck with makeup, she kept looking at herself in the bathroom mirror. *Simply Beautiful* played in her head, the song Gus always sang as she got dressed for special occasions. She released the tip of the foam rollers and watched her hair fall down her back.

She was ready to go. Placing a tube of Fire Engine Red lipstick in a small black clutch, Ruth turned the bathroom lights off, walked down the hall, and stood in the living room. She opened the closet door and grabbed a light overcoat.

"How do I look?" She was the only one in the house that night. The children were in Savannah visiting Frank and Rosa Lee.

"Simply beautiful!" She laughed, opened the door, and stepped onto the front porch.

He was waiting in the car. "You think you can do this?" he asked.

"Honey, I don't think. I know."

Later ....

Someone called her name. Right in the middle of the club as she celebrated Ida's 30th birthday. It could have been any of the seventy-five or so people gathered in the room but it was someone else. Someone she'd least expected to ever come to her for help.

Ruth stood in the club's small bathroom. It might be all in her head. There were days when it became incredibly hard to decipher what was real or make believe. Maybe this was one of those days.

Something was different. Usually, when she had a spell of some sort that affected her ability to know what was or was not real, she was in her own house. Now she was away from home, and, out of all the places it could happen, it happened in a juke joint. A place the saints were forbidden from going.

She heard the voice cry out again. She had to find from where she was being summoned. She had to find out soon because being paralyzed with fear was no longer an option.

Ruth snuck outside and peered into the parking lot. There was a couple leaning against the concrete building with their arms wrapped around each other. The man's hands were slightly above the woman's hips. Ruth turned away in embarrassment.

She walked over to a car parked in the front row, and stood next to it until the couple in front of her became alarmed, looked at her strangely, and walked away.

She heard the sound again.

Ruth looked up into the sky. An eerie feeling overtook her as she walked toward the building and then followed the paveway to the back. With the exception of the usual night critters, nothing seemed out of the ordinary. She turned back, and then she felt its power attacking her.

The muscles in her throat tightened. She grabbed her neck and gasped for air. Maybe she should turn around and go back inside. Another sound. Ruth fought to maintain her composure while looking around for possible witnesses. But there were none.

Something led her further down into the backyard towards the cornfields in the distrance. She could barely see the houses down the road. As she passed a wooden barrel, Ruth kneeled and picked up a stick.

Maybe it was the Devil himself finally paying her a visit.

"Cover me, Jesus!" she let out a faint whisper.

She could no longer hear Bill Withers crooning, *"Ain't no sunshine when she's gone."*

Another cry and this time much more powerful. Her throat tightened as Ruth reached up, grabbed her neck and opened her mouth to breathe. A sharp pain attacked her shoulders, but before she could do anything, her legs became numb. Walking further became a definite impossibility as she turned and stared back at the club.

"Ah ah." Ruth spun around and trotted toward the cornfields.

"Who?" she whispered and then yelled the same words with greater intensity. "Who is out there? Are you all right?"

The leaves began to stir, but there was no wind. Ruth knelt down. Then she saw a man lying in the grass.

"Ooh. Who's there? Let me go get help!" Fear crept inside her belly as she looked in the distance but could no longer see the club. She turned and once again walked toward the stranger lying on the ground.

He reached out to her. Ruth looked into his eyes and walked directly to where he lay on the ground. "What is going on?" she asked.

He never said a word, just looked at her as his eyes continued to plead for help. As he held one hand out toward Ruth, the other gripped his throat. Now she knew why she had struggled to breathe the closer she'd come to discovering him lying on the ground.

Ruth knelt down and reached for the hand he'd used to get her attention. She looked more closely at him and noticed the left side of his jacket was soaking wet. She placed her hand there. It was warm.

Realizing what the liquid was, Ruth jumped back. "Oh no! I must go get help!" she screamed.

Just then he attempted to pull her back with his free hand. Repeatedly his mouth opened, but he never uttered a sound as tears rolled down his face.

Ruth sat back down.

"You have to tell me what to do. You don't want me to leave you, but you're really hurt. Looks like you've been shot! I can't stand here and let you die. We have to get help." She wanted to cover him, but her overcoat was inside the club.

"Okay. Okay." She responded to his tightened grip on her hand, "I'll stay. I don't know what to do, but I will stay. They are going to be looking for me in a minute, ya hear me. Let's pray they come quick. You need a whole lotta help that I can't give, brother." She reached into his jacket pocket, removed the handkerchief, and wiped his forehead.

She moved over to his head, lifted it, and sat underneath him. "I don't know why, but I think God sent me here to be with you tonight. I recognized your troubled spirit when we met a long time ago. You had a lot of demons raging inside of you. I heard you saved, but did you repent for all of the meanness you been doing?" Ruth looked down at him.

His breathing was extremely labored, but he appeared at peace. He released her hand and pointed to his mouth.

Ruth leaned over. "What are you pointing to?" she asked. Then she heard someone else calling her name. "That's Ronald and the others looking for me. You're going to be fine," she lied.

He put his hand in his mouth and made a choking sound. Ruth reached down and pulled his hand out of this mouth. She removed her gloves and took her small hand and reached into his mouth. She could not see what she was doing but she knew something was lodged in his throat. She felt it.

"Great God! What is that? What did you swallow?" She struggled to see inside his mouth under the night skies.

She reached in again and pulled at what felt like mesh fabric. She pulled lightly and watched his reaction.

As she continued to pry the fabric out of the back of his mouth, he moved his arms wildly, forcing Ruth to stop.

"Does it hurt? I don't want to harm you any worse than you've already been harmed." She hesitated, but he took one arm and motioned that she try once again.

Ruth reached into his mouth and tugged again. Still no movement. All of a sudden, he began to cough and, with her fingers still lodged partially inside of his mouth, she yanked and the small piece of fabric became untangled and slid between her fingers. She pulled it out of his mouth, as he coughed uncontrollably.

She laid the cloth on top of his jacket and patted his chest. "There, there. It's out now. You can breathe better, yeah?"

He shook his head, and tried to speak. "I wanted tuh live right." His voice was extremely hoarse. "I never wanted tuh be like him. Lord forgive me!" His eyes rolled into the back of his head, his chest heaved upward and when his body returned to its normal state, Ruth knew that the end had come.

She sat there rocking him as if she did not know he was no longer among the living. She hummed softly until she heard her name again. The sound was closer. They would be discovered very soon. As the reality of what had just occurred dawned on her, Ruth started praying.

"Dear God, bless your name for the life of our brother. Lord, you heard his plea. He said he tried to live right. Lord, I stand in your presence and ask that you forgive him of all his sins and allow his soul to be free. Lord, you said if we confess our sins, you are faithful and just to forgive them. So please, Lord, forgive my brother for all the hurt he caused because of his own pain. Let his spirit finally be at peace. In Jesus name I pray. Amen."

"Ruthie, baby." Ronald Wilcox called again.

Ruth kept rocking the deceased man, humming a tune which she could not name nor recall where she'd first heard it. When she sensed that Ronald was near, she remembered the cloth she'd earlier retrieved from the dead man's throat. She spread it out on the ground to get a better look, but even in the dark, she guessed what it was.

"Ruthie, you okay, baby?" Ronald stood overtop of her watching.

She remained silent, picked up the piece of fabric and crumbled it in her hands.

No one, she promised herself under the stars of a crescent moonglow, ever needed to know.

III

Mary Brown Carter Wilcox

"Pastor Mary"

ONE

1972

Whack!

Smack!

Bam!

Blow after blow, all Mary Carter could think of was survival. She had to survive so that she could finish the collard greens just beginning to bubble on the stove. As she lay on the floor with her eyes closed, questions swirled around in her mind like a 'To Do' list: Had she turned the eye off on the stove? What about the white sheets hanging outside on the clothes line? She needed to go get them. Then, she remembered her son was due soon. What time did he say he was coming over?

She did not want him to walk in on this. Luckily for her husband, few were aware of the darker part of their relationship. In fact, until recently there were no witnesses to the horrors Mary endured at the hands of her tormentor. Stuck in a prison of hopelessness, her shame kept repeating, and there was no one she could ever tell.

Wham! Bam! Crack!

A loud noise rang through her ears. She braced herself and pondered whether her ribs had finally broken. He had kicked her in the same spot so many times before that she imagined one day his blows would finally sever a major organ. In fact, to protect them, she curled her body into a fetal position. He continued kicking her in the back, head, buttocks, and arms, unable to reach her chest or abdomen.

"You slut!" he ranted with each swing. Then he stood directly over top of her and yelled, "Get up and clean up this mess!"

For a moment the batting practice ceased, and that frosty December night in 1973 seemed normal; yet Mary knew that it was not over. He beat her in rounds and this was just the first one. As usual, it was a TKO. She had only a minute to reposition her body on the floor to give him a different target. The pain was unbearable.

With trembling hands, she quickly assessed the physical damage and discovered a lukewarm liquid strolling past her right ear lobe. There were several open sores across her forehead. She wondered how much hair she had lost this time around.

The clock on the wall struck seven. She had survived a forty-five minute round this time. It would take an hour of blows before she passed out all together.

Tonight was unusual: He had worn out faster than usual. Maybe he underestimated the hatred locked inside of his unequal opponent, who, for the first time in two years, had finally stood up to him.

She nearly succeeded. Yet, in the end, size proved to be the greater weapon, allowing her attacker to overpower her with ease.

It all started over a meal.

Dinner had to be prepared and ready to eat by six o'clock every day, no exceptions. He insisted that everything be finished when he walked into the house. In fact, when he opened the door, Mary had to place a hot plate of food at the head of the table as he stepped into the entryway.

Yet on this day, the electricity had gone out.

"Mer, get my plate!" Edgar Carter yelled as he walked by the kitchen. He resembled a lumber jack; enormously overpowering, tall, muscular, bald headed, and bronzed like the color of a new penny.

Mary busily worked on the collard greens and the yams. The potato salad, chicken, ham, okra and rice were already done. The yams needed a few more minutes; the collards needed even longer.

When he walked back into the living room, he surveyed the table and said, "Where my food, wench?"

"Power was out most of the day, Edgar." She kept stirring the collard greens and did not turn around.

"What that got to do with nothing?" His speech was slurred. Now she had a bigger problem.

"In a minute. Give me a minute. I had to send for help earlier just to get something done by sundown. It's going to be a little late, but it's coming."

"It's coming! That all you got to say? It's coming?"

"That's all there is to say." She opened the oven door to look at the yams. The butter on top had melted, but they had not browned.

"Say what? Dere betta be mo'." He walked over to where she stood inspecting the food. "You best git somethang on dis here table now or we gon' have a time."

"Okay, but it won't be cooked right." She started piling rice on a plate and opened the top to the okra.

"Woman, don't play wit me! Everythang you put on that plate betta be cooked and cooked right!"

Mary continued what she was doing. She scooped up a spoonful of yams from the oven but did not touch the collards. She set the plate down before his chair.

"There it is." She turned and walked away.

He sat down and began eating. "Where da dinner rolls?"

"No time. White bread tonight." She pulled the loaf of Wonder Bread from the top of the refrigerator and took out two slices.

"Ah be damned." He turned around and looked at her. "You pushing me, woman."

She handed him the bread on a saucer and walked back to the kitchen sink.

"Somethang missing. I just know it." He got up and walked over to the stove. He took the top off the pot with the collards inside.

"What's the matter with dese?" He grabbed a fork and tasted. "Tough as nails! Dese had to been on for less than a hour. What the hell were you doing befo' then?"

"Ah, let's see. Washing clothes, cleaning the house, and preparing dinner," she said sarcastically.

"Dat's what you s'posed to do! And you s'posed tuh have mah dinner ready when I git home." He turned and stared at her with hatred in his cold black eyes.

Mary kept her back to him and looked out into the yard. She knew if she gave him the slightest bait, he would bite.

Before she had another thought, Edgar walked over and tossed the pot of collard greens in her direction. She screamed and moved out of the way. The water had not reached boiling temperature, but she felt the sting. Only a small amount clung to her dress. He stood in front of her with his fists balled tightly.

They stared into each other's eyes. As he lifted his arm to land the first punch, Mary raised her hand and delivered the first blow with all her might. It landed somewhere near his chin. He flinched and swung back. His first blow landed directly behind her ear.

She tried to duck near the refrigerator. He blocked her movement and kneed her in the midsection. He went for a repeat. She tried to block the second blow with her hands. With his heavy steel brogan boot, he stomped her left foot. She screamed in agony and pushed herself around his body.

He grabbed her and pushed her onto of the dining room table, right on top of the food. As she tried to get her balance, he yanked the table cloth, pulling Mary, the food, and his enormous glass of cherry Kool Aid to the floor. She braced herself for the fall.

Before she even landed on the floor, he grabbed her by the neck and started choking her. She gasped for air. With both arms, she swung erratically, but, standing only five-feet five-inches tall, most of her punches missed the intended six-four target. He was tall and, at two-hundred forty pounds, enormously strong.

His grip around her throat tightened. Mary closed her eyes as he lifted her body into the air and slammed her against the wall.

"Look at me, heifer!" he yelled as tears streamed down her checks.

Mary did open her eyes. He released his hands from around her neck and grabbed her by the hair. She felt the follicles as they ripped away from her scalp. She would be bald soon. With both hands, she managed to free the strands of hair he so quickly snatched from her head.

She tried to run, but he put his foot in her path and she tripped, but caught her fall. He stood behind her, pushed her down, and raised both arms over his head. With the force of a lethal weapon, Edgar brought clinched fists down onto her back. Mary collapsed on the floor. TKO.

Awaiting his next move, she crouched into the fetal position. He bent over and tried to look into her face. She dared not look at him. He walked away and then turned swiftly and started kicking her as if she were a boxing bag. When she yelled for him to stop, he placed his size thirteen steel tipped boot directly on top of her midsection, raised it high and with a swift thrust, brought it down onto her body. The impact caused her head to slam against the wooden beams.

He paused while Mary braced herself for the next blow. She heard him tussling with his trousers. He took off his belt. The last time, he'd whipped her with his belt buckle. She was naked then. Tonight, fully dressed, she braced herself and thought about the potato salad on the counter. Did it need to be refrigerated?

First swing. The leather belt ripped into her calves, almost bringing her entire body off the floor. He raised the belt over his head two more times with the same intensity as the first swing. A noise outside of the front door caused him to lose focus, alter his swing, and strike the floor inches away from where his wife lay bleeding. He tried again, but missed. The remnants of the belt buckle struck her shoulder. Mary, trembling uncontrollably, buried her chin into her chest and prayed.

A pause was unusual. Edgar normally possessed far more energy than he displayed on this night. The last few licks merely grazed her flesh. It was a bittersweet relief. As she listened to the clock ticking on the wall, she calculated his next move, but still, he did not move. She was too afraid to raise her head and look around because he was still close enough to continue.

"I'm gon' take a piss and when I git back, you betta be in dat kitchen fixing my suppa and cleaning up the mess you caused." He turned and walked away.

Seconds passed as Mary, bloodied and bruised, lay on the floor. She thought of the yams in the oven. Then it dawned on her that she had to get out of the house.

When she heard him close the bathroom door, she struggled with all her might, to lift her battered body up from the floor. Her foot ached from the impact of his boot on her toes, yet, Mary used her arms to lift herself up. Barely able to stand up straight, she leaned against the wall and braced herself. She listened for movement.

She could hear him fumbling around in the other room.

Mary stared at the broken dishes on the floor as puddles of food rested on the tablecloth and the floor beneath. She tried to move but a sharp pain shot through her spine. She needed to focus on an exit.

She heard a loud crash. It was her cue. Mary limped to the other side of the room, grabbed her wool coat from the hall closet, picked up a butcher knife, and then stopped. An eerie silence fell over the room.

She stood still and waited.

Sweat dripped down her face and onto the floor. It dawned on her that every minute she waited around for his return was a quicker death sentence. Then, she heard movement. He was on his way back out to finish what he'd started. Round two.

Mary ran across the room, turned the door knob, and pulled to open it. She pushed the screened door open without looking back. It was dusk, but not fully dark. Putting her coat on as she hobbled down the steps, she was in the backyard before she could catch her breath.

Experience taught her that she had a better chance of getting away by running through the woods. There was a highway a few miles away. She ran faster, clutching the knife like a lifeline.

Through low hanging branches that shaded their back yard, she ran. As sharp pieces of wood and leaves brushed against her, Mary used her arms as a shield to protect her face. It was the only area Edgar never touched; he said it was too beautiful.

Her head, heavy and feeling like a ton of bricks, ached miserably, blurring her vision, but she continued running. The sounds of the winter night greeted her with each passing step. Yet the sounds of the unknown were far better than the sound of the man who would soon chase after her.

Edgar Roland Carter would never allow her to leave. He told her that many times. Besides, he had a reputation for how he handled his money, his business, and also kept his family in check. No one escaped from his grasp unless he sent them away or put them into an early grave. She discovered he had proven that to others in the Low Country of South Carolina and Georgia countless times.

Mary prayed a strategy would come to her. She could hear the sounds from the highway just up ahead but was having trouble thinking clearly. She saw the dark tar pavement in the distance and sprinted toward it. With a steady pace, she trotted down the lone highway. She had gone some five-hundred feet before she heard the sound of an oncoming automobile. She started to panic. What if it was him?

No, it could not be him. He was a creature of habit who would have targeted the homes of their neighbors whose properties bordered theirs. She prayed her strategy of deception worked.

A car came towards her. It made an abrupt stop a half of mile from where she stood. Panting and sighing heavily, Mary stopped running and looked around. The glaring headlights of the car obstructed her view of the driver. In an instant, a sense of hope overpowered her and she turned away from the road and headed toward a large oak tree nestled in the woods. As the dark brown color of her coat blended with the tree's bark, Mary closed her eyes and prayed to become invisible.

"Daddy, I need a little help!" she whispered. The car sped by her and continued on down the road. She ran up onto the shoulder of the two lane highway and continued. There were two or three small houses in the distance. She ran toward them. She heard another car approaching from behind. The sounds from the engine were familiar. She ran faster.

Up ahead was a thin patch of bushes. If she could only get to them before the car came any closer, Mary knew she would be safe. She ran behind them and knelt down, then she laid flat in the grass on the side of the road. As the car approached, she buried her head in the dirt and prayed.

"Our Father, which art in Heaven." She took a deep breath. The car slowed down.

"The blood of Jesus cover me now!" She did not look up to determine where the car was in proximity to where she hid.

The sound of the motor was closer now. Mary did not move. She tucked her legs up into her chest to resemble a slain animal lying on the side of the road and prayed for a miracle.

The car stopped but the engine stayed on. Mary opened her eyes. She could see the headlights shining in the distance. From the glare, she knew the driver had not spotted her. Within minutes, the car sped down the highway.

"Thank you, Jesus!"

Mary raised herself off the ground and ran toward the houses up ahead.

The first house was well illuminated with fluorescent yellow porch lights. Even in the dark, she could see its white clapboard structure. It sat low on the ground, but its foundation was supported by stacked cinderblocks. Mary ran up onto the front porch.

"Evening," she said just above a whisper.

The lights were on in the house and she heard voices casually speaking inside. Mary opened the screened door and knocked on the wooden door. The voices stopped.

"Who is it?" a male voice rang out.

"My name is Mary. I need your help!" she yelled. When no one responded, in a softer tone, she said, "I've been beaten pretty bad. Please help me."

She heard footsteps inside the house coming toward the front door, and then the door was opened.

A tall, bald headed man with a chestnut complexion and a protruding gut stood in the doorway sweating prefusely. Covered only by denim overalls, he wore suspenders over his bare chest.

He opened the door and looked out into the distance as if he did not see the short woman standing in front of him.

"Whatcha want, gal?" he said, finally turning his attention to Mary.

"I need help. I'm not from around here. My closest kin folks live in Yemasee. I just need to get cleaned up and out of this here cold." She stood shaking, holding the collar of her coat against her throat with her bare hands. Somewhere along the way she realized she had lost the knife.

"Who ya running from?" He stepped out onto the porch.

"My husband. He beat me. He is a bad drinker." Mary looked into his narrow slit eyes.

"Who ya husband and why he beat you?" He scrunched his bushy eyebrows together and examined the cuts and bruises that covered Mary's face.

"Sir, my husband is a drunk and plans to kill me! Can you please help me?" she pleaded.

He looked into the distance, scratched the top of his enormous head, and then stared directly into Mary Carter's face.

"Ah don't want no trouble, ma'am. You anotha man's propitty. Ah don't wan' no mess wid mah wife and chirren on yore account."

"Sir, I just need some place to rest for a little bit. My husband does not know where I am." Her eyes dropped to the floor.

"Naaw." He exaggerated the word, revealing the tobacco lodged in the right side of his mouth. "Naw, just can't do it. You should go back tuh dat man now! Ah'm sho' he worried sick about you. Men go off every now and then. You know by now dey calm down soon enough."

Without offering to get her a drink of water or bandages for the cuts and bruises that covered what he could see of her, he turned, opened the screened door, and walked back into his house. Within seconds, the porch lights went out.

Mary stood there in the dark. This was the Deep South she remembered. Most people in the Low Country thought a woman was to take what her husband dished out, till death do they part. Most often, it was the woman who broke the covenant with her death from one beating too many.

She walked down the stairs while the voices inside of the house continued as if she had never interrupted. She approached the next house. But, before she could climb the stairs, like clockwork, the porch light was turned off. She turned around and walked down the road.

As she headed toward the last house on the dirt paved road, she heard another familiar car sound. She turned around. A car raced toward her. Mary started screaming.

"Help me, please! Somebody, please help me!" She ran toward the last house.

She bounded up the porch steps and banged on the front door. "Help me, somebody!"

The door swung open. This time it was a woman.

"Who dis?" The short, dark brown, slender woman asked. Her eyes were bloodshot.

"Sis, it's Mary Carter from the church. I need your help!"

"Fo' what? Somebody afta ya?" She looked past Mary craning her neck to see what was frightening the woman in front of her.

"My husband." Mary almost collapsed but caught herself by grabbing the porch railing.

"Who ya husband?" Her attention was on the automobile that, seconds before, had come to a stop in her front yard.

Before the woman spoke again, a man came to the door. "Martha, who dat?" he said.

"Girl got husband problems," she blurted out.

"Don't you all," he hollered. "Look a heah. Yuh best git back wid'im. He da head of ya house not me!" The short freckle-faced man, half the size of Edgar Carter said, as he walked onto the front porch and peered out into the yard.

"Please help me." Mary was out of breath. "He will kill me tonight if you don't."

"Al, can't yuh try tuh talk some sense into da man?" Martha spoke again. There were years of experience etched across her face. She covered her large-breasted frame with a torn housecoat, her hair hidden underneath a bright colored turbin.

"Too late." Al, the younger of the two, said. "He waiting on me to walk toward him. He probably got a shot gun. I ain't gitting shot fo' no one." Then he turned and faced Mary. "You best go back and take this next lickin like yuh s'posed tuh. When he finish, y'all make up and everythang gonna be just fine."

"What is wrong with you people?" Mary shouted. "I need help and all you can say is go back home?"

"Look a heah," Al interrupted. He stood barefoot and watched the car door open. "I ain't no fool!" He pointed at the vehicle. "Dat Edgar Carter in dat car, right?"

Mary knew there was nothing else to be said. She walked down the steps and then turned back and looked at the two of them.

"I pray you never need the help of a stranger," she said as she walked to the car and her fate.

"You thank he gon' kill 'er?" Martha asked Al as Mary walked away.

"Eventually," he whispered as they stood awaiting the next scene. "If not tonight, soon, sho' nuff."

Mary was within one-hundred feet of the car when Edgar turned off the headlights. He would wait until she got closer then step out of the car and beat her right in front of the people she had attempted safe passage with. It was an all too familiar scene.

She slowed down. Something told her to turn around. Helpless, she took another step in his direction. She could see him slouched down in the front seat watching her every move. She heard her inner voice again. This time she listened. This time she obeyed.

Mary spun around and ran toward the back of the stranger's home.

"Ah no, missy." Al, leaning over the banister on the front porch, yelled after her.

She heard the car door slam. "I'll get her. Y'all go on back in yer house."

Mary sprinted toward a barn and a chicken shed. She smelled water. She kept going. She did not turn around. She could hear Edgar lumbering after her somewhere in the distance. She kept running. She closed her eyes and gave it her best shot. If she could reach the water, she would dive in and be with her daughter.

Free at last.

She raced to freedom. In the pitch black night, all Mary could hear was the voice in her head directing her to run away from this life, into the eternal. She grabbed the bottom of her coat and sprinted faster. Somewhere a sense of energy enraptured her spirit. And then she saw it.

Deep in the woods, in the middle of nowhere, as the sounds of the water dissipated, she realized she must have turned in the wrong direction. She was no longer headed toward freedom, but another possible rejection. Still, the voice told her to continue.

A few feet away, shining under the night's moonglow, was a white clapboard house with dark shutters. There was a huge screened porch on the side of it that Mary could see as she approached. Bigger than most houses in the Low Country, this one had an attic or an upstairs, something else rare in Jasper County, South Carolina.

The front yard was massive and even in the dark, Mary could see that it was sculptured with plants and rocks as if it were some type of hideaway oasis. Was she dreaming? She wondered if it was owned by a white family. Yet she continued running toward it. Her view brightened. All of a sudden, the sky lit up the entire front yard, and Mary knew that God Almighty had sent daylight to lead her to the front door.

Just a few steps from the front porch, she came to an abrupt stop. She was out of breath. Mary looked around in the yard. The porch light was off but there was a light on inside. She looked down at her feet. There was a wooden cross in the flower patch just below where she stood. Yes, the Spirit of the Lord was here.

She stumbled up the stairs, tripping over clay flower pots that lined the steps leading to the porch. She grabbed the banister and pulled her body to the top stair and stopped. She looked at the door. It was drapped with a colorful wreath that contained live flowers. The vastness of the colors caused a flashback. She had been here before. She turned to listen for her stalker. Yet, there was total silence, total serenity.

Mary struck the front door with all her might before collapsing onto the floorboards beneath her. She passed out. Dazed, she saw a light shining in her face. She tried to get her focus but could not. Something pulled her in a direction she did not know. It was too late; she had no strength to resist. She saw a blinding light all around her. Maybe this was what it was like to step out from the darkness into the glorious light. Maybe this was what it was like to finally rest in the hands of her Savior.

Freely, she gave in. Freely, she drifted toward the light. Relieved, Mary Brown Carter took a deep breath and closed her eyes.

TWO

1965

"A woman is not supposed to preach the gospel." The voice rang out from the small vestibule of the church.

"So I've been told." Mary continued sweeping the wooden floor of the small sanctuary. She did not turn around to acknowledge the person who spoke to her on that crisp spring June night.

"You are before your time, you know that right?"

"Maybe in these back woods, but women are preaching all over the country. One would think that by now everyone would know it."

"That may be the case in other parts of this country, but in the Deep South, folks call it blasphemy," the voice of a woman continued.

"Folks call anything they don't understand blasphemy. Jesus was accused of the same thing putting me in good company." She laid the broom against the wooden brown panels that formed the wall and sat down on a nearby pew, facing the altar. She did not bother to look in the direction of the woman who came to join the ranks of those that admonished her for engaging in a practice reserved for men.

"Women are supposed to stay in their place, at least around here. So I've been told," the woman continued.

"What about women like Harriet Tubman, Sojourner Truth? What if they had stayed in their place? Where would women be today?"

"I don't know. Lost, I guess. Folks around here say that's different. They say a woman has no business carrying the Word of God."

"Say what?" Mary turned around, but unable to see the stranger, stood to her feet.

"They say God never intended for a woman to carry the gospel!"

"Says who?"

"The mighty men of God in the South. They claim it's all plain as day in the Good Book!" The siloulette of a small statured woman could be seen. She had to be less than five feet tall. She weighed no more than one-hundred pounds and her body appeared to be draped in some sort of nondescript cloth that covered her from head to toe.

"Which book are you referring to? The Good Book I read says a woman, not a man, carried the word of God! In fact, a woman carried God!"

"Watch yourself. Your opponents will argue that God allowed a woman to carry God simply because only women can bring life into this world," she continued, without coming closer to where Mary stood peering into the vestibule.

"Think about it for a moment. A woman was good enough to carry God and scripture. The words in that Good Book, as they call it, tell us that God cannot be separated from His word. Therefore, if a woman could deliver the Word to the world, I think she can deliver the Word to a few backwater hicks living in this Low Country."

Mary walked toward the entrance of the small church, where her antagonists now stood in the parking lot facing the woods, back to her opponent.

"Maybe there are enough preachers living around here. Without Pastor Roy, townfolks have turned back to their old ignorant ways. They don't know who to believe anymore, so the safest thing to do is to just conform to whatever these cloaked men tell them to do."

"Well, I believe the Lord spoke through Pastor Roy and told him that I was called to preach the gospel. If I disobey that call, how can I call myself a Christian? Besides, if I run from this call I will never fulfill my purpose on Earth."

"So what is your next strategy to get these naysayers to listen?" The small woman turned to face Mary. "Without your husband, you have lost almost half of your fight. Now, you've lost that precious angel and your son does not want to have anything to do with the Low Country. Whatever you do, you must be certain that it is God's will or you will get eaten alive by these hypocrites."

"I know I am doing the right thing. I did not come to this town to be a preacher. I came to this town because God sent me here. Gave me a remarkable man of God to emulate and now I stand alone to continue what my husband started. If folk won't listen to me here, I'll just move where they will," Mary said.

"That's a good strategy. Go someplace where you can define your strengths. When you come back, they'll be ready to listen to whatever you have to say. One thing I am certain of is your day to preach the gospel, in this town, will most surely come. Just keep plowing!" She pulled a hood over her face, lifted the bottom of her makeshift gown exposing her peach-colored bare feet, and turned toward the woods. Within seconds, it was as if she were never there.

Mary kept staring into the distance. She had spotted the same woman sitting in the last pew of the church a few times listening intently while Pastor Roy preached Heaven on Earth. Each time, the mystery woman wore an outfit that covered her pale-skinned body from head to toe. Yet, it was hard not to notice her deepset haunting eyes. Now Mary had a voice to go with the stranger, and she was certain that eventually she would find out her name.

Two weeks later, Mary Brown packed up her belongings and moved to Savannah, Georgia. It was a larger city and one with an attitude of Southern culture possessed by a sense of urgency for change. Finally, in her new home, she found solace and a chance to grieve over her losses with privacy and dignity. Yes, once again, she was certain that God was calling the shots. This too would prove to be another trying assignment and she knew it.

A friend of Roy's, Pastor Keefe Jackson, suggested the move. He had been to the Chapel in the Woods on the few occasions while Mary delivered a sermon. When they reunited after Roy's death, he told Mary that Savannah had plenty of women preachers that could mentor her and teach her how to navigate through stricter cultures that believed women were to be silent in the house of the Lord. He said he believed she was called to preach the Gospel, and so he went out on a limb and offered her a chance to work in the church where he was one of the Pastor's Aides.

Several weeks after she arrived, the Pastor of the church informed her that she could teach weekly Bible study classes and, on occasion, or as the spirit led, some of the evening Tarry services. Tarry services brought back fond memories. Mary was elated.

It was a long time ago when she received the gift of speaking in unknown tongues. She would never forget, for her life was so different then. Now a widow, the gift reminded her of happier times. A time when she was a young married woman, head over heels in love with her husband.

Looking back, it seemed a lifetime had gone by. Memories like these reminded Mary that life was never to be taken for granted. Every life was precious, for human souls were often here today and gone tomorrow and that was something she would never forget. For when it came to living her life to the fullest, for Mary, death had been the best teacher of them all.

1945

"Come on, don't hold back. Let the Lord use you," Pastor Roy coached her.

Frustrated and exhausted, Mary sat on the floor chanting words that made no sense to her ears. As tears poured down her face, she wanted desperately to give up and accept that she would never receive this gift. It had been six long months. Six months of waiting, opening her mouth, releasing 'Ah' sounds, but nothing else. To the seventeen-year-old, everything that leaked from her vocal cords sounded like gibberish. She often wondered where was the Holy Ghost's power everyone in the church talked about? If it was available to any believer, why had she not been graced with its presence?

Six years her senior, twenty-two year old Prentiss "Roy" Brown easily read the expression on her face and knew that she longed to receive this awesome gift. He kept coaching until he noticed a look in her eyes that revealed she had reached a breaking point. Then he gently knelt beside her, covered her body with his medium-sized six-foot-two caramel brown frame, and prayed. A few minutes later, strange sounds emanated from her lips that caused tears to pour out of Mary's eyes and saturate her entire face.

1942

Prentiss "Roy" Brown worked on the marine base at Parris Island, South Carolina, but he never enlisted as a soldier. He said the military sent him home after discovering he had flat feet. Seems the recruiters felt sorry for him, having his dreams shattered, so they gave him a job helping new recruits and delivering equipment to the barracks. No one knew the difference.

Strikingly handsome, Roy was tall, light skinned, with strong facial lines that were graced with dimples on both sides of his sculpted jawline. Although he had an easy all-day smile, he managed to possess a serious look that told the world that, despite segregation, he was a black man to be feared and respected.

He received the call to preach at the age of seven and by the age of twelve folks everywhere said he was born with preaching in his bones. He preached at every opportunity, including on the street corner by the local grocer, before graduating to church parking lots where he delivered his sermons that later became famous.

Everyone in town liked him. As a teenager, he would strut across town, Bible in hand, dressed in a black three-piece suit and a crisp white cotton shirt, asking a question that would become his trademark opener, "Anybody told you they love you today?"

It was a simple inquiry and most folk answered him without giving his opener much thought. Yet to the young minister, it was his ticket into their world, whether they knew it or not. By the time he turned eighteen, folks knew that if no one confessed their love to them, when they saw Roy Brown, he would remind them that the God he served loved them and, to the surprise of many, that he did too.

He had a flair for detail. Meticulous about everything from his style of dress to his articulate speech, Roy asked every stranger their name twice and never forgot to address them by that name whenever he saw them. Those habits easily spilled into ministry.

Long before he reached adulthood, Roy Brown had won the entire Low Country over with his gift of affection and encouragement, demonstrated by the holding of hands, tight hugs, and kisses on the cheeks. There were many things about this young man that some townsfolk did not understand, but one thing was clear: God walked with Roy Brown everywhere he went and rumor had it, not even the Klan stepped in his way.

Negro soldiers on Parris Island claimed Roy paraded around as if he had an all access pass to the entire base or had been given a waiver to the rules of segregation. He frequented the segregated barracks and, oftentimes, he was the only colored allowed into the segregated mess halls. No one could deny there was something special about him.

"My God doesn't see color," he once said to a white officer who told him to go around to the back of the storeroom to deliver auto parts for the logistics unit.

The officer, an older, broad chested dirty blonde, standing a few inches shy of six feet, stared at Roy. "What that you say, boy?" he quipped.

"With all due respect, I don't think being nineteen qualifies me as a boy. Then again, I am not certain of your age so if you are quite older than I, you may address me as young man." Roy looked straight into the man's eyes and never blinked.

The officer looked at Roy suspiciously. He examined the sharpness of his starched white shirt and khaki pants. He looked at the way his face was clean shaven and even noticed the gold ring around his finger and the gold necklace and cross suspended from his neck. The man then turned around and yelled to the other men in the hall to move so that the equipment could be brought in from the front entrance.

"You gon' let that colored boy come through heah?" they asked.

"He says his God don't see color. I guess that's who sent him and I ain't gon' mess with that," the officer said, as Roy walked past him carrying a large cardboard box.

"Where can I put this?" he asked the soldiers who stood watching him.

They ignored him. Roy walked past them, and when he spotted other boxes of similar size on the other side of the wall, he placed the box right next to them.

"Who told you to come through that front door, darkie?" another soldier asked.

"Well, first God and then, let's see," Roy pulled out a folded sheet of paper from his shirt pocket, "I guess these orders from General Armstead himself." He smiled at the soldier who stood before him, fist balled tight, boiling with anger.

"You let me see that." He snatched the paperwork out of Roy's hands and then looked at his commanding officer.

"Jensen, go back to what you were doing and leave this young man alone!"

"Young what?" Jenson, a short stocky brunette with a spiked crew cut, spun around. "What did you call him, sir? What the hell is going on? This nigra claims he has papers from General Armstead! Why would a three-star general give some nigra boy access to this building?"

"Look, if he says he has orders from General Armstead, then he probably does!" the officer countered.

"But..."

"But, what? What trouble do you want to start now? Let the man make his delivery and leave! Don't stand there and cause no more foolishness, Jensen." The officer rolled his sea-blue eyes at Roy then turned and walked away.

Roy brought in three more medium-sized boxes and then walked toward the other soldiers who were standing around watching him. He held a clipboard with papers attached to it out to the small crowd.

Confusion flashed across the masks of them all.

"Seriously, gentlemen. I need to be on my way. I have too much to do to stand here while you admire me. Whoever normally signs needs to sign."

Just then a tall, lanky, blonde-haired soldier, weighing no more than a hundred and thirty pounds, approached Roy. He snatched the clipboard out of his hand. "Give it heah!"

Roy stood there looking at all the soldiers watching him. He then took the clipboard back and extended his hand out to the soldier who'd signed. He looked at Roy, turned toward the officer in charge, and reluctantly shook Roy's hand. The other soldiers gasped.

THREE

1940

While the elder generation of Browns were considered elitest by many in the Low Country, that term was an oxymoron when it came to describing their son Roy. Even though his parents rarely frequented the local establishments or talked to their neighbors, Roy knew just about everyone and visited almost every home.

"Good evenin', Miz Catherine," he once addressed a Caucasian woman in Ridgeland. "How you fairing now with Jules away at WestPoint? Been about twelve weeks now, huh? I am sure you miss him something awful."

The aging woman looked at Roy and immediately the harsh expression on her face softened as tears formed in the corners of her eyes. Few in town remembered her beloved son had been gone for so long. Initially everyone expressed concern and offered prayers, but now, three months later, no one bothered to inquire.

"Why thank you, Roy Brown, for being so considerate. I guess it has been twelve weeks, huh?" Her hazel, deepset eyes glossed over as she tried to behave as if the subject of son was no big deal.

"Well, it has been that long, Miz Catherine. I pray for him every night. I can see Jules sporting that brown bomber jacket you bought him for his eighteenth birthday. My, he wears it with pride." He held his hand out to her.

"You are too kind." She grabbed Roy's outsreteched hand. "I will be sure to tell Jules when I write to him." Moments later, a flash of fear crossed her face as she realized what she'd done and she dropped Roy's hand.

Roy was a businessman and a gentleman. On Saturdays, he traded in his khaki pants, starched white or blue cotton shirt, and shiny black rubber-soled dress shoes for demin overalls, striped cotton shirts, and a baseball cap. He volunteered his labor on a local farm and delivered fresh produce to needy families all across town. This was how he became so popular. It was also the beginning of his later famous outreach ministry. He was not afraid to walk onto someone's property, announce himself, and more often than not, stroll right into the front door. He had an open invitation. Very few would turn away someone with free food, even if he was colored.

On Sundays, he awoke before daybreak, prepared breakfast for his parents, and headed out to one of the church services in town. Since most started around eleven in the morning, he left the house around 8 a.m. in his father's station wagon to offer folks rides to church. He compiled his list on Saturday while he delivered food.

After the final trip of the morning, he sat in a back pew, opened his Bible, and read to himself. He read through the testimonies, the weekly announcements, and everything else except the sermonic prayer and the actual sermon. When the prayer began, Roy arose, turned around and kneeled down in front of the pew with his head bowed.

When the sermon started, he read along silently and then took notes in his composition notebook. He never said a word to anyone during this time and when the service concluded, he gathered his belongings and walked out into the vestibule to greet the parishioners.

On the first Sunday of each month, food was served either in the back of the church on the lawn, or, during inclimate weather, in a room behind the sanctuary. In addition to assisting the pastors, Roy helped the elderly church mothers with preparation. He brought food from Parris Island's Officer's Club each week which included the best dinner rolls and fruit punch or lemonade anyone had ever tasted.

"When I open my church, we will have service every Sunday," he told the church mothers one Saturday evening. His tall body draped over the metal chair he sat in and his long legs straddled both sides.

"Oh, boy, hush!" one of the mothers said.

"Serious, Mother dear! When the Lord says so, I am going to start another church that won't be a part of the rotation. Our doors will open every Sunday."

"You sho' the Lord is leading you, Roy? You don't want tuh be out dere by yo'self. Yuh need tuh talk tuh dese other pastors and see if opening every week is okay wid dem."

"Why, Mother? If God is for me, who can be against me?" He rocked back and forth in the chair.

"You still need to do thangs in decency and order, young man!" Another chimed in. "God don't like no mess. These folk been having church in rotation since slavery times, four churches, each open on a separate Sunday. That way all the families can fellowship together. They's good reasons for traditions."

"Then if that's the case, why don't we have one church built and just let the pastors rotate from the pulpit? We have four churches and four pastors, but they only have Sunday service once a month. Seems a waste. The only thing else they do is open for Bible study one day of the week. Churches are supposed to be about serving the people of God, but if the church is always closed, how are we serving the people of God?" His intense eyes penetrated his audience.

"You sho' you ain't holiness?" Mother Bell asked. The matriarch of the church, at eighty-six, she was the oldest living member in Jasper County and Roy Brown's favorite person. He smiled at the silverhaired woman and burst out laughing.

"I told you I might open a non-denominational church. Too much emphasis on sects. I 'm calling my church, "God's House," he beamed.

"That's good, son. You sho' got a whole lot of spunk! I reckon you gon' get yo' chance one day. But let me warn ya, church folk will take and take and never give back. Don't let them wear you out, ya hear?" She pointed her wrinkled index finger at him.

"Ma Bell, I hear ya. That's why I am praying for a strong wife!" He stood to his feet and walked toward the stove. " I need someone who's not afraid to speak her mind and get in the pulpit with her husband and govern the business of the church."

"What? Boy, are you fool?" another mother joined in. "Ya' talking blasphemy! A woman don't belong in no pulpit. We have our place, and it's taking care of the Man of God. Ya' sound like ya' want yo' wife to run thangs them deacons responsible for."

"My wife can do whatever the Lord lays on her heart, Mother Ward," Roy said as he bit into a sizzling hot piece of fried chicken straight out of the cast iron frying pan.

"Ya best be careful! You still wet behind da' ears!" Mother Ward stood near the stove. A tall, heavyset woman, her flowery print dress was just long enough to reveal the stockings that she tied together around the base of each knee. " Some fool gal come along and tell you da Lawd told her she can run da church. She'll run you next. Mark my words."

"You too nice anyway. You need to marry one of these young gals that is not mannish. Someone with a quiet spirit and her only concern is loving and taking care of you," Mother Bell added.

"Don't be no fool, boy! You betta make sho' ya' house is in order first. If ya' can't control ya' woman, ya' sho' won't be able to control the saints," Mother Ward said laughing.

"Long as my woman loves me, she will submit." Roy looked around the room and shook his head. "I just don't believe a man should try to control his woman, just gets in the way with what God is doing in her life."

"Boy, is that the way thangs run in your daddy's house?" Mother Bell adjusted the black turbin that she wore to cover up her gray tresses. "A woman's place is to take care of her man and help out around the house, in the fields, and whatsoever is needed to support her family."

"What about a woman's dreams, Mothers?" Roy stopped eating.

"Boy, God gave you a heart of pure gold! I guess most folks thank a woman's dreams are whatever her man's is. That may be right. My dreams were my husband's. I did what needed to be done fo' our six children, I did. I worked around da house and in da fields, and I did everythang fo' my family. Dey all up and gone now. My chirren have dey own families so sometimes I find myself wondering what to do with myself. Grands come around and even got great grands. I take care of dem but dey wear me out. Every once in a while I dream of what my life would be like to do something just for Ella." She laughed.

"Ah, Ella, that's just old age talking! You had a good life, a good man, good chirren. Ya' did what God sent cha heah to do. It's our reasonable service. Where would dese men be widout us?" Mother Ward, whose roots were from Jamaica originally, pondered.

"In the outhouse screaming for help!" Mother Bell hollered.

All of the women, and the lone male, burst into thunderous laughter. Mother Bell often told stories of her late husband, Robert Bell, a gigantic, six-foot-six man, weighing over four-hundred pounds, who found himself stuck in the wooden toilet of an outhouse one day. Unable to lift himself up, he yelled his wife's first name for seven hours until she finally came to retrieve him.

Roy studied the women in the small kitchen at the back of Second African Baptist Church that day. They had become his female sounding board. With a disabled mother, and a sister almost twelve years younger than he, there was no way for him to learn the female perspective when it came to one day becoming a husband, father, and even before then, a pastor.

Because of them, Roy decided he needed a strong woman by his side. She had to appreciate her role as a pastor's wife, yet understand that he expected her to walk by his side and not behind him. He was not attracted to pushy women. Instead, he was looking for someone that walked with confidence and whose silence merely represented her inner strength.

1941

Her name was Daisy Lyons. She was three years older than Roy, but that did not matter. He said age was nothing but a number. They met one Saturday as he delivered fruit to her family. She had spunk and did not back away as most of the young women did when he came around. That was not Daisy Lyons' way. She was a type of woman Roy Brown, at nineteen, had yet to lay eyes on.

The first time he saw her was at her mother's house when he came to deliver produce. He did not address her then, instead, he opted for a proper introduction. He did talk to her younger siblings, and played around with them as he devoured a small plate of okra and rice her mother prepared.

Daisy noticed him as well. She paraded past the small kitchen on three occasions, but Roy kept his focus on what he was doing. He did not allow anyone, no matter how pretty, to interfere with God's work.

The woman he came to visit, Ruby Lyons, weighed less than one-hundred pounds and stood about five-feet three-inches tall in high heels. Her body, aging before its time, was frail, reminding one of a slender old woman. She had given birth to five children before her husband was violently murdered. After his departure, unable to support her family, she sank into a deep depression, allowing her oldest daughter, Daisy, to care for much of the home as best she could.

Roy introduced himself to Ruby one day outside of St. Paul Baptist Church during the summer of 1940. He offered her his arm as she walked down the front steps. She was polite, but her facial expression was one of suspicion, as she cautiously strolled arm in arm with the extremely handsome young man. Yet, by the time fall rolled around, they had become old friends.

"I can take you on home now, Miz Ruby." Roy released her arm at the bottom of the steps.

"No, sir. We can make it up the way. Not far." She looked down at the ground. Three sandy haired little boys, all dressed in navy blue shorts with long knee socks played in circles where they stood.

"It doesn't matter. Distance is irrelevant," Roy smiled.

"What that mean?" she asked.

"It means the same thing he said before." A voice interrupted from behind them. "Irrelevant is the same as saying it does not matter, Mother."

The woman who had spoken stood on the steps, dressed in an orange A-line dress with a tailored bodice and ruffled hem that showed off her figure. The haughty way she placed her hands on her hips made her five feet six inch height appear as tall as Roy Brown. He quickly noticed her squared shoulders, pencil thin waistline and shapely long legs.

He turned around to face her, and, with all his might, tried to force a straight face, but she got the best of him.

"Called you out, huh?" She walked straight up to him. "You might impress these hicks around here with your big words, but I am not impressed, Pastor Brown."

"Hold on! I am not a Pastor yet. Haven't been ordained," Roy answered, humbled for once.

"They say you received the call. Is that right?" She leaned forward and grabbed the smallest of her brothers by the collar and tugged at him. "Stop it, I say. Stop it right now before I spank your behind," she threatened.

Ruby stood there watching Daisy with admiration. "You have not met my oldest, have you?" She smiled at Roy.

"No, ma'am. Can't say I have had the pleasure. Seems she knows who I am though." He walked a few inches in front of them before looking back.

"Whole town knows who you are. Do enough walking around town to wear holes in your shoes," she teased.

"It's God's work that keeps me so busy." He admired her wavy fiery red hair, and the way it appeared to lack direction, spiraling out and about framing her coppertone face.

"Is that all? Either you are on fire for the Lord or just plain nosey!" she added. "And yes, this is my natural hair color, in case you were wondering."

Embarrassed that she'd caught him staring, Roy glanced at Ruby as she raised her hand to cover her mouth and laugh. He noticed her outspoken beautiful daughter was not wearing a wedding band.

"This is the source of laughter in your home, huh, Miz Ruby?"

"She keeps everyone on their toes." Ruby shook her head from side to side.

"Don't speak about me as if I am not present!" Daisy swiftly interjected. "Whatever you want to know you can ask me." She walked toward the service road.

"My car is parked just down the road. Can I give your family a ride, Miss Daisy?" he teased.

"It's the least you can do! We could have been halfway up the road by now were it not for you holding my mother's attention with your southern charm." She walked over to his shiny white Cadillac and leaned on the hood.

"I see you know my name and my car." He smiled, put the key into the door, and turned the lock.

FOUR

1942

Daisy Lyons attended college at Savannah State and taught summer school in Ridgeland. She wore her confidence like a comfortable pair of shoes, and knew when to hold her tongue. Yet, when it came to getting what she wanted, she pressed forward unabashedly. In fact, she asked Roy out on their first date.

As Roy's visions of his future came to reality, he thought he had found the woman that would stand beside him in the church God would soon build. Sure enough, Daisy possessed the strength and the finesse to handle matters in the Old South, and it was no doubt that she was organized and could handle the affairs of a small church. Yet, something was missing.

For more than a year he courted Daisy, showering her with gifts and taking her on dates with and without a chaperone. The clock was ticking and he knew before long rumors would speculate in a small town so he wanted to maintain her honor. He wanted to do the right thing. That was marriage, but every time he gave it a second thought, he felt a sense of hesitation. Something was holding him back that he never understood, and as he continued to watch and pray, time for courting eventually ran out.

Daisy hated the church mothers Roy had become so fond of being around.

"They are just pure evil!" she lamented while they rode along the two-lane highway surrounded by large over-arching weeping willow trees enroute to Singleton Beach.

"Evil. Sweetheart, why do you say that? I've known everyone of them since I was five years old." Roy kept his eyes on the road.

"Yeah and they been evil since way before then! All they do is gossip and spread lies about folks. I can't stand the likes of them. Don't mention that Mother Ward. She is the worst of them all! I see the way she watches me as if I stank!"

"Stank!" Roy burst out laughing.

"That's not funny, babe! I am serious. Those hags are hell bent on keeping you to themselves. I know they don't approve of your choice of me. I am a college educated woman and they are just jealous. Keep it up. One day they are going to come right out and spill the beans! Don't act like I never told you!" She peered out the window at the vast landscape and bright sun miles shy of the Bryne Bridge that would lead them to the shores of Hilton Head Island.

"They are harmless, baby. I think you might be over-reacting a little, but some of what you say might be true. I don't know what I would have done without them. They were my rock as Mom's illness kept her in Hardeeville most of the time. When Dad would bring us here for services, those women cared for us. They fed us and yes, Lord, they preached non-stop. They made me see that women should have more of a leadership role in church."

Roy pulled the car off the side of the road and came to a stop. The smell of the fresh ocean breeze permeated the air.

"Tish tish, man. I totally disagree with you. There is nothing worse than a geechie!" She pulled out a brown silk scarf from her purse and neatly tied it around her long red ponytail.

"Hold on! That's not right and you know that's not a Christian thing to say. These women are proud of where they come from." He exited the car and walked around to open her door.

"It's not where they come from, man, it's the way they act. And I am not talking about Christians, I'm talking about hypocrites!" Daisy got out of the car, walked toward the back, and opened the hatch.

"Where were any of them when Roland Carter murdered my father?" she yelled.

"I don't know." Roy was soft spoken, and never raised his voice in a disagreement. "I only know what you told me about what happened to him." He carried the large wicker picnic basket and handed the towels and blankets to her.

"Those fools let that man walk up on our property and kill my father! Then he killed an entire family, because he did not like them. Simple as that. The man is the Devil and that whole town acts like his minions. They did nothing to protect my family and they did nothing to put Roland Carter in a hole big enough to swallow this ocean. That's why he's out and about town acting as if he just pulled off the crime of the century. Heck, he did!" She headed down to the beach.

"So, yes, I can't stand them. I can't stand how they look at my mother with pity, yet none of them ever offered her a helping hand. The only help we got was from the white people my daddy used to work for. Without them, we would have starved!" Daisy stopped and dropped their belongings on the sand.

"They probably didn't know what to do or say, considering how dangerous you said this man was. Some folks foolishly believe the scripture that says, "You have not because you ask not," means that unless you ask for what you need, no one should offer."

Roy put the basket down and spread the blanket over the hot white sand. Next he took the metal lounge chair he unsnapped from the base and stretched it out. He offered it to Daisy and when she refused, he straddled over the plastic seat and sat down.

"All I am saying is that those women are phony. They talk about everyone and don't you think for a minute, they don't talk about you. They say you are crazy. Calling you Joseph Brown, the dreamer. None of them believe in your vision. They think you have lost your mind." Daisy sat down on the blanket and removed her black leather sandals.

"Well, comparing me to Joseph is a compliment. You do recall that Joseph practically ran Egypt?" Roy smiled and pulled out his Bible.

"He should have after all he went through to get to that point!" She laughed and opened the basket and pulled out a bottle of Coca Cola.

"That just goes to show you that all of God's promises are yeah and amen. I don't expect the vision God gave me to happen overnight. I never expected it to. I am happy working on P.I., learning from the soldiers and officers about leadership, learning how to treat even those that don't like you, don't have a kind word to say about you or your race, and could care less whether you live or die, with respect. I know God's timing is perfect." He extended his tanned arms around her neck and gently stroked her skin.

"Don't worry about me, Daisy. I know one thing. When God says move, baby, the entire world won't be able to stop me!"

"I don't know, man. I don't know if it's worth it. We could do so much better living in Savannah or Charleston, even Walterboro. Folks travel down Highway 17 heading toward this island and act like us locals don't exist. To them we are nothing and that's the way these hicks act. Like they are nothing! You come here thinking you can preach a gospel that says all men and women are equal? Baby, you got an uphill battle before you."

Daisy stood up, took off the thin brown see-through fabric that covered her paisley print swimsuit, and ran into the ocean as the waves called her name in a language only she could understand.

Roy sat still lounging in the chair, watching the woman he loved enjoy the water. The radiance of the sun on Daisy's skin was like a blazing fire. Like the intense red sunrays,

Daisy's tongue burned anyone that she felt threatened her existence. Something major had soured her spirit.

When he was not reading scriptures, Roy focused on the twenty or thirty families walking along the beach and playing in the water. Then he looked over at the mainland and into the vast water that surrounded it. The side that was restricted to whites only. The longer he stared, the more his life made sense.

Behind Roy's sunshades, tears nestled in the corners of his eyes. The summers of 1940 and 1941 would forever be etched in his heart. Yet, he knew that soon they would become distant memories and one day fade away all together.

Daisy returned, soaking wet, as the droplets of water that covered her coppertoned skin appeared as sparkles of light. She reached into the basket, pulled out a flask of water, guzzled it down, and stretched out on a towel.

"Now, I must burn!" she said, laughing joyously.

Roy watched as she slept peacefully, inches away from his chair. He could not contain his sadness, for he knew he would never get the chance to see her awake in his arms as they lay in bed together or run his fingers through her fiery red hair. Those days were never to be. Just were not in the cards.

That sunny day on Singleton Beach was the last time they spent an afternoon alone together. From that day forward, Roy found himself engrossed in church work, while Daisy spent the majority of her time away at school. She concentrated on her impending graduation and a career afterward. They ran into each other at church sometimes and would spend a few minutes talking and reminiscing about the fun they'd shared together. Sometimes they talked politics, other times some new invention or event that would change the way Americans saw negros; changed the way negros saw themselves.

He never got around to calling the relationship off, in fact, he never had to. It was an unspoken language that the two of them possessed. In the spring, as he witnessed Daisy accept her diploma, her smile faded from his mind and he felt as if he were looking at a stranger. Gone was his original physical attraction, replaced by that of a woman he admired and respected but did not desire. The Daisy Lyons that he once drank grape Kool Aid with and pushed on the sliding board in the back of the church had grown into a woman of distinction. She was going somewhere big, and not even loving Roy Brown would stop her.

Later at a party given in her honor, they managed to dance together one last time. With tears in their eyes, they looked past each other into their futures.

"Roy Brown, there's a big world out there." A tear cascaded down Daisy's perfectly matched amber face powder. "Folks are starving for the kind of gospel God has called you to preach. You make me proud, ya hear?"

A tear strolled down his face too. Daisy removed the flower tucked behind her ear and handed it to him. "Something to remember me by."

That was the very last time he laid eyes on her. In the fall, he skipped work on the farm and his visits to families in need. The following morning he skipped church. Most of the town assumed he was ill, but Roy Brown never felt better.

He enrolled in Savannah State College to start a new life without the woman who inspired him to greatness.

FIVE

1941

Ethel Lee opened the door and saw her granddaughter stretched out on the ground below.

"What in God's name?" she screamed. "Mary, is that you?" She ran down the steps and picked the child up. Her trembling body pounded against Ethel Lee's large and full breasts.

"Come, child, you all right now. Just tell Grandma what ails ya." The elderly woman sat down on the glider and rocked the distraught child.

Mary could not get the words out. She saw the whole thing. She was the only witness, so in her twelve-year-old mind she thought she could never tell another living soul.

"There, there. You all right?" Ethel Lee held Mary's small, oval shaped, caramel-colored face in her hands. "Weeping don't last always. Whatever you crying for, you can rest assured that joy will come in the morning."

Mary buried her head further into her grandmother's chest. She was the only person who could comfort her now.

"Bud, come out here and take this child!" Ethel Lee handed a calmer Mary to her son. "Seems something happened that she can't tell me 'bout right now."

Once she placed the child in his arms, she reached over and opened the screened door so that they could go inside.

"Open that window so that child can rest with a nice breeze. She just need to sleep it off."

The elderly woman sat on the porch in a pair of denim overalls wondering what had her granddaughter so upset. Mary was her daughter Gwen's youngest child. They lived on the other side of town closer to the city of Yemasee.

A while later, Ephraim "Bud" Brown, a medium-build, tall, slender, thick wavy-haired man, chestnut brown with a stubbled face, returned to the front porch.

"Po' child," he said. "She's really upset. I washed her face with a cold rag to get her temperature down. Something sho'nough happened." He stood next to where his mother sat rocking in the glider.

"Bud, get in that truck and go see what is going on. I don't like the smell of this. That child look like she's been frightened out of her mind. I want to know why. Don't tarry long, you hear me?" Bud had already walked back into the house to get his car keys.

Ethel Lee stood on the porch watching anxiously as he drove away. Just then, a neighbor walked up the driveway.

"Did that chile come here?" the woman asked.

"Who?" Ethel Lee knew who she was talking about but she was very suspicious.

"I heard that chile crying and saw her running all the way down the street. I knew she was heading here. Before I could get my house coat on good, she was gone." She stood at the bottom of the porch steps watching Ethel Lee.

She continued. "I knew something was terribly wrong the way she was screaming uncontrollably like that. I put my hard-soled shoes on and came as soon as I could."

"Chile, I don't know what's goin' on! I heard her crying from inside my living room! That's Gwen's youngest. I sent Ephraim to check up on them. Nobody betta not o' hurt my grand, you hear me!" Ethel Lee declared.

Mary, dressed only in a thin white cotton slip, was sitting up on the bed, propped forward by toss pillows, when her grandmother and Delores Pickney, a much younger woman, walked in. Mary recognized Miz Pickney because she spent every summer playing with her twin daughters, Deborah and Delilah.

There was no way she would tell her grandmother the truth now.

"All right now? You wanna tell Big Mama what got you so bent out of shape like that? Who hurt your feelings?" Ethel Lee sat on the bed next to Mary.

"Nobody." Then Mary started trembling and shaking again. "Ma...." She did not finish the sentence.

"Ma! What, baby? Tell me! Did something happen to your mama?"

Mary started to scream. Delores Pickney walked over and sat at the foot of the bed.

"Calm down and talk, girl. You got to tell us what's wrong!" Ethel Lee gently shook the child. "Nobody gon' hurt you now. Just tell me. Did anything happened to Gwen?"

"Ma...." The child began again, then panted uncontrollably.

"What!" Ethel Lee shouted. "Baby, you scaring this old lady! What about your mama? She spank you again? What?" Ethel Lee stood up and walked back and forth alongside the bed while Delores continued to rock Mary.

"The, the, the river!"

"What about the river, Mary?" She bent over and held the child's feet. "Bless God, you gotta tell me now! What about the river? What that got to do with anything?"

"She...she gone, Big Mama." Mary's chest heaved up and down as puddles of tears trickled down her tiny face.

"Oh, Lord, no! You ain't saying what I think ya saying, are you?" She clinched her jaws tightly and stood looking down at Mary. "God in Heaven, give this chile the words to tell me what happened."

Mary sobbed uncontrollably. Delores sat holding her, also in tears. Ethel Lee sat down on the bed with her back to the two of them.

"This just can't be! Where she gone? Lordy, where my baby gone?" Trembling, she placed her aged hands over her bronzed face and cried.

No one said anything after that. They all just sat on the bed crying, praying it was some mistake. But Mary knew the truth. She had seen it all.

Saw her father beat her mother unmercifully throughout their house.

Saw him chase her into the woods.

Saw him choke her and push her against a tree, pull her hair and slam her face into the ground.

Saw her mother run for her life.

Saw her run to the river, turn around and look at her husband.

Saw her dive into the water near the surrounding rocks.

Saw the tide carry her body away.

She never saw her mother come back out of the water.

Darkness had saturated the earth when Ephraim returned. His chestnut complexion had gone pale and sallow as he exited the truck walking like a zombie. He did not enter the house, instead, he sat out on the front porch rocking in the glider.

By the time he'd made it home, the news had already been confirmed to Ethel Lee: Gwen was dead; gone without a trace. Not even a scrap of clothing had been found.

The memory of her mother's death left an indelible imprint on Mary's mind for the rest of her life. She never spoke to her father again. Never returned to the home she grew up in or walked in the yard where she'd spent twelve years playing. That part of her life became a distant memory that she tucked in the back of her mind. Never to be replayed again.

Months later, in the spring, Mary moved to Savannah to live with her uncle Ephraim and his three sons. His wife had died during childbirth a few years before Gwen's demise. He wanted a change of pace, new scenery, and better schools for his boys so Savannah was close enough. It was all part of his neice's divine destiny.

1944

"Anyone told you that they love you today?" The stranger stood in front of Mary while she waited for the city bus. She did not respond. She was wearing a full length emerald green coat, black patent-leather shoes, and her pressed, long dark brown hair hung beneath the green tam placed jauntily atop her head.

"One, two, three..." he counted.

"What are you waiting for?" Mary asked as she peered around him to look down the street for the approaching bus.

"Just your answer." He showcased a wide grin.

"Is that a pickup line or what?" She laughed. "That's a new one for me. And," she stepped to the side, "you actually expect me to answer it?"

"Simple question that requires a simple response." He kept his long fingers tucked away in the pockets of the blue linen slacks he wore. She noticed the sharp crease in the pant legs, and thought *impressive.*

"And God has answered my prayers, 'cause here comes the bus!" She chuckled.

"I declare that you shall never ride a bus again."

"And, who are you to declare such a thing?" She walked closer to the small group awaiting the approaching bus so as not to lose her place in line.

"Your future husband." He pulled his left hand out of his pocket, revealing a shiny set of car keys that he dangled in front of her.

Mary focused on the bus.

"Brown's the name." He reluctantly stepped out of the way so that Mary could step on the bus, pay the fare, and then walk to the back of the bus to enter again and sit down.

"You finally said something right. Brown is the name." She winked and boarded the back of the bus.

Mary sat down and looked outside the dusty bus window. The gentleman stood writing something in a composition notebook. From the look of his starched, pressed linen outfit, Mary suspected he was much older than she was and quite arrogant.

Three weeks later, Mary stood outside of that same bus stop with her uncle Ephraim. They were laughing when she heard a familiar voice.

"That's the same line he used on me," she whispered to Ephraim, while she grabbed hold of his muscular arm.

"You didn't fall for it, did you?"

"No way. That city boy must think us country folks are really slow, huh?" Mary turned and looked at him so that he could see she was listening to his conversation with another young woman.

Roy Brown shook the other woman's hand and when he noticed Mary and the gentleman standing next to her sporting a fedora hat, he started to smile.

"Oh, Miss Clayton, allow me to introduce you to my future wife," he said to the woman as he looked straight at Mary.

Embarrassed, Mary looked at her uncle, who leaned his head back and let out a hearty laugh.

"Seems someone has a huge crush on you, Mer," Ephraim joked.

"No, sir. It's more than a crush. That woman standing next to you is my destiny." He was dressed more formally, wearing a tan all-weather coat and a brown suit underneath. When he raised his hands to wipe his brow, Ephraim noticed the diamond cuff links.

Roy excused himself and walked over to Ephraim. "Pardon my intrusion, sir, but your daughter is the most beautiful woman I ever laid eyes on. She refuses to answer my questions or talk to me. If it's all right with you, let me introduce myself. I am Prentiss Raymond Brown, Junior, but everyone calls me Roy.

"Where your people from, young man?" Ephraim shook Roy's hand. Mary turned her head and stared in the opposite direction.

"We're originally from Atlanta. A family of Southern ministers. Father preaches in Beaufort."

"And you?" Ephraim asked.

"Sir?"

"Where do you preach? You said you were from a family of Southern preachers. Where's your church?"

"Well, right now I am in college over at Savannah State. I'm waiting for my assignment from the Lord. Hopefully, I'll get the wife before the church." Roy winked boldly at Mary.

"You sho' you ready for a wife or you just looking for someone to pick after you?" Ephraim now looked at Mary suspiciously.

"Sir, I cook and clean my own place. I work on Parris Island three days a week while in school, and serve the Lord the rest of the time. I don't need a maid; I need a strong woman that can stand beside me as my wife." Roy beamed.

"And how you know this here girl is the one?"

"I knew the moment I laid eyes on her. Then today God confirmed it." He winked at Mary again.

The bus came to a full stop. Roy reached out and placed his hand on Ephraim's shoulder.

"Sir, I would be honored to give you and your daughter a lift. I have my own car and it runs pretty good," he boasted.

Ephraim looked at the people getting on and off of the hot dirty bus. Then he turned to his niece. "It's your call, sweetie!"

Mary looked Roy up and down. She hated the bus drivers in Savannah. More than once she had paid the bus fare and been left behind as the bus tried to stay on schedule and crowds, particularly negros, took too much time paying and then going to the back of the bus. A ride home was a welcomed relief, yet she wondered about this man with such a distinguished name and the confidence of a con man.

"To answer your question," she smiled at her uncle, "someone tells me they love me every day."

"And might I ask who?" He reached into his front coat pocket and pulled out his car keys.

"I do." She walked ahead of him, arm and arm with her uncle, to Roy Brown's car.

Mary Brown never rode public transportation again.

Two months later, in the summer of 1944, they were wed in a small ceremony in the chapel on Savannah State's campus.

Ephraim Brown admired the young future minister immediately. He told his niece that marrying him would be a decision she would never regret. Two years later, he stood next to Roy's parents when he graduated from Savannah State College. A week later, Roy had his first fulltime assignment as a man of the cloth. Mary, the woman he swore was meant to stand by his side, was right next to him.

She adored her loving husband with all hear heart. He was one of the most remarkable men she had ever met. Everyone said Roy was pleasing on the eyes and Mary could not agree more. His eyes put her in a trance if she looked in them for too long. His deep baritone voice often sent chills down her back and his cool swagger made her weak in the knees.

The following year, 1945, Ephraim and his sons moved to California, taking the only real family Mary had in Georgia away. Without them, she was extremely lonely, but it lasted only for a spell. By the spring of 1948, she delivered a beautiful baby boy they named Micah. He weighed in at nine pounds and possessed his father's light brown eyes. It would be decades before Mary's feelings of lonliness returned.

SIX

1959

On Valentine's Day, Ramona Rose, slid into the world. She was named after her grandmother, Gwen, whom she would never meet. Mary had not spoken about her mother's death until she learned she was pregnant a second time. Now there was a sense of urgency to get everything out into the open. She could no longer carry the guilt alone.

"I saw my father do horrible things to Mama," she told Roy one day as they sat outside on the veranda, surrounded by tall orchids, hydrageneas, and a variety of plants with dramatic foliage color.

"I'm so sorry, baby. You rarely talk about them and I knew better than to pry. I believe God is the only one that can heal certain wounds. I wanted to give Him His chance with the woman I love with all my heart." He walked over and sat next to her on the lounge chair.

"Well, I vowed I would never tell another soul. I thought about telling Big Mama, but every time I did, someone else would pop up. By the time I had the courage to say anything, Ephraim had broken her heart and moved to California. She begged him to stay close to South Carolina, but...." She held Roy's strong hands and stroked them. "I knew he wanted to go to Hollywood. Always loved the movies, said he was the next Sydney Poitier."

"Yeah, now that the boys are practically grown, Buddy can live some of his dreams." He kissed her on the forehead. "Baby, you don't have to tell me unless you want to. I understand." He looked into her sullen eyes and tried to reassure her.

"Roy Brown, I love you. We share everything. For most of my life, I've kept this secret in a place that the world could not touch. A place where I thought no one could ever hurt me again."

He brought his head down upon her swollen abdomen. "You just let your heart do the talking. We got all day. Micah's with kin folks who don't want to give him back to us, I'm sure." He laughed. "So, I guess the two of us have all the time in the world."

Mary hesitated before she spoke again. She looked around and wondered how their lives would change once her perfect prince discovered she came from an imperfect family. From what Roy shared about his past, his family represented the normalcy she never knew. The Browns she originated from were totally different.

Tears filled her eyes.

"My father was a cruel man! He had a lot of women and plenty of children across the state of South Carolina." She kissed his forehead and stroked his hair.

"Mama was his floor mat. She even made space for his other women to stay with us. He said they were kinfolks visiting from out of town. She knew that was a lie after she caught him sneaking into their bedroooms during the night. Yet, she never said a word to him about it.

"She cleaned the house, washed his clothes, our clothes, and even theirs! I hated it. She ran after that man, picking up and doing whatever he wanted. He stayed out all time of night and came in drunk cussing everybody out. One night my brothers stood up to him and they whipped his behind! Mama begged them to stop, but they refused. They beat my father like he beat her, and then threw him out on the front porch in his drunken stupor to sleep outside like a stray dog."

Roy kept looking ahead. He never uttered a sound as she released waves of pain from her past.

"Next day, he kicked my brothers out of the house for good. They left me alone with my parents in a living hell. Daddy never put a hand on me; said I was too beautiful. He used to call me Precious, said I looked just like him, and then he would find a strap and beat Mama because he said she stepped out on him to have me. What kind of foolishness is that? I was the spittin' image of him!

"It never got better. For five years I wanted to die! My only out was Big Mama and Ma would send me to her house so I couldn't see what else was going on. But, sure enough, I found out." She picked up her glass of iced tea and drank from it.

"I found out more than I wanted to know. That fool man took her clothes outside and burned them one day. Left her with nothing but the housecoat she was wearing. She wore that until Ephraim brought her some of Big Mama's clothes. They were too big, but she wore them. And guess what? He beat her because he said the clothes were too big! Can you imagine?" She checked to see if Roy was still awake. He lifted his head and stared into her eyes.

"I'm sorry. It saddens me that you had to endure so much tragedy at such a young age. Now I know why you're such a strong and determined woman. Look at all that you have had to face, shelter, and get away from? You amaze me, Mary Brown. You simply amaze me!" He kissed her full lips, smiled, and turned back around to lie on her chest.

"I saw him burn her fingers one time," she went on, encouraged by his support. "Said she burnt the rice! You know how important rice is in the Low Country. Took her over to the stove, lit the eye on and placed her fingers against it. Never heard a scream like that! Mama ran over to the basin of water and put her hands in it. She was crying so hard she couldn't get her breath. He just looked at her and held the pot of rice in front of her.

"I think she was pregnant again after she had me. I saw him kick the life out of her. Next thing I know, some of Big Mama's friends came to stay with us. I snuck in their bedroom and there was lots of blood. That's all I remember. The enormous amount of blood that filled those basins, all coming from my mama's insides.

"Then, like clockwork, he was on top of her again. I could hear them sometimes. He would stroll in at some ungodly hour of the early morning and wake her up. I could hear him. He would yell that she get up and remove her underwear. If she took too long, I could hear her scream that he was hurting her. Then the bed would start squeaking. He even threatened her that if she did not open her legs wider, he would break them. Mama would always walk out to the kitchen later and get a basin, go outside and wash his stink off of her." Mary felt tears of sympathy and caring cascading down Roy's cheeks as she stroked his face.

"The day she died was the worst day of my life. One of his other children showed up. He wanted my father to come quick for his mother was sick. We later learned the woman had a heart attack and died. The boy never said it was urgent, he simply said his mother was not feeling well. Mama did not tell Daddy until he awoke from another drunken sleep hours later.

"Well, when my mother told my father about the earlier visit, he went beserk! Left and when he came back hours later, he had wet his pants. The stink on him was incredible! Mama kept asking what was wrong but he didn't say anything. Next thing we knew, he undid his belt, took it off, and started swinging at the furniture, breaking pieces and destroying every knick-knack Ma had around the room.

"When Mama peeked outside of the kitchen he saw her, dropped the belt and started after her. He caught her at the back door, slammed her face against the door, ripped her skirt, pulled down her panties and started smacking her behind. Right in front of me! Mama yelled to go get Big Mama but I was frozen and could not move. Her screams sounded like death throes. I begged him to stop." They both cried softly as she recounted these hardest moments of her life but still Roy said nothing to interrupt.

"I don't know what happened next. He turned around and told me to get out. I stood on the porch screaming for help but the neighbors paid me no attention. I ran down the steps and out of the yard, but I didn't know who to turn to with our family living on the other side of town.

"I ran to the house next door, but no one answered. Ran to the next house and the next. Then I ran back to my house. They were gone. The back door was opened and Mama's panties were lying on the floor near the couch covered in blood! I ran out onto the back porch to find them when I heard my mother's voice coming from way off in the distance.

"We lived near a river that was so deep we were told not to get into the water or the tide would take us away. I could not swim so I stayed away anyway, and played in the creeks behind our neighbors' yards." Roy lifted himself up and turned to face his wife. He lay next to her, holding her hands and crying on her shoulder.

For a long while, Mary remained silent. Eventually, she continued.

"I saw her in the woods. Running half naked, she looked like a wild woman. I called after her but she didn't hear me. I think she was beyond hearing. He caught up with her and slammed her to the ground. This time he put his foot on her neck as she choked and coughed up enough phlegm for an entire cold season! I screamed to him and he released her. He told me to stay back. Mama managed to get up and run toward the river. I begged her to come back. She slowed down when she saw he no longer chased her and raised her hands into the air. I could not hear the words that came out of her mouth, but she turned in my direction and I read her lips, 'God help me!' she cried over and over again.

"I picked up a stick, ran toward my father, and started swinging! He grabbed the stick away from me and threw it on the ground. He continued yelling demeaning insults at her. I took my fists and pounded on his thighs, pleading for him to leave her alone.

"He was just about to turn around and head back home when something happened. He grabbed me and slammed me to the ground. I lay there, kicking and screaming, until Mama must have turned around and headed in our direction.

"'You black bastard, get away from my child.' Then he lunged toward her and missed. She turned around and started running but he got up and ran after her. I stood up but could barely see them anymore so I ran after them as fast as I could. I saw him as he got closer to her, then he tripped. By then, she was too close to the river. It must have been calling her name because she turned around, looked back at him with hatred in her eyes, and then dived straight into the water."

Mary stood up and raised her hands.

"I ran after her. Then I stopped at the rocks and watched the tide come in and take my dear Mama away from me forever. I fell to the ground and screamed. He ran past me but stopped just shy of jumping in behind her. Oh, how I wished he had. To this day, I wish it was him in that water and not her." Her anger was evident now more than ever.

"He told the neighbors and the sheriff that they had a fight and Ma ran outside, through the woods and fell into the river. He never mentioned the hell she endured at his hands before bursting through those waves. He tried to make it sound like she went crazy and took her own life."

Mary sat back down. "I've never told anyone what I saw that day. I've never told the truth."

Roy sat up in the chair and peered into her eyes. "Mer, don't do this to yourself! There is now no condemnation to those who walk in Christ. Baby, you were a young child.

Helpless. Powerless. What would anyone expect you to do?"

"Tell the truth." She covered her face. "I could have told them what I saw! Oh, God! I kept quiet and I said nothing. I never even told Big Mama the truth! She went to her grave believing her daughter committed suicide."

"Mer, you know Ephraim would have killed your father if he found out. Nothing can bring her back. Rest assured, your father did not get away with what he did, as God sees everything. Vengeance is mine, He says. God will avenge all wrongs."

#

Roy ran into the small hospital room. Mary, face still swollen, was sleeping. He slipped his hand into hers and said a prayer. She opened her eyes and looked at him.

"They say her heart is very weak," she whispered as a lone tear descended down her cheek.

"She's going to be fine. We just have to trust God. We can't depend on what we can see. She will live and not die. You take my word for it, Mer." Roy placed his grey wool fedora on the white metal nightstand near the bed.

"She's so little. The doctors say her heart is struggling to beat. I just want to reach into her tiny chest and massage her heart so that it will beat on its own." She fought back the tears.

"Having done all to do, stand. Isn't that what the Word tells us?" Roy looked away from his wife as tears rolled down his cheeks.

"It doesn't say we have to stand with a straight face! We're standing because that's all we know how to do. I prayed, you prayed, and we prayed as a church family. Daddy Brown spoke to my belly when the pain started and he told me this baby was going to live! I guess the command has been given." Mary tried to crack a smile.

"I guess so." Roy turned and looked at her. "All I know is I trust God. What will be will be. He loves us, Mer. He really loves us."

"Yeah, baby, He does." She released his hands and laid back on the pillow. "And you know what, Prentiss Raymond Brown, Junior?" she whispered.

"What, Queen Mary Brown?"

"I love you."

As Mary dozed off, Roy sat next to her and admired the beautiful specimen God sent to him as a helpmeet. They brought Ramona home four months later. Still frail, she no longer required machines to breathe. In fact, the powerful screams emanating from her small lungs confirmed that she was doing better than breathing on her own. She had a strong spirit.

The next year, Roy thought it would help if they sought out someone to care for Ramona a few days a week. Mary was exhausted every night and barely had time for herself.

"Mer, you can only do so much," He told her.

"I know. They say a woman's work is never done!" She chuckled.

"Well, I think you are doing the work of four women! I don't want to see you tire yourself out. It started that way with Mama. She used to do everything around the church. Never even asked for help from the other sisters or brothers. When she fell ill, it seemed everyone else jumped in to help Dad as if they had just discovered there was work to be done in the Lord's house." He walked over to the bed, sat down, and looked his wife straight in the eyes.

"Don't ever be afraid to ask for help. That's what I am here for. Now, it's obvious you need help with Ramona. She will be all right if someone else looks after her a few hours a day."

"No, Roy! I could not disagree with you more. That little angel needs her mother, day and night. Her heart is too weak. I don't trust anyone with a child God gave me to raise." Mary sat up in the bed, alarmed.

"Mer, you gon' have to let go and let God heal that baby. You've done your best. She is walking and getting stronger every day. Besides…" he grabbed her hands, "she breathes on her own and can talk…man can she talk! She'll tell you if something goes wrong. That baby is way before her time."

Roy never had to say another word on the matter.

SEVEN

1956

Mary grabbed the pillow, buried her head into it and screamed with all her might. Trembling uncontrollably, she could not contain or control the throbbing in her chest. Death-curdling sounds escaped her lungs and filled the entire house with rage.

Seven-year-old Micah ran into the bedroom and stood patiently beside the bed. He too was crying, yet for different reasons. His mother was upset and he was too young to comprehend why or to know what he could do to ease her pain. Dressed in a short tweed jacket, white cotton shirt and brown shorts that fell just below his tiny knees, he resembled a child that attended a parochial school. He eventually leaned onto the bed, raised his small arms and caressed his mother's back. When she did not respond to him, he slowly walked over to the wooden rocking chair that she used to rock him in as an infant, and climbed in.

By the time Roy Brown dragged his tired, aching body through the front door around eleven p.m., Mary, exhausted from crying, was sound asleep. In her emotional state, she did not change her clothing, nor prepare dinner.

She did not know what time it was when she finally awoke from a fitful sleep. She was wearing a cotton nightgown and the black loafers she's worn that day were neatly placed on the floor across from the bed. Her quilted leather pocketbook was on the dresser to the left of the bed. In fact, all of her belongings were neatly resting in their rightful places.

She thought of Micah and how frightened he must have been over her sudden and sporadic earlier outbursts.

Startled, she jumped up and looked around the room. Then she listened for noises. It was silent. Slowly she tiptoed down the hall to his bedroom, turned the glass knob affixed to the wooden door, and saw her little man, sound asleep, snuggled underneath his favorite blue cotton sheets, holding a cuddly soft Teddy Bear. She heard a sound and turned around.

"Mer, you all right?"

It was 1956, they had been married for more than a decade, and Roy's concern for her wellbeing still had not waivered or diminished in the slightest.

"I'll make it." She avoided his eyes and stared at the parquet floors. "Rosetta won't so lucky."

"What do you mean?" Dressed in a paisley print silk robe and leather slippers, he walked toward her.

"She's gone, baby!" Tears began to swell in her eyes. "And I didn't even get a chance to say goodbye!" Now she could let go. Her king was close enough to console her.

Roy held her as she leaned into his arms and cried non-stop.

Later that same night, they lay on top of the covers while Mary reminisced about the woman who'd shaped her life.

"You talk about a good woman! Talk about smart! Oh Lord, that woman had a powerful brain! And she was strong and fearless! She had some seven or eight children and still managed to run a business!" She looked at Roy and went on. "I never met anyone like her before in my life. I mean, Rosetta was funny, God she was funny, and free spirited. It was almost as if she grew up on the other side of the world! I was shocked when she told me her folks used to live in St. George, not that far from Yemasee. She was just a girl when she and Frank married, and by the time she was in her twenties they had a house full of beautiful babies.

"Nothing could stop her! She did not care about Jim Crow. She took it upon herself to educate her own children! Yeah, she did! She said if her children were forced to walk miles to school and then squabble over paper and books, she would teach them herself!

"She loved to travel and she took those kids everywhere she went until they were old enough to stay home with Frank, attend school, or work in the fields. She was fierce, I say! I remember she told me she cooked three square meals a day! Didn't matter if she had to get up before the rooster crowed either. She was going to have cooked food on the table every day. Ha! That woman prepared enough food to feed an army!"

She sat up with excitement. "I loved it when she came to Savannah. So tall and beautiful, rich chocolate skin like fudge candy. She personified elegance. I would see her all dressed up in a colorful dress, matching hat, and gloves up to her elbows. Never left home without a hat! You couldn't tell her anything! And you never saw that long black hair out of place. Not to add how she wore those fishnet stockings around. I don't know how she did it!"

"What happened to her, baby?" Roy interrupted.

"I don't know!" She turned to face him. "Folks got so many stories. I heard she went crazy and stopped talking. I didn't buy that foolishness! I mean, I went down to Ridgeland to see her a few times. The last time I went to visit, I took Micah with me. When we got to the house, Miss Bea was sitting on the front porch and she said Rosetta was not taking company! I sat for about an hour while Micah played in the yard with the other children. Something was wrong though. I couldn't put my finger on it then. Everything about the house and the yard was different. More than that, a whole lot was missing now that I think about it."

"Did you ask Frank what was going on?" he interjected.

"No. Bea told me that the Klan took Rosetta one night. Apparently she was on her way home from Hardeeville. Nobody knows what fool things they did to her! They say she was beaten pretty badly and that they cut her hair! Can you believe that? They cut that woman's beautiful glory!" She was crying again.

Roy stood still, hesitated, and then asked, "Was she raped?"

"I was too afraid to ask. Of course, that's what I thought too. Miss Bea said after that happened, Rosetta stopped talking and spent all day in the house. Never gave the business or her family another thought. They said she looked at those beautiful children like she had never seen them before. Hmmm, whatever happened must have broken her spirit."

"That's horrible, baby! Poor Frank! I bet he took it hard. I mean, I know the Lord says we have to love our enemies as well as our friends, but those hooded bastards make me sick! I understand they are filled with hatred, but the devastation they have caused so many of our folks needs to be chronicled somewhere for all the world to see. I don't see a jail being big enough or hateful enough to hold them in." He clinched his jaws tightly together.

"Whatever they did to her eventually ended her life. She may not have died right then when it happened, but from what I hear, she walked around like the living dead for a long time. I can't imagine her not talking anymore. I can't imagine her not telling the jokes that we all loved to hear. You heard them before."

"Yeah, I remember. She was funny. She could really cook too! She had us all over to roast a hog one time, but she ended up doing everything herself. She made us men look weak that day. Frank warned us that if things were not done the way she wanted, she would take over and do it by herself!" Roy shook his head as a smile crept across his face at the memory.

"That's how she was about everything. It had to be just right. She paid close attention to the smallest of details. I'll never forget that."

"How long had you known her?" Roy walked over to the windowsill, sat, and stared out into the night.

"Seems like a lifetime ago. Ephraim met her at the market in Yemasee one day. She was the first black woman we ever saw in the open market selling without a white man over her shoulder collecting the money."

She continued. "Well, Ephraim sees this beautiful young woman and being Ephraim, a womanizer, he walks straight up to her. He found out soon enough that she was married! In fact, she lectured him about coming on to a married woman. When he asked where her husband was, she told him he was home minding the children! Oh, Lord, Ephraim hollered laughing at that woman. Next thing you know, she had talked him into delivering produce for her company. Said she needed a strong man to handle folk in Savannah. That's why we moved here." Mary smiled even as tears rolled down her face.

"Yes, Lord. The first time he drove for her was in '39. I know because I went with him. We stopped by her house and she gave him instructions for handling the Georgia customers. Said they were far easier than folks from South Carolina, but he still had to be careful, it was still Klan territory." She smiled as she laid across the bed facing Roy. "The minute she laid eyes on me, she laughed and said, "Ephraim, I like you already. You come from good people. I can tell by your sister's eyes." Roy handed her a handkerchief.

"Pretty soon, she talked to me about going to school and working too. She would take me around with her so I could see how everything was done. I was so happy. She was more than a big sister, she was the mother I had lost and I worshipped her. She even let me watch her children sometimes. When I turned sixteen, right before we met, she took me to the Five and Dime and bought my first face powder, stockings, and high heels. She was the one who taught me how to cook. She always scolded me saying, 'Mary, you gotta taste your food befo' ya serve it to anyone else.'

"Roy, she was the best friend I ever had! We didn't get to see each other much over the years, but when we got together, we had us a time. There was never a loss for words from either of us. Rosetta knew everything. I remember the trip we took on Greyhound to Atlanta in 1946, right before I had Micah."

She stood to mock her friend. "Rosetta strutted down the street like we were millionaires! Colored millionaires! She did not care how white people reacted. She glided by in those high-heeled shoes, sporting a hat tilted on her head just so, and probably a handmade leather pocketbook that she made herself. I marveled at the way people stared at her as we walked by. I think some folks thought she was famous or something, just a darker version of Lena Horne. Not only was she smart, she was beautiful, and not ashamed of it." Tears fell down her face. "And every minute we spent together, she led me to believe that I was beautiful too."

1963

"Micah, don't play in your daddy's study! I told you that time and time again. If I catch you in there again, I'm going to spank your hindparts, you hear me?" Mary picked up the newspaper on the couch and rolled it up threateningly.

"Ma, how old am I?" He was a shade darker than his father's caramel skin, six—foot-three, and built like a meticulously chiseled statue. His most appealing quality was a set of hypnotizing golden brown cat's eyes. "Dad knows I go into his study. There's nothing in there I want."

Mary swatted him with the newspaper. "You could be stealing his sermons to prepare your own," she teased.

"Absolutely not, Mother! I have no desire to do the 'church' thing and I told him so." Micah walked over to the black and white television set and adjusted the metal antenna everyone called rabbit ears.

"You never know. Your daddy comes from a long line of preachers. Pretty soon you could get the call." Mary walked into the kitchen.

"I doubt that very seriously. Church is just not for me. What fun did Dad have when he was young? What could he get into if he was on the street corners preaching all the time?"

"So you don't think church folk have fun? You think all we do is sit around and read the Bible?" Mary kneaded the roll dough on the counter.

"Something like that," he mumbled. "All I ever see Dad doing is waiting on folks hand and foot. Smiling in everyone's face, whether they like him or not. He did it in Georgia, and now that we live in hicktown U.S.A., he's still doing it."

"That's showing brotherly love, son." Mary shook her head.

"Yeah. What about an eye for an eye? There's something about the Old Testament that I love. The wars, the battles, the revenge. Those were real people that I could relate to."

"So you saying Jesus messed everything up once He came in the New Testament?" Mary, with a headful of premature gray streaks, turned and looked at her son.

Micah was slowly separating from the teachings his parents had long tried to impart into his young mind. A few years before, when he was fourteen, he'd asked to be excused from church services altogether. Of course, Roy would not have it and told him as long as he lived under his roof, he would attend church everyday and twice on Sundays.

He was close to seventeen, had finished school, and was preparing to leave for college away in New York. He said he had had enough of segregation and the Confederacy.

Roy tried to convince him to attend one of the excellent black colleges in Georgia or even a church school in North Carolina, but he refused. Said those states were Klan havens and that he did not know how much longer he could keep his mouth shut. The best thing he could do was leave and he vowed he would never return.

"What about your family?" Mary asked as she packed his belongings into a navy blue foot locker.

"What about them, Mother." He stared out of the window, hands shoved into his pockets.

"You're never coming back? This is your home! This is where your family lives, your kin folk live, and where we brought you up with everything most folks could never afford. You fail to realize that the Klan does not bother you because of your father. He is much respected in these parts. You think life is going to be so great up in the North? They hate black folks too, although they don't show it as much." She walked over to the solid oak chest of drawers and removed more of his clothes.

"Ma, I understand some folks will always hate us because we don't look like them. The problem with living here is that folks sometime tolerate us in the day and then dance in sheets on our land at night. Hell, I'm tired of ducking and dodging and being told I can't go certain places. I want to be a free black man, treated like a real man and not someone's slave." He took a pair of dress shoes out of the shoe box and put them in his nylon duffle bag.

He turned and faced his mother. "I remember I forgot to say 'Sir' to old man Gray t'other day. You would have thought I stole something out of his store! He went crazy! Told me to address him as Mister Gray or Sir every time he says something to me. 'Yes, sir, Mister Gray. No, sir, Mister Gray.' Ma, I got so tired of talking to him that day I just politely said 'yes' and walked away."

"Yeah, I remember that day," she said. "He saw your father getting gasoline at his filling station and he came over and told him you were being disrespectful. He said Daddy needed to talk to you about knowing your place." Mary looked at her son directly.

"Daddy never said a word to me. He came into my room, holding Mona's hand and talking about something all together different. Then he told me that Mister Gray was in the Klan as if I was supposed to be scared, shaking in my boots! I knew old man Gray was Klan the moment I laid eyes on him! Always calling us boy or referring to Dad as Roy Junior. My father is a man, not some boy he can call anything he pleases."

"Your daddy knows that! He doesn't care about the names white folks call him. He treats them with respect and eventually, one by one, the anointing that's on that man has those same white people calling your daddy Reverend or Mister Brown."

"That's the difference between us. I can't wait until they finally decide to respect me. I want respect now! Daddy tried to tell me to have patience. Said all things work for the good of the Lord and that black folks going to be free to go wherever we want *some day*. Well, Mama, I can't wait for that magical day to come. I'm leaving before I mess around and get hurt messing up with these folks."

"Micah, you can leave here, but never forget where you came from. You keep your Bible close. There is no place safe for a black man like you. God has anointed your steps and He has prepared your destiny. Now you be a good boy and honor your parents, ya hear me? You don't forget your home training now, trying to be grown. Just remember who you are out there representing." They both stood face to face as the sun poured down fresh rays of red and orange upon their faces.

"I can't walk in Daddy or Grandpa's shadow. I don't think I will ever get the call and if I do, I don't think I will take it."

"Raymond Micah Brown, if the Lord calls you, He has a time and a place for your ministry. Remember King David? Samuel anointed him King long before he ever took over Hebron or Israel. He spent more years in those fields with that sling shot!" She was laughing.

"Yes, developing." Micah leaned his head on his mother's shoulder. "Dad preaches more on David than anyone else the Bible. What is he? Stuck on Psalms?" he asked, laughing.

"Ha ha. No, he just likes reminding us that anything God promised us just takes time. It takes time for everything to manifest. Like David, you must wait too. God will let you know just when He is ready for you to walk into your destiny."

"And what if I say no? I mean, I don't do much alcohol. Really don't like it. Had some Moonshine once that made me sick as a dog! Don't like cigarette smoke, but every once in a while I likes me a good cigar." He waited for the expression of shock to appear on Mary's face.

"And don't forget the women!" She hugged her son and said a quick prayer.

EIGHT

1962

They were his greatest weakness. When Micah was a child, the little old ladies in the church said he was going to grow up and become a lady killer. His parents prayed otherwise. They did not want him to become another Ephraim Brown, a womanizer known for his uncanny ability to add women's names to his belt buckle.

By the time Micah turned seventeen, his great uncle had been married five times. With every visit came a new blushing bride. It got to the point that Roy refused to say anything to the woman until he was sure he had met her before or, until Ephraim properly introduced her.

Micah had a spirit all his own and, other than his looks, nothing remotely resembled his father, especially when it came to the opposite sex. Roy was attracted to smart, sassy, educated, and strong-minded women. Micah said that type of woman was bossy. He said he preferred a dumb woman. Someone to wash his clothes, cook, have his children, and not question anything he told her.

Then he had his first scare. In the middle of the night, Roy and Mary heard banging on the front door. Roy jumped up, put his robe on, and went out into the living room to answer the door. As he neared the foyer, he heard the sound of voices on the other side of the door.

He turned the porch light on and slowly opened the door. Three women stood on the front porch peering into his face.

"Are ya gonna marry my chile!" an older woman with a light colored bandana wrapped around her head, hollered into his face.

"That ain't him!" said a younger woman, no more than five-feet tall with dyed blonde hair.

"Who you be? You his daddy? Well, your chile done knocked this chile up." The older woman reached for the handle on the door.

Roy turned the latch, opened the door and invited the angry crowd inside. He then excused himself so that he could go and awaken Mary from her restful sleep. The women did not lower their voices.

"You didn't tell me he was a preacha! That boy gon' have to marry you, sho' 'nough. His daddy gon' see to it. Ah be damned. Sally done gon' and got knocked up by a PK," one of the women said.

"I don't know if he da daddy. I told yah. I ain't sho'." Sally held her hands over her fully extended stomach. She was wearing a pale green pajama top, matching shorts, and plush green slippers. "Dat's why I ain't wanna come over heah." The girl was now crying.

"Hell. Ah ain't care wut ya say. Somebody knocked ya up, and somebody gon' marry ya. Dat's all dere iz to it! Dese city folks not gon' come around heah wid dere chirren jumping from house ta house! Now he betta be a good Christian and take ya before the alta of the Lawd to be his wife."

"Ah don't wont 'im if he don't wont me! Ain't gon' have no shotgun weddin'," Sally cried.

"Ya gotta ha' somethin'." The last woman to speak, a medium sized, dark brown skinned woman spoke as Roy and Mary came into the room.

"Morning, ladies. I understand there is an issue with this young lady." Mary tried to start the conversation, but was immediately interrupted by Sally's mother.

"Dere ain't no issue! Your boy knocked dis heah chile up months ago and run off!" she yelled.

"You must forgive us, sisters. This comes as a total surprise. Micah is not here, but we will get to the bottom of this. I give you my word," Roy jumped in.

"Well, honey, I want to hear a little more. I have not met this young lady before. So when were you seeing our son?" Mary began questioning Sally. Roy stood next to her. He knew it would be difficult to rein his wife back in once she started her interrogations.

"Well, first of all, please forgive us. My name is Pastor Brown and this is my wife, First Lady Mary Brown. We pastor at the Chapel in the Woods. Have y'all been to any of our services before? We're open every day of the week." Nervously, he rambled on. "I don't recall seeing you there. I want y'all to know that we are very concerned about this situation and will do what is right."

"What is right is ya' boy marryin' dis heah gal before she drop dis barrel," the dark-skinned woman added. She wore a polyester turbin that covered her hair but could not hide the strawberry birthmark that splattered her left eye and the entire left side of her face and neck.

"Well, we are going to make sure everything is taken care of." Mary turned and looked directly at Sally. "I'm sorry, sweetie, what is your name? When did you tell my son of your condition?"

"Sally Hamilton, ma'am." She was fair-skinned with freckles laced across her nose and cheeks. "'Bout three or fo' months now. He ain't said much to me. I thought y'all knowed it."

"No. We are so sorry about what you must be going through. How much further do you have?" Mary had a very suspicious look on her face.

"'Bout two months. Hope I makes it."

"See, we needs to plan us a quick wedding," her mother interjected.

"Well, we need to make sure we are doing what is right. My husband and I don't believe in fornication. I guess that's too late to discuss now." Mary let out a nervous laugh. "I don't want us rushing to do something until we all have had the time to talk to these young people together."

"Ya boy had all dis time to tell ya he wuz gonna be a daddy. He ducking and dodging around town. Not fair. Not fair at all." One of the older women walked over to Mary and Roy as they stood near the fireplace.

"You must be Sally's mother?" Roy finally said.

"Yeah, I is. Look, we can git to know y'all later. I'm Bertha and dis heah my sistah, Geraldine. She come wid us fo' support."

"We understand. Well, Micah is away at prep school. He'll be back this Saturday. I'll arrange for us to meet on Sunday. I give you my word," Roy said.

Bertha looked Roy straight in the face. "Look, I'm sorry. The only word I want from y'all iz dese chirren gitting married befo' dis bastard chile land on Earth!"

1954

Roy Brown had become the South's beloved son. Many said he was definitely a man after God's own heart. He had a special gift and whatever he asked of the people, they eagerly gave. It was that way in Savannah and surprisingly, it was the same in Jasper County. The young pastor could stir up a crowd with a whisper; he was just that anointed.

The Chapel in the Woods became a household name as soon as they opened the doors. When blueprints were being done for the new building, Roy extended the square footage so that more than five hundred folk could fit inside the main sanctuary. It was the largest edifice around, and the size alone made it a structure everyone wanted to see.

As soon as word got out that Roy's church would not be a part of the customary church rotation, several pastors came to discuss the impact of his decision on their congregations. Roy countered that if he was placed in the rotation, he would only preach five times a year on fifth Sunday. His message, he explained, was far too important for occasional times during the year.

The other pastors agreed to give Roy's suggestion a try, for they reasoned he was young and would fall flat on his face. Who was he to try to change custom? It was hard enough to get townsfolk to attend church on a regular basis. Besides, many thought Roy's church would never garner a crowd because it was at least two miles from the other churches.

On the first Sunday the church opened its doors, two-hundred people were in attendance. Their critics claimed most of those visitors were from Roy's former church in Savannah. They said the following Sunday would prove otherwise. Until it came.

On the second Sunday, one-hundred and twenty-five people showed up; sixty of whom seldom attended church: the youth. Again, his critics claimed the numbers were attributed to the newness of the church and the interest of folks trying to see the insides of the building. "Curiosity is all 'tis," they mocked.

So they waited. For two years, Chapel in the Woods averaged one-hundred and fifty names on its church roster. The youth department, a first of its kind, had fifty people. It was the largest congregation of young people seen in the Low Country and the numbers grew rapidly in the years to come.

In addition to meeting with their neighbors every Wednesday, Roy sat outside of the Hawk's on Highway 17 and held a small impromptu service. It became so popular, truck drivers from all over the country dropped in and before long, Hawk's was jam packed with customers who came to hear Pastor Roy.

As the membership grew, he delegated more responsibilities to Mary and then suggested she enroll in Seminary School. She graduated at the top of her class, but when she returned to full time ministry, Mary insisted on handling the same duties she'd handled before going to college, never saying one word about having a piece of paper that read she now had a license to preach God's Word.

1961

"How much do you know about this Frank Wilcox?" Mary asked Roy a few weeks before the anniversary services.

"As much as I need to know," Roy smirked, with thin gray strands peppering his hairline.

"Is that your way of being smart, Raymond?" Mary walked over to the glider and sat down.

"You know me too well, Mer." He laughed. "That's my way of backing out of the conversation you're trying to have. I know it's wrong. Forgive me."

"There is no need to be forgiven." She reached out to grab his large hands. "There is something about that man that tells me he has a sinister side."

"All of us do." Roy sat down beside her. "What are you getting at?"

"I don't really know, darling. That's why I am asking. People look scared when Frank comes around. You notice how no one on your staff ever questions what he says?"

"Mer, I think every church needs a Frank." Roy looked down at the leather slippers he was wearing, the ones Frank had given him for Christmas, and laughed.

"Sometimes I think his spirit is the opposite of mine, and that's what I was looking for when I hired him to handle the church's affairs." He leaned on her shoulder.

"When we decided to hold tent services, we were out of our league. Only people doing them was Billy Graham and Oral Roberts, the white preachers I met on my travels. When I asked my assistants about it, they baulked. Said they wanted to have something in the back of the church, put chairs out and let people come from all around. I wanted something more structured, more organized. That's when I met Frank."

"Who are his people?" Mary continued, stroking Roy's hand.

"I don't really know much about them. Frank asked me to preach his sister's funeral. I don't know his parents. I got a call from Chaney's funeral home, seems the family did not want the homegoing services in a church for some reason," he explained.

"They're not believers?" Mary looked Roy straight in the eyes. "Is he?"

"Honestly, I never asked. He was my contact and I liked the way he set everything up for the funeral. Worked like he was used to organizing things. Then I saw him a few months later and he was downtown talking to the sheriff. From what I heard, the sheriff was taking directions from him. That was enough to impress me."

"I noticed how Old Man Gray reacts when Frank is in the store. Now he will rush customers and watch everyone that comes in the front door, but you let Frank step in that store. Oh, my God, Herber Gray runs around getting whatever Frank asks for, as if he's scared to death." she laughed.

"I heard he got some dirt on the Klan! He never told me though. Seems one day he walked into Herbert Gray's store and delivered a package. Gray was scared to open it. When he did, I heard it was a white robe with all the Klan insignia on it and everything. Question was, where did Frank get that robe?" Roy rubbed his forehead.

"What?" Mary, startled, looked up into Roy's eyes.

"Yeah, come to find out, the robe belonged to some high ranking Klan member. Now, rumor has it Klan will die before they give up their robes!" Roy said.

"Okay. That's enough! Now you're scaring me, Raymond. Do you think Frank has ever killed anyone?" She sat up, alarmed.

"Naw. Mer, don't over analyze this, baby! I just can't see him killing another soul."

"But you don't even know if he is a believer."

"If he wasn't, he has been around me enough to hear the Word over and over again. Besides, he has been over here and around our children enough for me to believe that he believes in God. Maybe he doesn't serve Him like us, but that's his right, Mer."

"Yeah, folk have a right to serve the Lord how they choose. It's just something else about that man. He's loyal to you, I'll give him that. Every time you go out of town and leave me in charge, he shows up like clockwork. He comes around and everybody gets to moving and preparing things. He even goes to pick folks up for church when they want to come but are afraid they will be mistreated for attending a church with a woman preaching the Word." Mary stood up.

"Mer, do you think I would leave you with someone I did not trust? Come on, baby. You know me better than that." Roy stood up too and kissed his wife softly on the lips.

"It's not you I am worried about. I mean, I like Frank, don't get me wrong. He's smart, run a business just like Rosetta did, only larger. He's a powerful man and I guess I should feel blessed that we found favor with him." She turned toward the cornfields in front of their house. "Sometimes I just don't know."

NINE

1964

Mary could see everything that transpired, but could not hear a sound. Not anything being said to her or to the others that sat next to her. Total silence. It was as if she were dreaming or watching a silent movie.

Dressed in all white, a color that represented another type of celebration, Mary looked over at Micah and Ramona who were seated on the opposite end of the same row. "With long life shall I satisfy Him and show Him my salvation," she whispered.

In front of her were some of the most distinguished looking men and women she had ever seen. She recognized their faces, but could not remember their names as she sat staring, watching their lips move with no sounds emanating from them. Yes, it was probably just a dream. She would awaken in a few minutes and it would all be over.

In an instant, she knew exactly what was going on. Frank Wilcox, the man who handled occasions like this on behalf of her husband, stood up and motioned to the others. Then he walked over to Mary and held out his arm for her to take hold and lift herself up from the pew. She felt weak all over. When she did not move, he signaled to Micah, who came over from the other side with Ramona tightly holding his hand. They looked down at her.

All of a sudden, Mary heard the piano playing *Precious Memories* softly pealing throughout the large auditorium. She recognized the bleachers behind her. She was sitting in the Ridgeland School for coloreds. She heard the cries and sniffles of onlookers as the fans whirred loudly in the windows and from the ceilings.

It was not a dream.

Mary tried to stand, but she fell backward onto the pew. Frank immediately grabbed her and Micah sat down next to her, fanning her face. She struggled to get up but there was no life in her limbs to make a move. She had to be dreaming. *God, please let this be a dream.*

She opened her eyes and looked around. She saw the casket in front of her, and then she saw him. He was wearing his favorite tan suit. There was a silk paisley print handkerchief in his left front pocket. She spotted the tan ascot drapped around his neck. From where she sat, Mary could not see his beautiful hands, wedding band, or college class ring, but she knew them by heart.

"I got you, Mom," Micah, wearing a nice gray suit and purple tie, whispered into her ear.

Mary turned and looked at him. He looked just like his father. She tried to stand to her feet. *Please, God, let me stand on my own two feet.*

Ramona, wearing a white satin dress with a purple sash, walked over to the casket ahead of them. She reached her tiny hands down into the side of it and placed something next to her father's body. She leaned toward him and spoke softly.

Mary stood to her feet. She could see him clearly now. All of him stretched out in the white casket with the gold trim. There lay her king. There lay her best friend. He looked as if he were smiling. *Please, God, tell me he is with you.*

Micah, dry faced, leaned over into the casket and kissed his father on his forehead. Then he stepped back. Mary walked closer, step by slow step, and stood looking down into the casket. Then she saw the photograph of the four of them; Ramona must have placed it next to his arm, she thought. Tears filled her eyes. No, this was not a dream.

She thought they would get to see forever, but surely, as Mary Brown stood in front of her husband's remains, she knew that forever, at least for them, had somehow faded away.

Summer 1964

Weeks went by and Mary Brown skipped church services altogether. Alone in the house with Ramona after Micah returned to New York, she felt like she would lose her mind. She picked up the telephone.

"Hi. Can you do me a favor?" She spoke softly into the receiver. For the first time in years, she had not combed her long coarse hair. "Go out to see Miss Ruth. See if she's having camp this year now that Roy is gone. If so, ask her can Ramona come a few weeks early and stay the summer." She listened for a reply, then continued.

"Yes, I mean the entire summer, I think. Mona goes to school this fall. She will need to come home then." She hung up the telephone.

The next day, Mary packed most of Ramona's summer belongings. She would miss her. Although the doctors had not changed their prognosis regarding her frail condition, physically Ramona appeared to be doing remarkably well.

"Are you going to be okay?" The subject of her telephone conversation stood in the doorway. She was close to three feet tall, fair skin with Mary's round face. Her long pigtails shined naturally in the sun.

Mary turned to face her. "Miss Mona, I am going to try," she said.

"You were the love of his life." The child smiled.

"And, you know this because?" Mary teased.

"He told me everyday. Jesus was his first love, we were his second, and all of God's people were his third." She laughed.

"Yes. He told you that too. Well, young lady, one thing is for sure, you are the apple of his eye." Mary sat down on the bed.

"I miss him so much! I'll be glad to see him again in Heaven. I bet he will have the same smile and that same anointing." Ramona swung from the bed posts.

"What do you know about an anointing, Mona?" Mary asked.

"I know a whole lot. I know it comes from God and I know it has the power to change the world! Daddy believed it and he lived to prove it." She walked over and sat next to Mary.

"Mama, do you believe there is a right time to die? Granddad said it was daddy's time. I wonder did daddy know that? Do you think he's mad with God for taking him from us?" She grabbed her mother's hand.

"No, baby. I doubt he's mad. Happy. Yes, I think he's happy. Death is a good thing if you're prepared to go. It's the return to the Father that sent you here. When he calls you home, that means you have finished the assignment he sent you here to do. Daddy truly did the work God called him to do. He brought thousands to Christ, fed the hungry, took care of the sick, and gave to the needy. Yes, I miss him dearly, but I think he finished his course on this here Earth." Mary started to hum.

"I love it when you hum like that, Mama."

"Humming brings me peace. I hum to calm my nerves or to hear from God when my mind won't get settled. Daddy used to hum to. You remember?" She looked at Ramona.

"Yeah. I remember catching him humming when I went into the study. He would sit at his desk and fake sleep!" Tears formed in the corners of her eyes. "Daddy loved to play games."

"Yes. He was quite the jokester. That was what made him beautiful. He knew how to laugh and make everyone else laugh. He just wanted everyone to feel loved."

"Anybody tell you they love you today?" Ramona mocked her father.

"Someone tells me every day," Mary recited.

"And, might I ask who?" Ramona laughed uncontrollably as they replayed the past.

They sat in her room playing and reminiscing about Prentiss Raymond Brown, Junior most of that day. Maybe Ramona would leave tomorrow. Today she was the solace, the release that Mary Brown needed.

Ramona stayed home until camp started in July. Before she left for Ruth's, she spent almost every waking hour with her mother. They adored each other and loved playing games, baking cookies, preparing fresh lemonade, and taking long walks together. Even at the tender age of five, Ramona Rose Brown knew that her mother needed time to heal for soon she would have to return to the ministry.

One day while Mary was relaxing in the bathtub, she packed her bags and called the church.

"She's ready for me to go." She hung up the telephone.

1966

Two years later, Mary finally got the call she never wanted to receive. Come quick. There was nothing left to be done.

The church had fasted together every month since Ramona's health took a turn for the worst. For a while, it seemed she would recover. She was almost seven years old and that's all she could talk about.

Seven. Mary repeated the number over and over again in her head. It represented completion and that made her wrestle with the thought of losing her husband and her daughter every night. During the daytime, like the prayer warrior she had become over the years, Mary never let on to anyone what the Lord had revealed to her: Ramona's time was soon approaching.

Ramona wanted a big birthday celebration that would last a full day. Mary wondered how her baby could make it through the day with all the other children and adults around. She suspected the excitement alone would tire her out physically and mentally. She picked up the telephone and dialed Ruth's number.

James and Ruth Harrison had faithfully visited Ramona since she was released from the hospital. Mary knew how much her visits meant to Ramona. She also understood what losing Ramona must have been doing to Ruth.

"Won't be long now." Mary stood in the kitchen window looking out into the back yard.

"No. Just don't make sense sometimes, huh? That chile is an angel. God sent her to us. You and Pastor Roy are so blessed." Ruth walked over and sat down at the kitchen table.

"Roy always said we had to take the rain with the sunshine." She turned to face Ruth. "I guess it's time to get wet."

"Oh Lord! I want to be selfish. I want to scream and ask God to keep her here longer. I want to see her grow up into a beautiful young lady and have children of her own. I want her here forever." Ruth started crying.

"You are her second mother, you know that right?" Mary put her hand on Ruth's shoulder. "God allowed you to do the things I could not do for her. You are the reason why that child has so much spunk." Mary smiled.

"But you and Pastor Roy are the reason she has so much Word inside of her! That child in there is not afraid of dying. She already knows. All she thinks about is her daddy." She grabbed a napkin from the holder on the table. "What kind of thinking is that for a six-year-old? I'm twenty-four and I can't comprehend a child dying. How can she?"

"I guess God prepared her for it. Then he tried to prepare me, but it didn't work. I want my baby to live!" Mary sobbed uncontrollably.

February 13, 1966

Almost seven years to the day she gave birth to an angel, Mary walked into Ramona's bedroom. The child had removed all of her vibrant crayon sketches from the wall. Her favorite toys were neatly placed in a cardboard box on the floor next to the dresser. Her jewelry box had a note attached to it and her clothes were neatly folded in the wardrobe closet.

Mary lay down beside her frail child and tried to remain calm. She could hear her faint breathing and knew that Ramona was resting in preparation for her journey home.

"Mama, don't be scared. Don't be sad. I never came to stay. I came to give you joy and to let you know that God really loves you. I came so that you would know that Grandma Rose never left your side. She was with you all along and when you could no longer see her, I came to be that reminder." Her breathing was becoming more labored.

"Don't talk, baby. Mama's here. I know God sent you and Daddy to me. I just don't know what to do without you two. Why can't I trade with you? You deserve a lifetime." She wept softly.

"I had a lifetime. Life was good to me. I never had an argument with anyone. I tried not to lie. Never stole and I did what you and Daddy told me to. I hope I was a good child."

"Mona, you are the best child any parent could ask for." Mary held her frail body closer.

"Hum to me, Mommy. Sing me your favorite spirituals like you and Daddy used to do when I was a baby."

Mary tried to hum the tune of the old hymn *Swing low, sweet chariot,* but it was difficult.

The she opened her mouth and sang:

Swing low
Sweet chariot,
coming for to carry me home,
Swing low, sweet chariot, coming for to carry me home.

She held her daughter closer. She prayed something miraculous would happen that would send life back into Ramona's body, but as the hours passed, the miracle never came.

As she listened for breathing sounds, Mary stopped humming. She was still breathing. On the third song, Roy's favorite, *Blessed Assurance,* she had barely started the first stanza when everything fell silent. The moon shone golden yellow into the window, and the night passed ever so slowly into morning.

TEN

1968

"Let the church say a-men!"

"I want you to know that if you don't have to struggle with it, there's no faith in it." Mary walked closer to the parishioners.

"Us preachers love to preach from up top away from the people, but I want to walk down and look into your faces to remind you that we are on one level in God's eyes. He does not rank us according to the selfmade titles man places on us. We are all his children! I struggle with the same things you struggle with. I have joy, sorrow, and pain. In fact, I used to think they came in circles: Once one leaves, another is sure to follow." She looked around the room smiling.

"But I can assure you that trouble don't last always, no sir! Weeping may endure for a night, but joy is coming in the morning, hallelujah!" She returned to the pulpit and wiped her brow.

There had been plenty of sunshine in Mary's life. God had been faithful to his word. She was a living witness. Her years in Georgia, like before, had been sweet. Folks welcomed her and her desire to preach God's word with open arms. What started as a small assignment to pray and teach Sunday school, evolved into requests to hear none other than Pastor Mary Brown deliver the Word of God.

She was standing in the back of the vestibule shaking hands when she saw him. He seemed taller. His eyes were wide and his grin was classic. Her heart skipped a beat.

"All right, Pastor Brown. I sho' enjoyed that Word. You got preaching in your bones!" He walked over to her laughing.

Several women stood watching as the debonair young man, dressed in an all black three piece suit with a black and white tie, approached Mary. As he neared, the women began to whisper.

Mary shook the last person's hand and hugged her son. He had visited before but had never come to hear her speak. She tried to fight the tears.

"Sometimes I think Roy's living inside of me preaching all this good Word," she held him and whispered.

"Naw. Mama, you got it honest! This is your gift. Yeah, my daddy could preach. He could bring down a house, but you...woman, you got something special." He kissed her on the cheek.

"Boy, what are you doing here?"

"Checking in on you, what else?" He had a coy look in his eyes that made her suspicious.

"Yeah, I bet. You never checked on me in the pulpit before."

"Well, that's because I never felt I had to. Daddy is with you. But I needed to hear a word from the Lord and who else to fill my soul than my gorgeous mother." Micah noticed the ever-nosy church women standing near by.

"Stop it, I say!" Mary struck him with the paper fan she was holding. "Must you do everything for the women?"

"I just wanted them to know that they can't compete with you on your worst days. Those women are trouble. I knew that before I laid eyes on them."

Mary laughed. "Maybe that's the anointing warning ya."

"Don't start. I think God took all the anointing he was giving to me and gave it to someone else; someone who was serious about using it." They walked back into the church hand in hand.

"You never know, Micah Raymond Brown, you still got some living to do. I just believe your time will come." Then she turned around and looked outside. "If you stay clear of the women!"

"Yeah, right. Women make the world go round." He grabbed her arm. "So, can I have the pleasure of your company this fine afternoon?"

"Of course. That's if you don't mind sharing me?"

Micah had a strange look on his face. "Don't tell me you still got ministry work to do. Don't turn into Dad. Take the rest of the day off after you preach," he lectured.

"Oh, honey, I plan to take more than a day. We just finished revival and I am worn out." She swung around. "Did you get my letters?"

"Guilty. I got them. Couldn't get off from work. That's why I showed up today. They saved the best for last."

"Well, I have a prior engagement." She watched him carefully.

"And I thought I was invited everywhere you went."

"You are. I just wanted to tell you that I agreed to have lunch with a gentleman caller this afternoon. I'm sure he won't mind if you tag along. Anyway, if he does, I won't go!" She took off her robe and hung it in the maple wardrobe in the corner of her office.

"And what do you want to tell me about this mysterious gentleman caller, as you say?" Micah sat on the elegant Duncan Fife sofa.

"Well, there's not much to tell. He's a faithful member of another church I attend on occasion. He's been coming around here off and on for about a year. He's nice and everything. Even drove me to a few meetings across town. We aren't dating seriously, in my opinion, but he has asked me to consider his hand in marriage."

"What? Already!" Micah sat up and surveyed the pictures of he, Ramona, and Pastor Roy that were neatly placed throughout the small office.

"Well, as I said, it's been a year. I guess he considered it courting me all along. He knew your daddy. Said they met a time or two when we lived here before."

"Who are his people?" Michah asked, quickly returning to his native Southern roots, then reached up and adjusted his tie. His hands, caramel colored, were massive just like his father's.

"I have not met them. He's from North Carolina, don't have many kinfolks here 'bout. He did say he had an aunt in Goosecreek, up near Charleston."

"Ma, I don't know about this. " Micah stood up, "A man with no past is hiding the past that he has."

"Micah, you been around your grandfather too long. I don't think he's hiding anything."

"Oh, yeah? How old is he?"

"Around thirty-five?"

"He got any chirren?"

"Children? Micah, who are you hanging with that has you speaking like that?" She picked up a cinnamon-colored blazer that was draped over a chair behind the desk.

"Doesn't matter, Mother. Does the man have any *children*?" He held the door for her as they exited the office.

"I don't think so."

"Has he ever been married?" He walked with his hands tucked away in his pockets. He had even inherited his father's famous swagger.

"Once, but he said they did not have any children. They tried, but she was barren, I think."

"What happened to her? Is that why they split up?" Micah stared ahead.

"Micah, I don't know. He said he's been divorced for ten years. I really was not interested in marrying this man. I still miss your father! I spoke to my spiritual covering and he suggested that I give marriage some thought. I don't know why. I am perfectly happy living alone. Without you and Ramona around, I am free to do so much in my life, but I must admit, I've been married my whole life and I really enjoyed it."

"That depends on who you're married to, Ma."

"You're right. I don't know about him yet. I'm just telling you because, I don't know why but, I value your opinion." They stood outside of the church in the courtyard that surrounded the building.

"You spoke to Uncle Bud about this? Frank Wilcox?"

"Micah, I'm a grown woman!" Mary walked across the street. She spotted her gentleman caller sitting inside the restaurant waiting for her.

1963

"Look at me when I'm talking ta ya, boy!" His grip tightened. "Another word outta you and I'm gon' slit your throat!"

The young lad, weighing less than one-hundred and twenty-five pounds, gawked at the enormous size of his attacker. His feet dangled in the air. He struggled to catch his breath.

"Yuh say one word, and dat's gon' be yo' arse! Killing come easy fo' me. You betta ask somebody. Yo' friend lying in his own blood. He ain't comin' back. That's gon' be yo' sorry tail you keep it up."

Tears fell down the young man's face. He tried to look over to where his friend lay beneath the tree. Through the sweat that saturated his face and stung his eyes, all he could see was the large amount of blood splattered around his friend's lifeless body.

"I'm a let ya live, boy. But you gonna 'memba me." Just then his assailant took out a switchblade with a mother of pearl handle and stuck it in the young man's upper thigh.

He yelled in agony.

1972

"I thank ya betta lay low," the police officer warned him. "I can't keep fending them offa ya. Pretty soon the sheriff coming fo' ya and he gon' lock ya up. Ya' hear me?" The officer, a brunette, pale-faced, medium tall man, looked directly at the man in front of him.

"Ya thank I's scurred?" His laugh was hearty and as vicious as a lion's roar.

"Look a heah. I'm tryin' to be yo' friend. Just letting ya know that thangs are gittin' pretty hot around heah. Yo' name keeps popping up. Strange thangs happening. Seems like old times wid yo' daddy. Sheriff said he not gon' let y'all reign wild like ya' did befo', going on killing sprees."

"Dat's not up to him. Anyone cross my family gonna sho' nuf die. Wut y'all got ta understand, we are the law! Ain't nobody fool enough to come afta us. Precedence, my boy, precedence." He winked a cold black eye, rolled the window up, took out a pair of black rimmed shades, put them on, and sped off down the highway.

The officer stood there shaking in his boots. Even in Klan territory, there were negros that no one bothered. Some were just too smart, while others possessed more hatred within them than the Devil himself. There was one undisputed fact: The man driving away in that 1970 Silver Chrysler gave even Satan a run for his money.

1968

Micah held the restaurant door open as Mary walked in. He watched her carefully until he was sure which table she was headed toward. Then he saw her suitor. Immediately, he recognized the man's face. Micah looked down at the floor.

"This is my son, Micah." Mary smiled as the man rose from the table.

"Well, well. We meet again?" Edgar Carter reached out to shake Micah's hand.

"You look familiar too!" Micah forced a smile. "I don't recall from where though. It's been so long."

"The pool hall in Savannah. I even saw you in Atlanta once or twice. Always had a pretty long-tall-Sally on your arms as I recall." He held the chair out so that Mary could sit down.

"You two know each other?" Mary was quite surprised. Edgar, dressed in a navy blue double breasted suit, white cotton shirt, and shiny navy leather floor shiners, did not seem like a person that hung out in pool halls.

"Yeah. I met him a time or two in my wilder days. That was before I gave my life to Christ and started living right." Edgar motioned to the waitress.

"So you don't remember Mr. Carter, Micah?"

"Not really."

"It's been a while." Edgar turned his focus to Micah. "You look like life's been real good to you, son."

"Better than most, I guess." Micah took the cotton napkin off of the table and placed it on his lap.

Edgar looked at Mary. "You look too young to have a son this old."

"So now I'm old?" Micah looked at his mother.

"You're right. But, you are a full grown man, I can see that." He raised his glass of iced tea toward both mother and son.

Micah stayed in town much longer than he had anticipated. After meeting his mother's suitor, he was left with reservations about leaving her alone. For the next week he purposely accompanied Mary almost everywhere she went, especially if she planned to meet with Edgar Carter.

He could not put his finger on where they met previously, but something told him it had not been a good experience. He thought of calling Frank Wilcox, but changed his mind. He would have patience and simply wait. A leopard, his grandfather always taught him, never changed his spots.

1969

Mary hung the wedding gown in the wardrobe and looked in the mirror at herself. She did not look anywhere near the age of forty-one. With silky smooth skin, bright white teeth, and an hour glass figure, no one believed she was over thirty. Her mind, on the other hand, seemed much older, for life had dealt tremendous blows that altered everything she believed, challenging her morals and her faith.

Roy had been dead for five year. Yet, she knew deep down inside that much of her continued existence began and ended with the love he had shown her. His gentleness and strong support epitomized her very nature and confirmed that love was more powerful than death. He remained her everything and when it came to true love, Prentiss Raymond Brown, Jr., was all she had ever known.

Her decision to marry Edgar Roland Carter was not an easy one. In fact, it was based on feelings of loneliness that pained her heart during the night ever since Ramona's passing. Her days were filled with ministry work so there were fewer moments in which she realized there would be no one at home waiting for her. No one cooking a meal for her or running bath water awaiting her return. No one, but the sounds of the birds that chirped nonstop on her back porch every evening.

One would not describe Edgar as extremely handsome. In fact, there was nothing attractive that stood out to Mary when they first met. Unlike Roy's enormously smooth hands, Edgar's hands were rough and calloused like someone who had worked in the coal mines. The color of his skin was a ruddy tone and when the sun hit his forehead, it was obvious that his once full hairline had tinges of clay-like reddish brown color sprinkled through it.

He made her feel safe. At six-feet four-inches tall, he weighed close to three-hundred pounds, yet he carried his weight on the tips of his toes as if he were as light as a feather.

There was something about the way he presented himself that made Mary take notice. Something about what he proclaimed as his favorite scripture that made her toy with the idea of a future together. She noticed those types of things more than his physical attributes.

He was stacking picnic chairs outside in the park when they were first introduced.

"Pastor Mary. This heah's a new member that outshines us all. Please allow me to introduce ya to Mr. Edgar Carter. He was a deacon up nawth before coming heah to Savannah. Seems he originally from this area and knew your husband." Pastor Dawson stood smiling.

"Is that so?" Mary, dressed in overalls and a white and red tee shirt with matching bandana, made minimal eye contact with the stranger.

"Yes, ma'am. That's so." He was wearing loosely fitted, ripped faded denims, with a tee shirt that covered his massive chest.

"Well, Mr. Carter. Welcome home, I should say. I know First Baptist is excited about having another hard worker join their forces. But..." She laughed. "If you ever need another church home, Providence would love to have you!" Mary winked at Pastor Dawson.

"Watch her, Edgar. She's quite competitive." Then he smiled at Mary. "Few men can keep up with the likes of Mary Brown. Many have tried, but she wore them out every time." He laughed.

"Well, that means I'm going to have to step up my game." Edgar walked toward the front of the truck. "Very nice to meet you, Pastor Brown." He wiped his hands and then extended one to her.

Edgar sat in the pickup truck watching Mary and Pastor Dawson giggle and kid around with each other. Mary could see out of the corner of her eye that the truck had not moved. She paid it little attention.

Unbeknownst to her, Edgar Carter was paying more attention to them than he let on. Three weeks later, he showed up at the Bible study class Mary taught on Thursday nights.

"Don't tell Rev you saw me." He stood, dressed in a tan striped shirt and brown slacks.

"You aren't considering leaving, are you?" Mary put her belongings in the nylon bag she had underneath the table. "Don't tell me you're checking out the competition." She smiled at him.

"I hear there is no competition if you're the challenger." He walked over to her. "I was bored. Our Bible study is on Wednesday nights. Thursdays the church is full with choir rehearsal and since I can't sing a lick that leaves me out. I was glad to know that this church's weekly events were just the opposite."

"You study the Word like that?"

"Well, I'm just trying to live my life like the Apostle Paul, who declared, 'That I might know him.' If I can just stay close to God, I know he'll give me a new life. That's all I really want is to know…the Lord is pleased with my devotion to the kingdom."

"You are really on fire for the Lord. You have to be a new believer."

"Is it that obvious?" He sat down on the pew. "Pastor Brown, you are quite perceptive, I must say."

"Well, I love it. The neophytes always immerse themselves into study and the Lord's work. My prayer is that the fire you now feel remains with you for a lifetime. It's going to get rough, but you hang in there." Mary stood looking down at him.

"I was sorry to hear about your husband. Talk about a preaching machine! I used to listen to him preach back in the day. I did not want to have anything to do with the gospel back then. Your husband preached wherever he went. I used to avoid him on the street and then he came into the barber shop preaching the good news! Once I had a taste of his message, I could not get away. About a year later, my wife and I moved to Atlanta. Then one day I found out y'all moved away."

"Well, thank you, Mr. Carter. Yes, everyone knew my husband. He was a remarkable man. He could get on your nerves too the way he preached nonstop. He vowed he would never be guilty of allowing anyone to go to Hell under his watch. That man was determined, I tell you." Mary had not mentioned Roy's name publicly in a long time. Feelings of loneliness and longing rushed through her body.

"Well, I hear you two were quite the pair. What became of y'all?" He got up from the pew and followed Mary toward the door.

"We started our own church near Ridgeland, South Carolina. Do you know where that is?"

"Yeah, been through Ridgeland a time or two on my way to Goose Creek. Quiet area, I say. How you like it?" He reached out to take her bag while Mary locked the side door.

"Too slow for me at times, but nice enough. We raised our son there." She purposely did not mention Ramona.

"I guess it was hard to stay after your husband passed on." They walked toward the metal fence and stood on the sidewalk.

"Very. I tried to stay but customs in the Low Country drove me out."

"Do you mind me inquiring as to what kind of customs you mean?" He pulled the gate shut and stood looking at Mary.

"Well, Mr. Carter, the kind that say a woman can't preach the gospel." Mary reached into her purse for her car keys.

"That's ridiculous, you know. Catholics worship Mary, the mother of Jesus. She's a woman. I also hear there were women pastors in the Bible that traveled with Paul." They headed toward Mary's car.

"That is correct. My, you know a lot already. I'm impressed." Mary stopped in front of her car. "Well, I have to get home. Thank you for waiting for me and thanks for walking me to my car."

"No need to thank me, Pastor Mary. I consider service to the Lord as my reasonable service." He reached over her and held the car door open while she sat down inside.

"Have a great night, Mr. Carter." She turned the key in the ignition.

"Thank you. You too. I guess if God is willing, I'll see you next Thursday." He smiled at her, turned, and walked off down the street.

ELEVEN

1965

Micah brought the car to a rolling stop. His girlfriend, Norma, vuluptuous and the color of burnt toast and coffee, sat next to him. He reached over and held her hand.

"Micah. Why all the preacher's kids just like you?" Her eyes followed his hand as it moved higher on her thigh.

"And, what am I like?" He quickly glanced over in her direction.

"You know what I mean. What kind of man of God expects a woman to lay down with him befo' he marry her?"

"A careful one." He winked at her. "I'm not my father. We have different beliefs and values. Don't get me wrong, I believe in God, for real. But I see nothing wrong with having sex in a serious relationship. You said it yourself, we're both too young to settle down and get married." He looked ahead at the road and took his foot off the brake pedal.

"Micah!" Norma screamed at the top of her lungs.

A woman came out of nowhere and slammed into the hood of his car. Trying to avoid hitting her head on, Micah swerved to minimize the impact. She collapsed in the street.

"Oh, my God! What is going on?" He reached down and pulled the parking brake.

"Baby, are you all right?" He looked at his girlfriend.

"She came out of nowhere! Is she dead?" Norma, trembling, was peering over the dashboard.

"I don't know. She walked right into the car." Micah heard the woman moaning. He slowly opened the door. Norma exited the vehicle from the other side.

"Are you okay?" He kneeled beside the woman whose head lay against his front tire.

She looked like a child, petite, less than one-hundred pounds. Despite the frigid winter weather, she was not wearing an overcoat. Bare armed, her magenta knee-length dress had been ripped in the front, exposing a white brassiere. There were large bruises alongside her face and her upper lip was swollen as if she had already been hit by something other than his car.

"Ya' gotta git me outta heah." She continued to moan as she struggled to keep her eyes open. "He gon' kill me," she said through labored breaths.

Norma knelt beside her, untied the polyester gold scarf she wore around her head, and wiped the woman's face with it.

"We need to call an ambulance," she said.

"No time." The woman, eyes pleading, raised her arm and grabbed Norma's hand. "He's coming. He ain't see which way I went, but he gon' find out. Git me outta heah, please," she begged.

"I can't move you! It's too dangerous," Micah shouted. "Oh, Lord, what are we going to do?"

"Ya either leave me in dis street to die or ya git me in da back of yo' car." She tried to raise her battered body off of the ground.

Micah and Norma looked at each other. There was no one around. They looked at the woman for direction.

"If I put you in my car, promise me you will let us get you some help." He took off his black London Fog overcoat and put it around her.

"I promise. We gotta move quick! He coming. I just know it!"

They helped her into the back seat. She rolled down into the floor. Norma removed her wool coat and covered the woman's body.

They jumped into the front seat and looked at each other. Neither knew what to do. The small hospital where blacks frequented closed at 10 p.m. Emergencies were taken to another hospital on the outskirts of town. It was twenty miles away.

As they pondered, they saw a man walking toward the car from the alley across the street. He appeared out of nowhere. Large as a giant, he carried what appeared to be a stick. Micah leaned over in the seat and grabbed Norma's face, pretending to kiss her.

"What?" Norma, caught by surprise, attempted to say something but he held her face close to his.

"Don't move," he whispered. To the woman in the back seat he hissed, "Stay down."

The man walked across the street and stood on the sidewalk watching the occupants in the vehicle. Micah could see him as he stood on the curb in front of the car. He continued to hold Norma.

"We moving anytime soon?" the woman whispered from under the coats.

"He's here. Just stay calm," Norma whispered.

Micah pulled away from Norma and looked the stranger straight in the face. He noticed the odd looking walking cane that the man held in his hand. The wooden handle was carved into the shape of a cobra snake's head. He was dressed in a blue three-piece suit, far too nice to be strolling down an alleyway like the one he'd come from.

Micah started the car. The man came closer to the edge of sidewalk. Just as Micah put the gear into drive, the man turned and started to walk away. Micah breathed a sigh of relief. As he put his foot gently on the gas, the man turned, ran up to the car and swung the cane at the back window.

"You wench!" He turned toward them and swung the cane again. The back window shattered.

Both Norma and the woman let out high octave screams.

Micah looked at the attacker in the rearview mirror. When the man leaned over to reach into the back window, Micah hit the gas and spun off down the street. Unable to catch them, he threw the cane at the moving car. Micah continued driving as sweat cascaded down the lower parts of his body.

"Who…no…what on Earth was that?" He held onto the steering wheel while waving one hand wildly.

"Boy, how old are ya?" The woman got up and scooted herself onto the back seat.

"What?"

"How old are ya?" she repeated.

He regretted getting involved. She was probably crazy too. "Old enough."

"I doubt dat. Ya look too young ta know da Devil when ya see him."

1968

"So, you ready?" Pastor Dawson smiled with pride. He had been Mary's mentor since she started preaching. A fatherly figure, he stood no more than five-feet five-inches tall, barely Mary's height. His crown was covered with a thick mop of salt and pepper curls, even though he was in his late seventies by then. He stood admiring Mary in the pastor's study.

"I reckon I'll never really be ready. When they put the dress on me this morning, all I could think of was my wedding to Roy. It was so nice. We didn't have much back then, but Savannah State went all out to make us think we were special." She looked wistfully out of the window and let out a deep sigh.

"You are special, Mary Brown. I know it's hard moving on to another chapter in your life. I think we both know that Roy's greatest concern was your happiness." He raised both hands. "I'm not suggesting marriage is the only way to be happy. I mean, Edgar Carter really loves you. Heck, he worships the ground you walk on."

He placed his hand on Mary's shoulder. "He's not perfect. Ha. I learned a long time ago there were no perfect people. But he's a decent man that wants to spend his life with you. He ain't afraid of your call and look like he wants to help out as much as he can."

"I don't know. Edgar is a real nice man. I just don't want to disappoint him. It's as if we are from two different worlds sometimes." She leaned on her mentor's shoulder.

Micah knocked on the door and walked in. When he saw his mother, he started to cry.

"My mama is the most beautiful woman in the world!" He smiled through the tears.

"Thank you, baby." She hugged him tightly.

"Mama. This is my last time asking." He lifted the veil Pastor Dawson had just placed on Mary's head, and asked, "Are you sure you want to do this?"

"I want to do this, Micah. He's a good man. A changed man and he wants to do what is right by the Lord." She kissed his hands. "He treats me almost as good as your daddy did. So you see, I'm still spoiled."

"I don't know." He shook his head. His tuxedo included a wide satin cummerbund around his slim waist. "I trust your judgment but I still think there is a lot more to this Carter fella than meets the eye." He kissed her on the cheek. "Just let me know if he ever does anything to make you cry."

There was a knock on the door. In walked Mary's favorite uncle, Ephraim, who had flown in that humid day from California just to meet Edgar Carter. His fifth wife remained behind with their sons. He smiled, revealing the gold teeth in the center of his mouth, but, like his great nephew, he too had his suspicions about Mary's choice of a groom.

"All right now! All of my bodyguards are here except for one!" she shouted.

"Yeah, Mer. Frank wanted to be here but he is away handling something big. Did he approve of the groom?" Ephraim asked.

"I never asked him. Frank is too much of a gentleman to behave like the two of you. I can read your faces." She hugged the handsome double-dimpled silver-haired man standing in front of her.

"And what do they suggest?" His tuxedo matched Micah's but he'd left off the cummerbund.

"That you both disagree with my choice."

"That's partly true. Well, Mer, I did not want to say it, but ole Edgar reminds me a lot of your father."

"That's an awful thing to say, Uncle Bud!" Mary spun around and almost tripped over the lace scallops that formed the hem of her off-white satin wedding gown. "How could you spoil this day like that? My father was a hateful man. I thank God he never married again. No woman should have to go through what Mama went through. No one. Period." She caught herself.

"Now, now, let's not upset the bride!" Pastor Dawson interrupted. "Mary will be protected by God. I pray more things are revealed as you both learn and grow together. Things are going to be just fine between you two, I just know it."

"There's the voice of reason. My, with all this doubt, I was going to call..." There was a knock on the door.

"You ready, Miss Mary?" One of her bridesmaids slightly opened the door but did not come inside. "Edgar look like he gonna pass out befo' long."

"What a sweet relief!" Micah, sporting a mustache and goatee, whispered to his great uncle.

"Well, I guess your mama is grown, now, huh? She has insight, sho' nuff." Ephraim walked over to the door and then turned back to face his niece.

"Now, this is my last time walking you down the aisle, you hear? The next time, let Micah do it." He laughed. "I'm putting in for retirement."

"Oh, be quiet. I told you I could get Frank to stand in for you but you would not hear of it! Bud, you are the best stand in father a woman could have." Mary placed her arm in his and motioned to Micah and Pastor Dawson that she was ready to walk down the aisle into her future.

1957

In another lifetime, the Browns were known throughout Savannah for their daily strolls through town. They held hands and walked through every neighborhood as if they were residents. Many folks noticed them.

Roy said it was a good idea to get to know folks that lived near their church. He also said it a good idea for folks to see Negros walking in public, not on their way to clean a white family's kitchen or with children that usually were not their own. No, he encouraged his parishioners to stride through the streets of Savannah as if they did not have a care in the world.

Mary used their evening walks as an opportunity to go places women did not frequent alone. There were 'patches', as they were called, throughout Savannah that were considered rough neighborhoods. She was always cautious to avoid them.

Sometimes she got the feeling that someone was watching them. Of course, a young, well-dressed Negro couple strolling down the street on a weekday often drew attention. Yet, after a few years of doing so, most people recognized them as the young pastors from Good Shepherd Baptist Church that was causing such a stir.

Mary placed her arm inside of Roy's. He was telling a joke and she balanced herself against him to keep her composure.

"Roy Brown, are you sure you don't want to be a comedian?" She laughed. "I sometimes think you missed your true calling."

Roy just winked at her. They were near their favorite spot. A diner that was surprisingly owned by a Negro family. They ate there at least two or three times a month.

Roy lead the way.

"So you really think I can do this?" Mary changed the subject.

"I know you can. God has gifted you with an awesome anointing."

"Roy, you sure? I think you have me on such a high pedestal you think I can do anything." She followed him into the diner.

"Evening, Jenny." They both waved at the petite waitress who always wore spiked five inch heels. Mary wondered how the girl worked in them but she seemed to manage.

"I'll wash off your favorite table," she yelled over to them.

"Mer, the Word says, 'He that has begun a good work in you is able to perform it.' It's not me. No sir. The anointing is on you. I'm just the one to open the door. The rest, my queen, is up to you." He kissed her on the cheek.

"All right you two love birds, your table is ready." Jenny pointed to the spot they sat everytime they came in, by the bay window.

Someone was watching them. In fact, every time they went anywhere downtown, he followed them. He watched how they laughed and joked with each other. He saw how attentive Roy was to Mary and the gentle way he held her hand, stroked her face, or looked into her eyes as they walked together.

He hated all the attention people in Savannah gave Roy Brown. He hated the fact that most people, of all races, adored this Bible thumper. No on, he reasoned, could be that good. Roy Brown had to have a bad side he was hiding from the rest of the world.

He watched them cross the street and stroll into the diner. Normally, he turned around and headed back to his car, but this day was different. There were many folks out walking around town that evening. It would be easy for him to blend in with the rest of them and never get noticed. He could get closer to his targets.

He knew where they lived and memorized their daily routines. He even knew when Roy was in town, and when he left his beautiful wife home alone.

It started out as innocent curiosity, but later escalated into envy and jealously. To their stalker, Roy Brown had the perfect life, and the more he observed him, the more he wanted that same life.

Sitting two tables behind the perfect couple, he listened to their conversation. He heard them as they talked politics, the Civil Rights Movement, and the private lives of Ralph Albernathy and Reverend Dr. Martin Luther King, Jr. Then, their conversation became romantic.

"You drive me crazy, you know that?" The pastor whispered into his wife's ear. They were holding hands when Mary turned and kissed him on the cheek.

"It's the dessert, Pastor Roy," she said as she laughed.

"No, it's you. You're the most beautiful woman I ever laid eyes on." He leaned closer. "Now, I'm a man of God, but I ain't blind. You are the sexiest woman I ever laid eyes on."

"Oh, yeah. Roy Brown, behave yourself! It's the chocolate. It brings out the beast in you." She kissed him softly on the lips.

"Oh, contraire. It's this gorgeous woman sitting next to me. The woman that I can't wait to take home and make passionate love to." They looked into each other's eyes oblivious to anyone who might be watching.

"Jenny, can we have the check?" Roy looked up and yelled.

Their stalker had heard enough. He wanted Mary Brown all to himself. She was every man's fantasy, and soon she would belong only to him. He just had to figure out a way to rid her of the good ole pastor.

TWELVE

1967

A tall young man walked up and down Sycamore Street in Savannah, Georgia repeatedly admiring the large Victorian houses that surrounded him. The sun shone brightly and several children were positioned alongside the narrow street engaged in a game of Kickball. A woman, concentrating on cleaning the mantle of a fireplace, stared at an old black and white photograph when she spotted him strolling past. She immediately dropped the cotton dusting cloth she was holding on the floor.

De ja vu.

As she walked over toward the front windows, she peeked her head outside. Just then, the two women on the front porch stopped talking. The woman just stood there looking straight ahead, dazed.

"What's wrong, Red?" the taller of the two elderly ladies asked.

"Nothing. Did you all notice that young lad who walked by? Maybe he's looking for someone around here." She sat down on the window sill.

"Dressed too nice to be up to no good," the shorter woman, fully round, less than five-feet-tall, said.

"You see, that's all Edith notices. She probably could tell you the color of his socks!"

"Well, they say the clothes make the man." Edith, an elderly woman that looked in her fifties but was actually over seventy-five years old, laughed. "I could not agree more."

"How many times has he walked by?" the red-haired woman sitting in the window sill asked.

"Oh, I reckon between five and ten times. He's a man, too proud to ask for help if he needs it."

"That's just the way men are! They will roam and roam, in circles if they have to, before they will stop and ask for help," Edith added.

"Well, my two favorite aunts, why don't you do your civic duty and ask him if he needs help the next time he comes by," Red said.

"Ask him what? The man is not bothering anyone. Besides, I love men-watching and he is making my day!" Joann, the shorter of the two with enormously full sagging breasts and a full circle midsection, stood with her hands on her hips facing her niece.

"Aunt Joann! You should be ashamed of yourself! That's a young boy you're talking about. His mother would not want you speaking about her baby like that!" Red's entire head was now outside of the window.

"She ain't heah!" Joann hollered.

Red got up from the window sill and stood surveying up and down the sidewalk.

"Y'all are too much. Just do me a favor and interrupt him if he walks by again. Ask him what he's looking for. I'll sit right here in this chair listening. I think I know his people." She walked over and sat down in a chair next to the fireplace.

Twenty minutes rolled by. Just then Edith tapped on the window pane. Red had dozed off, but she immediately opened her eyes.

"Joann, walk over to the edge of the porch so he'll think you just happened to be standing over there. We don't want him to think we're sitting here in the shade lusting over him," Edith, wearing a dark brown wig, teased.

"Hi, sweetie. I see you walking up and down the street. You okay? You lost?" She stepped down onto a lower step.

"Oh. Yes, ma'am. Is it that noticeable?" He laughed. "I dropped someone off on this street a few months ago. I came to check in on her, and for the life of me, I can't find the house." He looked up onto the porch at Edith as she rocked on the glider acting as if she had not noticed him at all.

"What's the address?" Joann removed her wrinkled light-skinned hands from her pockets.

"That's the silly thing. We never asked." He reached up and adjusted his hat. "My girl and I were giving her a lift. All I remember was the name of the street. These houses all look familiar now. I'm praying something about them jogs my memory." He looked at Edith again.

"Did she have a name?" Edith stopped rocking and looked directly at him.

"Cookie. Caroline? She gave us two first names but no last name."

"Don't no Caroline live around here." Edith sat up on the glider and looked at her sister. "No Cookie neither."

"So, what's your name? You're not from around here, huh?" Joann stepped aside on the concrete porch steps.

"Oh, forgive my manners, ladies. My name is Micah Raymond Brown. I live in Atlanta most of the time, but I grew up on the other side of town until my folks moved to Jasper County a good while back." He removed the broadcloth fedora hat he was wearing.

"Well, Mr. Micah Brown. Don't just stand there out in the hot sun. Come sit down on this here porch and let us get you some fresh squeezed lemonade." Daisy stood in the screened door.

She startled him. For a moment he thought he saw someone walk past one of the windows. Then he remembered seeing her on the front porch one time when he passed by earlier.

No doubt she was an older woman, but she was remarkably beautiful. He had never seen anyone that looked quite like her. With golden skin, her hair was the color of fire itself. It was long, straight, and cascaded down her back. She wore extremely high heels and the turquoise dress she wore could have been glued to her skin.

Micah opened the metal gate and walked into the yard. He was exhausted. The only thing he remembered was Buddy's, the corner store. He could never forget that name.

"So, is this woman someone special to you?" Joann sat down in a chair on the far side of the porch.

"Well, no, ma'am. Just someone I offered a ride to in the time of need. I told her that night I would check in on her and wanted to keep my word." He walked up the stairs and sat down in a reclining chair next to Edith. "Now I can't find her."

"That's mighty nice of you. You always keep your word?" Joann teased.

"No, ma'am." He watched Daisy as she carried the lemonade to a table at the center of the porch. "But I do try."

"Stop it, Aunt Joann." She put the tray down and walked closer to Micah. "She's just poking fun at you. She does that everywhere she goes."

"That's all right. My father was a jokester too. He did everyone like that."

Daisy could not believe her eyes. For years, she'd followed Roy's career. Heard he had an incredible wife and two children. Then she heard he died unexpectantly. It crushed her.

"So you did not travel this far just to see about this woman, did you?" Edith interjected.

"No, ma'am. I came to visit my mother. She's a pastor at Providence."

Edith raised her eyebrows at her niece. She understood why Daisy wanted her to stop the young man. Daisy was from Jasper County too, more than likely she knew this young man's parents.

Micah sipped the lemonade and watched the women carry on. He tried not to stare at Daisy, but her face was so familiar to him, he found himself unable to avoid her. For some reason, he suspected she recognized him too just by the way she said his name.

"So this Caroline, what does she look like?" Edith finally asked.

"She was kinda tall. Dark skin with a huge light colored afro hairdo," he recalled.

"Was it a wig?" Joann blurted out.

"I don't know about that. It was big and curly so, I don't know, I guess it coulda been." He looked at Daisy who sat across from them on top of the wooden banister that formed the wraparound porch.

"What did you say the other name was?" Joann asked.

"Cookie."

"That name don't sound familiar at all." She looked at Edith. "He can't be talking about Marilyn, could he?"

"Oh, Lord. I hope not. Such a pity what happened to her." Joann looked at Roy with a sad expression on her face.

"Who is Marilyn? I thought for sure she said Caroline." He shook his head. "Just seems she's gone without a trace." Micah put the glass of lemonade down on the banister.

"Marilyn lived down the street until about six months ago. Folks say she was messing with a married man from Jasper County. Pure evil. Say he walked straight into that house and slit her throat! Right in front of her family."

"Oh, God, ladies! That's probably not who he's looking for." Daisy stood up and stared at her aunts.

"When did you last see her?" Edith asked.

"It was around Thanksgiving," he said.

"Well, Marilyn was killed right before Christmas. She lived two doors down. That thing scared her peoples so bad they moved out of here! Been gone 'bout five months now. All of them just up and left, leaving no forwarding address.

They're hiding somewhere, but nobody knows for sure if they are dead or alive."

"That girl told her daddy that she met a rich man from up North. He was flashy. Wore expensive suits and drove a nice big Cadillac. I saw him one day in an emerald green car parked right out there on the street. He wouldn't get out, just honked and out she came running. I knew with manners like that he was bad news."

"What makes you say that?" Daisy took her mind off of Roy for a moment.

"What decent man drives up to a woman's house and doesn't get out the car?" Joann asked her.

"Maybe he already met everyone in the house before, or they were in a rush." Daisy laughed. "You old women always making assumptions about everyone in the neighborhood!"

"We're usually right, though. You can't deny that," Edith countered. "Now that Marilyn was with a married man or some man she shouldn't have been with, that's for sure. Her mama said she thought he was going to marry her. Then, about two months before she died, they noticed she didn't talk about marriage anymore. Seemed scared and confused. Started staying in the house. That's when they noticed the bruises."

"The rest was just a matter of time," Joann added.

"You said she was in need, young man? Is that what you are talking about?" Joann turned to face Micah.

"I'm afraid so. She was badly beaten when I picked her up. We took her to get help and brought her home early in the morning." Micah leaned forward and played with his fedora. "She warned us he would kill her."

"Did you see the man that beat her that night?" Daisy asked.

"Not really. I mean, he was a big man. Tall and well dressed like Miz Edith said. I don't remember much about his physical features. I saw him through a rearview mirror, but I swear, he could walk up on me right now and I would not recognize him."

1973

"What is that?"

"Cream. The sun does awful things to my skin." She kept looking in the mirror.

"You been working in the fields?" he asked.

"Yeah, sometimes. Beats working in the house."

"I thought you were going to be working on building a church here again." He stood behind her looking at her suspiciously.

"Well, I thought so too but things took a turn for the worse. Funny thing is, they kept on taking bad turns and I finally gave up," she continued.

"What's that supposed to mean? You knew what you were up against when you returned to this place. You were prominent in Savannah and had offers in Atlanta where I was. Why would you come back here? It thought you said the assignment back here was over."

"I thought so too. Then my husband up and changed his mind. Everything was wonderful at first. Then I found out he had more connections to this place than he'd let on." Mary turned to face Micah. "Seems he grew up here, parents divorced so he moved to North Carolina. Never had much to do with his father after that. Yet, when his father died, he left everything to him."

"But what about you?" Micah put his arms on her shoulders.

"What about me? I married him, right? I am supposed to go where my husband goes. Like it or not."

"Yeah, Ma, but this was supposed to be this awesome partnership. Just like you and Dad always had. I know Edgar's not a preacher, but he swore he would follow your ministry and support everything the Lord called you to do."

"That's what he said, son. That's what he said." She turned around and kissed him on the cheek.

1972

In the beginning, he idolized her, which made striking her a difficult task. It was four years into their marriage, when Mary realized she had married a wolf in sheep's clothing, for Edgar Roland Carter was nothing like the man he presented himself as when they first met. That painful discovery caused her make believe world of a knight in shining armor who loved her unconditionally, to shatter into a million tiny little pieces.

If truth be told, there were times she simply ignored her husband's violent propensitites. Then there were times when his outrageous behavior toward others forced her to accept the fact that she was married to a man that she did not know what he was capable of doing.

They were out one evening celebrating their anniversary when an older silver-haired gentleman, not tall, in fact, small in stature, accidentally stepped on Edgar's brown snakeskin shoes. Mary, dressed in a brown suede suit, was busy at the self-serve salad bar and did not see what happened. The sound of Edgar's cold voice caught her attention. She waited a few minutes and then walked over.

The old man seemed remorseful until Edgar raised his voice.

"Watch what ya' doing, fool!" He hovered over the shorter man.

"Fool? Who ya' calling a fool?" the indignant little man yelled back as Edgar wiped his shoe with a handkerchief jerked from his coat pocket.

"The one who just stepped on my new floor shiners. Folks have died fo' steppin' on mah shoes." His proper manner of speaking was now gone.

"Man, you must be crazy! You talking 'bout killing someone ova a pair of shoes?" The man started to walk away, shaking his head.

Edgar would not let it go. He stood up and with his barrel-sized arms, grabbed the man's left arm slightly below his arm pit.

"I is crazy," he hissed. "Ya' memba dat de next time you walk on top of mah shoes." He peered into the man's frightened face, nose to nose. "Keep it up an' I'm gonna give ya somethang to memba me by."

Mary came to an abrupt stop. She did not recognize the oversized bully shouting in front of her. The man she married had a gentle soul and believed in forgiveness. He would never behave this way. But he sure had on that crisp October night, and from that moment on, nothing between the two of them would ever be the same.

1969

On a blustery cold day in December, Mary Brown Carter walked into the lobby of the Capitol Hill Holiday Inn in Washington D.C. She was a guest speaker for the Natonial Baptist Convention which was being held in town for the next several days. Few women had ever received such an honor. She would make her small town proud.

She loved being in the United States Capitol, even though the District of Columbia was still a part of the mostly segregated South, there were many exciting events occurring to change the country into the place Roy predicted it would become for blacks; an America where equality would no longer be a dream, but a way of life.

The introduction of televison brought nightly action directly into the homes of many black and white families who were previously oblivious to the occurrences happening right outside of their front doors. Even the residents of Jasper County, while intimidated by the Klan who marched in their backyards, wanted to join in the ranks to end Jim Crow's segregation once and for all. Mary could not wait to check into her room and listen to the CBS news with Walter Cronkite.

Around four in the afternoon, she sat in the hotel lobby reading ***The Washington Post*** when a distinctively tall and slender woman walked into the reception area. She was surrounded by a group of men and women all dressed in business suits. Mary's jaw dropped. It was her idol: Congresswoman Shirley Chisolm, and she was staying in the same hotel.

A younger woman walked ahead of the group carrying a black leather briefcase in one arm and holding an all weather coat in the other. Dressed in a form-fitting black suit, multicolored scarf around her neck, and five-inch spike black patent leather pumps, she moved as if her feet were gliding across the marble floors of the lobby. She hastily approached the desk clerk. The congresswoman herself, wearing a tan dress with matching jacket and black heels stood several feet behind the woman with a look of total relaxation etched across her face. Mary just stood there watching the exciting scene play out.

After the desk clerk handed the woman an envelope, she rejoined the group and they proceeded to the elevator. Just then, she noticed Mary staring at the congresswoman. She stopped walking, handed the envelope to a gentleman closely behind her, and looked directly at Mary. A warm smile spread across her sunlit skin.

"Excuse me," she said as she walked toward Mary. "You're Pastor Mary Brown, aren't you?" She stopped a few inches shy of where Mary stood and adjusted the coat she was carrying.

Surprised, Mary looked at the woman fully embarrassed by her own behavior.

"Oh, yes. Yes, I am Pastor Brown." She tried to get her composure. "That's Congresswoman Chisolm isn't it? I would know her anywhere," she managed to get out.

"Yes, it is. I can assure you that the congresswoman knows who you are as well. Your husband was one of her favorite pastors and she was delighted to learn that you now preach as well."

"You must be kidding?" Mary was baffled.

"Not at all. You were both are an inspiration to folks everywhere." The woman extended her hand to Mary.

"Oh, forgive me." Mary removed the white elbow-length gloves she was wearing and shook the woman's hand. "You're Daisy Lyons, aren't you?"

"It is I." Daisy smiled.

"My husband told me all about you. He followed your career and was so proud of you. He said you persuaded him to get his college degree."

"And he influenced me to reach for the stars!" She beamed. "He was my best friend, and I was so glad when he found you. So sorry when he passed on." Daisy dropped her head and removed the black fedora that covered her fiery red crop.

"Thank you. He felt the same about you. Told me so more than once. I never thought I would get to meet you. Not after all these years." Mary stood smiling. "It must be fate, or perhaps the Lord's work."

"I believe it is the latter." Daisy locked arms with Mary and escorted her toward the elevators. "Miss Mary, could we have the pleasure of your company tonight for a late dinner? Shirley would consider it an honor if you could say a prayer for us during her re-election. In fact, would you consider coming back to Washington to do the opening prayer for members of Congress in the fall? It would be the first time a black woman has addressed the House and Senate."

Mary was speechless. Daisy Lyons was just the way Roy had described. She captured your attention with every word that came out of her mouth. No wonder she was the congresswoman's Chief of Staff. No wonder the congresswoman's career was going so well.

1973

"I have something to tell you. I don't know the relevance of what I am going to say to you, but I feel led to say something." They had kept in touch since meeting in Washington.

"By all means. Don't be shy. Speak your mind. I learned never to judge folks when they tell you something you don't want to hear. May come in handy one day," Mary said slowly.

"First, thank you. From the moment we met, I knew we would be lifelong friends. I knew Roy would want it that way." She started to cry.

"What is it, precious?" Mary grabbed Daisy's soft well-manicured hands and held them tightly. "Anything you say to me will remain between us. I'm not one to gossip or let things slip out that' none of anyone else's business."

"It's just I hate myself for having to tell you and not telling you earlier. I don't want to bring up old ghosts, especially bad news." She looked away.

"Well, if it's old, it can't hurt either of us now, can it?" Mary leaned over and kissed Daisy on the cheek. "Besides, there is nothing that God is not aware of anyway."

"You sure, Pastor Mary? I should maybe just leave it buried in the past and we can pray about it."

"No. I think some buried stuff needs to be dug up sometimes." Mary forced herself to laugh in spite of a sense of dread in her belly.

"Yeah. This has been buried for quite a while and it really stinks." Daisy looked about the small patio at all the colorful hanging baskets above them. Slowly she began her story.

"A long time ago when I was growing up in Jasper County, my mother used to say a man followed her. Then one day that man was so bold he told her that he was going to steal her away from my father. She paid him no mind. Thought the man was being fresh. Never gave it a second thought.

"I don't know if she even told my daddy. But the man wouldn't leave her alone. Kept going on about how beautiful Miz Ruby was and that he knew she was supposed to be his wife. Ridiculous, huh?" She glanced at Mary, who stayed silent, then went on.

"Well, one day the man came by our house and told my daddy that he was in love with Ma. Of course Daddy laughed it off. Then, a couple of weeks later, my daddy lost his job. Seems the man told his boss some lies on him. So Daddy did what any man would do and confronted him, asked him what he had against him. The man said my daddy stole something from him." She bit her lip. "His wife."

She sighed and regained her composure then continued. "Daddy told the man that he and Ma had been together since she was eleven years old and that she had never mentioned this other man. He said there must be some kind of mistake. The man said he chose my mother and that once he'd made the choice she was his. Only thing was, Mama was a married woman with four kids so how could he choose another man's wife?

"Anyway, Daddy couldn't convince the fool man that he was mistaken. Even asked Mama about it and she said she never had more than a few words with the man over the years. So I guess Daddy left it alone. The man disappeared, Daddy got another job, and things went back to normal. Or so we thought."

Mary listened intently. "What happened?"

"Man showed up on our doorstep one day and told Mama to pack her bags, he was taking her with him. He was a big man, wearing nothing but overalls and brogan boots. He had a head full of red hair, like mine. Anyway, Mama thought he was crazy. Daddy was not home so she told me to go get Mister John, our neighbor. I went to get him while Mama tried to reason with the man, to no avail. He came in the house and started throwing pieces of furniture around, all the while telling Mama to pack her stuff. My little sisters and brothers ran outside screaming and yelling for someone to help us.

"Finally, our neighbor came over and confronted the man. Mister John was a big man too, standing nearly seven-feet tall. They started arguing and the next thing we knew, they fought all over the house, breaking our furniture.

Finally, the man jumped back in his pickup truck and left. No sooner than he drove away, Daddy pulled up.

"Mama told him the story and he got his shotgun and sat out on the front porch. First night, nothing. Daddy didn't go to work the next day. Then on the third day, Daddy went back to work, but sent us to Aunt Chelly's house on the other side of town. We stayed there for two more days and then Daddy came and told us to come home that Saturday. So, Saturday morning we got up, ate breakfast, and headed home. Everything seemed so quiet. We got out of my uncle's car and ran into the house. That's when we heard the screaming. Poor Mister John was screaming at the top of his lungs.

"We ran to the back of the house and found him standing over my daddy, a big hole in his chest where he had been shot. I turned around and ran back to the front yard to stop my uncle, but he had already driven down the road. I ran up the steps to Mister John's house and his wife was putting her clothes on. I told her and we ran over to another neighbor's house because they had a telephone.

"The police came and Mister John told them that he sat in the window and saw the man, Roland Carter, sneak into the back yard around five that morning. By the time he got his clothes on good, he said he heard my father and Carter arguing. He ran over to the house. As he walked up to the front door, he heard shots fired in the back. By the time he ran around to the back, all he could see was Roland Carter strolling back into the woods and Daddy lying in a puddle of blood.

"Police came and later the coroner showed up and took my daddy's body away. Police arrested Roland Carter, but then they let him go. Right after my father's funeral, it seems someone walked into Mister John's house and killed his entire family! No one would say anything about it. Then someone told my mama that the same person that killed my daddy had killed Mister John's family. He wasn't home when it happened, but when Mr. John found out he had a nervous breakdown. Next thing we knew, he walked out onto Highway 17 and jumped in front of an eighteen wheeler. The driver never had a chance to apply the brakes."

"Oh, my God!" Mary put her arms around Daisy. "This is terrible." She rememberd the name of the assailant in the story. "You say Carter was his name?" Her face was soaked with tears.

"Yes, ma'am." Daisy used her small hands and wiped the tears from Mary's eyes. Sternly she said, "From what I hear, the fruit don't fall far from the tree, Miss Mary."

THIRTEEN

1973

He placed his foot on her throat and pressed down.

The small crowd stared in disbelief but no one moved toward him or raised any objections. He tasted their fear and was emboldened by it.

"This here is mah woman! Anyone got a problem with dat, let me know now!" The enormous brute looked around. "She is mine, God gave her ta me and none o' y'all hicks betta not come between us."

Mary lay in the ground, kissing the earth. There was enough dirt in her eyes to seal them, but she tried to focus on the bright sunshine piercing through those August skies.

Earlier, she'd tried to run away from him. It was after two rounds of a beating, with no place to go, that she ran toward the workers in the fields hoping for an intervention.

If they did not hear her approaching, they at least had to have heard the intense screams coming from her lungs. By the time they spotted the half-naked woman, running with no shoes on, she appeared out of her mind.

Mary yelled for help. When she was close enough to the small crowd, she kneeled down and clasped both hands together, eyes swollen, yet pleading.

Ten people stood looking down upon her. Four men and six women. Not a man smaller than two-hundred pounds. The women were medium sized, but she did not expect much from them. There was an old beat up pickup truck a few feet from where they stood in the sugar cane field.

"I need to get out of here," she cried.

"We working," a short, stocky man shouted. "Need to get this harvest up and out before sundown."

"Please help me! I don't know how to drive a stick shift! I swear he's going to kill me." Mary collapsed on the ground.

"Pick her up!" a woman, no more than four-feet tall, holding a rake, yelled to the men who stood by.

"Wut? You outta ya' mind? We don't know wut iz goin' on heah. Whur she come from?" another man spoke. He was short too and the color of shiny black coal.

"Don't matter. We can't stand heah and watch this po' woman die!" Another woman broke through the crowd and looked down at Mary.

"Mable, stay out of it. Brotha iz right. She could be a hag, possessed by the Devil hisself. Look at how she dressed," the stocky man answered.

"Dis woman need our help. Whut we gonna do? Let her die in this heah field? Den huh blood iz on our shoulders." Mable, dressed in overalls, a plaid shirt, rubber shoes and a straw hat, ran over to Mary and tried to lift her off the ground.

"Dat Mable gonna git us all kilt! Keep on. Say you not 'fraid of hags. Dey gon' hunt you down and drive ya crazy. Mark my words." The same man spit out a wad of tobacco onto the dusty row they'd been picking.

"I ain't scurred of no hags, Nate. Help me get dis woman in da truck, I say!" Mable lifted Mary's head up. "She still alive. Still got the breath God give huh."

A heavy set woman, over two-hundred pounds, square shouldered and dressed in a pair of cut-off shorts and a cotton shirt, walked forward. She kneeled down beside Mary.

"We gon' git ya outta heah. Where your peoples?" She pulled Mary's thinning hair away from her face.

"Yemasee and Savannah. I know a few folks. Frank Wilcox," she blurted out. "But you can't take me to him."

"Why not?" Mable yelled. "Seem like a safe place tuh me! Ain't nobody fool enough to mess with Frank! You safer dere than anywhere else if you ain't got family."

Mary had a stern look on her face. "Frank will kill my husband."

"Looka heah. I owns dis heah truck. I says where it goes. I ain't driving no wheres. I just don't like the smell of dis," a balding man in his fifties, walked up and declared.

"Thomas, we gotta do something! We got to at least git her to safety. You see she can't walk good wid all dose bruises and cuts on her legs," a woman with long, thick cornrows hanging down her back said.

"Edna, you mah wife, so you do as I say," Thomas said.

"I agree wid your wife," the last man finally spoke up and said. He looked half grown, barely out of his teens. It was obvious that he had little exposure to the hot sun of the Low Country. "Let's git her outta heah then we'll sort it out. Not all of us have to go. Just one man and one woman. Dah rest can stay and work."

"Well, y'all can take mah truck but I ain't going. Ain't getting involved wid dis mess." Thomas dropped the car keys on the ground.

"I'm going. I needs to know she safe," Mable said as she helped Mary to her feet.

The youngest man picked up the car keys and headed over to the truck. As Mable closed the passenger door, someone in a dark blue Chrysler drove up and parked behind the truck.

No one moved. Nate motioned to the young man behind the steering wheel to drive away, but he sat frozen, unable to move. His eyes were stretched wide open as if he had seen a ghost.

"Drive this truck, Buddy!" Mable shouted.

Edgar Carter stepped out of the vehicle and walked up to the driver's side of the truck.

"You ain't fool enough to put your foot on that pedal and drive away are ya? I'll slit your throat befo' you put the gear in drive."

Tears ran down the man's youthful looking face. He did not look at Edgar.

"All right, Edgar. I'll go with you!" Mary shouted. "Leave these folks alone. They are minding their own business."

"Then why yah in dis truck?" His Low Country accent returned.

"They bringing me home, but you here now, so come on." She faked a smile.

"Woman, I was born at night, but it won't last night.! You tryin' ta leave me! You gon' pay and dem wid ya gon' pay too." Edgar walked around to the passenger's side.

Mary whispered to Mable to get down in the seat. Then she swung the door open. Before she could step down from the truck, Edgar reached in and threw her out onto the ground. She fell beneath him. He stared at Mable.

"You got it coming too!" He addressed the crowd. "Wut y'all looking at?"

As they watched in horror, he took off his belt, wrapped it around his wrist and struck Mary repeatedly. The impact of each blow tore into the sheer fabric of the housecoat, revealing her naked body underneath. When he finished, he picked up her bloody body and threw her into the back-seat of his car.

No one uttered a sound. No one did a thing to help.

1974

Everyone in the store turned around when they heard his voice.

"Evening, Mr. Frank," Herbert Gray said as the medium-tall brown skinned man walked into the General Store.

Frank Wilcox stood looking around. Then he walked over to the counter where Herbert sat counting dollar bills.

"You heard anything about a man beating his wife in one of your fields?" His eyes were focused on Herbert's trembling hands.

"I knows my workers leave the fields early, a few months ago. Dang near ruined the crops." Herbert Gray did not look up.

"What reason they give you for leavin' early?" Frank raised his hat revealing the stern look on his face.

"Said some cockamamie story about some big feller coming and threatening to kill 'em over some woman."

"You get a name?" Frank reached out and placed his hand on top of Herbert's hand which held the dollar bills. He turned and looked about the store.

"Y'all go on now. Get what you come for and leave us be," he told the customers.

Everyone in the store dropped what they were doing and ran outside. They were aware of Frank's reputation. The less they knew about what was going on that day, the better.

"Name," Frank repeated.

Herbert was sweating perfusely. "Naw, didn't say no name. They say he wuz driving a Chrysler. A new one. One most of y'all can't afford."

"Speak what you know, white man." Frank removed his hand from around Herbert's.

"I done told ya wut I know. Some Nigra in a Chrysler. I thank they lying 'bout the entire affair. Thank they made it up to leave early. Just lazy is all."

"What about the woman? Any description?" Frank stared outside at the gas pumps. His 1973 Cadillac was parked on the side of the building in the shade.

"Hell naw. She won't nobody. Just another man's propitty, all I heard." Herbert trembled as he put the dollar bills into the cash register.

"Anything else you care to tell me befo' I'm forced to come back and ask again." Frank opened his jacket and revealed the gun in the holster around his waist. "Won't be so nice next time."

"Mr. Wilcox, I ain't teasing ya. Dat's what I done heard. I heard dis fella someone ya really don't wanna fool wid." Herbert looked nervously outside. "See dat gal right dere?" He motioned with his head.

Frank looked at the crowd. Some people walked away, but a few remained. He saw the woman Herbert Gray was referring to. She looked familiar. Then he remembered where he knew her from. It was a long time ago. He could trust her. She stayed around to tell him everything he wanted to know and more.

Fall 1974

She heard the car coming into her driveway. She was in the bedroom. As usual, she went to the side window and looked out. She prayed Edgar would honor his word and stay away from her for good. It had been a few months since she'd left him. She was finally finding her strength, rediscovering the peace she had traded to be with him seven years before.

It was a dark color, four-door automobile. It looked brand new. Mary started to panic.

The car pulled up just outside of her front door but no one exited the vehicle. She ran into the living room and grabbed Micah's shotgun. Then she stood behind the front door and held the gun tightly in her arms, aimed squarely at the front window.

She heard voices as the door on the passenger side opened. A large gentleman with salt and pepper hair stepped out onto the grass and looked around the front yard. Mary put the gun back in its usual hiding place behind the door.

The man walked around the front of the car and opened the driver's side door. After a few minutes, a second man, medium height, face hidden by a tilted hat, stepped out of the car and also looked around.

A smile crept over Mary's face as she opened the metal door. "You gentlemen into scaring old ladies these days?"

"When I see an old lady, I'll scare her." He had a wide grin and pearly white teeth.

He walked up the stairs, opened the screened door, and pulled her body close to him. "Hey, beautiful, how's life?"

"Well, it has its challenges, but I'm making it, Praise the Lord." She reached up and stroked her hair to see if the curls were still in place.

His hands fell from around her as he stood looking into her eyes. His look escalated to serious. "Anything you wanna tell me?"

"Excuse me?" Mary looked around to see what the other man was doing. His back was turned to them.

"I heard something I didn't like. Something that broke my spirit. Now, before I take some action to rectify the situation, I need to talk to you."

"Hold it, Frank! I don't want your kind of action around here! I love you, but I know your other side." She stepped back into the living room.

"Is it true?" He raised his voice slightly and stepped inside. Mary was silent. "Did he put his hands on you?"

Mary stood in the center of the room. Frank Wilcox had become one of her closest friends. He had moved back to South Carolina two years before, but lived further north in Florence. She vowed not to tell him unless he found out and even then would she tell him only what she thought he needed to know.

"Don't take that tone with me, Frank. I'm not these other folks around here. I'm not afraid of you." She stood facing him with her hands on her hips.

"What have you ever had to be afraid of? I devoted my life to your family. You know I made Roy a commitment to protect you and Micah. What kind of man would I be if I did not keep my word?" A tear paraded from beneath the shades he wore.

Mary sat down on the sofa and looked up at the man that seemed taller than a giant to her. This was a conversation she never thought she would have.

"How long has it been going on?" He removed his dark shades and sat down in the wingback chair across from her.

"Frank, it's nothing now. He's gone. I've forgiven him and he has not bothered me since I moved out of our house."

"Nothing! Mary, from what I hear, that beast whipped your tail unmercifully out in public and you call that nothing? What has gotten into you?" he cried.

"Frank, folks are just exaggerating. You know the Low Country." She reached over and grabbed his hand, but he pulled it away.

"I know men like him. There's not that much exaggerating in the world! He hit you out in public and then threatened to kill everyone that was around. Give me their names. When I finish with them, they gon' know I mean business!" He stood up and walked over to her.

"No! Frank don't come in here with that foolishness! This is a house of God! We don't do things like that. 'Vengeance is mine' says the Lord." Mary moved away from him.

"Yes, and I will repay."

"You talking blasphemy, brother! Don't play with God. Leave it be," she begged.

"Or what? "

"Frank, please leave it be!" she screamed.

"Mary, you know I can't do that." He grabbed her face and turned it toward him. "Not knowing what I know. They say he's the Devil. Family killed folk in this town and got away with it. Nobody is going to protect you from him."

"And what are you going to do, Frank? Are you going to take the law into your own hands? Two wrongs don't make a right and you know it. It's over. I filed for divorce." She looked up at him hopefully.

"You think he will ever let you get away? Edgar doesn't have the sense God gave him. What makes you think you'll be any different?" He placed his arm around her shoulders. "Mer, just how much do you know about his past?"

"Oh, God. More than I ever wanted to know. I heard so much that if I don't hear anything else, I will remember what I now know for a lifetime. Yes, sir, I heard a lot."

"I'm sure you don't know the half of it. He fooled you real good, Mer."

"Yeah. I know that now." Calmer, she leaned into him. "That's my shame that I'll take to my grave. I should have been more watchful. Funny thing is, he said he knew Roy back in the day."

"He lied about that too." Frank laid his head back on the sofa.

"What? What are you speaking, brother?" Mary leaned forward and turned to look at Frank.

"I'm saying Roy never had one conversation with that man!"

"Oh, come on! Roy knew the whole town of Savannah, like he knew everyone around here." Mary was baffled.

"He didn't know him, I tell ya. We talked about Roland Carter, his father, because he killed a couple of folks in town including someone close to a friend of Roy's."

"Daisy. You can say her name. We are good friends." Mary shook her head and laughed.

Frank sprang from the sofa. "You know Daisy Lyons?"

"Yeah. It's a small world, huh? That's why I left him. She told me everything I needed to know." She stood up.

"You didn't tell him what she said, did you?" He faced her.

"No! Don't be silly. I told him I wanted out. He didn't ask many questions after I made it clear that I was leaving dead or alive."

"He won't stop until you're dead. Word in Atlanta is that he killed his first wife and some other folk too."

"What? The Blood of Jesus! Frank, you can't be serious." She grabbed his hands.

"Do you know where he is now?" He looked into her intense brown eyes.

"I don't know. I think he moved away."

"He's plotting his next move. As long as he's alive, you're not safe and neither is Micah."

"What? Oh, my God! That's why Micah kept hanging around in the beginning. He knew something was up with Edgar."

"Did he ever tell you his theory about when they met?"

Mary raised both arms and put them around Frank's sculpted waist. "No. And I never asked."

FOURTEEN

1975

Mable walked to the outhouse, opened the door, and sat down on the wooden toilet seat. She was careful to fasten the latch on the door. As she reached to pull down her pants, she heard violent screams which shook the earth beneath her. She jumped up and got dressed.

Shaking, she grabbed ahold of the latch, but it would not open. She started to panic as she recognized the voice of the person screaming out in agony. In shock, she pounded on the wooden door wildly but it would not give. She was locked inside of the outhouse as something horrific was happening in her own house.

"Help me!" she screamed. The sounds on the other side became blood curling. Mable, grief-stricken and terrified, bent over holding her sides and yelled, "Oh, dear God. Help me somebody!"

When she could no longer take it and the screaming continued in her ear like an echo, Mable turned around, grabbed a two by four that was propped against the wall and swung violently, hitting at the door. Then it dawned on her to strike where she knew the latch on the other side was placed. She swung three times before the door came ajar.

Running toward her home, she bounded up the stairs taking two at a time, and reached for the metal door handle. Nothing happened; it too was bolted. She ran over to the edge of the porch, reached down beneath the house and pulled out a baseball bat. Then with everything she could, she struck the front window with the bat. It shattered into pieces.

Turning the latch, she lifted the broken window and climbed inside. She jumped over the couch and headed in the direction of her daughter's voice.

"Mommy, he hurt me!" her daughter screamed repeatedly. "Where were you? I called out to you and you were not there!"

Tears rolled down Mable's face as she looked around the small room. Everything was dishelved. The bed linens were tossed about the floor and there lay her daughter, garments ripped to sheds, and blood running down her legs.

Mable opened her mouth to scream, but instead, she fainted.

1974

"You looking at life, boy. Life, and that's a long time for your punk behind to spend with men that pray meat like you show up in a prison cell everyday." The Sheriff threatened the young teen.

"But I didn't do anything, sir! I swear fo' God, I didn't." His body trembled all over as he wept before the larger man menacing down upon him.

"Tell that crap to someone who gives a damn. I'm going throw your black butt in jail and laugh when I hear how many times them hoodlums rape ya." Sheriff Bryant, eyes fixated on the young man, snarled.

"What do you want from me, sir. I told you the truth. I come home from Savannah State College, work in the fields during the summer, and mind my own business. I don't hang around nobody that's headed down the wrong path." He starred at the steel table he was seated in front of, arms behind his back, secured by metal handcuffs.

"Well, well. I never thought you'd get where I was coming from. The ball is in your corner. Save your nigger behind and give me what I want. Stop acting like a punk, sitting here choking down wads of spit. Your'e pathetic!" Without warning, the Sheriff smacked the young man across the back of his neck, causing him to fall forward onto the table.

Charles Bryant knew this young man was not a suspect in the stream of burglaries that were taking place. He picked him up for another reason. Like an elephant, he had an enormous memory bank that recalled facts like an enclycopedia. It was years ago, but he clearly recalled the medium height, flawless coppertone- skinned, young man seated at the base of an Oak Tree right next to a slain teen, whom the sheriff later learned was the lad's first cousin.

Freightened out of his mind, the teen consented when offered a ride home. That ride, was the ticket Charles Bryant now used over the same young man's head as a ransom. It was time to pay the piper, and, unbeknownst to the frightened teen, the Sheriff demanded full payment in blood.

September 1976

"I've got to be on my way. Y'all know I have to get over the Savannah Bridge before midnight. These roads are too dangerous for a woman driving alone all time of night."

"Then stay heah. You ain't got no man waiting at home for ya," the woman said, laughing.

"No, and not sure I want one either," Mary shot back.

"Girl, you can't let the Devil win. He sent that counterfeit to you. But the Devil is a liar! That man was sent to destroy you. But look at God!" the woman said.

"Look, I may never want another man after what I went through. My focus is on Micah, that wayward child of mine, getting married and blessing me with some grandkids. That's the only company I want right now." Mary sat down in the front seat.

"You sure you gonna be okay? I mean, I can ride back with you, if you want me to. The kids not in school tomorrow," another friend added.

"No, sir. I'm covered by the blood. Like I tried to tell Frank, I cannot live my life in fear. If it were up to him, I would be cooped up in the house night and day. Shoot. I have to get away sometimes."

"Yes indeed. Now Daisy coming through in a few weeks and I know she will kill me if I don't invite you over for supper so she can talk your head off."

"Yes, Lord. That child can talk. I miss her when she is not around. I know she's off saving the world. Talk about retiring. That'll be the day!" Mary waved goodbye and closed the car door.

She was on Highway 17 before she knew it. Once she had a good view of the Savannah Bridge, she popped in an eight track tape of The Staple Singers and sang along with them.

South Carolina state line. She loved to see it coming and loved to see her leaving it. The state would never be a place she loved, it was an assignment from God Almighty and more and more, Mary Brown Carter was beginning to understand.

As she drove into Hardeeville, she looked at the gas tank. Most filling stations were closed by then. She could sense the clock had to be on the verge of striking midnight.

She drove to the stoplight and looked around. Everything was peaceful. The new hotel on the corner brought more travelers to Jasper County. Hawk's stayed open until one a.m. Times were changing. Mary turned onto the two-lane service road.

That is when she noticed a car was following her. It was him.

She tried to remember which of the driveways to turn into for safety. He would never follow her there. As sweat prickled her forehead, she tried to remain calm.

The car behind her sped up. Realizing she was in danger, Mary pummeled the gas pedal and almost lost control of the wheel.

"I shall live and not die," she proclaimed, but he was gaining on her.

Mary swerved into the opposite lane and screamed. She was going too fast to make the turn. She passed it.

Edgar was within inches of the back bumper of her Lincoln Continental. She had to do something, and quickly. Just as she looked in the rearview mirror, she thought of slamming on the brakes. Instead, her stalker pulled his car around hers and honked the horn. Mary's heart raced.

She tried to keep her eyes on the road. He steered his front tires in the direction of her vehicle. Mary lost control of the wheel and, barely missing a barge on the side of the road, drove over the gravel onto the shoulder and brought her car to a sudden stop.

He sped past her and headed down the road into the darkness.

Panting frantically, Mary called out, "Thank you, Jesus."

Just as she was about to turn around and head in the opposite direction, an inner force overtook her and she pulled back onto the service road and sped after the very person who had chased her moments before.

"What are you doing, crazy lady?" she asked herself as she slowed down.

About a mile up the lone road, she watched as he turned left onto a side road. Mary followed. She followed him until he turned onto a major highway, headed toward Beaufort County. She wanted to turn back, but once again, the voice told her to keep on going.

After crossing the Jasper County line, she watched as Edgar turned right into a driveway, less than a mile away from the Beaufort County line. Mary kept driving straight ahead, and then without warning, she turned the car around.

As she passed the driveway he'd turned into earlier, she saw a billboard and unable to read it, slowed down and turned onto the next dirt road. On the sides of the road were mile markers placed every few hundred feet. She read the advertisements, "Private Restroom," "Cold Beer," "Live Music", "Disc Jockey every night." She knew where she was. She had been here before with Frank.

She drove into the well-lit parking lot and turned around. Feeling uneasy, Mary knew she had no business in a place like this, so she turned around and headed back to the highway. Then it happened again.

Instead of turning onto the highway in the direction of her home, Mary spotted a driveway at the end of the road, turned there and pulled her vehicle over into the cornfields. She was determined to find Edgar and confront him no matter the costs.

She could sense his presence as a spirit of evil lurked around her. She turned the enginee off and leaned over into the floor in seach of a flashlight. She reached under the driver's seat, and as she expected, felt the steel coldness of the small revolver Frank had hidden there when he thought she was not looking.

"Father, forgive me. I know you said you would handle this. I've never done anything like this before." She let out a nervous chuckle. "Probably won't do this ever again, but I can't live in fear any longer."

She got out of the car as a spirit of calmness filled the air. She had no plan as to what she would do if and when he spotted her. Yet she kept walking, out in the pitch-black night, looking for a man who promised her he would kill her if she meddled in his affiairs again.

Slowly, gripping the gun with both hands like a police officer on a stake out, Mary walked down the driveway toward a small red house she spotted in the distance. She stopped and surveyed the land. There was a barn behind the house, a small bicycle and a few children's toys in the front yard, two white wrought iron chairs on the porch, and an old car parked next to the porch steps. The front window of the house was covered with cardboard.

And then she noticed the big Chrysler parked on the side of the house next to the woods. Bingo, as she suspected, this is where he had come.

There were muffled voices coming from inside of the house. Then everything fell silent. Mary ran and hid near an oak tree in the front yard. When she peeked around the tree, she spotted Edgar burling down the back porch steps carrying a flashlight in one hand and another object in the other. Behind him was a small frail girl, dressed in a housecoat. They walked towards the cornfields.

Mary knelt behind the tree until she could no longer see them. Then she ran onto the back porch and peered into the window. The house appeared empty. She turned to follow them.

From where she stood, she noticed they were not talking to one another. It seemed Edgard knew exactly where he was going. As they came upon a wooden outhouse, he stooped down and pulled something from underneath the structure. He pushed the girl in front of him and continued walking, giving orders as to where she should go.

Less than a hundred feet, they stopped. Edgar unfolded the blanket he retrieved earlier and spread it out. He motioned to the young woman to lie down.

Mary heard his infamous laugh as he unbuckled his pants and kneeled in front of the woman, tugged at her housecoat and laid ontop of her. Mary, horrified, felt sick.

Frozen, she watched everything from behind the cornstalks. He made the same grunting noises he uttered when he used to climb on top of her at night. She knelt down and cried.

Suddenly the young woman let out a loud wail, as Mary watched Edgar place his hand overtop of her mouth. Mary stood to her feet. At that moment, she knew she would not leave that night without him knowing she was there.

"Get up!" She ran over, trembling with the gun in her hands, and stood facing the two of them.

Edgar, bloodshot eyes, caught off guard, looked at Mary, and upon recognizing her, jumped to his feet.

"Wench, wut you want? You done lost your mind! Now I can give ya wut I owe you!" Partially dressed, he staggered toward her. "I'mma give you some and then slit yo' throat right heah in dese woods. Wut the church gone say about that?"

Mary took a few steps backward before pointing the gun directly at him.

"Back away, Edgar! You tried to kill me on that road tonight. You're not going to stop, are you?"

"I'mma do what I wanted to do when I saw you in Savannah wid dat punk sorry excuse of a husband."

"That would be you. You aren't half the man Roy was," she interrupted and then stopped.

"Dat's why he dead and I'm still heah! And I took his woman too." He continued to stagger towards her, yet at a slower pace than Mary remembered.

He fiddled with his trousers and then lunged towards the gun. Mary jumped to the side of him as he collapsed on his knees.

With the gun pointed directly at his forehead, Mary threatened, "this is your last chance to get the hell out of Jasper County alive, Edgar! I don't care where you go, but if you stay here, I can guarantee you'll be dead before daylight."

"And who gon' kill me? You? You ain't got the nerve to pull that trigga. Killing come easy for me!" He struggled to get back up again, all the while swinging punches in Mary's direction.

Mary closed her eyes and pulled the trigger. Everything went black.

When she woke up the next morning, her car was not parked outside. She was in the house alone, but someone had been there with her. Ten years later, she would find out who it was.

III

The Book of Life

ONE

1972

Micah drifted in and out of a state of consciousness. He could hear voices around him. He heard the doctors say he had a slim chance of survival, and a nurse say what a shame it was to watch such a young man die like this. He heard it all, but never opened his eyes and acknowledged the wonderful truth that God had given him a second chance.

A woman strolled into the room dressed in a green paisley print dress that gripped her waistline like a corset. Her shoes were bright yellow and she carried a matching yellow purse. Her hair was pulled neatly together on the top of her head with the remaining red locks flowing freely in an afro puff.

Micah sniffed the air and smiled.

"L'air du temps," he whispered.

"Oui, oui," she laughed.

Daisy Lyons stood looking at him. She came to visit every week since she'd heard the news. Roy would have wanted her to. More than anything, she and Mary were close friends.

"I see there are less bandages than before." She kissed him on the cheek.

"Yeah, my doctor said I can go home in a few weeks if this keeps up. I'm just happy that I no longer feel like King Tut wrapped in so much stuff." He smiled.

"True healing takes a lot of time. The bandages only cover the physical bruises. It's the mental ones that seem to hang on." She sat down in the chair next to the sole window in the room.

"Right on. I'm done with running the streets with all kinds of loose women. As those knives tore into my flesh, all I could think about was that I was dying just like Sam Cooke, killed by someone who I thought loved me." He looked up at Daisy and continued. "At least I thought she did!"

He turned and looked away. "She reminded me of you and Ma, head strong, and for once in my life, I was not afraid to love a woman like that. I don't know what happened to make her do this to me. Maybe it was payback for all the things I did to other women."

"Well, you know what they say; it's a thin line between love and hate. What's important is that you are alive! Very few of these doctors were hopeful you would survive, but not your mother. She never gave up. She was here everyday, while her girlfriends held vigils in front of the hospital. You should have seen the look on the faces of the police. Those women scared them half to death with their singing and chanting! They had the entire parking lot filled with folks from everywhere praying that God would restore your life."

He held his sides and laughed. "My father used to say when Mom prayed, the heavens moved and God stood at attention."

"Your father was right. I've never seen anyone like Mary and Mother Ruth. I remember the time I went to visit them, called myself getting some rest before the next campaign. I had no idea what was in store when I got there in the middle of what seemed like an all-night prayer service. I walked in the door and saw folks stretched out on the floor or kneeling all over the place. There were even folks outside on blankets praying. It was a sight to see! Those women prayed straight through the night. Seems they do this every month without fail." She put her hands on her chest, sighed and stared out the window.

"I've seen my mother pray so hard, sweat pours off of her like rain in a thunderstorm!" Micah Brown knew without a doubt he was alive because of that kind of praying.

He had a lot to digest as he drifted in and out of consciousness. There were things that happened throughout his childhood that he never understood. Three months in a hospital bed caused him to have more flashbacks than he could handle. Images that he had long forgotten of a life he had run away from so many years before.

Ministry was just not the way he wanted to live his life. He had watched his father sacrifice everything for the church, never getting proper rest, until it sucked the very life out of him. Then he witnessed his mother's own rejection and scorn as she fought to pursue her dreams to touch the lives of hurting people everywhere.

If truth be told, Micah had been angry with God for a long time. Angry for all the losses his family had endured. Angry that miracles, at least when he made the request, were few and far between. He would never forget the last time he prayed for a miracle. God's rejection of those prayers still plagued his mind as he replayed the heartwarming desperation of his own cries while Ramona's innocent face vanished from his memory.

He wanted her to live more than anything. So he asked, even begged. He pleaded with God to give his sister a second chance. When nothing happened, he bartered with that same God to trade places with her, but once again, his prayers went unanswered. Right until the final hour, young Micah prayed that she would be healed. He prayed as she slipped away into the night, and yes, in enormous pain, he prayed as he looked down upon her frail remains lying in a beautiful white casket.

Growing up as a preacher's kid, he was no stranger to prayer, but he often wondered what, if any, were the benefits. He had not held or read a Bible in years, although he frequented churches when his mother preached. When she asked him about his sword, he always said he left it in the car, but he was lying. He was lying every time.

She must have known. When he awoke from surgery, there was a brand new Bible resting on the nightstand beside him. He wanted to reach out and put it near his heart, but anger said otherwise. It told him that God was punishing him. It whispered to him during the night that God wanted revenge, and it yelled out loud that he would never leave the hospital alive.

It was Daisy that noticed the plastic cover had not been removed. The first time, she simply pointed at the Bible and upon seeing his reaction, she smiled and continued as if she had not noticed. The second time, she was more deliberate. She picked it up, held it in front of him, and when Micah said nothing, she removed the plastic, opened it up, and read Psalms: 23 out loud.

Tears drenched his face. By the time she said the words, "Goodness and mercy shall follow me all the days of my life," he cried out to God to forgive him. That was the moment he forgave his parents for sacrificing everything to a God that he thought did not care about them. On that very day, as he heard the promises of God drop from Daisy's lips, Micah Raymond Brown became a free man.

1975

"I need you to pack your bags and head home."

"Say what? Look a heah, man, I'm not one of your flunkies from the church." Micah jumped up from the bed and put his pants on. "You can't just bust in here like some law, demanding that I go home. I'm home right now, man!"

"You know what I mean. You need to go see about your mother."

"My mother reminds me all the time that she is a grown woman. She can take care of herself. She married Edgar Carter and Lord knows no one is going to mess with her now." He stood up, walked past his intruder and headed to the bar.

"That's what I'm afraid of. I heard some things that have not settled in my spirit for a long time."

"Can't believe everything you hear, man." Micah poured Vodka into the small crystal glass.

"Well, like my crazy mother said, there is some truth in every rumor." The intruder walked into the living room and sat down on the sofa.

"Exactly what are you hearing, Frank Wilcox? From what I've been told, you have your pulse on Jasper County. If you heard something, then I know it's true."

"It took a drink for you to figure that out?" he asked as he leaned toward Micah.

"Man, I'm half asleep. You come in heah, waking me up, talking about heading back to the country that I loathe. That place was my parent's choice, not mine. I don't have any business in Jasper County, and I told them that." He poured another drink, and then turned to Frank. "Ahh, look a heah, I'm sorry, I didn't offer you a drink."

"Don't mess with alcohol. Never did. I'm no saint, just not a drinker. Don't believe I could hold my liquor good anyway." Frank lay back on the sofa.

"Yeah. This is one secret Mom doesn't know about."

"You sure? Mer knows everything about you. Even the women you hang around."

"That's why I live in Atlanta, far away from her eyes."

"She knows about them too." A suspicious grin was on Frank's face.

"I bet she does. That's how you knew where to find me."

"Man, you're like a moving target. Anyone looking can find you though. You got your business all in the street. Too many women never meant any man any good." He winked.

"I could do worse." Micah walked over and sat next to his father's closest confidant. "Tell me, Frank Wilcox, what really brings you all the way to Atlanta?"

"A friend in need is a friend indeed." He gave Micah a stern look.

"Is my mother that friend?"

"She is. I went to see her months ago when I heard the rumors that Edgar struck her down right in the street. She denied it. She said something like what you said. I didn't believe her. I had my people keep a watch on her. Turns out it was not the first time he'd hit her. Seems her younger husband comes from the Devil himself. I used to hear horror stories about his father, Roland Carter. Folks said he gave Lucifer a run for his money."

He demonstrated with his hands. "Man used to grab a person by the neck and squeeze the life out of him right in front of the law. None of them Jasper County hicks ever did anything about it. Just let him roam the Low Country, committing more crimes than someone on the most wanted list."

"This can't be true." Micah slapped his forehead. "Man, I knew it! I felt something was wrong the first time she introduced me to him. I knew I had seen him before. Couldn't put my finger on it, so I assumed it was from one of those dark and smoke filled billiards rooms I love so much. It didn't dawn on me that she was hiding something 'till last time I was there. That's when she mentioned she was leaving him; said he was something different than what she first imagined." His voice escalated with each word.

Michah jumped to his feet and screamed, "That night!" Then he turned toward Frank and cried, "You gotta get her away from him! He is the Devil! I think he killed another woman I met in Savannah."

"What?" Frank stood next to Micah. "How long have you known this?"

"I just connected the dots two minutes ago." Micah walked away, pacing frantically.

"Do you think he remembered you?"

"I'm positive he did. He even offered me a toast. That sorry bastard. How long did he think it would take for me to figure it out?" Micah opened the closet and took out a suitcase.

"It obviously took a long time. You mean to tell me Mer has been married to a suspected killer and nobody knew it?" Frank walked into the kitchen. "Now I need a drink!"

"Help yourself. I said I think he killed this girl. Had enough evil in his eyes one night to rip her skin apart. I don't know if he ever found her, but she swore if he did, he would kill her. I found out the next year she was dead." Micah threw items of clothing into the piece of luggage without looking back at Frank.

"Maybe the fruit don't fall far from the tree. His daddy was the Devil, and it appears Edgar is running a close second." He reached into the refrigerator and grabbed a pitcher of iced tea.

"He fooled her! Said he was a changed man! Always talking about the Lord. Treated Mama like a queen the whole time he courted her. It seemed like he supported her ministry and couldn't wait to work side by side with her in the church. I wonder what happened to make him snap?"

"He must have resurrected his father's demons." Frank walked back into the living room holding the glass of iced tea.

"I thought you needed a strong drink." Micah snapped the locks on the suitcase and walked into the living room. He picked up the telephone receiver, dialed a number, and waited.

"I need you to stay here while I'm away."

"Don't know. Might be a week, might be longer."

"Will you do it for me, baby? All right." He listened for a moment.

"Don't tell anyone that I'm out of town. Just answer my phone and say I'm not here and take a message. Nothing else." He listened to the person on the other end.

"Just business, don't worry, I'll be fine. I'll call here tomorrow and give you a number where you can reach me. Don't give it out to anyone, regardless of what they tell you. I'll give it to my mother, so she won't call looking for me." He stared at Frank and added, "The key is under the mat. Me too." He hung up.

1974

Frank stopped the car in the driveway, but did not exit the vehicle. He kept his eyes on the twenty something women kneeling around the oak tree. Something about their posture on the ground confirmed to him that there was little to worry about. The one he worried most about would be all right.

Too much was going on around him. He had some issues to deal with in New York, a ton of problems with customers below the Mason Dixon line, and a problem or two lurking in Jasper County. Something had to give and give way quick.

He was daydreaming when she tapped on the window. It startled him. He rolled the window down.

"She left. Said she didn't want to bring no more trouble to Mother Ruth or her kids, so she just left. Moved further into town. Nobody knows she lives out there. Not even him."

"How do you know what I'm here for?" A smirk was etched on his face.

"Why do you continue to ask questions to which you already know the answer?" She bent down and stared directly into his eyes.

"Because I know you'll never answer them. You can fool most of the people some of the time, Beulah, but none of the people all of the time. You got a lot a folks fooled into believing you some sort of demented root doctor," he chuckled. "I know the truth and don't you ever forget it.

Only difference between me and you is I stay away from my enemies."

"Keep your friends close and your enemies closer," she laughed.

"What are you doing here?" He reached for the door handle.

She backed up and waited from him to get out of the car. "These women are fascinating. They just might sum up some real power if they keep praying like that." She turned and stared at the women.

"Why aren't they in church?"

"Pastors started to ban them. Said they could not come if they spoke in tongues and refused to accept a man's instruction." She linked her arm inside of Frank's.

"Church folks don't like change. I never understood church folk. Never spent too much time around them until I met Prentiss. He knew the Lord and because of him, I got involved." He stopped walking. "What about you, Chaney? Why you never had any use for church folks?"

"Church folk killed Jesus. Tradition rules them. That's why these women have taken to the streets. If they can't pray the way they want to in church, they come outside to be free to worship any way they want." She rubbed his arm and continued.

"I like it here. Nobody bothers me. Nobody curses the ground I walk on, or calls me and Mama witches or Devil worshippers. These folks just accept anybody that shows up on Ruth's property as if they are family. I never experienced that before." She smiled at him.

"Oh, I see someone's defenses are coming down." He laughed.

"Don't get beside yourself, Frank Wilcox! I'm no fool. This probably won't last and you know it. Good times never last for long around here."

"Well, you're going to have to change that! I've traveled around the world, and met a ton of folks. People are pretty much the same. They just want to be loved and accepted above everything else."

"Now who's getting soft?" She yanked his arm when she stopped walking.

"You know better! I'm saved but still hardcore. Don't play with nobody."

"Did you locate our package?" she whispered.

"I did. It's safe and sound. I doubt if anyone will ever discover it."

"As long as it's safe, that's all that matters."

Ruth Garrett walked toward Beulah and Frank with her arms outstretched.

"Oh, great God!" she screamed. "Frank, is that you? You can't go away and not come back home every once in a while."

Frank released Beulah's arm and hugged Ruth. He had been living in New York for four years. Other than a few late-night visits, not many people knew when he was in town.

"Ruthie, you are still a sight for sore eyes!" He hugged her again.

"Frank? You home for good?" She winked at Beulah.

"Maybe an extended visit. The jury is still out on my decision."

"You been by to see Ida Mae or your mother?" She fussed with the collar of his jacket.

"You know the answer to the latter question. I plan on visiting Ida and Timmy at the club."

"They roasting a hog on Saturday. You should go then. I don't believe Ida is going to the club afterwards. You know Timmy is going to be there. He goes to the club every night without fail. Said he's afraid Sheriff Bryant is going to raid the place again."

"Old troubles. Bryant has been warned, you hear me?" They formed a semi-circle below the front porch steps.

"That never stopped him before! Between Bryant and Edgar Carter, we have a lot to pray and fast about. I just wish I could pour some oil on the both of them at the same time."

"Watch yourself," Beulah interjected.

"Ah, hush up, Beulah Chaney! You know I'm speaking the truth. Both of them are pure evil sometimes. They have gotten such a bad reputation that one of the women put their names down on a piece of paper and nailed it to that oak tree. When it rained last week, paper still dry. You tell me, what kind of spirit is that?"

"The kind of evil that only a bullet will stop," Frank added.

"No, no!" She raised her voice. "Frank, don't you start that foolishness. We are not taking this on, no sir. The Lord has declared that vengeance is his to repay. When he gets finished with all these sinners, they will be too busy fighting him to ever pay us attention again."

"That's not what y'all praying about, is it?" Frank took both of Ruth's hands and held them in front of her.

"Oh, we pray for a ton of things all at once. We even have you and this thang here on our altar," she said with a chuckle.

"You can remove my name now. I've gotten about as much as I'm going to get out of your prayers. Tell the women it's working too." Beulah sat down on the steps.

"Are you dead?" Ruth screamed.

"You're standing here looking at me, what do you think?"

"Well, sistah, you said you no longer needed prayer. And, honey, only a dead person no longer needs prayer. All of us living need as much prayer as we can get."

"Well, I guess it won't hurt," Beulah said shyly.

"I don't believe my ears! Beulah Chaney has backed down in an argument? I never thought I'd live to see the day!" Frank, arms above his head, danced in a circle.

"What's all that dancing about, Frank?" Ruth looked at him suspiciously. "A man acting like that is in love."

"Funny, you say that all the time. You know marriage ain't fo' me." He looked at the women gathered beneath the oak tree.

"Don't have to be married to fall in love," Beulah added.

"Lots of good, single women out here. You are a good man, Frank Wilcox. The Bible says marriage is honorable, so what do you find so difficult about it?" Ruth asked him.

"Nothing. Remember, I did it once. Not interested in doing it again. I'm getting too old and tired to chase after children. It would have been nice to raise some grands though." His voice trembled with regret.

"Be careful what you pray for, you just might get it." Beulah laughed.

"Who said I'm praying for it?" He put his hand over his brow to block the sun.

"Only time will tell, huh." She looked at Ruth.

"Well, if you are, just keep holding on. God answers prayers. May seem like a lifetime to get what we want, but when it comes…it comes in a big way, I tell ya!" Ruth turned around and focused on the women underneath the tree. "God always has a plan. He never takes something away from us that he is not prepared to give back to us when we are ready."

Frank ignored Ruth at that point. She knew his secret. She knew why he never wanted to marry again. No amount of words could console him, even after all these years.

He finally spoke. "Who is that woman standing near the cornfields?"

"Who's asking? Frank, my cousin, or Frank the private investigator that thinks he's Columbo or Petrachelli?"

They all laughed. Frank kept his eye on the woman standing near the cornfields. He knew her. Although it was a long time ago, he remembered the night she arrived on his doorstep. He remembered, as if it were yesterday.

It had become his lot in life to rescue women in distress. She was the first, and, all these years later, he was certain that Mary Brown Carter would not be the last. Something drove women to his home. He never turned one of them away. He never refused to shelter them from the dangers around them, regardless of the cost.

Despite what was said about him, despite what anyone thought about the mysterious, powerfully low-keyed individual, Frank Wilcox was the one man in Jasper County that personified integrity. The women were the first to discover this truth, but years later, the entire county found out.

TWO

1958

Christmas delivered two terrible blows to the Wilcox family. The first came when Anne was killed in Harlem; the second hit Frank Wilcox right between the eyes. Over time, he became too familiar with the set of twins known as Pain and Loss. In fact, by that time he was a young man he knew much about the both of them. Knew each time they crept into his life, and knew the devastation they brought with them, destroying everything within their path and doing permanent damage that could never be erased.

The decorations were made from solid pieces of wood. He carved them himself and painted each a vibrant color, red, gold, green, or blue. When he finished, he hung the tiny ornaments from the tree branches, and then placed miniature wooden statues of the Nativity around the room. The Wilcox's had something big to celebrate, but it never came to pass.

Two weeks shy of Christmas day, Frank's wife, Leslie, became ill and was forced to deliver the baby two months earlier than expected. Since Ridgeland's hospital offered no neonatal services, Frank drove her to Savannah. She died two hours after giving birth.

Their baby girl survived the birth process, but remained weak from complications during the delivery. Although she weighed five pounds, a condition known as Apnea of

Brachycardia diminished her chances of survival. Eight days later, while resting on her father's bosom, in the nursery they built just for her, the little angel returned to her home in Heaven.

Frank left the entire house the same way it was before his life was tragically torn apart. The Christmas tree stayed up until it rotted, and the gifts remained underneath the tree's remains, until he moved away almost three years later. He never entered the nursery they decorated together, nor opened any of the packages purchased prior to Leslie's illness. In fact, he slept in the living room until his new home was built, and after he removed a few belongings out of the old house, he burned the structure, that held all of his precious memories, down to the ground.

1962

He saw her sitting on his front porch. She had been there for a little over an hour, after knocking on the door for ten minutes while he sat watching her from a chair next to the front window in the living room. He dared not open the door, for whatever she wanted would have dire consequences for him and he knew it.

She eventually arose from the glider and walked down the steps out into the yard. After she walked a good twenty feet, she turned around and watched Frank open the front door, look at the package she'd left for him, pick it up, and take it into the house.

A few nights later, Frank was awakened by loud banging on the back door. He grabbed his shotgun and ran toward the back of the house. Then he heard her faint voice.

"Mistah Frank. It's me," she whispered into the door. "I come tuh warn yah. They coming fo' yuh, sir. Klan not happy yuh heah. They plan tuh burn yuh house down tuh da ground."

Frank stood in the doorway, but never opened the door. When he heard her turn around and walk down the steps, he stood in the window watching.

She was wearing a thin white tee shirt and cut off denim shorts. As she placed her foot on the bottom stair, she turned back and said, "I was hopin' yuh was home. I know you don't like me, but I don't want nothing bad tuh happen tuh yuh, sir. Just wouldn't be right. You seem like decent folk. I thanks people got a right tuh live where dey wants."

"I think so too." He finally spoke. "You best get on before they arrive. I don't want them finding out about you."

It was silent the entire night. The next night, around midnight, Frank watched as twelve men jumped from a pickup truck and headed into his front yard. A few marched onto the front porch. Frank, fully dressed, was seated inside with a loaded double-barrel shotgun tightly held in his hands. He turned on every single light in the house. He even turned on the black and white television set that he rarely watched.

"Yuh don't belong heah, boy! This not yuh side o' town," someone yelled from the porch.

"Yuh got two weeks tuh move! G'wan back tuh your own kind's side o' town. Go where yuh belong," another voice yelled.

Frank never moved. In fact, he never blinked the entire time. With a steady finger on the trigger, he looked straight ahead at the front door awaiting the Klan's intrusion.

After a few minutes, he heard a lot of banging in his yard, looked out of the window and saw the wooden cross as it was being driven into the ground. Then, he watched in horror as the men set the torch against it. Frank sat still and closed his eyes.

The next morning, he arose from the chair he'd spent the night in, walked into the bathroom to shave, and walked outside onto the front porch. He looked at the charred cross and smiled.

When dusk fell, Frank gathered what was left of the cross, placed it in the back of the truck, and drove four houses down the road. He entered the long driveway, grabbed his revolver, and pulled up to within a few feet of the front door. When he came to a stop, he stepped out of the truck, removed the cross, took out a shovel, dug a hole and stuck the cross into the ground. Then he remembered something.

Frank ran back to the truck. He opened the glove compartment and pulled out a photo of two women, two little girls, and a man standing behind them. Frank stared at it for a few minutes. Finally, he stepped out of the truck, took a nail out of his pocket, stuck it into the photo, and pushed it into the charred cross.

He drove off the property, the same way he'd arrived: Extremely calm. He had sent a message that even the Klan understood.

1975

Mary stood in her small backyard looking around. Solace was once again becoming a good friend. She now felt confident that she could stand alone outside without the fear that Edgar would charge upon her. It had been nine months since she left, and she vowed to never look back at her horrid past seven years again.

As suspected, he chased her. Showed up each time she settled down, followed her in his car, and even walked straight up to her in Piggly Wiggly and threatened her.

"Yuh not free." His eyes looked as if fire burned behind his pupils.

"I am." She looked at the contents in her cart for a weapon if needed.

"Yuh still mah wife. Mah property. I let yuh go. Got too much going on to be dealing with yuh foolishness. Yuh can leave the house, run from me, but I ain't giving yuh no divorce papers. As long as I live, another man ain't gone put his hands on you, either." He stood close behind her and placed both hands on top of hers as they rested on the grocery cart.

"Leave me alone, Edgar! I don't want to deal with you. You can do what you want. As for another man, you ruined that from ever happening. I don't know how you fooled everybody, but I pray one day folks learn just how much foolishness you got your hands into."

"Who gon' tell 'em? Surely not you." He stood directly on the side of her so that she could feel the pistol lodged in the waistline of his pants.

"I won't have to. They will find out on their own." She finally got the courage to look into his eyes.

"By then, I'll destroy yuh and that son o' yours too. Just remember no one can protect you, I got the law in my front pocket. Anything I want tuh do tuh you when I feel like it, I'm gon' do. That means honoring your wifely duties if need be." He released her hands.

"Ha!" Mary was agitated and spoke through gritted teeth. "I'm not afraid of you, Edgar, and as far as wifely duties are concerned, if I ever have to lie with you again, one of us is going to die!"

"Yeah, we'll see about that." He was distracted and walked beyond Mary to the short, brown skinned woman on the other side of the isle.

Later...

Mary heard a car drive into the driveway and ran into the living room. She had no weapons, but Ruth had given her a baseball bat and taught her how to swing it. She grabbed the bat and headed toward the front door. Then she stopped.

Whoever was on the other side of the door did not move. Mary peeked out of the window, and seeing no one, noticed the brand new Cutlass Supreme parked in the front yard. She burst out laughing and placed the baseball bat down next to the door.

"I hear women like fancy cars!" She opened the door.

"I hear they do. This one is not for one of my women; I bought this one for you!" Micah stood on the other side of the metal glider holding fresh cut flowers.

"What am I going to do with a fancy car like that, man? You must think I am still a young gal." She reached for the flowers.

"In my eyes, you will always be a young woman. Age cannot defy your God-given beauty." He stepped into the entryway and planted a huge kiss on her cheek.

"How did you find me?" She walked toward the kitchen in the back of the small house.

"I didn't. Frank did." He looked around. Other than two pictures of his father and Ramona hanging on the wall, everything else appeared to be newly acquired.

"So, this is your new beginning?"

"Yes. I guess you can say that. It's been a long time coming." She turned around and displayed the flowers now resting in a vase.

He looked around and then said, "Why didn't you tell me?"

"Tell you what? That I married a man I thought I loved, but he turned out to be someone else? I'm a little too old to make a mistake like that. I mean, Edgar is a wolf in sheep's clothing, and you know something? He's a hurting wolf at that. I don't even think he knows how to stop the pain in his life. So, yeah, been through a lot and I'm sure you and Frank heard the rumors. Some true, some not so true. Bottom line, I'm free and none of you have to worry about Edgar coming after me."

"You can't believe that, Mother! This man has shown the whole town that he can do what he wants. Not even Sheriff Bryant is big enough to step to him. I hear the entire police department is afraid of Edgar. I wonder what he has on them." He sat down at the kitchen table.

"Something. I tell you that. They say his father ruled this town for many years. Not even the Klan came after that man. He was able to go about murdering entire families. Edgar is the child of one of his women, but he grew up in another area. He thought he was safe returning here. Boy, oh boy, was he wrong!" She sat down and put her head on her son's shoulder.

"So you never suspected anything was up with this man?"

"Not at first. Not for a long time. Then I heard him speak very poorly to another man one day. Even his accent changed. I watched in horror, but I never said a word. I just thought he was mad, you know? Never thought that demonic spirit I witnessed that day would ever rear its ugly head again. But I was wrong. It reared its head from the moment we stepped foot in Jasper County. Must be some kind of curse, I just don't know."

"Why did you suffer so many years in silence?" he asked.

"Because I was waiting on the Lord to show me why I had taken this path in life. I wanted to know what role the Lord had assigned for me in Edgar's life. I kept trying to save him, but it was no use. He hated me and everything I stood for."

"I knew it from day one." Micah looked at the vase in front of him.

"What do you mean? You knew what from day one?"

"I knew he was bad news. If I'd have said anything to you, you wouldn't have listened though. Remember your wedding day? I gave you a way out, but you went ahead and married him. I just wish Frank could have been there to stop you."

"Oh, come on! Give me a little more credit. I knew he was not a Prentiss Raymond Brown. No one could ever replace that man. Edgar was a distant third that presented himself quite well. By the time I realized he was a pathological liar, it was too late. I had already taken vows before the Lord to honor him."

"Mother, marriage is no death sentence. I am sure God gives ways to divorce in the Bible. He never intended for His children to be caught up in so much pain. You didn't have children, so why not..." She interrupted before he could finish the sentence.

"It's more complicated than that. I wear a cloth around my neck that declares to the world that I am a woman of God. That means I have to be careful about the things I do and say. I had to know for myself whether his behavior was something he was just going through, or future evidence of his vile spirit. When I was certain that he was practicing and living evil in our home, I left. Found out he was in Charlestown with some woman. Stayed a week. She must be fooled too."

"He hit you?" Micah slammed his fists on the table.

"Yes, son. He struck me a few times."

"What? You say that like it's nothing! That demon put his hands on you a few times? Why didn't you tell me then?"

"Because I knew what your reaction would be. I've already lost a husband and a daughter; I don't want to lose my son." She started to cry.

Micah remained silent for a while. "I'm so sorry, Mother. I'm not judging you. You've dealt with this mess for years; I've only had a few days to process everything. I know I should have been here with you all those years."

"No, son, honestly, I was fine. The Lord protected me. It may have been rough, but God kept his hand on me every step of the way. I'm still here, aren't I?"

1977

Ruth sternly watched the women seated around the kitchen table. Their small circle had tripled in size making it impossible to pray in the house, but they always ate breakfast in the kitchen, living room, and on the back porch. Breakfast became a tradition of the prayer circle; one that continued for more than fifty years.

Barely eating anything, Ruth suspected that something was brewing right underneath her nose. The women were behaving odd and she noticed how they avoided certain subjects when she was in their presence. It was the tiny subtleties that troubled her the most. The sharp pains alongside her abdominal walls confirmed that whatever they were hiding was something big.

She spoke a few words, but mainly watched, as an observer, focusing on each woman's mannerisms. She watched each one of them carefully; the way she held her eating utensils, held the tiny teacup to sip coffee , and even how she wiped her mouth with the handmade cloth towels Ruth placed in the center of each eating station.

Surveying the room and ignoring the nagging pains in her stomach, Ruth eyes shot straight open when it dawn on her that someone was missing. But, who was it? All of her favorites were assembled in the crowd. While the women busied themselves fussing over the linens and the food, she silently took a head count. The circle normally consisted of thirty women who faithfully attended breakfast. Today, there were approximately twenty nine women in the room. Who had she forgotten about?

Ruth got up from her seat and walked toward her bedroom, then, without warning, she spun back around. The women noticed. She said nothing, just looked at each one of them carefully.

Pauline Davis was not in her usual seat next to the television, nor was she hovering over the stove, or leaning against the back porch door, head turning back and forth in an attempt to participate in the conversations in the house and on the back porch.

Nothing about her absence seemed positive. Ruth strutted into her bedroom and knelt down beside the mahogany poster bed and prayed. She could hear the women resume their normal conversations as they washed, stacked and dryed the dirty dishes. When she still had not returned, she heard them as they put the dishes back into the china cabinet that surrounded the sink or in the wooden cupboard Augustus built that sat right next to the kitchen table.

Ruth reappeared in the entrance of the large hallway.

"Y'all seen Pauline? I wanted her to lead prayer today." She looked around suspiciously. "Where is she?"

The shocked looks on their faces gave it away.

"Oh, I'm sure she'll be heah any minute," a voice rang out from the back porch.

"I never knew Pauline to miss breakfast. She never miss my hoeke cakes, swears they the best on Earth. I wonder what's keeping her?" Ruth walked over to the living room window and stared out into her front yard.

"I'm sure it ain't too serious, Mother Ruth, or we would know by now," Mable added.

"Hmm." Ruth started to hum.

Everyone present that morning was familiar with Ruth's humming. They knew they had failed to convince her that Pauline was on her way to the prayer breakfast. Ruth Fields Garrett paid close attention to tiny details and Pauline was always the first one to arrive.

They looked at each other for direction.

Ruth turned around, raised her arm and then pointed into their faces one by one.

"You must have a pure heart when you go before God in prayer. Y'all know that. Now march your little selves out to that oak tree and decide how you're going to tell me whatever has happened to that child! She's been acting strange for weeks! She's even taken to missing evening services. You think I didn't notice?" She raised her voice. "I noticed!"

"But, Mama Ruth..." Molly tried to interject.

"No, ma'am. You won't try to clean this mess up now! You started off wrong. Now I hope you repent for sitting here acting as if you did not know what happened to that beautiful angel. Y'all need to remember your Bible stories right this minute! I am that shepherd that will take my entire herd of sheep just to find the one that's missing. Now you better go on out there and pray for forgiveness and direction! Y'all want to keep secrets? Okay, but the God I serve is going to expose that lying spirit, ya hear me?" She opened the door as the women filed out onto the front porch, heads hanging.

They walked out into the yard never looking back at Ruth as she stood behind the screened door watching them. After forming a circle around the tree, the women cried out in loud voices, begging for forgiveness. Ruth stood watching for a few minutes and then closed the door. It was their private time with the Lord. Whatever they were hiding could only be revealed to her at their own free will. She knelt down in front of the sofa and continued praying.

Moments later, as Ruth lay prostrate on the floor, speaking in the Holy Spirit, she was interrupted by violent loud screams from outside her front door. She jumped up and opened the curtains only to see women running up the stairs onto the front porch. The door was unlocked.

"Mama Ruth, help us!" Mable was the first to enter the house. Some of the women even stormed up the back porch steps and ran through the door in the kitchen. They were hysterical.

"What's wrong?" Ruth stood before them in shock. "What is all the screaming about?" she demanded.

"We are so sorry! Please forgive us, Mother Ruth!" they screamed in unison.

"God have mercy on our souls!" One of the women collapsed on the floor in front of Ruth.

Another woman was crying hysterically, but tried to get the words out. "We...we didn't mean no harm. She begged us not to tell you!" She sobbed uncontrollably.

Ruth put her arms up into the air. "Everyone please calm down! What has y'all so upset? You know I forgive you for what you did. So why you running and screaming, falling out on the floor, lying prostrate all over this room?"

"God spoke to us!"

"What?"

"He caused the wind to blow hard and the branches made a humming sound and then he spoke!" The woman dropped to the floor.

"Who spoke?" Ruth was furious.

"God spoke through the tree!" someone yelled.

"What? What fool thang you talking? Hush up your foolishness and tell me what happened!"

"Ma Ruth, the tree spoke back to us, telling us to repent! It was God, I know it!" Mable cried.

"That Devil is a liar!"

Ruth ran onto the front porch, stared at the aged oak tree, and gazed up into the air. The skies were clear and heavenly blue with patches of white running through them. She walked back into the house to witness most of the women now huddled together in prayer.

"I don't know what is going on. That oak tree did not talk. Maybe the Spirit of God spoke to each of you, but I am sure the tree never opened its mouth, if it had one." She walked over and lifted Mable's body from the floor.

"And they call me crazy! Get yourselves together this minute! We are going back out there."

"No! I ain't going out dere! Whatever is out dere can stay! I ain't fooling wid no spirits, Sistah!" Pearlie said, holding her abdomen and panting uncontrollably.

"Chile, sit down! Everyone in here, sit down! If you want to pray, fine! Just sit yourselves down and let the Lord calm your spirits! This spirit of confusion is not God, I tell ya!" Ruth stormed out of the house.

She stood underneath the oak tree.

"Father, in the name of Jesus, please tell me what is going on? I thank you for these women, they really love and adore you, Daddy. You said you would give us perfect peace if we kept our minds on you. Do it now, Heavenly Father. Satan, the snare of the fouler is broken. I rebuke you in Jesus's name. You cannot put fear in our hearts. We are protected by the Blood of Jesus."

Before she concluded, she heard movement in the branches of the oak tree. Ruth opened her eyes, raised both arms to block the sun's glare and looked around. She caught a glimpse of the women gathered together in her living room window watching her every move. She purposely stood with her back to them so that they could not see what she was about to do.

The frown that had consumed her face softened. The memories in her mind took her back to a childhood she had long forgotten. A faint smile crept on her face as Ruth looked up at the branches of the enormous old oak tree and whispered, "Don't break your butt trying to get down out of this tree! You should be ashamed of yourself! Mark my words sistah, I'll deal with them now, but I'm coming after you later."

She turned around, hid the delightful feeling that had overtaken her, and marched back into the house.

THREE

1978

Ida sat on the bar stool moving her hips in the seat. She loved fast music, but rarely stood up anymore and danced. She was afraid Timmy would complain that she was having too much fun and not contributing to the club's overall profit margin.

Over the years, Timetheous Tilley had become obsessed with having money and discussions regarding it became a daily ritual. He started each day reviewing the club's receipts from the night before, before focusing on ways to bring in more customers, offer more entertainment, and expand the operations beyond the limits of Jasper and Beaufort Counties. He made no qualms about it. He was a businessman and would do just about anything to make his dreams of owning clubs throughout the Deep South come true.

Ida was just the opposite. To her, money was good, but she had everything, with one exception, that she could ever want in life. Thoughts of expansion actually scared her, for she knew with each club, there would be more enemies lurking about to destroy everything she and Timmy had worked so hard to build. She was certain of this.

It was a Saturday night, the busiest night of the week. When the crowd reached the 250 limit capacity, the hired hands would start a line outside, awaiting a departure before letting anyone else inside. Normally, this was not something they paid attention to, but after four encounters with Sheriff Bryant, even resulting in the club being closed for three weeks, they learned the hard way to obey whatever rule he said pertained to them.

Thoughts of his resurrection always made Ida nervous. As long as he was around, she would always have to look over her shoulder, regardless if she had done anything wrong or not. He made it clear that he wanted to destroy her at all costs and, to Ida Mae, his words were not a threat, they were a promise.

Timmy had gone to one of their suppliers earlier that day. He called an hour before the club opened to say that he was running late. Ronald assumed his responsibilities at the bar and their youngest brother, Jerrold, replaced Ronald as the nightly disc jockey. Everything was going smoothly, but Ida was not at ease.

Dressed in a form fitting burgundy sweater dress, she wore her hair up in a bun that evening. She had worked all day to get the new kitchen ready and had no time to deal with hot combs or curlers. In fact, she intended to leave the club as soon as Timmy arrived.

To the right of her sat a table full of women, congregated together and gossiping. Ida noticed that none of them had danced the entire night, nor had they purchased any alcoholic beverages. She kept watching them, until she noticed the eyes of someone on her left, fixated on her every move. Ida looked out of the corner of eye, but never turned to acknowledge the observer. She continued dancing in her seat and checked on the women on her right, until it was obvious that the person eyeing her from the left was headed in her direction.

Ida turned around in the seat and saw a brown-skinned, average height woman, approaching middle age, walking directly to where she was seated. She kept her composure and then looked back at Ronald. Like clockwork, he had spotted the same woman.

"I'll have a Budweiser." The woman addressed Ronald. She kept her back to Ida.

"Enjoying yuhself?" He asked her.

"Definitely. Nice club. Interesting name," she said.

"That's what my brother thought when he renamed the original club. Thought the name would pique folks' curiosity. Not your average Low Country establishment, you see." Ronald put a coaster on the bar and then sat the bottle of cold beer in front of her.

"Mmm. Just the way I like it." She smiled.

"Club name the only thing that brought you heah?" He waited to connect with her eyes.

"Had a friend from here. She's long gone, but I thought I would check out her hometown once I took vacation."

"Vacation!" he screamed. "You must not be from around heah. Folks vacation right in the house!" He continued laughing.

"I'm from New York, Harlem, U.S.A. I grew up a few blocks from Lennox Avenue before moving to the Gardens." She turned and looked at Ida.

"What's the Gardens? Ida's brother visits Harlem sometimes, don't he, Ida?" He watched the woman's reaction.

The stranger turned around and looked at Ida. She half smiled and extended her short arm, filled with silver and gold bangles, out to Ida. Ida hesitated before shaking it.

"I'm Freda Dunne. Did you catch me staring at you earlier?"

Ida was embarrassed. "Sho' did. Bet you thought I was somebody else. Folks make that mistake all the time."

"I apologize for staring. You're a spittin' image of a very special person I used to know. I was shocked, that's all. They say northerners lack manners you know."

"No problem. You ain't need tuh apologize. No harm done." Ida turned her body toward the woman.

"I appreciate your kindness." Then she pushed the half empty bottle toward Ronald and said, "I never could handle my liquor. You better take this before I do something I will regret."

"How long you in town fo', " Ida interrupted.

"Until Monday. I promised a friend I would escort her to church. She seems to think churches down here are better than the ones in New York. She calls my pastor siddity, being a United States congressman and all."

"Your pastor is one of them congressmen too? An' he black?" Ida seemed puzzled.

"There's not many of them, I tell you. Yes, he's black, don't look it," she laughed, "but he's black for sure." She started to walk away.

"You came here alone?" Ida stepped off the bar stool and stood face to face with the woman.

"No. You see that boy dancing like he's lost his mind?" She pointed to a very stylish young man on the dance floor.

"Yeah. He wild. I saw him dancing earlier. You see that group of women in the corner?" Ida pointed at the crew she surveyed earlier. "They can't stop talking about 'im. Won't dance wid anyone, thinking he gon' come and ask one of them tuh dance,"

"What? That's funny. He's usually shy. That's Floyd Williams. He has roots down here. His parents live in New York too. Mother disappeared after a few years and Floyd's father raised him on his own."

"Ronald, you recognize him?" Ida looked back at her brother in law.

"Nope. Never seen him a day in my life." Then he leaned on the bar and asked Freda, "He over eighteen, ain't he? We can't go to jail for a Yankee." He smiled.

"Yes, sir, he's legal," she said.

"He sure got some big hands on him to be so slender." Ida watched the way he snapped his fingers while dancing.

Floyd saw them staring and headed over to the bar. "You ready to go?" he asked Freda.

"I was, but I hear you need to ask one of those women at that table for a dance or you'll break their hearts." Freda looked at Ida and smiled.

"I'm tired. Besides, they obviously don't mind sitting there, they have not moved all night! I've seen brothers ask them to dance. I don't want to have my face on the ground after they tell me no." He turned and looked at them. The women at the table all giggled.

"Oh, come on, Floyd, be a gentleman and ask one of them. I promise we will leave afterwards." Freda turned to face the dance floor.

Floyd was hesitant. He finally looked at Ronald, who gave him a coy look, and marched over to the table, said hello, and escorted a tall robust woman out onto the center of the dance floor. The other women, shorter and much slender than his selection, watched in shock.

"You think he can handle huh?" Ronald stood watching.

"Ah hush up man! That big girl can dance like a skinny woman." Ida chuckled.

"Ya think? He better check with Joe Tex and stop bumping with them big fat women." Ronald held his head back and hollered loudly.

Freda took the opportunity to get a closer look at Ida Mae before speaking again. "You do church in the morning, Miss Ida?"

"Nope. Never have. Been about twice with a cousin of mine as a girl, ain't been since," Ida answered.

"Wow! I didn't think there was a person in the South that skipped church." She kept her eyes on the excitement on the dance floor.

"Other than my brother, Frank, none of us goes. Besides, I run a juke joint. What kind of witness would I be?" Ida laughed.

"The kind the real world needs, Miss Ida."

"I can tell yuh different than folks around heah. They say we sinners and going straight to hell for running these clubs. Nobody, 'cept my cousin, talk about us going to church." Ida sat back down on the bar stool.

"Well, Miss Ida, I was told God will wait a lifetime for us to get our acts together. It's never too late to come back. I used to ask my friend every Saturday without fail, but she never got the opportunity. She promised she would make her debut on Christmas Day, but it never happened." Freda turned to face the bar.

"Why? Something stop huh?" Ida was perplexed.

"Yes. Life stopped her. Unfortunately, she died too soon." Freda avoided looking directly into Ida's face.

"So she went to hell, huh?" Ida put her chin in her hand and leaned on the bar.

"I don't know. I believe she found Christ and accepted Him, just by the way she behaved before she died. She was a changed woman. Said she was going back to school, even enrolled in one of the city's programs, but never had an opportunity to finish."

"Tomorrow ain't promised tuh none of us, huh?" Ida looked directly at Freda.

"I learned that the hard way, Miss Ida."

1976

Ruth sat on the sofa and gazed out of the window. She hated high rise buildings, but curiosity caused her to peer out of the window of the twenty first floor in amazement.

"What happens if a fire starts? How will you get out?"

"Not many fires in the Gardens. I guess you can say we're blessed. We can't get on the elevators, so we take the stairwell. Pray we make it, huh."

"But you have small children. Doesn't that bother you?" Ruth opened the curtain again.

"They are trained what to do. By the time a child is three in New York, he knows what to do in case of a fire."

"Well, I plead the blood of Jesus over this entire building. I bind up every demonic spirit that comes to kill, still, and destroy this place through fire. It will not happen! In Jesus name, I pray." Ruth opened her eyes and looked at her friend.

"I'm so glad you took Daisy's advice and came to stay with me. You can consider this your second your home. My husband met Gus when he first joined the military. That's all he would write home about, Duke Garrett. When I met him, I agreed, Gus was someone special. He had a unique way with people, it didn't matter where they were from. He was a natural gift of God." She looked at Ruth. "I still can't believe he's gone."

"I laugh sometimes to keep from crying. Gus used to say he just wanted to see the world before God called his number." Tears formed in Ruth's eyes.

"I heard him say the same thing one day. Didn't seem worried about dying at all."

"He wasn't. He loved the Lord. The Apostle Paul said to live is Christ, and to die is gain. We gain the entire kingdom when we leave this earth." Ruth stood up and put her hands on her hips.

"Is that the hint to for me to start dinner? Even when you are not at home, you have a set time for everything. Your'e so organized, I can't keep up."

"Francine, children forced me to be organized. If not, they'd run circles around me, you hear me?" She walked toward the kitchen.

As Ruth walked through the large apartment, she felt her friend slip her hand inside of hers. Ruth smiled inside. In Francine, she had found someone who shared her pain. They met before she married Augustus and even after having children, Ruth and Augustus visted the Dunnes in Harlem every single year.

Francine's husband, Douglas, was violently murdered during an attempted robbery four years before Augustus was killed. It happened right outside of the brownstone they lived in, yet there were no witnesses.

Francine shoved Ruth to the side and started to run. "Last one there is a rotten egg!

Ruth just laughed. In the hallway, she noticed a picture on the wall that made her stop walking and gasped.

"Francine, come back here for a minute, please." She continued staring at the picture prominitely displayed on the wall.

Francine walked back and stopped in front of Ruth.

"We were best friends. Not a day goes by that I don't think of her. She came from the South, not sure where. She acted like she had something to prove. I tried to school her on the evils of city life, but she thought she knew it all. She was so naive."

"What happened to her?" Ruth could feel a strange sensation in her gut.

"She was killed in the heat of an argument. Apparently, her boyfriend associated with some evil people. They eventually turned against him. She was just an innocent victim! What happened to her should never have happened." Francine grabbed Ruth's hand and they walked into the kitchen and sat at the small table next to the stove.

Ruth looked into the distance for a long while. She forgot about cooking. She even forgot about her children playing in the bedroom at the end of the hall. She could only think about one thing: How God strategically placed Francine in her life all those years ago. Tears flooded her eyes as she watched her friend sob uncontrollably as if Anne Deveareaux Wilcox had been murdered only yesterday.

1980

Benjamin walked out onto the front porch where Ruth was resting. He checked to see if she was awake and then came closer.

"Are you tired, Mother?"

"No, Benjamin, I'm doing just fine. Thank you for checking. When I write to your brother Larry, I'll be sure to tell him how much you take after him." She opened one eye.

"Larry is over protective, but I know when to give you space." He sat next to her.

"What are your comrades in there doing?"

"Trying to get Jonah to put her shoes on." He chuckled.

"Jonah!" Ruth yelled. She could hear commotion in the house just from the sound of her voice. "If you don't want to sit under me the entire time you're in church, you better behave yourself now!"

Benjamin grabbed her hand and lightly planted a kiss. "Did I tell you my homeroom teacher keeps asking questions about me?"

"What kind of questions?"

"About where I come from, do I know my biological parents, how long have I been in Ridgeland? Stuff like that." He shrugged his shoulders.

"When did this start?" Ruth felt her temperature rise.

"Soon as she saw me." He looked at her.

"What's your teacher's name?"

"Miz Harley."

"Who? That was not your teacher's name at the beginning of the school year!" Ruth opened both eyes and sat up.

"Yeah, Miz Hawkins left."

"Watch what you tell folks. I told you the truth about everything I know. When the time is right, I am sure the Lord will reveal the rest. In the meantime, you tell Miz Harley if she wants to know anything about your origins, she needs to contact me, you hear me?" Ruth stood up and waved at Mary Brown Carter.

Ruth and Mary strolled toward Second African Baptist Church. It had become customary for the women in the prayer circle to stop at Ruth's house before services for devotion, sing songs of praise, and finally pray before heading to Sunday School. The children were allowed to go ahead of the adults, and if they behaved, they could sit with other children on a pew especially for them during the actual services.

Mary, dressed in all tan with matching hat and cape, seemed extremely happy about something. She looked at Ruth and smiled.

"I asked Pastor Jones if I could assist sometimes. I told him I don't want to be out front right now, just too soon, but I can handle some of the administrative responsibilities of the church and help the deaconess with planning for the week."

"Oh. What did he say?" Ruth was still thinking about what Benjamin told her earlier that day.

"He acted strange at first. Then he said he had enough hands now, but would consider me when the need arises."

"Liar! His wife died almost a year ago. She refused to help around the church and those deaconesses are a joke. All they do is compete to secure a ring from that man. Why can't they give him a break! Let the man mourn, why don't they?" Ruth wondered if she needed to telephone Frank to check into this Harley woman.

"Those women better seek God first! I heard Clarence Jones is one ornery man. He always had that poor woman looking like she was going to a funeral, dressed in black every Sunday. And, I am not so sure she did not want to help out; I think he would not let her." They stopped walking and waited for some of the other women to catch up.

"You sure you want to work close to him?" Ruth looked around. She was becoming suspicious of everything.

"What choice do I have? None of these other preachers will give me the time of day. At least he calls and asks me to do Sunday School and prayer services. That's the most requests I've had since we returned." Mary headed into the vestibule.

Ruth stood outside of the church and greeted those coming in. She did this at every service she attended and since Sunday services rotated between the four churches in town, Ruth often singled out new faces that she had not had the pleasure of meeting on prior occasions.

She knew rumors about her illness surfaced every now and again. She saw a few people attempt to avoid her and even intercepted their child's hand to prevent direct contact. This did not bother her one bit. During those years, there was little understanding, if any, of the disease with which she had been diagnosed. Folks were afraid of things they could not understand, and Ruth was all too familiar with the enormous amount of ignorance and fear in the South.

She thought again about Benjamin. Since he was old enough to understand, she told him that his mother had moved away to Savannah, because that was the last place listed on the postmark. That was fifteen years ago. There had been no communication from her since then.

It took a while before Ruth was able to put some of the pieces of the puzzle together. The young woman, barely in her twenties, lived somewhere near Frank Wilcox. When she conceived a child out of wedlock, she went to him for help. Frank hid the woman until she gave birth. Afterward, she returned home to her parents, but never breathed a word about her newborn. Months later, she disappeared with the child's father en route to Atlanta. When their plans fell apart, she returned to the low country and married someone else. As soon as her husband discovered the truth, he threatened to kill the boy, which at that time, the woman sought refuge from the one man who always came to her aid, Frank. He sent her to Ruth.

Frank never disclosed the woman or her family's identity, or why the child posed a problem, other than the fact that she was unmarried. Yet over the years, Ruth noticed strange things about Benjamin that gave away the woman's secret.

In 1970, she took Benjamin down to City Hall to obtain full custody of him. Frank assured her that she would have no problem getting the proper documentation, although Benjamin had been in school for years and no one ever said a word. However, since the integration of South Carolina's public schools, stricter rules applied requiring legal documents for every child enrolled.

His secret remained well kept while he attended the segregated Thomas Haywood Academy, yet it unraveled the moment Lula Peters saw him playing in the yard one day. He was a Peters, and there was no getting around it. In fact, he was the son of Marion Alice Peters, Chadwick and Lula's estranged daughter whom they had not heard a word from in over a decade.

A week later after she discovered the truth, Lula Peters made another visit to Ruth's house. This time, she handed Ruth an envelope and the keys to a safe deposit box with explicit instructions that she would deposit money into the account every month to assist in her grandson's wellbeing. Ruth objected, but Lula insisted that she use the money to keep Benjamin as far away as possible from Chadwick Peters. That request would prove to be virtually impossible.

FOUR

1979

For three years the police made no arrests in the death of Edgar Roland Carter. Sheriff Bryant maintained the investigation was still pending. But that changed when, after believing he had put together all of the pieces to the puzzle, he made his move.

He drove down the dark service road around four-thirty in the morning. He knew if he wanted to catch her off guard, he would have to come knocking before she opened her eyes to face a new day. It was rumored that she worked at the high school as a substitute teacher. He had to get there before she left.

As he turned into the driveway, he turned off the front lights. When he was within a few feet of the house, he put the car's gear in neutral, gliding the rest of the way until he was able to coast around to the side of her small house.

Although the front of the house was dark, as soon as he stepped out of the vehicle, he noticed a back porch light and, upon a closer look, saw that a small lamp was dimly lit in one of the rear bedrooms. Tiptoeing, Charles Bryant walked around to the front door and removed the small revolver from the holster affixed to his belt.

With one swift knock, he raised the bullhorn up to his mouth and called her name. He heard movement. He then let go of the bullhorn, and put both hands on the pistol and pointed it at the screened door.

"This is Sheriff Bryant." The porch lights came on.

"Come outside with your hands up!" he demanded.

The door slowly opened and Mary Brown Carter stood before him. She was wearing a pink terry cloth robe. Her hair was covered by a multi-colored silk scarf.

"What's going on, Sheriff?" she asked as she unlatched the screened door.

"Mary Carter, you are under arrest for the murder of your late husband, Edgar Roland Carter." He took one hand off of the revolver and opened the door.

"There is no need for you to point that gun at me. I am not resisting anything. There is a baby and two children inside. I need to get someone over here to care for them." She backed away and let him come inside.

Sheriff Bryant went from room to room, verifying Mary's story. He noticed the small infant peacefully asleep in her bed.

"How old is that girl in there?" He walked back into the living room.

"She's fourteen." Mary gripped the top of her robe.

"Then she's old enough to watch that baby."

"She doesn't know anything about caring for a baby. We need to get an adult."

"You need to come with me now!" he shouted. "You can make a phone call from the station."

"Sheriff, I need to call someone now. We can leave, but I need to be sure that child is not stuck caring for that baby for more than an hour," Mary walked up to him and said.

"One call. That's all the time you get. No time to get dressed then, I suppose." He watched as a young boy came into the room.

"Honey, it's okay. I have to go away for a while with the sheriff, and you and Jasmine keep an eye on the baby until Pauline gets here, okay?" Mary grabbed the child, lifted him to her, and planted a reassuring kiss on his cheek.

She dialed a number and waited. After a few minutes, she said, "Hi, it's Mother Brown. I'm being arrested and taken down to the sheriff's department. I need some help with the baby. Can you come early?" She watched the sheriff carefully.

"Time's up." He gave the little boy an evil look. The little boy returned another.

Mary put the telephone down and looked at the sheriff.

"Let's go," he demanded. "You have the right to remain silent. Anything you say or do can be held against you in a court of law. You have a right to an attorney and if you can't afford one, the court will appoint one for you." He locked the handcuffs. "Do you understand what I have said, Miz Carter?"

"Yes, I do. My name is no longer Carter, it's Brown. Mary Brown." She dropped her head and walked outside with the Sheriff.

LATER.....

Simultaneously, there was banging on the door, while the telephone rang. Ruth was seated on the toilet and could not move.

"Ben, get the door. Elijah, get the telephone. Tell everyone to hold on until I come out." She laughed to herself. It seemed there was no privacy in her life.

She walked out of the bathroom and heard Ida, Pearlie, and Mable in the living room. She reached across the bed and pulled the curtain back. There were five women gathered around the oak tree.

Ruth put her clothing on in a hurry, then stopped and decided to wear something more formal. Something told her that she would be leaving the premises.

She walked out into the open space and looked at everyone.

"Y'all don't look good. Whatever is going on is in God's hands," she said to the women, and then looked at her son. "Eli, who was on the telephone?"

"That was Mother Brown's son. He said to tell you, they won't let her have visitors."

"What? Great Scott! Ida, is that what you come to tell me?"

Ida just shook her head. "Ruthie, I can't deal with that devil. I hear he locked her up and refused to let the woman even get dressed. Carried her out in her robe! Came at the break of dawn, before the rooster crowed, and stormed the place like she was a fugitive."

Ruth sat down at the dining room table. "Sometimes I lose my breath when I hear the foolishness of the Devil. Now, does Sheriff Bryant realize that in a few hours he is going to have the whole town on him?"

"Apparently he don't care. I heard the police chief demanded that he close the investigation into Edgar's death," Mable added.

"I thought he closed it a long time ago. Why now? What did he discover to make him think Mary killed that man?" Ruth was puzzled.

"Said it was new evidence," Ida said.

"Oooh. Who has the baby?" Ruth stood up.

"Pauline. Mary called before she went down to the station. When she got there, she called Micah too," Mable said.

Ruth turned and looked at the children. "You know y'all don't have any business sitting here listening to this stuff. Go on in your rooms and do some homework. Isaiah, you one step from being put on punishment for the rest of the year with the grades you brought home." She looked back at Ida.

"So Micah must be there now. Why won't Bryant let her have visitors? Something else is going on here." She walked toward her bedroom. "I'm going to get some fresh clothes and we are going to march on that sheriff's office. He better take these clothes so Mary can get freshened up."

"I called Frank," Ida said as Ruth walked away.

"Oh, God! That's all we need now."

"His assistant said he's in Canada. New Hawk's opened this past weekend. She said she would call him later."

"Let's pray we get Mary out of there before he gets back here." Ruth gathered a pair of slacks, a top, and a sweater for Mary. She placed them in a brown paper bag.

"Who called the women?"

"Pauline called everyone except you." Mable looked at Ida and then looked down.

"That's all right. Time heals all wounds, I guess."

1977

Beulah removed the bandages. The damage was severe. She placed gauze throughout the woman's abdominal area, and then took out the surgical needle and thread. She motioned to Edna to bring the sterile equipment into the room.

"You must have been extremely desperate to allow someone to butcher your body like this."

The woman just lay still, not uttering a word.

"I feel sorry for you. It must have been a painful decision." She continued cleaning the wound until Edna brought in the surgical equipment.

"I'm going to have to stitch this up! Then I am going to have to do some tricks on the other mess I see. Edna will give you something to make you drowsy. There is no way you can make it through this without a little help." She looked at the woman.

"Thank you, Miss Beulah." She opened her eyes and tears poured down her face.

"You're quite welcome. Like they say, this too shall pass." Beulah rose and allowed her assistant to administer the anesthesia.

Pauline slept for two days. Beulah had no idea if she would ever be able to conceive a child again. The abortion clinic took care of that. Beulah felt sorry for her, but she knew for many women it was the only option. The clinics were dirty and often did more harm than good. At least Pauline made it out of there alive.

Three days before when she'd arrived on Beulah's doorstep, she insisted that no one tell Ruth what had happened. She said she could not endure what Ruth would say when she found out. Beulah assured her that Ruth finding out should be the least of her concerns. She had been cut incorrectly and now infection had set in, thus, Beulah's first priority was to save her life.

Pauline would have to deal with her spiritual reputation on her own.

1979

Charles Bryant felt a cold hand on his shoulder and jumped up from his chair.

"How did you get past my deputies?" he asked as he moved further away.

"Easy," she said.

He walked over to the door, opened it and looked down the corridor. Then he yelled out to the deputy seated at the end of the hall, "Everything okay down there?"

"Yeah, boss. You all right?" The deputy turned to face him.

"Yeah. I was just checking." The sheriff closed the door to face the inquisition he knew Beulah Chaney would conduct.

"I don't know what you want. This is official poh-lice business. I don't owe you or anyone else that comes here today answers about an ongoing investigation." He sat in the chair behind his desk.

"Is that your official response?" She let out a holler. "Tell that to the folks that don't know what is going on. You and I both know that woman in that cell did not kill her husband, although she would have been justified if she did."

"Well, she succeeded, so that makes her guilty of murder."

"I thought everyone in this country was innocent until proven guilty?" Beulah sat down in one of the high back chairs facing the sheriff.

"Well, the prosecutor agrees with me on this one, so I got the law on my side," he boasted.

"You sound like a broken record, Charles." She leaned toward him, "Or shall I call you Chuck?"

He did not answer. His face grew pale as he seemed dazed by her response.

Beulah leaned in closer. "Just how far do you want to take this? You drag an innocent woman in here, practically naked, for a murder investigation in which you should have been one of the key suspects. There were several folks that wanted Edgar Carter dead and you know you were one of them."

"What does that have to do with nothing?" he sneered.

"It has to do with everything! Edgar Carter did not die from that gunshot wound and you know it."

"Her fingerprints were on the gun," he mumbled.

"And it took your office almost three years to discover that? Yes, her fingerprints were on the gun. But did the bullet match the murder weapon?" She stood up. "And when did she touch the gun? Fingerprints don't tell time."

"What is it to you?" He looked around the room suspiciously.

"Do you really want to know? You are going to dig a hole so deep, it will bury you alive." She walked around the desk.

He stood up and faced her. "Get the hell out of my office!"

"I will leave the same way I came."

"On a broom I bet."

"Ha. Was I on a broom when that young girl died in my arms after she told me that her boyfriend raped and sodomized her? You remember his name, right? Chuck.

Tell me, was I on a broom when I saw your car following Edgar Carter on the night he died? Or when you planted his weapon on another murder scene? You don't want to go there with me. You may think you have the law on your side now, but just wait until you do battle with me!"

"Your threats don't mean nothing. Who is gonna believe you? You're a sinister witch doctor that everyone knows is crazy. You got no formal education and you can't compete with a college educated man with enough credentials to run the entire pohlice department of this state."

"Then try me. I know everything about you. Long before you ever returned to Jasper County." She headed toward the door. "Now do the right thing and set that woman free. Just say the evidence is tainted and drop this. It's been too long and no one cares anymore anyway."

"There is no statute of limitation for murder." He held the door open.

"That's good to know. You ought to remember that should evidence happen to drop on the Chief's desk proving you had something to do with the Spellman murder all those years ago. "

"You're crazy. You think the Chief is concerned about a murder in Atlanta?"

"He would if the family ties could be traced to Jasper County." She gave him a wicked smile.

"Well, that's not going to happen." He stood in the hall to see if anyone was standing around. "Anyway, I doubt you could prove something as complicated as that. Where would you get the medical records?"

"As if I am stupid enough to tell you. I can get anything I want, including the death certificate that proves how our old friend gave up the ghost." She walked past him and stood in the hall.

"He died from a single gunshot wound to his heart," he whispered.

"The bullet never reached his heart. It ricocheted into a non-vital organ." She turned around and looked at him. "Now then, you still think I'm uneducated?"

"You're out of your league, witch woman." A smile crept across his face. "There is one thing you forgot when you started playing detective with the pros." He paused, "I lack motive." He turned and walked back into his office.

"Already covered that one." She headed toward the cells in the back.

He spun around on the heels of his cowboy boots. "So tell me, since you know everything, voodoo woman, what was my motive to kill that sorry Edgar Carter?"

Beulah kept walking toward Mary's cell. "Go home and ask your wife."

FIVE

1979

Charlie Peters pulled the cruiser next to the crowd of women as they headed to the Sheriff's Department. He turned the engine off and rolled down the window. He exited the vehicle, walked around to shoulder of the road, and faced the crowd.

"Good morning, ladies. I take it y'all on yuh way tuh see the sheriff?" He surveyed the crowd.

Ruth walked ahead of the group. She wore dark shades and was holding a brown paper bag.

"Good Morning, Mother Ruth. Ah just thought ah would save yuh a trip. She done been released a few hours ago." He looked beyond Ruth at the other women.

"You sure, Charlie Peters?" She looked perplexed. "We were told she was being held and could not have any visitors." Ruth sat the bag down next to her and took off the shades.

"Yeah. Seems Sheriff didn't want all the confusion so he released her into her son's custody about three hours ago," Charlie said.

"Well, praise the Lord! God always beats me to the punch!" She laughed and looked at the women behind her. "Well, we will need a car to get to her house."

"Now, this car can't hold all o' y'all, but Ah can take about four o' yuh ova tuh huh house."

"Mother Ruth, you, Pearlie, Ida, and Mable run on to her now. She might need a little more prayer than Pauline can give," one of the women proffered.

"No." She picked up the bag and started walking. "I think we should give Mary some time alone. I'll call her when I get home. Let's just stroll back the way we came, praising the good Lord all the way. Hallelujah!" she shouted.

Charlie Peters stood watching the large crowd of women as they turned and walked in the opposite direction. He was glad they had not made it to the sheriff's office, which was a good mile away. He was familiar with the woman leading the crowd. She had left an indelible mark on everyone she'd ever met in the Low Country. In fact, when Ruth Garrett gave instructions, folks followed whatever she told them to do, even white people.

1959

She was not sure why she was driven to her. For some reason, all the talk across town about a young, strong willed, black business woman piqued her interest more and more. It was the first time she had ventured to the side of town where blacks lived in a long time. For the past ten years, she had remained locked up in a house with a family she had grown ashamed of. But, if she was ever going to meet the mystery lady, Lula Peters would have to leave the house and find her.

She spotted her walking down Main Street on an extremely cloudy day. She was pulling a red wagon with children inside. The confidence that she exuded convinced Lula in that moment that she was who she thought she was. There was no need to search any further. She had found the missing link to the puzzle.

She followed her all the way to the front steps of the IGA grocery store. Then Lula turned around and headed back to her automobile. She would not endanger the young woman's life, because the last time she was spotted in public with a woman of color, her life changed forever.

A year later, as she drove down Highway 17, she saw her again. This time she was alone and off the beaten path, away from suspicious eyes. Lula pulled onto the shoulder of the road and got out. Then she turned around, walked back to the car, drove to the corner grocer a few yards up the road, parked the vehicle, and walked back toward the Coosawhatchie River.

Ruth was seated on the grass near a barge, looking across the muddy waters.

"Anythang biting?" She kept her eyes focused on the water.

"Not much. I'll catch supper if I'm lucky." Ruth, dressed in cutoff denim shorts and a pink ruffled blouse, tugged at the fishing pole.

"Are you that woman that designs those beautiful dresses?" Lula looked down at Ruth.

"It is I." Ruth kept looking at the water. "Can I help you with something?"

"I would love to get measured, but honestly, I don't know where I'd go. A long time ago, my sister used to bring me dresses from everywhere she visited and to this day, I've only worn one of them." She paused as a tear fell down her cheek, "Wore it to her funeral."

Lula, at five-feet-six, appeared taller as she stood in a brown pair of three-inch heels, a green a-line skirt, and a gently pressed, short-sleeved white cotton blouse.

Ruth turned around and put her hand above her eyebrows to get a better look at the woman. Something about the way she spoke caught Ruth off guard.

"I'm so sorry for your loss," Ruth said, putting the rod down by her side.

"She was a remarkable woman. Sometimes I think I'll never meet another woman as fearless as she was." Lula sat down next to Ruth.

"I know what you mean. Some people just radiate this earth wherever they go. When the Lord calls them home, we all suffer until we realize that they were never meant to stay here in the first place."

"Well, darling, that was spoken like someone who knows what I'm talking about." She smiled at Ruth. "How did you start designing dresses?"

"Well, that's what everyone else called it. For me, it was ministry. I just needed something to keep me busy so that I could get over my mother's death. Her absence left a huge hole in my heart. Just seemed I didn't have anything to live for." Ruth removed the straw hat that covered the four cornrows that held her thick hair together.

"My sistah loved hats. In fact, she wore one wherever she went." Lula could not help staring at Ruth's shiny black braids.

"So did my mother. Maybe it was a sign of the times. Women were just getting a little power and they wanted to show it to the world. Didn't matter what color you were, freedom is something every human being longs to have." Ruth pulled her shades down over her nose, winked at Lula, and covered her eyes again.

Lula was silent for a while. How had so many years passed by and she had not tried to reconnect with any of them? She pointed at Ruth's wet toes and then began taking off her heels.

"That looks fun, do you mind?" She removed her shoes and placed her pale small feet into the water.

"Help yourself. This is God's free country. My daddy's people own this land, but they don't mind who fish at this river. Said it belongs to all of God's children."

"Do you think everyone is a child of God?" Lula asked.

"That's an interesting question. Before my mother died, I would have answered yes. That was because I had no idea that there were people on this Earth that were truly evil, so bent on riding with the Devil, that nothing can turn them around. But, anyway, none of us are perfect and salvation is a process." Ruth sat admiring Lula's pretty olive-toned hands. She wore a ring on every finger.

"Well, I wonder how many chances a person gets before God dismisses him all together." Lula leaned back on her elbows and stared into the water.

"I guess as many chances as the person is willing to repent and ask for God's forgiveness."

"Some folk never give what they are doing a second thought. I doubt repentance is in their vocabulary." She watched Ruth's reaction carefully before continuing.

"Let's just say I know someone who is evil personified, I tell you. Now, he was never perfect, but over the years he grew worse. I used to pray, but it didn't do any good. Next thing I knew, he had traded places with the Devil himself! One day, I found something that made me hate him with all my heart. But, I still couldn't bring myself to admit the truth…" She was cut off.

"There yuh go! Not too safe out heah by yuhself." He walked up to the two women.

Ruth looked up for a moment and then pulled her wet feet out of the water. She knew who he was. She picked up the fishing rod and threw the line back into the water.

"You have a good day," she said to Lula Peters without looking at her. Within minutes, she saw Chadwick Peters manhandle his wife, half dragging her, as they hurriedly raced toward her car.

1980

Timmy opened the car door for Ida. He walked around to the driver's side and sat down in the seat. Ida was beaming with joy.

"The more you hang with Ruth, the less any of us see of you at the club." He looked out of the rear view mirror as he backed out of the yard.

"Not true. Besides, sometimes I just need a break. We've spent so much time on opening and running clubs, that I forget what it's like to just relax every once in a while." She reached into her purse and pulled out a tube of lipstick.

"Them clubs pay for everythang we got, the lifestyle we now live." He turned onto the service road.

"I'm not complaining, Timmy. I'm just saying there is a lot going on around town that I think we need tuh pay more attention to." She wiped the end of the tube with a napkin.

"Like what?" He finally looked at her.

"Like all the foolishness with the sheriff and the Klan. Just like what happened to Mary Brown. Not many of y'all men folk opened your mouths. You know that woman was locked up over some foolishness."

"What could we do? The pohlice handled that! We got our own problems with the sheriff. Now I don't want to end up in jail again messing with that fool. I say you stay outta his path."

"I wanted to, but I can't run all my life, Timmy. I can't keep running from him. His evil spirit has haunted me for years." She knew she had slipped.

"Years? Tilley, the man only been sheriff for a lil' ova eight years now. You talk as if he's been heah as long as we have." He slowed to the stop sign and looked both ways.

"Well, it seems like that long. Look at how many citations he has given us? It's ridiculous. If we run from him, then we are just as guilty as everyone else. What he is doing around town is wrong and one day, I kid you not, this town is going to have to pay for all those underhanded negotiations he entered into."

"What this town got to do with any o' the Bryant's shady business dealings?" He drove faster down the lone highway.

"Ha. A whole lotta folk took bribes and gonna go down right alongside wid 'em. Too many of us suffered at his hands, while the rest o' the folk stood by playing dumb. Most of us know he's crooked, but will defend him every chance we get." She put the tube of lipstick back inside her purse.

"Hold on, Ida. I am not defending that man! He's got a lot tuh deal with as the sheriff of a county dominated by the Klan. Do you know how vulnerable that man is?"

"What? Vulnerable! That man has a heart of steel. All the deals he's brokered with the Devil, the Klan can't touch him." Ida looked out of the window and shook her head.

"You wrong, Ida. He still have tuh obey the Klan. Chad Peters gon' see to that."

"Chad Peters! Hush your mouth. That devil is dying a slow death! I'm talking about the Klan too. Something tells me they going down soon." She adjusted her straw hat and looked over at Timmy. "How long we gonna allow them tuh rule us widout fighting back? If Frank could stand up tuh them, the rest of us can too."

"Your brother got something on them folks, you heard Herman. Frank smart too. He aligned himself with the biggest family feud around. Everyone knows how much Wallace Hawkins hate Chadwick Peters. I heard that feud only rekindled the feud that started centuries ago between their fathers." He turned into the driveway.

Ida ran inside to get Ruth. She was only half listening to Timmy by then.

1965

Frank stared at Lula Peters as she stood in the line at the bank waiting to see a teller. After all her heartache, she was still a beautiful woman. For years, he'd thought she was just someone in a fairy tale, a tale that he often heard whenever Wallace Hawkins detailed his past.

Their love affair had definitely transcended time. For although Lula married Chadwick Peters, everything she did showed her heart never left Wallace Hawkins. She was very cautious to protect him and the child they shared together in secret. That had to be the only reason she stayed trapped in a marriage to a man she practically despised.

Over the years, it became obvious to Frank that Lula suspected Wallace had shared their secret with him. She often winked at him if no one was around, and the few conversations they had, she never failed to give him a message to deliver to Wallace. That was just the way she was, one very classy lady.

Frank walked out of the bank and into the courthouse. He exited the elevator and ran into Kathryn and Betty Hawkins, the women he promised his mentor he would protect for the rest of his life.

"Why, Mr. Wilcox!" Kathryn beamed. Betty, a short and stocky girl with dingy blonde hair, was shy, never opened her mouth, but stood silently watching the encounter.

"Is Mr. Hawkins still around?" He played the game.

"Ah, yes he is. He's waiting for you in room 214." Kathryn pointed down the hall. She resembled a fashion model, tall, slender, with the most captivating brown eyes anyone had ever seen.

"Sure is nice to see both of you lovely women on this fine day." He smiled at them as he walked away.

From the corner of his eye, he could see Kathryn as she watched him walk down the hallway. She was like that. Whenever he was around, she watched his every move. He doubted she was suspicious of him; he had proven countless times to be the big brother she never had, or, at least the only one she would ever know about.

Wallace Hawkins, in a race with time and death, sat next to one of the clerks. Strikenly beautiful with sandy brown short hair and wide golden brown eyes, the young woman was the only black clerk miles around, in fact, Wallace had her brought in from Dekalb County. Next to her sat two of his middle- aged Caucasian lawyers.

"Gentlemen, this is Frank Wilcox. He manages our stores along the coast. Frank has been with our family for many years. I thought he would like to be here when we sign this new deal. He'll be responsible for getting a copy to the board in our New York regional office that opened last year." He smiled politely but did not look at Frank for long.

"Yes, of course," one of the lawyers said. The shock was written all over his face. "I heard you had someone local managing the stores around here. I thought you were gonna get one of them college boys from USC or Clemson to protect such a valuable investment." He let out a nervous laugh.

"I got someone that is college educated." Wallace motioned to Frank to take a seat next to him. "Mr. Wilcox is a graduate of Morris Brown College."

"Say what? Well, that's mighty fine of you, boy. Too bad Mistah Wallace don't have a son to continue his legacy," the other lawyer,balding with a pencil thin long nose and a non-existent top lip, commented.

Wallace Hawkins stopped smiling. "But I do indeed, gentlemen. Now, shall we get on with the business at hand?"

Unbeknownst to the smartest guys in the room, on that day, Wallace Hawkins had relinquished fifty-one percent of ownership in his prized Hawk's stores to Frank Wilcox. No one would have suspected it. The small board in Jasper County only consisted of four people: Kathryn, Betty, their father, and a silent partner, which twenty years later, everyone discovered was Frank Wilcox.

Frank was the sole owner of four stores in Virginia, Maryland, and Delaware. Titles were conveyed as a birthday gift from Wallace a few years back. However, once the news of cancer was confirmed, Wallace thought it necessary to make some permanent changes. His daughters knew little of the business and lacked any interest in taking control of operations should he become unable to do so.

That left him with one viable option: Reveal to the world that he had a blood son that was contaminated by a man he hated, or turn over ownership to the one man he trusted with his life.

For him, staring at Frank Wilcox proudly; it was an easy decision.

1961

Frank held the photograph in his hands. He studied it for a few minutes, but did not recognize the faces on anyone in it. Wallace told him it was insurance to protect him when trouble came, as he predicted it surely would. He did not have to go into detail, for Frank understood what type of trouble was headed his way.

The land he built his second house on originally belonged to Wallace. In fact, he insisted that Frank build Leslie a home secluded from the rest of town. Yet, Leslie wanted to move closer to family, so, reluctantly, Frank bought a smaller lot closer to Coosawhatchie. Wallace advised him to hold onto the land he had given him originally, for who knew what the future would hold.

Frank turned the photograph over and noticed the small writing on the back. He had to squint to make out the faded letters. He dropped the photo, looked up and yelled as loud as he could.

In shock, he forced the gear into reverse and hurridly backed out of the driveway. There was only one person, other than Wallace Hawkins, who could confirm the authenticity of his new revelation. He had to get to him quick.

He drove down a windy dirt road until he spotted the massive house that belonged to the one person he knew he could trust with such sensitive information. Turning the engine off, he stopped directly in front of the house, but hesitated before getting out. Suddenly, it dawned on him that the secrets shown in the picture could also bring pain to several people in his own family. That was if no one knew the truth, but he suspected otherwise.

"Evening, Cousin Frank."

The younger Frank, sweating perfusely, stood on the porch contemplating what he would say to his older, wiser, cousin of the same name.

"Frank? Herman's boy? Is that you out there in the dark? Everythang okay, son?"

Frank Fields opened the door.

"You alone?"

"Naw. James and John visiting. They're in the back room. Edna and Sam on their way, but that's what they said hours ago. I don't expect them to show up until tomorrow morning for breakfast. They'll get here the same time as Ruthie and James."

He walked into the foyer and headed toward the empty parlor.

Frank could hear the television blasting in another room and spotted his two cousins sprawled out on the floor.

"They half drunk by now." The older Frank turned around while walking and said. " Been drinking moonshine goin' on half a day. Don't expect much movement out of them two."

Frank Wilcox laughed as he entered the parlor and sat down in a recliner next to the window.

"I'm sorry I been kinda low on visits, sir. Just really getting the nerve to go out much and be around folks." His remorse was plain to see.

"That's all right, son. I've been through your kind of pain and it ain't easy at all. You just keep putting one foot in front of the other. That's all you can do."

"Thank you, sir. I rushed over here to show you something that came to my attention. Something really private, might even upset you..." He stopped midsentence.

"Why is that? I've suffered the loss of my life already. Hope you didn't come to tell me anything about my children." Frank Fields sat up in his chair and looked suspiciously at his namesake seated on the opposite side of the parlor.

"No, sir. Nothing about them. I was given a photograph and I couldn't make out anybody in it until I turned it over and read the back." He pulled the photo out of the manila envelope Wallace Hawkins had given to him.

"Hand it here, son, let me take a look." Frank Fields reached over, took the photo out of his cousin's hand, pulled out his reading glasses, turned on the lamp next to him, and examined it. He never turned the photo over to look at the writing.

"Where did you get this from?" He took his glasses off and handed the photo back to Frank Wilcox.

"My employer gave it to me for collateral against the Klan."

"Smart employer. Chadwick Peters would die if this got out." He looked directly at his cousin. "I've known for a long time. That's how we started the business. Old man Simmons was good to black folks, but he couldn't keep his hands off our women. Gave up everything he had for her, even his Southern reputation. After a while, he didn't care who knew."

"Then he up and disappeared," he continued. "Of course his family separated the girls, but eventually they found each other again. Folks never caught onto the connection between the two of them either. Just seemed like a white woman and her childhood maid." He forced a laugh. "They were insperable. There was nothing those girls would not do for each other, regardless how everyone tried to keep them apart. "

"Does Peters know?"

"Heavens yeah! That fool knows. He found out the same way you found out. Peters stole Lula from Wallace, and when he found out she was pregnant, he married her to avoid the shame. Only thing was, it wasn't his baby. By the time he found out about her bigger secret, there was nothing he could do. If he told anyone, it would have cost him his life back then." Frank Fields rubbed his eyes and laughed.

"Why did the Klan go after Cousin Rose?"

"I'm not too sure. I think they messed up. They didn't cover their trail too good, or something. You see the day Rosetta went missing is the same day she and Lula met each other in Hardeeville. I think someone was following them or they got caught being too friendly towards each other in public, Lord knows."

Frank Wilcox stood up. "You think Chad Peters had something to do with her death?"

"I know he did! If he did not hurt Rosetta with his own hands, he had someone else do it for him. Setta would not tell me for sure, but I knew she was hiding something, just couldn't put my finger on it. Long after she died, I finally realized she was not protecting Chad Peters; she hated him. She was protecting the woman she loved with all of her heart."

SIX

1972

It was well past midnight when Micah returned home. He was slightly inebriated, but had good control of his balance. He opened the door and then pulled the key out of the lock. The curtains were pulled throughout the open living space of his apartment. He turned on the hall light and stepped inside.

He had been in this apartment for two years, then recently decided to purchase a home on the other side of town. Mary often complained about his single status, so he planned to make the purchase of his new home synonymous with the announcement of his impending nuptials. Finally, he had found the woman of his dreams.

As usual, the first thing he did was walk into his bedroom and look around. Tenanciously neat, with everything in its proper place, something that night seemed out of order. He ignored the warning because he had felt that way everytime he came into his bedroom for the past six months. He kept believing someone had somehow violated his personal and most intimate space; but he never acquired sufficient evidence to prove it.

He turned on the lamp on the nightstand and sat down.

There was no use to turn on the television. He had already missed his favorite variety show, *The Tonight Show with Johnny Carson*, and most of the other stations would lose their signals in a few short hours. Exhausted, he put his head face down on the pillow and immediately dozed off to sleep.

An hour had zoomed by before Michah felt the pain of a sharp object as it pierced his back, arms, and neck. Dazed, he felt someone sitting directly on top of his one hundred-eighty pound frame holding him down. He tried to lift himself up to no avail.

"You one low down dirty dog, Micah Brown! The fruit ain't fall nowhere near the tree when your daddy birthed you! You a disgrace to that man and his memory," she ranted as she continued stabbing him.

Micah jumped in shock when he recognized the voice.

"What is wrong with you, woman?"He cried out in pain and utter confusion as it became evident that he was being stabbed.

"Your behind got caught! " She stabbed him again. "The chicken has come home to roost!" She stopped for a moment, and then place the knife against his neck.

"Move one inch and I will slit your throat!" she threatened.

Micah could feel drops of blood drenching his arms and neck. He could barely see anything in front of him because the curtains and shades had been pulled together purposely blocking the brightly lit fluorescent lights from the parking lot outside.

"Yeah! What you got to say now?" She struck him in the side just below his arm pits.

"God, Bonita, let me up!" He spoke through sobs as the pain in his side intensified. "You got this all wrong! I have never cheated on you!"

"Shut up, liar! Everyone was right! You a dog! A low down dirty one that hides behind your preacher mama! Wait till she hear you died the same way you lived: Like a low down dirty, disgusting, nasty, dog!" The knife entered his throat.

She got up, tossed the bloodied butcher knife, she took from his kitchen hours before, down beside her betrayer, and stood next to the bed. "Next time, tell your ho not to leave anything behind!"

As she walked out of the room, she turned around, reached into her purse and removed a pair of ladies underwear. She tossed them on top of Michah's haunted face as he lay dying in a puddle of his own blood.

1979

Ruth talked to Mary on the telephone. "Why now? After all this time, why did that fool wait to arrest you now?"

"He said I had motive. Seems the murder weapon had my fingerprints on it, and he also mentioned there was new evidence that came from Atlanta linking me to the crime."

"What? You have not been in Atlanta since Micah was stabbed half to death. What does Micah's story have to do with yours?" Ruth motioned to Elijah to turn the volume of the television down.

"I don't know. When I left Edgar, he was breathing and very much alive. I don't know if I killed him. Maybe I did. But, I never hid the gun. I threw it at Edgar, who shot after me, missing every time. I honestly don't know what happened after that." She seemed out of breath.

"Mary, you and I both know that God is on our side. Something else is going on. I don't know what any of this has to do with your son, but we are going to get a hot-shot lawyer and find out."

"I asked Michah earlier. All he remembered about Atlanta was getting stabbed forty times and being left for dead. I remember asking the police department repeatedly if they could tell me what happened to him but, they just said the person who called was not in the apartment when they arrived."

"Where was Bonita when they found her? Maybe she felt bad about what she had done and called the police once she got home." Ruth stared at the floor.

"I thought that too, but the police said after she left the apartment, apparently she went on the run. They caught her down in Macon, Georgia, at one of her relatives' house's a week later. They said when the found her, she was hysterical, ranting and raving about stabbing the only man she ever loved."

"That's a spirit of confusion! Did you ever talk to her?"

Ruth gave Elijah an evil look and then said to him, "I'm two minutes from spanking you, ya hear me, mister? You go out there and get me a good switch to pop your behind with!" She turned her attention back to Mary.

"I went to see her after Micah's condition improved. Poor child, all she could do was cry and mumble something about finding a pair of women's underwear in his bed. I could not stand to hear the rest."

"Underwear? What? Ah, God, Mary." They were both quiet for a few minutes until Ruth started praying.

"Father, we come to you to give you glory for everything you have done. You have showered us with your love and taken excellent care of our families, and for that we give you thanks. Now, Lord, we ask that you would forgive us for any sins that we have not confessed or admitted earlier. Purify our hearts, Father, and saturate us with your loving kindness. Ensure, dear Lord, at all times, that we are vessels fit for the master's use. I lift up my sister, Mary. She has already asked for forgiveness and confessed her sins regarding this matter. You have forgiven her and wiped the slate clean. We know your promises are yeah and amen and that you will deliver her from the trap the enemy is trying to set. Father, you are the author and the finisher of her faith so give her peace in her mind, in her body, and in her soul, about this situation. Your word declares that whom the Son sets free is free indeed. We believe the report of the Lord, and know that every report that contradicts your word is a lie. No weapon that is formed against us

shall prosper. Now, Father, we ask that you forgive Sheriff Bryant for what he has done, forgive and cleanse his mind. We continue to pray for his salvation. Father, anoint him with a passion to know you Lord, in Jesus name. We consider all things done. Amen.

After a few minutes, both ladies, exhausted from the events of the day, hung up the telephone. Ruth looked in on her children as they played in their bedrooms and then walked into her own bedroom and stood directly in front of the large oak chest of drawers. Tears flooded her face as she opened the top drawer, placed her hands toward the back of the drawer, and felt around her lingerie in search of something she had long forgotten about.

1975

Mary sat on the bathroom floor sobbing. The more she thought about her past, the longer she cried. Since leaving Edgar, she had bouts of depression that often sought to take control of her happiness. There were times when she felt like the past eight years had all been a big mistake. It was her past decisions, she reasoned, that now affected not just her own life, but sought to destroy the life of her son.

Edgar promised her that he would harm Micah if he ever got the chance and Mary believed he would. While Micah no longer lived in Atlanta, Mary knew he was still close enough to fall into the grasps of her demented husband.

She hated to admit it, but she did not feel safe no matter how hard she held onto the promises of God in the Bible. She knew she was covered by the blood of Jesus but something nagging on the inside of her told her that she had good reason to fear another attack.

At times, she questioned God about the confusion she now felt. How was Satan able to get so close? If she remembered correctly, when she met Edgar Carter, she was busily doing the work of the Lord. She did not remember any spirit she harbored that would bring that type of evil into her life.

At forty-eight years old, she wondered if she could ever love or trust another man after all she had endured. She felt so alone in her thoughts.

She dabbed a cotton tissue on her face and prayed.

"Father, send help! I don't know where to turn. My heart is lonely and my mind is at a loss. I don't understand all that is happening to me. I pray you teach me how to love and trust again. I long to be used by you again. Please forgive me for any wrong thoughts that continue to plague my mind. Allow me to forgive freely. Finally, please forgive Edgar and all the people who hurt him causing him to hurt others. Free him from the enormous anger he harbors on the inside. Set him free to serve you Lord. In Jesus name, Amen."

As she stood in the hallway outside of the bathroom, she noticed the headlights of a car shining through the living room window. She was not expecting guests.

Mary ran into the bedroom and looked at herself in the mirror. Her hair was strewn all over her head, her eyes were sullen, and, without tinted face powder, she looked extremely pale. She ran to the closet and took out a navy blue pair of slacks and a silver tunic.

She could hear the visitor's footsteps as they approached the front door, then everything fell silent. Half dressed, Mary laughed outloud.

"Micah, is that you?" She leaned in the doorway and yelled down the hall. He never knocked for she could sense his presence every time.

"Open the door and see," a male voice answered. It was not Micah. Mary jumped back into the bedroom and looked around for the baseball bat.

"Who is it? May I help you?" She put on her slacks and turned out the light.

"A gentleman caller. Who else knew you would be home?" the man continued.

Mary stood in the hallway for a moment. She did not know what to do. She walked toward the telephone in the living room.

"Mary Brown, don't pick that telephone up and call the police! It's Frank. Do I have to say my last name?" Then he tapped on the door.

Mary gasped and then put the telephone back onto the base. "Frank! What are you doing here?" She tried to contain her laughter as she opened the door.

Frank Wilcox stood on the other side of the screened door holding a large bouquet of flowers. "I wanted it to be a surprise. Bad idea, huh?"

"Very bad! I don't even have on face powder. You know I don't open the door for strangers looking like this!" she teased him.

"I thought I was family." He opened the door and walked inside.

"Then if you family," she ran toward the back, "you won't mind waiting while I freshen up."

"But you didn't get a good look at the flowers!" he yelled.

"Didn't have to. They are beautiful."

He knew she loved movies, knew that she and Roy frequented them every chance they could steal away from the church. He knew a lot about the family of the man he vowed he would take a bullet for if he had to.

LATER...

They were strolling down the sidewalk near Oglethorpe Mall in downtown Savannah. Mary kept turning around and looking behind them.

"Mer, there is nothing to be afraid of. I have complete control of the situation. Besides, I know where he is at all times." Frank stopped walking and looked directly into her eyes. "Do you want to know where he is tonight?"

"It's not that I care, but I just don't trust him. He shows up all the time." She put her hands up to her face.

"He only acts crazy when you're alone. He won't come near you when you're with me. I know too many people that will take him out of here quick."

"Frank! Don't go there. We should never have to resort to violence." She grabbed his hands.

"Spoken like a true woman of God. Mer, I'm a realist. Some folks won't stop until they are forced to stop. Edgar's been threatened. He's not coming near your house. He's not coming after you, unless he loses his mind, and I'm not certain that he won't lose it again."

"Frank, thank you. You take your responsibilities so seriously. You are not responsible for us anymore. My husband's death freed you from that obligation." She put her hands on his cheeks. "I am so grateful to have you in our lives, but you can't be with us everywhere we go. What about the wonderful life I hear you live?"

"You are my life. Caring for you and Micah is not an obligation, it's a commitment. I'm a man of my word. Roy knew that better than anyone. The Lord blessed me when you two came into my life. That blessing did not end with his death."

Mary tried to change the subject. "So where is he this fine evening?" She laughed, opened her purse and took out a piece of chewing gum and handed it to him.

"So now you're giving out hints?" He turned around in a circle and laughed.

"Frankie, you sure are happy tonight! What have I missed out on? I tell you what, if it's a woman, she's one lucky sister." She patted him on the back and continued walking.

"You women are all alike! Every time I visit any of you, you swear I have somebody that is making me happy. What if I'm happy in Jesus alone? What if I finally found peace in my life?" He opened the wrapper to the gum and stared at it.

"It won't bite, I promise." She laughed. "What if you have, but woman's intuition says otherwise."

"You actually believe in that?" He laughed.

"Despite all that I have been through, I still believe it exists if we obey the signs." She put a stick of gum into her mouth.

"Sometimes there are no signs and when you discover the truth, you have already dug a hole too deep to get out of." He bit off half of the stick.

"You didn't answer my question," she said.

"I was trying to avoid it. Well, the good news is, I think Edgar has found himself in love again. Seems he can't keep away from one particular woman. They never meet in Ridgeland, just in Charlestown, and he was even spotted with her on Hilton Head Island and in Walterboro."

"You have to be kidding? Why all the sneaking around?" She linked her arm inside of his and continued walking.

"Why else would they have to?"

"She's married." She laughed out loud. "He's really crossing the line now. He told me his first wife was unfaithful. Never got her name, but after seeing the demons come out of that man, I doubt she's still around, and if she is, she's not doing too well."

"Well, this woman is very married. Married to a powerful man at that. I did some checking and it seems this relationship is nothing new. Some of my men showed a picture to some of our Atlanta crew and were surprised to learn they knew who she was."

"So you're telling me he was cheating on me the entire time? When did he get the time to do all this courting?" Mary was getting angry.

"I don't think he was. Seems folks remembered them years ago. No one knew them in Savannah. She must have gone back to her husband by then." He tried to look directly into her face but she avoided his eyes.

"Who is this powerful husband of hers and why doesn't he know about this?"

"What makes you think he doesn't know?"

"No man is fool enough to let his wife gallivant across town with another man, if he can stop it. Definitely not a powerful man." She finally looked at Frank.

"That's what I want to know. I would have left him alone until he threatened you that day. He opened up a can of worms and ever since then, I have been watching him. He's got more skeletons in the closet than a haunted house."

"That doesn't surprise me. Edgar is hateful and there is no other way to describe him."

"And so is her husband. If it were possible, these two cats could be fraternal twins."

"Oh, Frank! You must tell me who it is! Don't get me this excited and keep the secret." Mary stopped walking and grabbed him by the collar, laughing.

"You promise you won't blab to my sister or my cousin?"

"I promise on the Word of God that I will never let on that I know anything about Edgar's other woman."

"Or her husband," he interjected.

"Or her husband. Now come on and spill the beans." She was close enough to kiss him.

"Edgar's been seeing Anita Bryant." He watched for her reaction.

"Anita Bryant. That name doesn't ring a bell, Frank. Who is she?"

"Focus on the last name." He put his arms around her.

"Oh, my God!"

1980

Charlie Peters stood listening intently to the young man as he confessed to what had become the most popular killing in Jasper County over the past ten years. Something told him the young man was speaking the truth, regardless of the Sherriff's doubts.

"So, where did you get the gun?" He asked slowly, as he chewed a wad of tobacco.

"Kinfolk give it to me." The young man, caramel colored, slim, medium-height with hazel colored eyes, spoke through sobs.

"Wut you had against Carter?" Charlie asked.

"Nothing and a whole lot. He killed my cousin long time ago. Slit his throat for no reason. Threatened to do the same to me." He looked up at Charlie and mimicked the stabbing with his fingers directed at the base of his neck.

"But, why now? What were you doing out at Mable's property that night?" Charlie walked over to the metal chair on the other side of the folding table and sat down.

"I been seeing Shirley. We off and on, ya understand? Things kinda settled down 'tween us, but I still come around every now and again."

"So you went to see Shirley? Was she home? Was Carter there?"

"I didn't know who's car was parked next to the house. I guess it was his. I saw another car down the road, but couldn't make the tags or the color. " He wiped his soaked face and starred straight at the Deputy Sherriff.

"What'd you do next?"

"I knocked on the door and nobody answered. I stood there for a few minutes and then I heard screaming coming from the fields. I ain't recognize the voice, but I would discover it was Shirley. She was running straight towards me." His eyes were wide open.

"She say anythang?"

"Yeah, she told me to git out of there. Said Edgar Carter just raped her and she got away!"

"What happened next?" Charlie started writing on the notepad.

"I sent her to her cousin's house down the road. I did not want her in the house alone. I was headed down towards where she said Carter attacked her." He said.

"You were going after Carter? What made you think you could take on a man twice your size?" Charlie dropped the pin and starred at the young man.

"I didn't. I had the gun in the car and all I could think about was Shirley. He raped her! I ain't care about calling the poh lice or anything! I just wanted to get my hands on Carter." He started crying again. "He already killed my ace boon coon!"

"So you went out into the fields and found Carter? What was he doing?

"He was on his knees swinging at some woman! I saw him from the back. I didn't see the gun in the woman's hands until I got about ten feet away. She was begging him to stand back, but he kept swinging like a fool, after her."

"So you shot him in cold blood! That's your statement?" Charlie started to rise and leaned toward the young man. "That don't look good for you, boy!"

"No! The woman shot the gun and nothing happened. He didn't jump or back away. He lounged for her again, grabbing the hem of her dress, trying to pull her down on the ground with him. He swung again and she fell down. I yelled for him to stop at that point. He turned away from her, saw me and tried to get up off the ground. I shot him, at least I think I shot him."

"Why you say that? You think you shot him? Your gun matches the bullet found in his chest." Charlie said.

"Then I shot him. I won't sure at first, but now I remember,yeah, I shot the bastard. I shot him dead." He seemed defiant.

"And you just figured this out. Four years go by before we get a lead other than his wife. You graduated from college now?"

"Yes sir. I'm finished school. I guess I never said anything because I don't remember pulling the trigger. I think I did. I mean, I saw him fall..."

"And? You don't seem certain, son. Your'e confessing to a crime that is going to get you put away for a long time, and you don't seem so sure." Charlie headed towards the outer door. "Maybe I should give you more time."

"I don't need more time. I just need to write my statement and be arrested." He pleaded.

"Why would I arrest a man who ain't half sure of what he is confessing to."

"Because, cuz, I swear for God." The young man turned his body in the chair to follow Charlie.

"That you killed Edgar Carter with this gun?"

"Yes sir."

"You shot him how many times?"

"Once or twice, I think." He turned back around to face the wall again.

"You see, that's the problem. You think. I need you to be sure." Charlie opened the door. "You need some time to get your story straight, young man. Take a few minutes, and I promise you I will be back.

"But, but, please. I am sure, Deputy Peters. I shot the man and later learned he died."

"You sure? I ain't got time for your foolishness today. Either you confessing or you not. You shot him twice? You saw him fall to the ground? What else? There's somethang you aint' telling ." Charlie stood between the hallway and the door's entrance.

"I heard another gun shot right after I pulled the trigger the first time. I don't remember anything else."

"Say what? Another gun shot. Did the woman ever get back up?"

"No she was out cold. " The young man pounded his fist against his forehead.

"Then if that story is true, you were not alone in that field that night. What did you do next?"

"I honestly don't remember anything from that point."

"Yup, cuz I bet you were knocked out cold too." Charlie turned back towards the hall in time to see that the Sherriff had arrived.

SEVEN

1982

Sometimes the spirit moves in ways no one can predict. It happened one Sunday and changed their lives forever. The worship schedules and agenda had been set for the day, but nothing went as planned. It seemed something or someone showed up that was least expected, and that presence changed the future of every person in attendance.

Ida's eyelids tore through the web of sleep around five-thirty that morning. She had been up most of the night, so it was most unusual. She looked over at Timmy, who lay peacefully in a deep sleep that almost resembled a coma. There was something drawing her out of the house.

It moved her to get dressed without cooking breakfast, and even moved her to skip her favorite television shows that aired on Sunday mornings. The ones that occupied her time while everyone else she knew went to church.

Having never been a part of a congregation, Ida never missed that type of fellowship. Church folk had proven to her on countless times that Eula Mae was somewhat correct in her assumptions that some folks were plain hypocrites and no amount of church could ever change that.

Ida walked over to the wardrobe in the guest bedroom and picked up a brown paper bag. She opened it and pulled out the small black leather Bible tucked neatly inside. Ruth gave it to her in celebration of her twentieth birthday. She opened it the first time ten years later when Edgar Carter's body was discovered at the club. She only read it when Timmy was not in the house.

She had completed the book of Psalms and had begun reading the New Testament. She understood so little of what she read, but over time she discovered that a sense of peace would fall upon her as she held the Bible in her hands. There were even times when she could feel teardrops as they crept from her eyes and careened down her face, causing her to stop reading and close the book all together.

Although she never joined a church, she felt comfortable around the women in the prayer circle. It seemed each of them had a story, filled with the types of secrets that Ida understood. Each woman had endured her own prison to finally arrive at true peace. This was definitely something Ida could identify with, for the cells of her own prison had just begun to release her.

She put on a powder-blue dress and pulled a matching hat out of a box on top of the wardrobe. Timmy started purchasing hats for her after Ruth showed up in one that awful night at the club. Ida replayed that night in her mind over and over again until she could not get the images to leave her alone.

She stood in the mirror and allowed her fingers to caress the locket that she wore around her neck. Li'l Boy gave it to her when she turned seventeen. Since then, the thin piece of gold had become the only surviving reminder of the life she lived before her innocence was destroyed. Over time, it served as a constant reminder that fairytales could come true.

She missed Li'l Boy and the easy way of life he represented. Memories of him, sometimes, were the glue that held her life together when things became difficult. She could see his face as if he were still around. She could hear his voice as if he were standing next to her, and she even remembered his fingers on the trumpet that never released a sound.

Something about his spirit resonated within her whenever she stood underneath the oak tree in Ruth's backyard. Oftentimes as she watched the women praying, she had a strange feeling that someone was watching her. Someone she had no reason to fear.

She hurriedly dressed and for some reason, felt the desire to kneel down and say something to God. She was in desperate need of direction. Li'l Boy used to say that God had already designed the blueprint for our lives. All each of us needed to do was seek His guidance, and the path to our destinies would become as clear as the skies above.

Ida walked into the living room and, for the first time in over a decade, she humbled herself and prayed.

1962

He only engaged in this particular activity when the house was empty. Never when he suspected anyone was around. During the day, with Ida in school and both Herman and Eula Mae at work, the house was free until four p.m. Ida was always the first to arrive. Everything had to be picture perfect, or at least appear that way.

He tried to ignore the urges. Even tried to pray them away, yet nothing worked. They had the intensity of harsh labor pains, and each developed greater speed and impact than the one before until he could no longer resist.

He sat on the toilet for a few minutes, shaking as he pondered his next act. Then, slowly, he stood up, unbuckled his pants, unzipped them, and pulled them down below his knees. He was forcing himself to ignore the urges at that point and then he freely gave in to them.

He had to believe, at least in his mind, that he was engaging in normal activity. Not something that made him feel dirty inside, causing him to run bath water afterwards, and sit for hours in the bathtub, soaking away the shame that each act released. His bedroom was off limits. For one, he believed such pleasure was most unnatural, and two, it brought back too many painful memories of a time when sexual activity was a normal act between he and his wife.

As Dexter's body exploded with satisfaction, he thought he heard sounds coming from beyond the bathroom door. It was too early for anyone to be home, so he dismissed his fears, and continued in his shameful pleasure. When he was finished, he grabbed an old towel he hid underneath the cabinet and leaned over into the bathtub to run the water. Tears streamed down his face as an enormous amount of shame rose within him.

Unbeknownst to him at the time, Eula Mae returned home to retrieve an item she'd forgotten and was on her way back out the door when she thought she heard someone moaning. She turned and walked back down the hallway, then noticed the bathroom door was ajar. She was about to knock, when she heard the sound again. Shocked, she turned and ran out of the house.

A few days later, she convinced Herman that his uncle was a threat to their family, particularly Ida Mae. She said Ida was a very impressionable teenager in whom someone could easily take advantage. For that one single factor, Dexter would have to leave their home immediately.

As Herman tried to explain the uncomfortable position he was in, shame and horror was written across Li'l Boy's face. He apologized profusely and explained that he had only engaged in that activity a few times, but never when anyone was in the house. Ida was too important to him. He would never hurt her or expose her to anything of that nature.

Eula Mae would not budge. She demanded that Li'l Boy stay as far away from Ida as possible. In fact, he was to never allow Ida to even step foot into his bedroom again. She even demanded that he take back all of the gifts he had given Ida over the years, but to that ridiculous request, he refused.

Otherwise, Li'l Boy did as he was told. He kept his bedroom door closed most of the time, and when Ida dropped by for her usual visit, he simply ignored her knocking or opened the door and behaved as if she had interrupted an intense jazz session.

Before his shame was discovered, Ida had so easily become his sounding board. Her innocence was the catalyst that restored the large amount of love that he once harbored in his heart for mankind way before hate destroyed his family. He even resented God for allowing him to live after everything he knew and loved was taken away. Yet, through young Ida's childlike unconditional love, Dexter "Li'l Boy" Wilcox was somehow able to see the first glimpses of a new life.

He stayed on through Ida's seventeenth birthday party, gave her the last remaining memory of his family, and then left in the middle of the night, without ever saying goodbye. He planned it that way. Herman drove him to the train station in Yemasee in route to Jersey City. It would be a long time before anyone in his family would see him again. And when they did, no one would recognize the man he had become, except, the woman who had been able to breathe life back into his already dying spirit.

1960

When spring finally blossomed, Frank Wilcox spent much of his time getting to know the layout of his new surroundings. Even back then, New York City was a complicated maze within a maze. It was important that he knew his way around every borough, became familiar with the lingo, and understood the culture of the families residing within them. It was the only way he would get what he wanted.

After two trips on a Greyhound bus, he drove his brand new 1960 navy blue Cadillac the next time. He was going to stay for a while. Sufficient time had passed and he felt comfortable enough to start asking questions about her death.

He went to the local newspaper and requested a copy of archived articles, specifically, homicides of young black women. He was given ten articles, but none of them mentioned a woman being thrown out of a thirtieth-floor window in Harlem. In fact, there was no mention of her death at all.

Frank refused to give up. With the money he saved from doing business with Wallace Hawkins, he leased a large apartment in a high rise building adjacent to the Gardens. He had to appear as a local for fear of what reaction an outsider would cause.

As he sought answers, a popular club called ***The Blue Note*** trickled off of the tongues of many and continued to drop suspicious clues into his ears. It was a private dinner club that restricted access to the public and required some sort of exclusive invitation just to get inside of the front hallway. Once inside, access was limited to certain parts of the establishment. Full access had to be earned, and that could take years. Yet, it only took Frank Wilcox three days to become an invited patron.

On his fourth visit, he finally got the nerve to inquire about his sister. A member told him to be very careful when asking about missing or presumably dead folks, so Frank hid the truth of his actual origin, telling folks he was searching for a long lost cousin. When they asked where he was originally from, he said he was from Sparta, Georgia, worked for the Pepsi Cola Plant, and was living with a fictitious aunt near the Gardens. The rest of his story, or whatever question someone posed about him, he made up as he went along.

Six weeks hanging out at ***The Blue Note*** and all Frank had found were a few women looking for a good time. He still had no concrete information, until he overheard a conversation that sent him straight to the men's room.

Eight people were dead.

Seemed they all shared an apartment together in the Gardens. Two were shot multiple times in the head, four were stabbed, and the remaining two were set on fire. By the time the police arrived, the place was wiped clean as if each room appeared to be a stage for a gruesome horror flick. But this was no make believe; it was execution style murders that sent a message throughout every borough in Harlem that someone was determined to get revenge.

Frank leaned over the commode and released the fragments of the dinner he had just finished devouring. He hated the feeling of vomit and the smell sickened him even more. He tried to keep his balance, but he was losing the battle.

He knelt down, flush the commode, and spit into the bowl. Then he went over to the sink, ran the water, and put his face directly underneath the faucet. As the water stimulated the inside of his mouth, someone walked into the room. Frank reached up and grabbed a cloth towel from the adjoining table, and then he stood up.

As he continued to pat his face with the towel, he noticed a very large man standing behind him. He gauged from the awkward silence that something was wrong. All of a sudden, Frank stopped moving, took a deep breath, and turned to face the man who stood at full attention watching his every move.

"Weak stomach," the man said as he turned and locked the bathroom door from the inside.

Frank was nervous, but played it safe. He threw the towel into the bin, pushed back the coattails of his jacket, and exposed the gun resting in the waistband of his pants.

"You quick tuh go for that gun, huh?" The man cracked a smile.

"If I have to." Frank positioned himself where he could reach the other two weapons he was carrying.

"I bet you packing heavy, my man." He stopped smiling.

"Depends on who's asking, and who's brave enough to find out." Frank stepped forward.

The man burst in laughter.

"Is something funny? I didn't tell a joke." Frank stared into his face, before he noticed the man's enormous fists. "Look a heah; I got no beef with no one in this establishment. Just minding my business. Don't know what you want, but I assure you, I don't have it."

Someone knocked on the door. Frank watched the man's reaction.

He did not flinch. Instead, he mimicked Frank's earlier gesture and pulled back his coattails revealing a silver revolver with a pearl handle.

"Nice gun," Frank said as he reached into his pocket and pulled out a pack of Wrigley's Juicy Fruit chewing gum.

"Much obliged. The gum is a dead giveaway. No one from the city chews that mess." Before Frank could respond, he added, "and I doubt they chew it in Sparta either." He came closer to where Frank stood.

"You're not scared of me," he continued, sounding puzzled. "I can't find a lick of fear in your eyes."

"Is that what you were looking for? If you were going to kill me, you would have done so as soon as you caught me in here alone. The fact that I am alive means you don't want me dead so what else is there to be afraid of?"

"But I do want something." He offered Frank a packet of chewing tobacco.

"What's that?" Frank declined his offer.

"Meet me at this location tomorrow. Don't come as packed as you are tonight. Too much metal gon' give you away."

"And why should I come anywhere you say, much less unarmed?" Frank now looked puzzled.

"Because I have all the answers you need." He walked beyond Frank, headed to the sink, and began washing his hands.

"Who says I'm looking for answers?" Frank turned toward the man's broad back in the mirror.

"You did with every calculated move you have made since you landed on this island. Let's cut to the chase: I found out about you the first time you showed up." He paused, "and I knew you would come back too."

"Then tell me now what I want to know and I'll leave."

He turned to face Frank. "Slow down, man! The walls have ears." He walked toward the bathroom door.

"Hey, man, who shall I say I'm looking for when I get there?" Frank asked.

"They'll know. Just come in, grab a stick, and find me." He unlocked the door.

"And you are?" Frank followed behind him.

"I could ask you the same thing." He held the door open.

"Wilcox is my name. Frank."

"Yeah, Frank. I already knew that." He walked down the dark hallway toward the back door.

"And how do you know that?" Frank stopped walking.

The very large man took a key out of his pocket, put it into the lock on the emergency door, turned the switch, and looked back at his nephew. "Wilcox was my name too in another life."

1982

Ida sat on the wooden bench underneath the oak tree. No one else was around. She wanted to move from where she sat daydreaming, but her legs would not release her from the position they had taken that day. She was compelled to remain still and listen to God's voice all alone in the early morning hours of a clear, crisp day.

Pauline, resembling an adolescent with a box figure and small limp breasts, was headed toward the front door when she noticed someone sitting underneath the oak tree. She put down the Bibles she carried and looked out into the

backyard. Looking at herself in the mirror before exiting the house, she hastidly walked down the steps and approached the woman.

"Hey there!" she yelled, but did not know to whom she was speaking. "Praise the Lawd! You up with the roosters today! God must have something just for you." Dressed in a loose fitting Natural colored cotton dress with penny loafers, Pauline still did not recognize Ida Tilley.

Ida looked up and smiled. She liked Pauline. Without fail, for the past seven years, Pauline had asked her to join the prayer circle, but she repeatedly refused. Membership did not seem like something she ever wanted, at least until now. She had to fill a void in her life.

She reached out her hand to shake Pauline's.

"Oh, my God!" Pauline screamed. "Ida Mae, is that really you?" She got closer, lifted Ida's hat, and started to dance in a circle.

"Go on now! Stop your mess! I been coming fo' a while now. Y'all see me, I know ya do. I sit on the back porch and don't bother nobody. That's the way I like it." Ida shook her head.

"But why are you out here now? You needed time at the tree alone? What? Too many of us women, hooping, hollering, and praising the lawd fo' yuh to be around?" she teased her.

"Shucks no. Y'all don't scare me. In fact, I like seeing yuh worship like that. Y'all seem free." Ida looked up at Pauline.

"We are fee, Ida Mae. So are you. You just need a push. Mother Ruth was on to somethang when she started holding prayer in her home. Suddenly, the spirit moved and more and more folk wanted to be a part of this prayer chain, they used to call it." She continued. "I don't remember it all, but one day, that kitchen inside Mother's house was packed. We were having us a time, I tell yuh! That's when Mother Ruth told us to go outside to the oak tree. Said it needed some love." She sat next to Ida.

"What? Needed love? That cousin o' mine is crazy. Plain old cracky sometimes. Then again, she was on tuh somethang, huh?"

"Yes, she was! God was directing huh fo' sho'. Out of all the churches I've been tuh growing up, none of them allowed women tuh just have a Holy Ghost good time and express their feelings before the congregation. We always had a proper place tuh meet and yuh had tuh act like yuh was holier than thou when yuh came together. There was no way yuh could talk about some of the real problems we had, especially women. No, sir! We were told that the Lawd would make a way." She faced Ida. "What exactly does that mean tuh someone who is grieving or going through?"

"That was my problem. I went tuh church one time fo' help, and got nothing. In fact, no one would help me." Ida grabbed her hand. "It was a long time ago, but I remember as if it were yesterday."

"Yes, Lord. I don't think most saints know how tuh help anymore than saying tuh pray and wait on the Lawd to answer. Most of them were trying so hard tuh live this holy life full of rules and regulations that they never learn how tuh address the problems going on right befo' their eyes. What's that Beulah said the other day? 'Someone can be so heavenly bound that they are no earthly good!"

They both laughed uncontrollably, while Ruth watched from the kitchen window.

Pauline had not seemed this happy in a long time. Despite all of Ruth's invitations, they had not discussed the problems that lead to her disappearance. If it were not for Beulah, Ruth may not have been able to put the pieces of the puzzle together.

She tried to dismiss her inability to help a woman in her circle as a coincidence, even told herself that God had intervened so her help was not needed, but it did not make Ruth feel any better. Somewhere inside she felt like a failure; felt like she lost a sheep and was unable to recover it. To Ruth, it was as if her inability to help Pauline was a sinful act for which there was no forgiveness.

LATER...

At least fifty women of all ages stood underneath the oak tree as the sun softened the skys above. Releasing shouts, praises and tears of joy, they could have easily been mistaken for the cast of a broadway production. It was the scene of a women's liberation movement occurring in the backyard of someone who understood first hand the real value of being totally free. Head raised high, eyes tightly closed, Ruth beat the tambourine with all her might. Something on her insides said this would be a day like no other, for on this day, God would answer her prayers of deliverance for everyone present, including those that did not believe He was capable of setting the soul free.

There was no structured prayer circle that day, no concrete agenda for them to follow. Many of the women eventually knelt down in the grass, as some even lay prostrate on the ground, tearings soaking their identities, worshipping God in unknown tongues. God was up to something and no matter how many times they tried to conclude the service, they would discover that to be an impossible feat.

Mary Brown walked over to the oak tree and stood in front of the women. "There is a spirit of heaviness in this place. God is about to set us free! This very day, God is about to set us free!" she shouted.

"Bow your heads as we go before the Lord in prayer." She looked out among the masses and then turned when she heard the sound of cars in the distance. Ruth and the others noticed too.

One by one, seven freshly polished automobiles turned into Ruth's driveway. All bore license plates from the state of Georgia. Mary looked at Ruth and smiled.

The first car was a sage green Cadillac. When it came to a stop, Daisy Lyons opened the door and stepped onto the grass. She was wearing a red polkadot dress with ruffles at the hem. Her hair was down, and for the first time, it was hot combed and flowing freely down her shoulders. She motioned to the other drivers to exit their vehicles.

Thirty-three women walked toward the fifty or so women already assembled. As if it were the first day at a new school, both groups stared at the other in anticipation of their next move.

Mary started clapping. "I will look to the hills from whence cometh my help, my help comes from the Lord who made Heaven and Earth," she said, as she raised her hands high into the air.

Pauline sang as loud as she could. "*Victory, victory shall be mine. Oh, victory, victory shall be mine. If I hold my peace and let the Lord fight my battle. Victory, victory shall be mine.*"

Within minutes, the song united the group and the Georgia women joined together with the women of the Low Country in a full circle around the enormously aged oak tree.

For three hours, the women testified and encouraged each other. Around midday, when it was clear that they would not attend one of the rotation services, they all sat down on benches and spread-out blankets to listen to Pastor Mary deliver a sermon.

"When I started out this morning, I told the women that there was a spirit of heaviness in this place and, I believe there was. There are times when we, and I am included, just don't feel like praying. We don't feel like celebrating the Lord, for life has given us enough blows that all we can do is lie down. Bow down to whatever it is that has taken ahold of our minds and brought us so low. No, sometimes we just can't seem to pray. We feel like we can't go on any further, existing in a prison of confusion, so we freely give in. We simply throw our hands up and declare that we have been defeated.

You know, a few years ago, there was a movie starring an actress by the name of Irene Cara. Yes, ***Sparkle****, that's what it was called. Now most of us broke our necks to see that movie. Y'all remember the pretty sister who had everything but still fell for that drug dealer? Yes, I know you do. Well, remember right before she died, she sat in the mirror all beat up and a song played in the background that said, 'giving up is so hard to do.' Well, when it comes to loving a man who isn't right for you, maybe that's the only time when giving up is so hard to do. But, when it comes* *to fighting the enemy, I can attest to each of you assembled here today, that oftentimes, giving up is easy to do."*

"Amen," someone shouted, followed by thunderous applause.

"You better preach, sistah," another added.

When they announced the altar call, several women went to the front to allow Mary and Ruth to anoint their foreheads with oil and pray for them. Ida was still seated on the bench, watching and listening to the women. She did not say much the entire time.

Her head was bowed low and occasionally she would move it from side to side as if she agreed with whatever was being said during the service. When she heard the altar prayer, she looked up toward the sky as tears cascaded down her face. She lifted both arms to remove her hat, placed it next to her, and with her head still raised, cried out in a loud voice.

Her scream startled the women. A few of them standing near her turned and walked over and put their hands on her shoulders. Ida continued to moan and cry out before them. Ruth, cautiously watching her cousin, eventually walked over, sat down and placed Ida's trembling head on her shoulder.

"He's listening, gal. He never left your side. He's always been closer than you could ever realize. God loves you, Ida Mae, and so do all the women you see here today. You're home, sister. You're finally home." She rocked back and forth.

Ida cried softly as the altar call continued. Just before Mary did the benediction, Ida stood up and walked toward the front of the gathering.

"I've been heah all morning. Waiting fo' somethang, but I just ain't know what that somethang was. I ain't like the rest o' you. Church not something I do or ever did in life. Seems mah folks ain't have much use fo' church, so we never went. Then everyone around me started disappearing and it just seems like everything I want in life leaves, dies, or simply don't come back. I am so empty. With all the worldly possessions I got, I still feel empty inside. I wanna thank Sistah Ruth and all y'all for making me feel so welcomed. So loved. Ruth know since my sistah Anne pass, I ain't been close to no other woman for fear I'll lose huh too. Ruth been wid me the entire time; she never left my side and she never judge me or mah family 'cause we didn't go to church." She started to cry again.

A woman walked up to Ida and put her arms around her. Without looking up, Ida collapsed into her arms and they walked back to the bench and sat down together.

"It's okay, Miss Ida. I miss her too," she whispered into Ida's ears. "She was the best friend I ever had and I miss her too."

Ida took the handkerchief she held and dabbed her face. Then she looked up at the woman. It took a while before she recalled where they had met before. A smile slowly spread across her damp face.

"Yuh knew Anne? Where you know huh from?" she asked.

"New York. She lived across the way from my building in the Gardens. Saw her one day, spoke to her the next, and we became instant friends. I knew the moment I saw you, that you were the sister she always told me about. You were Li'l Anne, as she would say."

Tears fell down Ida's face as she grabbed Freda Dunne's hands.

"I thought I could tell you the last time, but I couldn't. I didn't have the courage to bring it all up again. I bet you wonder how I found you?" Freda asked.

"I wonder about a lot of things. So us meeting was not a coincidence, I take it." Ida smiled.

"No. I was friends with Ruth for ten long years before I discovered she was related to Anne. I wondered why I liked that woman so much. It must run in your family. Just nice and decent, good-hearted folks. Don't meet many of them in the city, unless you lucky. I was lucky. I met two women that changed my life. Ruth wrote to me one day and asked me to visit her. When I got here, she told me who you were and about the club you and your husband owns. I couldn't wait to meet you. But I was so scared to say anything, all I could do was stare, and when I finally got the nerve to introduce myself, you sound so much like Anne, I couldn't bring myself to tell you who I really was."

"Anne used tuh write me every week. Told me all about a woman named Francine. That's the only name she ever mentioned. Francine this and Francine that. That girl loved somebody named Francine a whole lot. She even said that Francine was huh other sister. I got mad, but I never said anything. So I guess I have a sister somewhere name Francine that I have yet to meet, if she's still alive on this Earth."

Freda smiled and started to cry. "She's very alive, Miss Ida. I have been using my nickname, Freda, for so long that most people forget my real name. But not Anne! She found out my name and that was the only name she ever called me: Francine." She looked into Ida's eyes, "It's me, little sister. Your other sister is very much alive."

With a newfound energy from a divine source, the women all gathered around the reunion and hugged each other.

EIGHT

1981

Ruth walked in the front door and removed her hat. Multicolored with feathers wrapped around the brim, it was surely a conversation piece, which was her intention.

Edna was resting peacefully in the front bedroom. Ruth had not slept in that room since Augustus' death, opting for the other large bedroom located on the opposite side of the house. She walked into the room and looked at her sister. Even while she slept, pain had a way of revealing its presence. Ruth knew too well the pain Edna was going through. It had visited her home twice.

Sam was fifty-five years old. He had been hospitalized and bedridden for four years, suffering from alcoholism's famous cousin: cirrhosis of the liver. No one knew he had a drinking problem until his bad choices cost them the family business. The business that Rosetta put everything into before fate drove her away from it. After her death, Ephraim Brown, the Chief Distributor, proved to everyone that he was the only capable person who could fill her shoes. Then he got married and moved to California.

Reluctantly, Frank Fields turned the business over to his daughter and son in-law. Without Rosetta by his side, he could not regain interest in anything that reminded him of her. When Sam proved he could produce a sizeable profit after three years, Frank willingly relinquished control. It was a mistake he would live to regret.

Long before the business was losing more money than it was bringing in, Frank discovered Sam was skimming from the top. Rumors surfaced that Sam only recorded the sales from customers that paid by check. He pocketed much of the cash payments.

Frank had been out of the loop for a while, but he knew the local customers better than anyone. Some of them had been around for more than thirty years, and he took every opportunity he got to show how much he appreciated their business. Occasionally he personally delivered produce to their homes, or sent greeting cards, and even gave them special gifts during the holidays. It was a tradition Rosetta started, and one he promised himself he would continue until the day he died or the day the business closed, whichever came first.

Three of his most loyal customers approached him about discrepancies in their receipts. It seemed the amount on the yearly statements provided by Edna did not reflect the totals found on the actual receipts. Frank spoke to Edna first, who retained the cash flow journal and all of the receipts, and then he questioned Sam.

Sam maintained that he required the drivers to include the total amount of the purchase, together with any additional compensation, such as tips, on the actual receipt. The accountants would then reconcile those amounts when preparing the yearly report. Frank did not buy his story.

He hired a driver from Goosecreek to deliver most of the products and to oversee the receipts of the other drivers. It worked for a few months until that driver discovered the receipts she had written and the ones later produced by Sam had been altered. In addition to stealing cash, Sam had a system that overcharged customers by roughly $100 a year, which he then pocketed.

Frank was outraged, but he did not fire Sam. Instead, he purchased carbon copy receipts and required all drivers to give the copies to Edna and the originals directly to Frank. That pretty much ended the problem. But other problems came and came they did for ten more years. In the end, rather than going completely bust, Frank Fields incrementally phased out all operations, with the exception of his famous pecan rolls which he sold exclusively to Hawk's.

"Did you see all those people at the funeral?" Caroline stood in the hallway watching Ruth as she unwrapped many of the dishes taken from the repast held at the church.

"Well, most of them did not know Sam. Those were customers who came out of respect for Daddy. Some of them been around since before you and I were born." Ruth laughed.

"I counted twenty-six white folks in the room. It seemed some of them could not stand the sight of each other!" Caroline sat down at the kitchen table. "Hand me some of that Jelly Cake. I know your cooking when I see it."

"What that you talking? Folks don't seem to care when races mix at funerals. Long as none of the long-lost secrets come out at the same time." She handed her sister a slice of cake.

"Ha! Ruth, you always think there is a conspiracy in every family."

"There is. I bet there's a few in our family too." Ruth poured two cups of coffee.

"Oh Lord, sistah. That's what I miss the most. Living in Virginia, though still the country, is nothing like living here. The people are so different. I miss this. I miss the smell of the well out back, the trees, the flowers, and even the hogs. Oh, I just miss home so much sometimes." She took a sip and looked wistfully at Ruth.

"Virginia is beautiful too. It's not South Carolina, but all the same, it's beautiful. I guess it depends on who you ask."

"Well, I have taught at Paul Lawrence College for ten years and every day I miss this place more. All I ever wanted to do was be a teacher. Nothing else. Never dreamed I would get married and move so far away." She held up the fork with a piece of the cake on it and yelled, "So far away from this cake!"

"Well, now that Larry has transferred from Morris Brown College to Virginia State College, he can bring you cake every time he returns."

"Oh, he's going to Petersburg for school now? Most kids that attend Virginia State come from up north. He is in for a rude awakening," Caroline said.

"Hush your mouth. God's got everything in control. I don't care where my children attend school if they believe God is sending them. I plead the blood of Jesus over them every day. It's my guarantee for their safety." She smiled.

"Safety is not what I'm worried about. They have a lot of parties at that school and fast women everywhere, I hear."

"The same floozies live right here in Jasper County. Larry better not bring home any babies or he is getting married as soon as I find out." Ruth knocked on the table.

"Oh, Ruthie. You wouldn't do that to him, would you?"

"What's my name?" She arose from the table and pointed toward her sister, "Remember who ya talking to. I don't play around with sin."

Caroline was seven when Rosetta died. Ruth was the sole mother figure she remembered growing up in the Low Country. She knew very little about her mother's death until Ruth told her years later.

When she graduated from Ridgeland High School, Ruth drove her to Spellman College in Atlanta and told her that she could not return home until she had a piece of paper with her name on it declaring a degree had been conferred. In three years, she did just that.

Caroline met her husband one day while delivering pecans to Hawk's for her father. He was the son of a southern preacher who played football for Grambling College in Louisiana. He took one look at Caroline, dressed in overalls and wearing a wide straw hat, and asked her to marry him. Six months later they moved away to Cincinnati where he played professional football. He retired five years later and they moved to his hometown in Virginia.

At the time Caroline moved to Virginia, Ruth was living in North Carolina with Augustus and the children. They would often visit each other's families. After Ruth moved back to Jasper County, they saw each other less and less. Though she never said anything, Caroline was sick with grief and wanted nothing more than to be around her entire family, but more than anything, she wanted to spend most of her time under the anointing of her sister Ruth.

She stopped daydreaming and stood up. "Ruth, did you see that woman staring at me in the cemetery?"

"What woman?" Ruth turned around from the kitchen sink.

"The one in that fancy dress. Where did she think she was going dressed like that?" She picked up the dishes and carried them over to the sink.

"Hush yo' mouth!" Ruth laughed. "You are talking about Lula. Lula Peters is her name." Then she turned around and faced her sister. "So, what did you think of the dress?"

"Bad to the bone! I guess she had to find someplace around here to wear it. That dress looked like something straight out of a fancy catalog." Caroline opened the refrigerator and took out a bottle of milk.

"Catalog my foot! Shucks, I designed that dress and six others for her a few years ago. Said she only had one nice dress that she wore to her sister's funeral decades ago. I felt sorry for the woman."

"Who is she?" Caroline asked.

"A lonely old woman married to a monster, that's all."

"Who?"

"Chad Peters. His father ran the Klan. Chad's far worse I hear. That poor woman had no clue what she was doing. She's so sweet. I just wish she had married Wallace Hawkins. She told me they were real sweet on each other, but her parents forbid them from marrying after someone spread lies about his father and then claimed Wallace was already married. Devastated, she up and married Chad."

"Just shows you oughta never make an emotional decision. No telling what can happen."

"Seems we women do that a lot. We think with our hearts, men think with their ...well, you know." She burst out laughing.

1982

Ben drove out of the school parking lot heading into town. He was supposed to run errands for his mother and then take his girlfriend to the drive-in theatre in Beaufort. Ruth did not allow him to hang out often in Jasper County; for some reason, she said it was not safe.

When he turned sixteen, she gave him a brand new emerald green Ford Mustang. It was a replica of a model car he'd built with her first father, James, when he was four or five years old.

Although he loved both of his fathers, he idolized James Harrison. That was who taught him how to build cars. James said building an automobile from scratch was far better than being an auto mechanic. From that day forward, Ben put his hopes and dreams in one day building cars for people on every continent. It was his tribute to the man that inspired him.

He was headed toward Route 336 into Ridgeland when he noticed the gas tank read empty. Immediately, he pulled the car off the side of the road at a local filling station. Ruth had given him a list of stations that she said did not cheat its customers. He examined the list. This particular one was not mentioned, but, he felt he had no choice.

As he pumped the gas, he noticed the machine cut off around three dollars before he pulled the hose from the car. He paid it no mind, flipped the operating lever up, and screwed the top back on the tank. He walked inside, paid the attendant, and then returned to his car where he noticed a man watching him from the full service side of the station. He opened the car door and stepped inside.

The gas gauge read one half full. He had purchased five dollars worth, which usually just about filled the entire tank. It was then that he realized why this station was not on Ruth's list. He turned the ignition switch.

Before he changed gears, the man he spotted a few minutes before approached his car with one of the gas attendants. Nervously, Ben rolled the window down.

"Afternoon, son." The attendant looked directly at Ben and continued.

"Seems yuh might have a problem with the pump you were using. Kinda slow."

Ben looked at both men cautiously. He did not say anything.

'It's all right. The gentlemen standing heah thought he saw the machine accidentally turn yuh pump off."

"I thought it was strange; I usually fill her up on seven dollars; five takes it right below the full mark. For some reason, it's reading a half tank of gas." Ben looked at the man standing next to the attendant.

"Well, tuh make it up tuh yuh, we gon' let yuh have a full tank." The attendant beamed down at Ben.

"Sir, I really just want what I paid for."

"Well, this heah nice man wanna make thangs right." He looked at Chad Peters.

"That's really not necessary." Ben forced a smile. Chad Peters fixation on him made him feel uneasy.

"Already taken care of, boy." Peters finally spoke. "He's gon' pump it too. Yuh just stay in the car." He watched Ben carefully.

"All righty then. Thank you, sir." Ben wanted nothing better than to turn the ignition on and drive away, but his mother taught him better.

"You from around heah, boy?" He was still eyeballing Ben.

"Born and raised, sir." Ben looked straight ahead at the black people walking by.

"Who ya peoples?"

"My father is dead."

"An yer mama?"

"Very much alive, sir." Ben blew a bubble.

"You ain't tell me huh name." He leaned into the car.

"Mother Ruth."

"Well, son, come on now. She ain't your real ma. Look at huh. She's colored, but I'm sho' yuh can see that." Peters looked over at the attendant.

"Sir, she's the only mother I have ever known and when I leave this green Earth, her name will be the only name listed as my mother in the obituary." He turned and gave Peters a stern look.

"You got some nerve, huh. Guess you don't know any better. They not too smart so they can't teach yuh much. Yuh shoulda stayed at that private school she put yuh in. Not many colleges want yuh from that other place they call a school. Kids running around like apes, dumb as a doorknob."

"Well, let's just say I get along well with the apes, sir. Feel right at home." He smiled and blew a bubble in Peters' face.

Chadwick Peters backed up and turned around. Then he turned back to face Benjamin. "Kids tease you about dem blue eyes?"

"Nope. Some days they're blue, some days they're green. They may turn brown by the time I grow up."

"Yeah. I doubt they'll be turning brown anytime soon. I had a daughter wid beautiful blue eyes. When she turned fifteen, they up and turned green like an emerald." Sadness filled his face.

"Oh yeah, what color are they now, sir?" Benjamin turned the ignition switch.

"Hell, I ain't seen huh in years. I ask mahself the same question. When did yours start tuh change?" He looked at the ground.

"Around the same time as hers." Ben hit the pedal hard and drove off.

1978

Ms. Harley motioned to Benjamin to remain after class was over. She smiled so he would know there was no cause for alarm.

The bell rang and Ben remained seated. He whispered something into his girlfriend's ear and turned to face his teacher.

"Benjamin, do you mind if I introduce you to my very best friend? I've been telling her all about you and she's just dying to meet yuh?" She walked toward him.

"Well, okay, I drove to school today." He tried to hide his agitation.

"Well, darling, she'll be here in a few minutes. If you could be so kind and just hang around and say hello, I would appreciate it." She stood in front of him, giving him no choice but to stay put.

For ten minutes, he avoided her eyes until it became obvious that Ms. Harley was nervous about something. He looked at his wrist watch.

"Someone expecting yuh?" she carefully asked.

"Yes. My mother expects me home around a certain time every day unless I have to go to work or run errands for her." He looked up from the book he had just opened.

"Well, I do declare. We'll wait five minutes longer and if she isn't here by then, you can go on. I'll give you a note to carry home to Mother Ruth."

The classroom door opened and a strikingly beautiful woman walked in. She immediately looked at Benjamin, who was busy reading.

"Gloria, I am so sorry that I am late." She walked toward them as she tussled with her hair. She was wearing a turquoise fitted dress with a white sweater, it was clear that her dirty blonde hair had been dyed a few times to hide the obvious brunette roots.

"Ah, heavens, Alice, you had me worried." Gloria raced over to where she stood.

There was no need for an introduction. Benjamin remembered Alice Peters from the playground at Thomas Haywood Academy. The last time he had seen her, she'd handed him a photograph of herself and a darker gentleman holding a bouncing baby boy. Ben barely looked. When he got home from school that day, he hid the photo underneath the mattress of his bed, and never mentioned the woman or the photograph to another living soul.

1983

Ruth put the bookmark in the Bible and then bowed her head. She prayed for a while, then opened her eyes and looked around. She could hear the children playing in the back room.

"Jonah, it's time for your nap." She stood in the doorway looking at the toys spread across the floor. "Y'all pick up a little before taking anything else out of those boxes." She reached out for Jonah's hand. "Off you go, young lady."

"You so pretty, Mama," Jonah said as she climbed into bed.

"So are you, little angel."

"Was your mommy pretty just like you?" She laid her head down on the pillow.

"She was prettier than I. When you get older, I'll tell you all about your Grandma Rose." Ruth turned and walked out of the room.

Lately, all she thought about was her mother. Despite all of the wonderful people who had come into her life, she still missed Rosetta terribly. There were times when she wondered what her mother would look like in old age; what she would say about all the changes in their lives, and how she would feel about the paths each of her children had taken.

A tear fell down one side of her face, as Ruth stood in her bedroom window. She had so much to be thankful for. Her life had come full circle in many ways. The Lord had healed her mind and she was able to bring hundreds of people into the fold. In fact, with all that she had going on, it was hard to think about what was missing, but every now and again, it hit her like a ton of brinks that the person she wanted to hold the most was gone.

She knelt down, reached underneath the bed, and pulled out a cardboard box. It was the same box that she used as a hope chest so very long ago. After she was diagnosed with schizophrenia, she put all her mementos inside a suitcase that she kept in the bottom of the hall closet. When she had trouble remembering things or sorting out exactly what was real from what was make believe, she would open the suitcase and see her entire life laid out before her very eyes. It was then that she knew everything she witnessed in that moment was not in her head, but had actually occurred at some point in her life.

She thumbed through the box until she came upon the obituary of Lula Peters. Although she kept many of them, Ruth never read the inside of the program. Something drove her to open the one in her hands and read it.

Her maiden name was Simmons. Her father died when she was a teenager and she moved away to live with her mother's parents. She had one sister, Rose Marie, but she died sometime ago, no date was given. Other than the marriage to Chadwick Peters and the names of her two children, Charles and Mary Alice, no other information about her family was mentioned. She was affiliated with the First Baptist Church of Ridgeland, the church where the funeral was held.

Ruth attended, as did several members of the prayer circle. For once in his life, Chadwick Peters made no objection to the presence of blacks being around him. He sat on the front row with a smirk on his face the entire time.

Ruth thought of Lula's last words to her and wondered why she used as a dying declaration a formal apology. She looked back in the box and noticed the black velvet jewelry case that Lula had given to her on her death bed. She had not opened it since the old woman went home to be with the Lord.

Slowly, she opened the box and pulled out the long white satin glove. Without giving it much thought, Ruth knew it belonged to her mother. She recognized it the first time she laid eyes on it. Next, she looked at the two chain-linked necklaces. She did not notice before, but the pendants were exactly the same, eighteen inches or so in length, fourteen carat gold, with a heart-shaped locket attached. Puzzled, looked past the lockets in her hands and noticed three aged photographs.

The first photo was of a very handsome, Caucasian gentleman dressed in all black, as if he was on his way to church. It was Lula's father, no doubt. Ruth carefully turned the photo around and read the faded inscription, 'Dad' on the back. The second photo, folded in half, was of two women, two older girls and a little girl sitting on the ground playing in the dirt. Ruth stared at it more carefully. All of the women in the photograph resembled one another.

She looked at the two older girls standing next to the women. Rail thin, they had their arms wrapped around each other's shoulders. Dressed exactly alike, they both wore petticoat dresses and high heel shoes. The taller of the two was darker in complexion with very distinctive eyes and legs so long and thin that they reminded Ruth of the cartoon character, Olive Oil, Popeye the sailor man's wife.

Ruth noticed they each had extremely long-silky dark colored hair. Then she noticed something she had not noticed earlier, they were all wearing elbow length white satin gloves! Ruth turned the photo over immediately and read the word, 'sisters' on the back. She flipped it back over to get a second look.

This time she looked at the women closer. She had seen one of them before, but could not remember where. She looked at the little girl seated on the ground. Still nothing. She looked back at the two girls and noticed for the first time, the necklaces hanging around their necks. She looked down at the heart-shaped pendants on the bed. "Oh, God!" she whispered.

Ruth took one of the necklaces out of the jewelry box, looked at it and then looked back at the picture. She put the picture down and stared at the remaining contents in the box. Then she picked up the last remaining photograph. It too was folded in half. Ruth opened it up and dropped it immediately. Then she opened both lockets.

"Jesus! What in God's name?" she gasped.

In her shock, she carefully sorted through the momentums strewn across the bed until her eyes fell upon a white gold, small solitaire diamond ring. She picked it up, chest heaving upward in slow motion, and started crying. Slowly she slipped the ring onto her finger and placed her hand on her chest. At that moment, the truth she'd sought all those years ago was finally revealed as her hand caressed the outside of her heart.

"Oh, Mama!" She looked up and cried over and over again.

NINE

1965

The sign to the pool hall had a neon arrow attached pointing down into the stairwell. Frank was unfamiliar with this part of town. He slowly walked down the steps.

He entered the dark, smoke-filled room and looked around. He could barely see the people standing near the pool tables, but he had a clear view of the woman at the bar. He walked over to her.

"Hey, how you doing?" He looked at the hundreds of bottles of alcohol stacked up on the bar behind her.

"You're a cutie. Have not seen you in here before. Come for a drink?" She leaned over toward him, exposing her red brassiere underneath a sheer white blouse.

"No. I'm looking for someone. Where can I get a stick from to play?"

"Take your pick. They are hanging in the back. Just grab one and tell the player at the table you'll take the next winner. That's the only way they will let you in. If you stand there saying nothing, they will ignore you and you'll never get a chance to play." She tossed her curly locks.

"Thanks for the advice." He turned to walk away.

"Thank you." She had coy look on her face.

Frank walked to the back of the room and retrieved a pool stick. There were three tables with games being played. He looked at the table in the far back corner and saw the man he had come to see. He was dressed in all white, white shoes and a white fedora hat. When he saw Frank standing there, he motioned to him to join him.

"Wasn't hard to find you." Frank said with a crooked smile on his face.

"Wanted it that way." He turned around and headed toward the tables that lined the back wall.

"So you ever gone tell me who you are?" Frank sat down facing the front of the room.

"You haven't figured it out?" He removed a pack of cigarettes from his front pocket.

"Nope. You said you were a Wilcox, but I've never met you. Maybe the last name is a coincidence."

"Trust me, it is not. Herman is my first cousin. You do recognize that name, huh? Herman Coles Wilcox?" He let out a slow-winded laugh.

"So you some kinda kin to my father?" Frank relaxed in the chair.

"That ought to make you feel better." He laughed and then continued speaking. "So I heard you were asking questions about a murder at the Gardens, hanging out at ***The Blue Note*** and even inquiring from that crowd." He puffed and returned the cigarette to the ashtray in front of him.

"Only way to find out is to ask."

"Wrong answer." He lifted the cigarette and inhaled.

"What do you mean? It's the only answer I have. Everyone around here is tight lipped. I need to know what happened to my sister. Tried the cops, tried the papers, still nothing." Frank shook his head.

"It's almost as if it did not happen at all, right? What you must realize is that folks are smart. They know after a murder the cops will send snitches around to gather information. You might think eight years is a long time, but not around here. Eight years is like yesterday. Folks know to keep their mouths shut." He put the cigarette out and leaned back in the booth.

"I just want some answers. She was here for close to three years. Someone had to know her, or even hear about her. I can't believe she lived here and never met anyone outside of the fool that should have stood by her side."

"She knew a lot of people, Frank, they just not willing to divulge information about her or the circumstances leading to her death." He leaned forward. "You're not in Kansas anymore, man."

"I know that. I just want to know what happened. I heard eight people got killed right after she died. One of them was thrown out of the thirtieth-floor window. This can't be a coincidence."

"It's not. They died because of her," he whispered.

"What do you mean? What did her death have to do with them?" Frank leaned in closer to hear.

"Revenge."

"On who?"

"Anyone that saw her die and did nothing to save her."

Frank looked at Mark Wilcox very carefully, and said, "And who was after revenge?"

"Her father." He put his enormous hands on the table.

"What? Man, I don't get it! You mean to tell me, my father had something to do with all of this? What would that genteel man, who can't seem to control his loud mouthed wife, do in a situation like this?"

"You are so wrong about him." He held up his glass and motioned to the waitress to refill his drink.

"Man, that's another story. My father ain't got that kind of courage. He came up here to pick Ann's things up and maybe talk to the police. When I asked him what happened, he never could tell me anything concrete and I believed him. He doesn't know what happened. I'm telling you, her death nearly destroyed him."

"Me too." The waitress brought two glasses of drinks, to which Frank shook his head declining the offer.

"It's pop, Mr. Wilcox." She winked and smiled.

"Pop?"

"Gingerale." She looked back at him as she walked away.

"How does she know what I drink?" He looked around suspiciously.

"She works for me. I told her before you came in."

"Who are you? Stop all the crap and give it to me straight, no chaser." Frank took a sip of the drink to make sure it was a ginger ale and not alcohol.

"I'm not sure you can handle it all that straight." He laughed. "Here's the crooked truth, Anne was killed in a feud between some drug lords. Seemed her friend was not too wise and got mixed up in some real funky mess. She called me about three days before she died. I was going to pick her up and bring her back to Ridgeland to be with y'all for Christmas. I was hoping Herman could talk some sense into her. Then I remembered Anne vowed she would never step foot in South Carolina as long as Eula Mae was there."

"How you know all of this?" Frank was agitated.

"How do you think? Man, you not as smart as I thought." He raised his voice.

"Man, look a heah; I ain't got no time for games." He was interrupted.

"What makes you think I'm playing games? Now either you're going to listen to this story and never ask about it again, or keep on asking and get your butt killed."

"All right. All right. All this jive is really knocking me for a loop. How long had you known Anne?" Frank calmed down.

"Before she was born." He looked down.

"What?"

"I told you her father wanted revenge, right?" He looked up at Frank.

"Oh, hell! You? I heard Eula Mae when she told Anne that Herman was not her father."

"What? When?" Mark Wilcox could not believe his ears.

"The last time I saw her. They were all outside in the middle of the morning. I had just come home. I was about to cross the field when I heard the commotion. I didn't stick around. Matter of fact, I left as soon as I saw the look on Anne's face after she found out she was someone else's child. I couldn't take anymore. She was like a mother to me and in one instant, Eula Mae destroyed her."

"Yes she did. No one was to know. Anne was so crazy about Herman, but for some reason, she couldn't stand Eula Mae. I never understood it."

"But hold on! You know about that night? That's why she run off with that fool to New York?" Frank looked straight at him.

"Probably. All I know is she found out everything once she got here and it just made her love Herman even more." He removed his hat and rubbed his balding head.

"Who told her the truth?"

"Her father did." He put the hat back on.

"And I wonder what she thought of him? That bastard decides to tell her all those years later." Frank leaned back and tapped on the table.

"I told you no one was supposed to know." He focused on Frank's fists and the angry sound of the taps. "Your mother does that."

"What?" Frank stopped tapping when he realized what Mark was talking about. "How do you know? "

"Old habits are hard to break. Eula Mae always knocked on wood when she was frustrated about something."

"Y'all were friends too."

"More than that." He winked.

The light went off in Frank's head. He crossed his hands together and looked around the room. In that instant, he had learned more than he had come to New York to find out.

"Did Herman know?"

"He knew Eula Mae was pregnant before he married her. I doubt if she told him who the father was." He looked around. "Herman was always the smartest person in our family. One day he just figured it out. Came to me and told me to look after Anne in the streets. I knew then he was not asking for a favor, he was issuing a demand based on obligation. I respected him, so I never said a word. I did what he asked, even watched out for Ida Mae, then one day, I ran into Anne and we started talking. As she got older, we talked more and more. I guess we became close friends. I never had the guts to tell her back then."

"What made you finally tell her?"

"I didn't. She told me. Said she had finally put all the pieces together. Said thank you and if I didn't mind, she didn't want anyone to know but the two of us. I kept my word until you showed up looking for her."

"She was the only mother I ever had." A tear fell down Frank's face. "It's hard for me to look at Eula Mae without hating her for what she did to Anne. If Anne had never found out Herman was not her father, she probably would not have gotten on that bus. She would be alive to this day." He looked at Mark Wilcox, "You should have stopped her from leaving."

"I was in the hospital, remember? By the time I got out, it took me a while to find out where she had gone. I came up here, found her and even rented a place for her to stay in, but it did no good. She liked the Gardens. Had some friend there and thought she'd be safe. I knew it was mistake from the beginning."

"Why did they kill her?" Frank fought the tears.

"Dumb boyfriend took the wrong package. Whole gang of drug lords showed up. When he wouldn't give it back, they threatened to kill Anne. He tried to call their bluff and when they smiled and let him think he had fooled them, they grabbed my daughter and threw her out of the window." He removed his glasses so that Frank could see the tears as they fell down his face. "They took the best of me. My life ended on that day. I didn't want to live any longer. She was the only daughter I had, and she was the only person I ever let get that close to me."

"Is that why you changed your name?" Frank finally asked.

"I needed a new identity. Williams was a common enough name. I had to disconnect myself from the past. It was the only way I could survive."

1990

Herman walked down the street. He had taken to walking after he retired. His second wife, whom he never officially married, died of a heart attack leaving him alone in one of the biggest houses in the entire Low Country. With the exception of Ida, Timmy, and occasionally Frank, he entertained few visitors.

His doctor delivered the worst blow of his life: Six months to live. He walked faster. He stopped at the park on Main Street and sat down. He was too weak to go any further. When he spotted a taxicab, he waved it down and got inside.

When the taxi arrived at his front door, he noticed Frank's car on the other side of the yard. A smile came to his face. He paid the driver and walked toward true consolation.

Frank opened the front door and stood watching Herman walk slowly up the stairs. By the look on his face, he knew something was wrong. He opened the screened door and allowed his father to walk inside.

"You wanna talk?" he said just above a whisper.

"In a minute. Let me take these good clothes off and get settled." Herman never turned around.

Frank was sitting in the back room watching television when his father returned. He could see the worry lines etched across his face. He turned the volume down and waited to hear the news.

"Cancer." Herman broke the silence.

"Okay. That's what we expected. Now what?" Frank was trembling.

"Six months."

"What?" He stood up and walked over to where Herman sat.

"Yeah. It's too far gone. I waited too long they say. Nothing much the doctors can do." He appeared extremely calm.

"That's what these hick town doctors say. Let me take you to Atlanta or to New York where the specialists are." Frank leaned on the wooden column and knocked.

"You think that's gon' do me any good? I had a good life, son. I raised three beautiful children, and now I have two grandchildren, that no one thought I would ever see. God's been good to me. Never even went to church until I was over fifty years old. Seem like I was just living on borrowed time anyway."

"You sound like you have given up! You got a lot of living to do. Why you gonna throw in the towel now?" Frank could no longer hide the tears.

"I'm almost eighty-five, son. Living to see eighty was a big deal for me. All that stuff you and Ida Mae did for me, I'll never forget it." He walked over and put his arms around his son. "The Bible says there's a time to live and a time to die; I just think this is my time. I was hurt when I heard the news, but then I sat on that park bench and thought of the fact that my eldest never got the chance to see all of this, so I'm feeling pretty blessed right now."

"Let's get a second opinion, please?" Frank pleaded.

"Okay. One more opinion only. I don't want to spend the rest of my life in and out of hospitals taking tests to tell us the obvious. We take one more test, and then we accept the truth, whatever it may be." He stared solemnly into Frank's face.

1984

Timmy held onto Ida's waist and swayed to the music. Occasionally, he would look down at her and plant a wet kiss on her lips. He loved her more each year and as the years passed by, he knew she was his soulmate and that they would be together forever.

Clubs in New Jersey were quite different than the ones in the Low Country. Timmy visited northern clubs for new ideas to use in the seven clubs he now owned throughout South Carolina and Georgia. His dreams had finally come true.

This particular club was known for its live music. They owned one club in Savannah that used live bands, but the cost of overhead made using extra personnel for entertainment seem like a less attractive option.

They stood in line for an hour before getting permission to come inside. There were large men, bouncers, who stood outside of every popular club in the north. It was a practice that did not exist in the south. Finally, they both were admitted into the vestibule, patted down, charged a twenty-dollar cover charge, and then allowed to roam freely throughout the establishment.

This club was one of the largest they had frequented over the years. With an upstairs lounge, the bottom floor had a large dance floor and bars positioned on each side of the room. The upstairs was more intimate, the lighting was lower, there was one small bar with a few stools surrounding it, and twenty or so small tables spread out in front of a circular shaped stage.

Timmy and Ida stood watching patrons dance and fellowship among each other. Unable to withstand the thick smoke that congregated in the air, they walked over to the bar, ordered drinks and headed upstairs.

"This feels much better," Ida said once they got to the top of the stairs.

"Yeah. Too many folks down there bumping into you, not saying excuse me, and whatnot," Timmy commented. "This is just my speed."

A waitress came over and escorted them to a small round on the side of the stage. She informed them that the band had taken a break, but the second set was scheduled to begin in fifteen minutes.

Ida looked at the women around her. It was clear that she was out of place. Many of those women were dressed in blue denims and high heels. Ida was one of the few women wearing a dress. She also stared at their hair. Women in the north had long said goodbye to the straightening comb.

The band resumed its session on the stage while Timmy and Ida pulled their chairs close together and hugged one another. They stared into each other's eyes and enjoyed the music. This was a great night.

After playing a series of songs, each band member did a solo of his particular instrument, playing alone for a few minutes. The crowd clapped and screamed for more of what they heard. Finally, the saxophonist stood center stage. The background music came to a complete stop. He stood there for a few minutes with his head facing the ceiling and then said into the microphone, "This one's for you, Hannah."

His hands stroked the pieces of steel and he began to play with such passion that the room was transformed into a religious experience; folks stood clapping, arms raised to the ceiling, and shouting in excitement. It reminded Ida of the spirit that flowed in the prayer circle. She looked at Timmy to discover that he, too, was crying.

"What's a matter, baby?"

"That brother plays like he's been touched by God. I mean, I can actually feel his pain in that sax. Wow! They got something special heah. No wonder it took us ova' an hour to get inside of this place!" He put his cheek against hers.

Ida watched the audience's reaction and agreed that the man playing the saxophone had a special gift. This Hannah person must be someone special. She looked back at him as the solo came to an end. She watched the way his fingers stroked the keys, effortlessly, as if he was not playing at all!

"Timmy!" she almost shouted.

"What? What's wrong?" He saw the way her hand trembled.

"I know him!"

"What?"

"I know him, I tell yuh." She grabbed Timmy's hand and held it tightly.

"Where you know him from, Ida Mae?" He put his other arm around her.

"Only one man play like that. I never heard the music, but I know the moves of his hands better than anyone. Ain't seen him in years, but I know it's him! No one can tell me otherwise." She was almost crying.

They walked hand in hand down the long dark corridor. Ida told the waitress that they were there to surprise the saxophonist. The waitress said his name was Big D. Ida told her what the D stood for and she let them go into the back dressing rooms.

His name was on the door. Timmy knocked softly. No one opened the door, but the door next to his room opened and someone peeked outside.

"Didn't mean to disturb you," Timmy looked over and said just before the person shut the door.

A few minutes later, a woman opened his door and stood looking at the two of them.

"Can I help you?" she asked.

"Hey. We are from South Carolina. We just wanted to thank the saxophone player. He really moved us to tears out there," Timmy said.

"That's what they all say. How did you two get back here?"

"We told the waitress we knew him," Ida said.

"And how do you know Big D?" She opened the door further.

"If he could come to the door, he'll find out," Ida snapped.

"Maybe he isn't here. As a matter of fact, Big D done left already."

"Is he coming back? We're only here for the weekend. If he's gonna be heah tomorrow, we can just come back," Timmy said.

"Big D doesn't play on Saturday nights. Sorry you missed him." She was about to close the door.

Ida fumbled in her purse and said, "Give him a message, will you?"

"I'm not his secretary." She closed the door.

Ida raised her fist to beat on the door, but Timmy grabbed her hand. "No, baby. Don't get her upset. We don't know what we up against. Let's just go. If it's him, we'll try to see him again."

"I wonder why he left so soon?" Ida put the paper back into her purse and stood looking at the door.

As they turned and walked away, she rested her head on Timmy's shoulder and fought back the tears.

They walked down the street from the club and stood on the corner looking around. Timmy put his hand up to hail a taxicab.

A taxi pulled over to the curb. Timmy opened the door and Ida slid into the back seat.

"Hold the taxi!" A man came running from around the corner.

"What?" Timmy sat down next to Ida.

"We can share," he said to the driver as he opened the front door. He put a case down in the floor and then sat down. The taxicab pulled off.

Timmy had a strange look on his face. The man in the front seat removed his hat and turned toward them and said, "I'm sure Li'l Anne doesn't mind."

TEN

1987

Mary stood in the airport at the ticket counter. Numbness had taken control of her entire body. As she tried to fight the tears, she leaned her head on Frank's shoulder and smiled.

"Thank you," she whispered into his ear. "I don't know how I would have made it without you this time." She looked up into his strong face.

"Don't have to worry about that, Mer. I told you, that's what I'm here for." He kissed her on the forehead.

They walked toward the terminal gate and sat down. Mary opened her purse and took out a letter. It was over thirty years old.

"When my mom died, Uncle Bud gave this to me. It comforted my spirit and declared that God had a plan for my life. I didn't know what he was talking about. I read this letter so many times that my grandma, Ethel Lee, took it away from me. She said the letter was a crutch to my dealing with the loss I had suffered." A tear rolled down her face.

"That must have been a difficult time for you." Frank sat across from her and listened.

"It was. It's hard to lose a parent at that age. I lost two. I vowed I would never step foot in our home again. I hated my daddy for what he drove my mother to do. He didn't even try to stop her. Just let her dive into that river, into her death." She took out a handkerchief and blew her nose.

"Some things happen that no one comprehends."

"If it wasn't for Ephraim, I would not be standing here today. You see, he was real close to Grandma Ethel Lee. He used to live with her on and off, in between his marriages. But when my mother died, he moved in, fixed the house up, and took care of me. I was shocked when Grandma let him take me to Savannah with him and the boys to live."

"And that's where you met Prentiss?" Frank looked around.

"I'll never forget that day." She laughed. "Uncle Bud always knew Prentiss would be a great husband for me. He was right. In fact, sometimes I think he was right about everything. When he said people were good, they were better than good." She looked up and continued.

"He said Rosetta was good. Yep. I remember. He introduced me to her. She changed my life and so did he."

"When was the last time you saw him?" he asked.

"Well, after Grandma died, he stopped coming down south, seems he fell in love with California. Retired on the water, married and settled down. Shocked all of us." She stood up to board the plane.

"So he never came back?"

"He did. He came for my wedding to Edgar, came to Micah's college graduation, and came when Micah was stabbed. I guess he came about once a year if he could manage. Didn't come last year or the year before so I went out there. I think I've been to California nine times over the years. Prentiss took me the first time." She grabbed his arm and they boarded the plane.

Ephraim Brown died the way he lived: In a complete state of bliss. He was a successful developer, married with six sons, and he invested much of what he earned from running Rosetta's business into what became the largest real estate brokerage firm in San Diego.

He knew he was dying, but he never told anyone. Found out one day and started writing a guide on real estate the next. In thirty years, he never missed one day in the office, yet on the morning of his death, he told his wife that he wanted to stay in bed. She never suspected anything until she returned home around three that afternoon to find that he was still asleep.

Next to his body was a neatly folded piece of paper that she opened after she called the ambulance.

"If I reflect upon what the good Lord has allowed me to experience, I can only stand in awe and praise his name!

Life for me has been a crystal stair. When they ask you how I died, tell them happy and full. I really know what it means to have it all. A life most dream of, wealth people desire to have, and a family that represented the meaning of true love. Tell everyone that death for me is a welcome friend. Whatever you do, don't grieve for me, for I am not gone, just walking on the sands of Heaven with my savior. I'm free. I love you so!" Bud

He started to pen the words to one of his favorite songs, *"Goodbye till we meet again in tomorrow's crystal sea. As always, I'll be yours to love, knowing that you must be free..."*

The pen drifted off the page and remained gripped between his long, stiff fingers.

1985

On February 1, 1985, Daisy Lyons called it quits. She had been the campaign manager of nine successful bids for everything from state legislatures, members of the U.S. Congress, and even the President of the United States of America. There was nothing left for her to conquer.

After President Jimmy Carter left office in 1980, the highlights of her career were quickly coming to an end. She stayed in Washington, D.C. until the end of President Ronald Reagan's first term, and then, after witnessing the unthinkable, she decided it was time to move back to the

South she had so impatiently run away from all those years ago.

She first thought of retiring after Shirley Chisholm left office in '82 but someone convinced her to continue to ensure that more blacks had an opportunity in deciding the future of this country. Reluctantly, she stayed on, remaining Washington, all the while looking forward to what she and so many others believed would become a Democrat Party takeover in a few years.

Her career escorted her to the uttermost parts of the world and she and loved every minute. There were times during her travels when she envied women around her that had families, but she knew she would have never been satisfied with a life in the South, nor would she have been fulfilled by having a family without having a successful career. She made a sacrifice and when she looked back over her life, there were no regrets. She had lived the life that God predestined for her to live.

She telephoned the movers to take residency in a foreign state she had not lived in for thirty years. From the television and her short visits it seemed South Carolina had finally changed. Many things about the old Confederacy were now distant memories, yet Daisy knew the remnants of Jim Crow could still rear their heads at any given moment.

June 30, 1985

Micah stood in the foyer staring as she walked in. As usual, she was elegant. Wearing an emerald green taffeta gown, Daisy walked with the authority of a person who controlled everything within her distance.

"Anais Anais," he whispered into her ear as he took her arm and escorted her down the stairs.

"As usual, the gentleman from Georgia is correct," she teased.

"As usual, the red haired woman is stunningly beautiful and the envy of every woman in the room."

"I doubt that. This redhead is tired and old, and feeling it every minute." She looked at him.

"Well, you have come a long way, baby!" He laughed. "The world is a better place because you were here for all the black silenced voices of our past. Thank God that you were here."

Four-hundred people gathered in the Capitol Rotunda that day to bid farewell to Washington's most devoted political strategist. She promised them that she would never return to the District of Columbia or the halls of justice which she so loved visiting. Her new life, Daisy joked, would be confined to beautiful scenic locations, preferably beaches, with warm water, hot sunshine, and easy living. She would not miss the hectic life of politics, she chimed; but those listening to her did not take such talk seriously.

Frank and Micah chartered a plane to bring most of the women from the prayer circle to see Daisy's last hurrah. It was a surprise to celebrate her sixty- fifth birthday. She was overwhelmed as she looked out into the audience and spotted the faces of the sixty Southern women whom she'd heard about more than twenty years ago.

Ruth, Ida, Beulah, and Mary stood together on the sidelines watching her every move. They had arrived two weeks earlier to help pack Daisy's belongings. She objected to them doing household work in her home, but they overruled much of what she said claiming the Lord had sent them to give her a proper send off.

She had not told them until their arrival that she was looking for a place near their new church. She wanted that to be her very own surprise. After years seeing the power of the women and their impact on thousands of lives, Daisy knew that retirement for her would consist of doing the Lord's work. She smiled every time she thought about it.

"You know, my dear Southern belles, I feel love is in the air. Somebody is about to jump the broom." At the reception, Ruth laughed and looked at Ida, Mary, and Daisy suspiciously.

"Oh, no. I don't think I would know how to be a wife." Daisy laughed as she looked across the room at Micah. "Y'all see that? Maybe that's what Ruth means."

"Pauline. That girl is too old for Micah," Ida chimed in.

"Ladies! Age is nothing but a number." Beulah lifted her glass to them.

"You have a problem with that, Mary?" Ruth asked.

"Heavens no! I just want him to be happy. Pauline has been good to me, taking care of Mona like she does. She's been a life support to the church. Maybe that's what Micah needs." She looked over at Frank sitting alone at the bar.

"I'm not talking about Micah. I missed that one. But, yes, Pauline would be good for him." Ruth winked at Mary.

"Stop it, sister. I see what you're doing. No." She looked at all of the women. "No. Don't even say it out loud. We are just friends. We go way back and y'all know it." Mary played with the peplum on her dress.

"That's the best kind of man to marry. Someone you know for sure will be there through thick and thin," Beulah said.

"Amen to that," Ruth and Ida said simultaneously.

"He's been there, but I don't think he's interested." Mary looked at Ruth and rolled her eyes.

"Any fool can see that Frank is in love with you. What's wrong, Mary? Why are you not willing to admit it?"

"Admit what?" She saw Frank looking over at them with a wide grin on his face.

"That you're in love with him." Ida burst out laughing.

"Now that's not fair, sisters, and you know it. Don't believe Ruth's clairvoyance this time. Some of that stuff I think Ruth just wants to happen." Mary winked at Frank.

"Well, the authority of life and death, and I guess we can add love, lies in the power of the tongue," Daisy said while looking over at Frank.

"It depends on who's doing the talking." Mary walked over toward Frank without looking back at the women around the table.

"Mmm. I didn't know the old girl had it in her," Beulah said.

"Watch it now. You almost her age. When you gon' get married again?" Ruth turned her attention to Beulah who was sitting right next to her.

"Who says I'm not married?"

"What? What crazy man stays home all the time while you run the streets?" Ida interjected.

"That's for me to know, and you to find out."

They drank a toast and continued talking into the wee hours of the morning.

1954-1986

Her outward mask was pure deception. Inside, she masked far more intelligence that she let on. The Low Country rumormill suggested she was a self-proclaimed healer who possessed supernatural gifts that allowed her to heal the sick and raise the dead.

But she was far more than a Low Country root doctor. She was highly educated, holding a doctoral degree in nursing. By the time she was forty, she was the highest ranking nurse in the state of Georgia, responsible for more than five-hundred hospital staff across the state.

She kept her life a secret because of the rejection she faced in her home town. Rejection that started with her mother, who was also blessed with the gift of healing, and later chased Beulah every chance it got.

At sixteen, she left Jasper County, and while passing as a white woman, she attended the University of South Carolina, where she received her first degree. The following year, she enrolled in graduate school in Georgia, with enough face powder that fooled the natural eye into believing that she was of Caucasian descent.

By the time she received her last degree, Beulah had been married three times. She used the money and the prestige from those marriages to work with some of the most sought after physicians in the country. She thought of going to medical school, but later changed her mind. Instead, she practiced holistic healing on the very people that rejected her as a child.

In some ways, practicing in the Low Country was easy. There were few persons in the sixties that achieved college degrees. In fact, because the Low Country consisted of many self-taught farmers, few people questioned the powers of a root doctor. Her powers were believed to be supernatural, and that was something that was highly accepted back then. To some, even superior to book learning.

Until she met him, that is. Brought to her doorstep in the middle of the night, he had a fever that made his skin feel not just hot, but like a small fire to the touch. Beulah had never seen anything like it. She did her usual practices on him, and when nothing worked, she emersed his body in a bathtub full of ice cold water. Initially, despite the freezing cold, his body temperature remained the same.

He sat in the water for thirty minutes longer than the time it takes to stop the human heart, but nothing changed. He said his soul was on fire. Never seeing anything like it before, Beulah called for an aloe plant, cut open the stalks, and placed the open, oozing branches directly onto his skin. Within minutes, the fever disappeared.

He fully recovered, but unlike other customers who were not allowed to convalesce in her home, she did not ask him to leave once he got well. Instead, she told him he could stay until he felt he could deal with the outside world. It took five years, and as she suspected, as soon as he no longer was haunted by the demons from his past, he disappeared into the darkness from whence he'd come.

Seven years later, he returned. They married, but by 1974, he had taken to the road again. This time, Beulah knew where he was and she understood why he felt he had to go. He had a destiny to fulfill. She wouldn't let anything stand in his way.

It was the suspense that drove her to keep the secret from everyone, including his own family. Once they married, she often traveled to visit him on the road, but would find herself with little to do so she returned to the Low Country where she felt the most comfortable. When she retired from nursing in 1987, she devoted herself to him, and surprising the entire small town, she finally opened a tiny window into her very private life.

1984

Ruth looked out of the window and saw Beulah sitting alone on one of the benches under the oak tree. She watched for a few minutes and then busied herself with housework. After a while, she looked again and saw that Beulah was gone.

"Ruthie, come out and play," she heard from the back of the house.

"What in God's name?" Ruth headed toward the kitchen. She walked out onto the back porch and looked through the screened door as Beulah sat on a swing in the back yard.

"Come on out here and keep me company. You can do housework any time. Jonah's half grown now. You got an empty house. Come play with me." Beulah swung high into the air.

"Great Scott, Beulah. You never cease to amaze me! First, climbing trees and scaring the life out of folk, and now the swing. Is this your way of telling me you want to me to take you for a ride in my airplane?" She laughed and walked toward her.

"Ruthie, you're the only person I would fly with in those small crop dusters, but no thanks. I like the bigger jets, if you don't mind." She laughed.

Ruth sat in the swing next to Beulah and rocked slightly. "This branch is not strong enough to hold the two of us, you know that, right?"

"Who says so? I keep my figure, I don't know about you with all the company that's in this house. I don't see how you get any rest. Between the kids, your family, the women, and everybody else who thinks you can heal them, you should look like you're ninety years old."

"And you should look a hundred, from what I hear about your root business." She let out a holler.

"I don't have a root business, you nut. I practice holistic healing. You of all people should know that." She stopped swinging and faced Ruth.

"You practice a little more than that, sistah! Why didn't you just become a doctor? You had the intellect and the skills."

"I don't know. I became bored with school and bored with having to be someone who I was not."

"Oh yeah, I forgot about that. I thought I blew your cover when I asked about you at the hospital." Ruth bent over and picked up a stick, spread her legs apart in the swing, and started to doodle on the ground.

"By that time, I didn't care. I stopped wearing face powder too. Those fools just thought I had a tan. That was that bronzer I was using. It worked so good on the Klan." She burst out laughing.

"Where do you find the energy to keep up fuss with these crazy people?" She stopped writing and looked around. "I kept our secret all these years, but I wanted to ask you about that girl. You remember?"

"How could I forget? She was brutally raped. Those scum took everything she had. I'm surprised she's still alive."

"Well, that's good. I bet she moved far away from here."

"Hatred is widespread, Ruthie. I learned you can never outrun it." She rose from the swing and stood up.

"Maybe. I think of that girl every time I look into the woods. I used to hear her screams in my head whenever I saw a pickup truck. Then, like so much in my mind, the sounds disappeared. I have not heard them in a long time. I thought maybe she was dead."

"Nope. She's very much alive and right underneath your nose."

"What that you talking, Beulah?" Ruth stood up.

"All I can say is that she is closer than you think. Now let's talk about something else, why don't we?" They walked to the back porch.

"Tell me who she is, wench." Ruth took both hands and pushed Beulah.

"No! And don't abuse a witch. It's bad luck!" She ran up the stairs.

"You ain't no witch, just half crazy out of your mind."

"I'm not so crazy, sister. Some things I never divulge unless I think it will change a person's life for the better."

"And so now you're going to change my life, huh?" Ruth sat down on the old worn out sofa she placed on the back porch after purchasing her first leather sofa.

"No. You're going to change someone else's." Beulah sat very close to her.

"What are you up, Beulah? I bet you got some hair-brained idea inside that head of yours. We are too old for some of that mess you conjure up."

"Baby, this is not in my head."

"Where is it then?"

"Somewhere in your house." She pointed into the house.

"Stop your foolishness. What is in my house that you think is going to set someone else free?" Ruth leaned away from Beulah.

Beulah grabbed her hands. "The missing piece of the puzzle."

"What? I knew you were up to no good when I saw you outside. You tell me what I'm hiding this instant," Ruth snapped.

"You don't scare me, Ruthie. We're old friends. I trust you with my life. Now I come to ask you to give Mary's life back to her."

"What? Mary? What does Mary have to do with me hiding something?"

"You thought you were protecting her." She looked at Ruth suspiciously.

"From what? I honestly don't know what you're talking about, sistah!"

"I believe you. You probably forgot all about it. It's been many years."

"What?" It finally dawned on Ruth what Beulah was talking about.

"Bingo! I can see it in your eyes. You didn't have a clue at first, but now you know." She released Ruth's hands and lay back on the sofa.

"Oh, God! How do you know these things, woman? I did not know what to do with it. I planned to give them to Sheriff Bryant, but I learned he was the Devil incarnate and wanted nothing better than to see Mary rot in a jail cell. After she was exonerated on the murder charges, and that boy confessed, I just left the matter alone." A tear rolled down her face.

"Mary needs peace so that she can go on with her life. The guilt is eating her up. She was exonerated, but she never got over shooting Edgar. In her mind, even if he did not die at her hands, she contributed in his death."

"When she told me the police had new evidence, she told me about some underwear in Micah's apartment when he was stabbed. Something seemed so strange; I just could not put the pieces together. What does one pair of ladies underwear have to do with the other?" She leaned closer to Beulah.

"The person who took the underwear off of those women is one and the same."

"Yuck! How did Edgar get a pair of underwear into Micah's apartment?"

"He had the key!" She waited for a reaction. Ruth just shook her head.

"He stole that child's key in a pool hall, made a copy. When Micah got home, he probably thought he'd left his keys home and that they were not lost as he suspected. Never changed the locks. Edgar used to take his women to that apartment when Micah was out."

Ruth moved away. "Say it ain't so! What in God's name?" She put her hands over her mouth and breathed loudly.

"That child received all those stab wounds for something he didn't do. That's a terrible shame."

"Mary told me she caught Edgar on the ground, right in the act!"

"She did, but that was a different girl. Looks can be deceiving. That was not consensual. Edgar was blackmailing that girl's family."

"How do you know all of this?"

"How do you think? Her mother came to me for help two weeks before his demise. I told her it would be over in fourteen days."

She continued. "Ruthie, that man was evil. He had a lot of enemies. More than one of his enemies were there that night to make sure Edgar Carter would never again see the light of day."

Later...

Ruth knocked wildly on the front door. "It's me and Beulah. Open the door."

Mary peeked through the window and then opened the door and stared at the two women.

"Y'all beating on the door like the sheriff. There must be something really wrong."

Beulah stepped forward and then turned to point at Ruth. "She has something to tell you."

Mary appeared puzzled. She stepped backward into the foyer and waited for them to come inside.

"Mer, I need you do something for me." She hesitated. "I owe you an apology. I am so sorry!" Ruth started to cry.

"Sorry for what? Ruth, you're one of my best friends. If you wronged me, it was by accident." She looked at Beulah with an uncertain look on her face.

"Marry Frank," Beulah whispered.

"What? What does he have to do with this?"

"You didn't kill Edgar. He died from asphyxiation."

"Oh! That word sounds familiar." She turned away and walked to the sitting room.

"He suffocated on a pair of underwear he had in his throat that night," Ruth finally said.

"Who told you that?" Mary swung back around.

"He died in my arms. I couldn't bring myself to tell you back then. All the pain that man caused you. I didn't want you to suffer anymore."

"Ruth, was Edgar alive when you saw him?"

"Yes. He was suffocating, but I did not know it," Ruth cried.

"So he couldn't talk?" Mary seemed perplexed.

"Barely. He struggled to find his breath, even after I removed the pair of underwear that was lodged in his throat."

"What? I don't even think I want to know more." She turned away from them. "So after that, was he able to say anything?"

"Yes, he told me he was sorry and that he wanted to live right."

"So he repented?" She turned back around.

"Yes. It seemed like he was asking for forgiveness, so I prayed for his soul, right then and there." Ruth sat down and looked at her friend.

"I still don't understand. Did Sheriff Bryant know this?"

"I told the bastard. That's why he dropped the charges." Beulah sat down on the chaise lounge.

"You knew too?" Mary looked shaken and then a smile appeared on her face.

"Well, father." she let out a slow deep laugh and said, "I guess you do reap what you sow."

"That's the first unkind word I have ever heard come out of your mouth, Mary Brown." Ruth walked past her and sat down on the sofa.

"That's about all I can muster up. He was sleeping with a lot of women. I guess he had lots of underwear." She laughed. "Oh, this is really disgusting. I wonder did Anita Bryant know about them too." She put her hand over her mouth in shock.

"Anita Bryant!" Ruth yelled.

Beulah pushed herself up from the chaise and stood up.

"He's not the only one that's going to reap what he sowed," she yelled.

Beulah Chaney ran out of the room, through the front door, down the steps, into the car, and spun away down the road.

ELEVEN

1993

On the day Herman Coles Wilcox was laid to rest, the sun refused to shine. The clouds were a cast of gray and there were no patches of blue to seen by the naked eye. Even the Earth shed tears as a misty condensation was released from the heavens. Not even the summer temperatures of eighty and ninety degrees could maintain their levels. In fact, nothing that day was ordinary, especially not the tears that cascaded down Eula Mae Wilcox's face.

At the burial, Frank Wilcox did not sit with his immediate family members on the first row. Instead, he drifted in and out of the tent next to the six-foot hole as if he were a spectator. He never looked anyone directly in the eyes and whenever someone offered him a hug, he merely consented by patting them lightly on the back.

Since the day Herman told him the news, he prayed desperately that this day would never come. Prayed that Herman would outlive him, because in some way he felt his father deserved to. They had become close friends in the last ten years, talking to each other every night on the telephone. It was the closest relationship he had with anyone in the Wilcox family since Leslie died.

They celebrated Herman's life every six months. When he outlived the expected first prognosis, Frank took him to Los Angeles, California, because he loved the movies. Six months later, they flew to Paris and six months after that, to Madrid. They took six trips in total, all a full month in duration. Their last destination was Johannesburg, South Africa, and it was a trip that would remain with Frank for the rest of his life.

After the first father-son celebration, Eula Mae packed her bags and moved back in with Herman. Unbeknownst to anyone, they never officially divorced. Frank objected to her presence, but Herman behaved as if he had won the lottery. He said Eula Mae was his best friend and the only person he trusted with his life.

For months Frank thought it was just a phase caused by the guilt Eula Mae felt for all the wrong she had done, but as time drifted by, one thing was crystal clear: His parents were madly in love with one another. He watched as Eula Mae labored in the kitchen to prepare whatever dish Herman requested. Then he watched the careful attention she paid as his condition worsened and she dressed him for outings, or the way she carefully held onto his arm so that he could continue taking his daily walks. And during the final year of his journey, she held him every night and read his favorite stories to him. As he drifted off to sleep, she sang Stevie Wonder's *You are the Sunshine of My life.*

Despite her closeness to Herman, nothing changed the way Frank felt about his mother. She was someone he never wanted to be around and could not fathom ever getting to know the woman his father referred to as 'loyal.' He questioned what happened to her loyalty when it came to his sister Anne. Those thoughts intensified the hatred he felt in his heart for her more than anything he could see with his own eyes.

1985

"Where are we going?" Frank slipped his wristwatch on and followed behind Mary as she headed out the front door of his house.

"To the courthouse," she yelled without looking back at him.

"For what?" He grabbed the grey pinstripe jacket to his suit, slipped it on, and glimpsed at himself in the hall mirror as he walked out of the door.

"Frank Wilcox! Why do you ask so many questions? Today you are going to follow me, right?" Mary opened his car door. "I'll let you drive if you behave yourself."

"By all means, Miz Brown. I'll drive to the courthouse, but if you need anything, you should let me know now. With Chad Peters and all the rest of them crooks dead, I no longer recognize a single face in City Hall."

"Oh, there's still a face I bet you'll recognize when we get there. Just get in before I change my mind and drive myself," she teased.

Frank got into the car and looked over at Mary. He smiled as he noticed the way she was dressed.

"That sure is a beautiful dress. It's not one of your usual ones." He caught himself, "I mean, you always look radiant, but something is different about you today. That dress looks like you are going to a ball or something." He leaned toward her and said, "You're not going to share the surprise, beautiful lady?"

"Flattery will get you no where, Frank Wilcox." She motioned for him to put the key into the ignition and start the automobile.

"You're not right, Mary Brown. First you show up early this morning with breakfast in a basket. Then you go into my private wardrobe, pick out a suit and demand that I wear it. Now you tell me that we are going to the courthouse, but you refuse to tell me the purpose of that visit."

"You'll find out soon enough." She winked at him.

Frank drove into Ridgeland smiling the entire way. He had no clue what Mary was doing, but he would do anything she asked him to. In fact, he had done everything she had asked him to do, including accepting the fact that there was little chance that they could be together, something he wanted more than anything else in the world.

As they strolled down the halls of the courthouse, Frank noticed that the woman behind the main desk smiled when she saw them enter. He did not recognize her so he kept walking without acknowledging the friendly gestures she made. When Mary reached the desk, she pulled out a piece of paper, handed it to the young woman and waited for further instructions

"Judge Richards will see you in a minute." Then she looked down at the papers Mary handed her and said, "You both need to sign this before going before the judge."

Mary looked at Frank. His hands were trembling during the back and forth between Mary and the clerk.

"You ladies want to tell me what's going on?" Before he could get another word out, Kathryn Hawkins came from the back room.

"Well, if it isn't my favorite person." She held her arms out.

"I bet you recognize her." Mary looked at him and smiled.

"You took old man Peters' place?" He walked over and hugged her.

"Heavens no! I'm the Clerk of the Court," she screamed.

"What?" Frank looked at the women standing in front of him.

"He doesn't read many newspapers." Mary laughed. "You would think a man of such prominence would keep up with local politics." She and Kathryn hugged each other.

"Well, I thought something was strange. I have not heard from you in a while. All I knew was that you were running all those stores like a champ!" She beamed.

"I'm just doing my job," he replied, looking embarrassed.

"Frank, you are the boss. You can take a vacation every now and again," Kathryn chimed in. "Come check on us commoners." She patted him on the back.

"Okay. What are you all up to? I'm here now. I'm sorry. Yes, one day, I'll take a vacation," he said.

"Get it in writing, honey. Frank is workaholic," Kathryn warned Mary.

"Well, the paper is still waiting for his signature." The young girl held the paper out to Frank.

"You ladies know I never sign anything I have not read." He took the paper and stared at the writing on the top, and then he gave Mary a surprised look.

"But… but." He shook his head, smiled, and looked at Kathryn who had tears in her eyes.

"Sign the paper, you old fool, " she said.

Frank looked at Mary, reached into his coat pocket and took out a pen. As tears came to the corners of his eyes, he walked past the women and headed over to the counter, bent over and signed the marriage certificate. Then he turned around and said, "You didn't let me get a ring."

A tear dropped onto his collar.

1993

Timmy held Ida tightly as she sat in the metal chair a foot away from the shiny burgundy colored casket adorned in fourteen-carat gold trim. He could feel the enormous energy from her sobs as they penetrated against his body with the rhythm of a clock.

She kept her eyes closed. During the service at Second AB, she collapsed twice as she struggled to say goodbye. Now, as Mary said the final prayer, a sense of peace took over her body.

As the mourners began to drop flowers into the vault that would hold her father's remains, Ida looked around for Frank. She spotted him early as a pallbearer although his name was listed no where on the program. Apparently someone had not shown and Frank, being the man he was, jumped in to fill the void.

Ida reached down into her purse and found the tissues she had placed inside of the front pocket. Then she touched the Bible she'd hidden in the paper bag all those years before. It was her father that made her publically acknowledge that she had become a believer to the rest of the world.

"If you ashamed of God before men, he will be ashamed of you when you get to Heaven," he told her one day when he discovered her crouched down in the parlor reading her Bible.

"Why do you hide it in that paper bag?" Herman asked her.

"So it won't upset Timmy. I don't want to argue over this. I made up my mind to give the clubs up and live for God. Timmy still out there in the streets. He thinks that's the only way he can make money. I tell him to just run the clubs and allow these young fellows to manage them, but he don't trust nobody. Whatever I say go in one ear and out the other."

Tears filled her eyes as she thought of all the advice Herman had given her over the past three years. He used the last days of his life to resolve many issues that she had not addressed. They talked about everything. He even told her that Mark Williams was actually his cousin Marcus Wilcox, and Anne's biological father.

Ida turned to look at Mark as he sat behind them. He'd arrived a month before once they were certain that Herman's condition had taken a turn for the worse. There were times over the years when they assumed he would not last much longer, but Herman managed to recover every time.

Mark and his son, Floyd, traveled to Madrid with Frank and Herman a year before Herman died. It was then that Ida learned they had resolved their issues concerning Anne. She also learned what happened to her sister the fateful night she was thrown out of the window.

Herman made sure that Ida knew everything, knew why he and Eula Mae were separated all those years, and knew what happened with Li'l Boy.

Although she saw her Uncle Dexter a few times over the years, she had not laid eyes on him recently. Eula Mae told her that while she was away with Ruth and the women in Washington, D.C., Li'l Boy visited Herman and stayed for over a week. By the time Ida returned, he was gone again.

"Ida Mae." Timmy lightly tapped on her shoulder.

"Look over yonder, Mae." He pointed toward where the cars were parked in the front of the church.

She could see him. Knew who he was before he came any closer. He was carrying a potted plant and walking with someone she knew quite well.

"Well, Lordy. God just answered my prayers." She got up and ran toward them.

"You came! I knew you would." She fell into his arms.

Dexter Wilcox handed his wife the plant and held his niece tightly. "Anything for you Li'l Anne. Anything," he cried.

When he released her, Ida could see that Beulah had tears in her eyes. She let go of her uncle and walked over to where she stood.

"Miss Beulah, thank you for coming. Thank you for all you done for my father. He loved you so much. I'm so glad we got to spend some time getting to know each other. I didn't know you knew my uncle too." She reached out and grabbed Beulah's hand.

"Ida Mae, Beulah knows the whole family." He hesitated, then added, "She's family herself." He walked over to them, took the plant out of Beulah's hands, and kissed her on the cheek.

"Did I miss something?" Ida stared at the two of them as they held hands.

"Ida, Beulah is the only woman brave enough to hang with this mixed up musician all these years! She believed in me when I was too afraid to live any longer. This is the woman who taught me how to love again after I left y'all almost thirty years ago."

"What?" Ida turned around when she felt someone touch her on the back. Timmy stood behind her smiling.

"We never told a soul, Ida. I don't want you to think I was keeping secrets. It's just we have been through so much together that we kept our relationship hidden from everyone we knew. I guess we are more best friends than husband and wife like you two," Beulah said.

"You two in love?"

Timmy laughed out loud. "Tilley, these two are married."

"How you know, Timmy?" She spun around.

"Herman told me a long time ago and I just kept the secret. When we saw Dexter in Jersey, I thought they were no longer married so I went to Miss Beulah to tell her that I saw him, but she already knew because he telephoned her the minute he left us that night. She said he was so happy to be reunited with you."

"I would be mad at all of you if it were not for that man lying in that casket." Ida shook her head.

"What do you mean? Did Herman tell you?" Dexter asked.

"No. He told me why you left and I understood after he told me. I know you love me. I knew it when you got into that cab after us. Nothing else mattered." She took the plant from Beulah and smiled. "Now this marriage is a whole nutha matter all together. Beulah, you are something else."

"That she is. She's the love of my life, Ida Mae. She told me to think of Hannah every time I touch those keys and it worked. It really worked," he said.

"You play like you've been touched by God," Timmy said.

"Well, I was touched by an angel," he said as he laughed.

The four of them stood watching the people walk back to their cars. Ida noticed the look Dexter gave Mark when he walked by.

"He know too?"

Dexter laughed and said, "Ida, that's who convinced me to play again. I never play at a club he doesn't own."

"Wait!" Timmy yelled. "Mark owns ***Club Sapphire***?"

"And ***The Blue Note*** and all them other fancy clubs in the north. Mark is Mister Nightclub, you hear me?" He laughed as they turned to walk to the limousine.

Ida turned back and watched the men sealing the vault that represented her father's final resting place. "You did good, old man. You hear me, you did good."

1992

The chemotherapy weakened Herman's body, but never affected a strand of his thick salt and pepper hair.

Frank purchased new suits for him so that church folk could not tell the amount of weight his father had lost. His skin had become pale, his face sullen, but his eyes sparkled with passion. It seemed he would live forever.

Herman insisted on going to two churches every Sunday, whatever service was in the rotation that week, and to The Oaktree Prayer Tabernacle, which opened every day.

He loved the fact that women ran a church. Loved the fact that his son was married to one of those women. He had waited a long time to see the joy spread across Frank's face. Mary Brown brought that joy and for that, Herman was eternally grateful.

"One thing I learned about a good relationship," Herman said to his son one day as they sat on an empty pew in the Tabernacle.

"What's that, old man?" Frank leaned closer to him.

"Never keep secrets, you hear me? They will destroy everything. No matter how insignificant you think the secret is. The other person in the relationship might disagree. Just not worth taking the chance." He looked at his son and smiled.

"Nope. Don't have any of those," Frank proffered.

"You sure? You told that woman everything?"

"Everything that pertained to us. I even told her that Edgar was the man we discovered stalking her and Prentiss years ago. That was the biggest secret I kept from her." He had a strange look on his face.

"You never were a good liar," his father said.

"I'm not lying." He refused to look Herman in the face. "What else do I have to tell?"

"You told her all about your dealings with Wallace Hawkins and what not?"

"What not? Dad, my business dealings were legal. Yeah, we did things to beat the system because a black man could never run a business like that if white people knew about it. I don't think having silent partners and hiring white folk to attend meetings is illegal." He put his hand on his head.

"I'm sure it's not. That's all you did." Herman started laughing.

"Wait! You tell me what you think I was doing all those years." Frank reached out and slapped his father's hand.

"I don't know. I do know that you were untouchable. No one in Jasper County or this entire state could touch you. That was long after Wallace died. You had something on Chad Peters and the Klan and you know it."

"I did. That collateral died with the Devil himself." Frank looked around. "I used it while I needed it. Then I relied on God for protection."

"That's who we always relied on, son. God is the only real protection any of us have. Despite what happened to Anne, God protected my family over the years, even when Ida was raped."

Frank boiled with anger. "What did you say?" His voice escalated.

"Oh, God! Lord forgive me," Herman uttered, realizing he had said too much.

"Raped? Is that what you said? Someone raped my sister? Who? Is the bastard still alive?"

"It was a long time ago, son. You were off on your own then. Some college kid from up north had his way with her. She got pregnant, but lost the child." Herman tried to balance himself to stand.

"How come I'm finding out almost thirty years later? What other secrets are my family keeping away from me." Frank could not contain his anger.

"Calm down, now. That was not a secret. I thought by now Ida Mae had told you about some Richards boy that raped her."

"She never told me! One time she told me Timmy had fathered a child by... Wait!"

"Richards. That's the name," Herman said. "Yeah, same family. When the brother found out Ida Mae was expecting, he had a fit, tried to rip the baby right out of her!"

"Timmy knew about this?"

"Yeah. Timmy was there when she lost the baby. I think afterwards both of them thought the Lord was punishing them when Ida Mae had all those miscarriages."

Frank walked over to the door and looked outside. He had to talk to Ida. He had to know the truth.

TWELVE

1988

If there is a stage beyond utter exhaustion, Mary Brown Wilcox had reached it. After numerous legal battles between townsfolk who claimed ownership of the property Chapel in the Woods rested on, Mary finally decided to give up her fight to reclaim the old church and, instead, decided to purchase land somewhere else. She had no idea how difficult it would be to locate a prime spot in Jasper County. In fact, everywhere she and Ruth looked was occupied or owned by someone who refused to sell, leaving the only spot available right next to a juke joint. No matter how much thought either woman gave to the idea, they would never consent to it.

Yet, like all the other times in the past, Frank Wilcox stepped in. The same man whose suspicious character she'd questioned her late husband about more than thirty years before, yet later found enough integrity within him to marry him without seeking the approval of another living soul. That man, the one she later learned was destined to become her soulmate, came to her rescue and delivered a piece of prime property in a perfect location.

"Frank Wilcox, what are you saying?" They sat in the front of Hawk's right off the Route 462 exit in Coosawhatchie.

"This is a perfect spot for the church." He pointed at the store and gas station.

"What? Are you crazy, man!" Mary opened the car door and looked around.

"Well, what do you think?" He beamed.

"This is Wallace Hawkin's store, right? Did you buy it after he died?" She walked over to the driver's side of the car.

"I owned it long before he died." Frank stood up and kissed her on the lips.

"Frank Wilcox! What have I got myself into? You own this Hawk's?" She turned around and looked at the newly remodeled store which sat on four acres right off of Interstate 95.

"I own every Hawk's in the United States."

"What? My God! Who is the white man that does all the commercials then?" She looked at him suspiciously.

"A good friend I met years ago. He had the look. I don't look like a Hawkins, do I? Besides, I'm camera shy." He reached out and grabbed her hands.

"What about his daughters? I thought he left his stores to them?"

"Naw. I acquired them before Wallace died. This was the first store he ever put in my name, then each year, I took over another store. That was in the beginning before I owned the manufacturing plants we buy our foods from. Today, very little of what we carry comes from folks outside of South Carolina and Georgia. Our entire inventory is generated from suppliers that I own or manage in some kind of way." He kissed her again.

"So you're rich, you old devil." Mary turned away from him and admired her new store.

"God is good, that's all I can say. I intended on donating this land to you and Cousin Ruth a long time ago when I saw that oak tree out yonder. " He walked behind her.

As he walked toward the tree, he turned to look at her. "You didn't have to marry me to get it, either."

1990

Prayer Circle members from around the region stood in anticipation of the march. Hundreds of marchers, men and women, gathered behind Mary, Ruth, Ida, Daisy, Pauline, Mable, and Samantha Gray, who stood on the front line awaiting the signal to begin the march. They planned to sing all the way to their new edifice, and then kneel in the streets to give praise and thanks to God for allowing them to witness such a miraculous event.

Micah Brown stood directly behind his very pregnant wife, Pauline, and held Lauren's hand, who held her brother Larry's hand on the other side. Ruth's long lost son , Jacob, stood next to Benjamin, who held the hand of his young wife. Next to them was Jeremiah, Jonah's new husband, who held Jonah's hand, who held the hands of all six of Ruth's siblings as they stood proudly behind their sister. Timethous Tilley held the hands of he and Ida's twin girl and boy, while their oldest son looked about the crowd with anticipation. After them were long rows of people from all walks of life, all races of the universe.

Ruth squeezed Ida's hand and smiled. The two of them leaned into the other as the singing began. Ruth mouthed the words of each song to Ida. She knew how much of a statement Ida's presence made to the entire town, just by standing in that crowd. She was now a founding member of a place she swore she would never step foot inside.

Frank Wilcox stood on a flatbed that carried the church's new sign. He was at least one-hundred yards away when he turned and blew the trumphet to start the processional. Another gathering of folks stood on the sidelines and clapped their hands and as the marchers passed by, they followed them down the road until there were no longer any bystanders for everyone appeared to be a part of this joyous celebration.

Mary started crying. It had been a long journey since she and Prentiss came to Jasper County in the early fifties. She returned years later while married to Edgar Carter, but after years of physical abuse and shame, she decided to call it quits. Yet, the faith demonstrated by the women in the Prayer Circle gave her the strength to start over again.

As they neared the intersection of Highway 17 and Route 462, they could see balloons all around their new building. Mary raised her hands high into the air as Ruth, Ida, and Daisy gathered around and cried with excitement.

"It's the Lord's doing, and it's marvelous!" Daisy said through sobs. "I am so honored to stand before you women and see this great moment. I thought power had to be achieved through politics, but I have learned that real power only comes from God Almighty."

"Amen! Well, it took more than us women to get this accomplished. If it had not been for Frank, I don't know whether we would have seen this day so soon," Ruth added.

"Yes, Lord. I thank God for that man every single day." Mary beamed. "I am the woman I am because he is my best friend and I have each of you who believed in me before I knew how to believe in myself. I'll never be able to repay you." She watched Frank open the door of the van as Herman exited.

"Great God! Look over the bridge!" Ida shouted as hundreds of people marched on the other side of the Route 462 bridge to join the swelling crowd.

"Where did all of them folk come from?" Pauline asked.

"More supporters!" Micah yelled into the crowd.

There was thunderous applause from the crowd. Frank turned around and looked at the people on his right and then the sea of faces marching toward the church on his left.

City officials were present, and to everyone's surprise, the mayor and the town aldermen were in attendance. People from as far as Ridgeland, Hardeeville, Walterboro, Bluffton, Charlestown, and Savannah stood among the smiling masses.

Mary walked beyond the crowd as they crossed the street. Frank greeted her with a kiss as she walked onto the front steps of the church to face the crowd. As they came closer, she knelt on the concrete stairs and said a prayer. By the time she was back on her feet, the crowd surrounded her. She approached the podium and awaited Frank's nod to begin.

Good Afternoon, Saints:

Get as close as you can. We only have the street closed for a little over an hour. I promise you I will keep my comments brief today.

First and foremost, let me thank God for giving us this beautiful weather and this wonderful new edifice to praise His name even more. Thank all of you for being here with us on this momentous occasion. Welcome to the Oaktree Tabernacle of Prayer! We are delighted to have the saints march with us as we celebrate the beauty of God and the awesomeness of His power. One word, saints: Faith! We made it because of Faith! We believed we would see the goodness of the Lord in the land of the living.

This church was started in the backyard of Mother Ruth Garrett's house as just a group of women who came together to pray before church on Sunday. Years later, those women started praying outside underneath an oak tree, seven days a week. That was almost thirty-five years ago. After my late husband, Pastor Roy, and I built the Chapel in the Woods, we encouraged the women to continue to pray and allow the Lord to use them. I never suspected that one day I would become one of those women.

Today we are more than just women. As some of you know, our second place of worship was burned to the ground two years ago. That's when we headed to the Coosawhatchie River for service. That was fun, but some of you complained about the bugs biting you. So one day my amazing husband, Frank Wilcox, decided he would move one of his stores, formerly called Hawk's, now Herman's, to the other side of the street, less visible from the highway, and bless us with this incredible piece of holy ground.

Although we have held service here for a year, today is my official installation as pastor, but most of you know, we have had pastors from all over the North and South come and deliver a Rhema Word to all of us this past year. They have blessed us tremendously. I am humbled to serve as your pastor and I take this oath of office knowing that the Board of Trustees, chaired by Mother Garrett and Daisy Lyons, will do what is best for this congregation and consistent with God's word. We are a community church and our arms shall extend beyond racial, gender, and cultural lines. We are the people's church and everyone is welcomed in our sanctuary. In fact, our doors shall remain open for prayer twenty-four hours a day, seven days a week."

The crowd shouted cheers as hundreds of balloons were released into the sky.

1983

Love is the only emotion that survives death. Sometimes its powerful force mysteriously lingers on and grows with each passing year, causing the loss of a loved one to seem all the more painful than the heart could ever imagine.

She never did let go, and when he was no longer physically in her presence, she resorted to spending hours alongside his final resting place, remembering the promises of a life together that was never meant to be.

Oftentimes she laid down in the grass next to a tombstone that confirmed that he had once graced the earth; while othertimes, she sat for hours releasing poetry into the air, in hopes that he would hear her desparate calls for him to return.

She never noticed the pale face woman watching her on the other side of the cemetery. Never knew that someone was mentally recording her actions and one day would figure out her deeply hidden secrets and possibly expose them to the world. Or did she care? In seven long years, the earth beneath her had become her solace, removing her ability to care about the opinions of others.

She was a few feet away from her car, when someone approached her.

"Cemeteries are places to release, not hold onto something that has already been set free." Buelah Chaney appeared out of no where.

"Is that so?" The tall slender dark-skinned woman looked at Buelah and then turned her stare to the door handle of the car she was driving.

"That's so. If you're here to let go, then you are on the right path, but something tells me you are still holding on. Life, is for the living, you know that right? No matter how painful the loss of a loved one is, we must go forward and learn to live and experience, the blessing, the Lord has given to each and everyone of us called life."

"That's funny. I'm sure your'e right, but that does not apply to those of us who are the walking dead." She opened the car door, then turned around to face Buelah.

Buelah reached out and grabbed her wrist. "Yeah, I feel a heartbeat. No one with a heartbeat can call themselves the walking dead. You still have a purpose on this earth."

"Huh!" She put her hand over her mouth, revealing a half carat diamond ring.

"I felt more than life in that pulse, sister. The rage you feel is just as strong." Buelah come closer.

"So it's true. You really do read minds? All these years I thought it was just Low Country gossip going around about you. Somefolks swear you the second coming and some think your'e the devil incarnate. " She became withdrawn and spoke in a still, small voice. "It's not hard to read my mind. I wear it on my sleeves. I wish I had the courage to end this thing called life. Never was good at it. I probably don't have the guts to do anything about it, but if I did, I would do it today. The funny thing is, no one cares whether I live or die anymore. A lone tear shed down Juanita Bryant's face.

"Those are the remnants of hate and revenge. You surround yourself with those two and they will bleeed you dry. " Buelah starred into her lifeless eyes.

"Well, too late now. I'm holding on for the last act of revenge I need to witness and then that's it, there is really nothing else to live for."

"That's one of the saddest statements I ever heard come from another human being." Buelah looked out into the vast landscape of the cemetery to avoid Juanita's cold stare.

"Well, it's the truth. I have no family, no friends, thanks to the devil of a husband I married, and since I gave up leaving his fool behind a long time ago, the only other option was to stand by and watch his demise...and baby, it's taking too long to come."

"Watch yourself. Revenge has an awful pricetag that I'm not sure you've considered. " Buelah slowly turned around, back now to Juanita, and faced the opposite direction.

"Well, all I can say is, it's done now. Yes, the train as already left the station. It's only a matter of time now." He once, soft spoken voice, was an octave higher.

Buelah never turned around to see her leave, but she heard the tires as Juanita drove over the dirt and gravel out of the cemetery. She stood staring into the distance until something dawned on her: She had witnessed the Sheriff's wife standing over two different grave sites.

She hurridly approached the one she spotted her at several times. The infamous last name she knew by heart. She turned and began retracing her steps to the other gravesite she saw Juanita visit on occasion. It was on the other side of the sloped hill she now stood on near the older gravesites.

Buelah walked until she became exhausted. Maybe she had gone too far? Sighing heavily, walking in a full length linen black skirt, she stopped and looked around. It was then that she spotted the faded rose etched on the tombstone she remembered seeing a few weeks ago. She took a few steps further up the hill, but nearly fell backwards as she read the family name carved into stone: Pickney.

"Well, I'll be damn! Still waters run deep."

1986

At three-thirty in the morning, Ruth sprang from the bed, ran through the house, and headed onto the back porch. She forgot about putting on a robe to cover her body, and to protect her from the frigid elements outside.

It was winter and many plants on the back porch were covered up. Ruth smelled smoke and her clairvoyant spirit convinced her that something else was being covered up.

She stood on the porch facing the woods as the smells permeated the skies. As the cold air embraced her raw skin, she ran back into the house and dressed. Finally, she looked in on Jonah, grabbed a wool coat from the front hall closet, and then walked out the front door.

A car traveling down the driveway startled her, but she kept her eyes focused on the driver as she walked down the steps and stood in the front yard.

Pauline got out of the vehicle.

"Momma Ruth, something is wrong." She had been crying.

"What, child? What are you doing out here this time of morning?" Ruth reached out and pulled her closer. "That child is coming and you out here alone. Where is your husband?"

"Micah ain't come home last night. I don't know where he is. We had a fight. I told him about what the sheriff did to me a long time ago."

"Ooh. You didn't tell him about that before you jumped the broom?" Ruth looked at her suspiciously.

"No. We were so in love, I only told him about the abortion and that I may not be able to conceive a child again. I told him how the prayer circle prayed over my womb, but I didn't want to get his hopes up high. He never asked who the baby daddy was."

"So why did you tell him now?" She put her arms around Pauline and walked back up the front porch steps.

"We were talking about the sheriff being retired and all. Micah was praising him for his accomplishments, so I started telling him just how evil that man was and one thing lead to another and...you know." She stopped midsentence and looked around.

"Yeah. I know. It's hard to live with that kind of shame and keep it a secret. I understand completely. Now, we must find Micah. I kid you not, that baby is on his way."

"Mamma Ruth, I love Micah so much. He is such a good man. Who would have thought I would be having a baby at this age? I mean, all my peoples chirren grown now. I'm the oldest pregnant woman I know. I should have had grands by now, some say."

"What do these people know? Everything happens in God's time. You were meant to be a mother. The Devil tried to seal your womb but God said not so. You just focus on what the Lord is doing in your life and not what the Devil is trying to do." Ruth stood next to the fireplace and put more wood inside.

"I hated to relive what happened to me. That man pulled me over on the side of the road and bribed me. I thought he was being nice. Then he showed up at the house. I tried to get him off of me. His dirty hands were everywhere. Then he threatened to put me in jail if I told anyone." She started crying and added, "And to think I had to carry his seed inside of me! There was no greater shock. When I went to that clinic, I felt I had to do something to end my misery once and for all. I regret taking my child's life, but God knows, I felt I had no other choice."

"Let's not focus on the past. You are a healed and a forgiven woman now. God has blessed you with a man who loves the ground you walk on. Look at all you have. You're driving around in a new car and there's nothing you have to ask for that Micah won't make sure you have." She walked over and faced Pauline, "God is showing you that the slate is wiped clean."

"Mamma Ruth, I'm so sorry I could not bring myself to tell you the truth back then. You kept telling me to stay away from Sheriff Bryant and to stop being so trusting of these men. You warned all of us that he was evil, but I did not listen. I had to learn the hard way, and I tell you, as God is my witness, I never knew such shame after what he done to me."

"Well, that shame has been removed by the blood of Jesus. Let's get you back home where you'll be safe. I don't want you driving this time of morning." Ruth walked Pauline to the door, grabbed her car keys and headed to the car.

They were riding down Route 336 into Ridgeland when they spotted a burning vehicle in the distance, engulfed in flames. Fire trucks and police cruisers were parked a few feet away as the fireman sprayed water onto the flames.

Ruth pulled the car over on the side of the road and waited inside until one of the officers approached her vehicle.

"Can't get through here right now. Road's closed, ma'am." He leaned into the driver's side of the vehicle.

"Anyone hurt?" Ruth turned the ignition off and rolled the window down further to get a better look.

"No, ma'am. I think someone done run out of gas. Car sitting on the side of the road empty. Must have exploded some sort of way. It's the strangest thing. The entire trunk was engulfed in flames by the time the fire trucks arrived."

"You check around the vehicle in case someone was thrown out of the car?" Ruth continued to stare at the scene.

The officer took out a flashlight and shined it into her face. "You ladies best be on your way. We can handle this. If you circle back a few feet, you can take Route 21 as a detour," he said.

"Okay." She put both hands on the steering wheel and then spoke. "Are those plates from out of state? You think someone unfamiliar with this area ran out of gas on these roads? Something just doesn't seem right to me, that's all." Ruth looked the officer straight in the face.

"Those plates are from Florida. Probably someone visiting Hilton Head or family. No sign of anyone when we showed up."

"Ooh. Something tells me where there's smoke, there's fire and fire is sometimes

used to cover something up that can not be seen with the naked eye."

1986

As Ida placed programs on the empty chairs surrounding the Coosawhatchie River, a white Cadillac appeared heading slowly toward her. Ida noticed the woman at the wheel and immediately stopped what she was doing.

"Excuse me, what time does the service start?" she yelled from the window.

"Nine if you coming for prayer and Sunday school. Actual church services git started 'round eleven." Ida stared at the two children sitting in the back seat.

About an hour later, several people crowded around as the deacons began putting out additional chairs to accommodate them. Ida busied herself in the make shift tent that housed the outdoor church's temporary kitchen. Ruth insisted that they provide breakfast for the parishioners every week in the event someone did not have the ability to make their own, or the means to afford it.

As Mary Brown approached the podium, the same woman that arrived earlier drove up close to where the crowd was seated, and, upon seeing the look on the parishioners faces, whispered to her teenagers and then quietly walked towards the back of the group and found a seat. Although the children seated with her were casual, the woman was dressed in a semi-formal multi-colored polka dot dress,with matching hat and shoes. Her sandy blonde hair was conservatively worn in a single bun behind her ears.

When the altar call was announced, she walked up to altar and knelt down. Ruth approached her and then placed her hands, covered in white gloves, on top of the woman's head and prayed. After she finished, the woman arose and threw her arms joyfully around Ruth's neck as if they were long-lost friends.

Ida was busy canvassing the crowd, placing white cotton sheets on people that had collapsed or fainted during the altar call, when she noticed Ruth's interaction with the woman. She stopped, looked around for Mary, and then stood watching the their interaction with each other. A strange look crept upon her face. She walked over and, after Ruth introduced them, she carefully shook Samantha Gray's hand.

"Can we get you something to drink?" Ida asked taking her politeness cues from Mother Ruth.

"No." Startled, Samantha appeared shaken. "I want to join the church, but I did not hear the invitation." She searched the crowd for her children.

"Well, since we don't have an official edifice, we consider everyone a friend until we get a building we can finally call home. We still meet in the back of Mother Ruth's yard for prayer during the week, but we stopped extending the right hand of fellowship until the Lord blesses us with a place to accommodate everyone.

"Well, I want to become a member of this church the minute you open your membership roll again, and if it's alright, I'd like to come to the prayer services too."

"Fine. What brings you here today?" Ida signaled for the other women to join them.

Mary was first to walk over. She smiled vibrantly and extended her hand toward Samantha Gray.

"Missus Gray! What a pleasure it is to see you again. I'm glad you found us. I hope you don't mind our temporary location. Since the weather is so nice, we just set up shop out here." She looked at Ruth, Daisy, and Pauline who stood by watching.

"These are some of the church's officers, they keep everything going."

"Afternoon, ladies. Of course I know Mother Ruth. We have known each other for many years. When I heard you had a church, I just wanted to join. No questions asked. I know wherever Mother Ruth is fellowshipping is a good place. Honestly, I've been trying to get here for weeks. I came this morning, but I got caught up at home before I could get out again. But, I made it, y'all, here I am!"

"Well, welcome!" Daisy extended her hand to Samantha.

"Thank you so much. I can't wait to volunteer my time and work wherever you need me to."

Samantha Gray shook the hands of the ladies standing around and exchanged telephone numbers. She knew she was right at home with this group of people. Fear had kept her away for more than ten years and now she was ready to take the biggest faith walk of her life, and join a predominantly black church.

THIRTEEN

1992

Ida ran down the stairs after her brother. "Frank, don't do this! Let bygones be bygones," she cried.

"Timmy, you have to stop him!" she yelled out the screened door.

Frank jumped in his car and sped down the highway. He had heard enough. No one was going to treat a member of his family in such a way and get away with it. He pushed the gas pedal harder.

In his fit of rage, he forgot that Ida's attacker, Sheriff Bryant, had long left the borders of Jasper County, South Carolina, retiring from office seven years before. Rumor had it that he left amid another round of scandals that had become synomyous with his name during the latter half of his career. By the time he returned his badge, no one was surprised nor cared the reason for his departure.

Over the years, Frank Wilcox had mastered the art of finding missing persons. He knew how to track a person with the faintest scent. He had done it before, and he promised himself, after discovering the truth, he would do it again.

Ida recanted the entire story to him. She said she was not raped; Herman had gotten the story wrong. She confessed that she lost the baby as a result of the vicious beating she received at the hands of her angry assailant, and she even told him about the years of torture Sheriff Bryant later subjected her to.

It played in Frank's head like a broken record. Over and over he envisioned Ida being assaulted by a man of Charles Bryant's stature. He pulled the car off onto the shoulder of the road, turned off the ignition, laid his head upon the steering wheel and cried.

1980

The DNA results confirmed that the samples submitted to the lab matched that of a Charles Nathaniel Richards, a black male, who was believed to have been killed in an automobile accident in downtown Atlanta in the spring of 1962.

That information hit her like a ton of bricks. It could not have been a coincidence. Her twin sister was raped and killed in Atlanta during the fall of 1961. It was a year the Pickney family would never forget. Even though they tried desparately to uncover answers surrounding her death, no one at Spellman College could shed light on the horrible situation. In fact, the police eventually closed the case, listing it as an unsolveable homicide.

To cope with losing her twin and soul mate, Deborah Juanita Pickney packed her bags and headed to Atlanta, where she enrolled in Clark Atlanta University, minutes away from where her sister spent the final two years of her life. Graduating in 1967, she met and married someone who, at first glimpse, seemed like the answer to her prayers. College-educated, he openly discussed his plans of becoming the first negro police chief below the Mason Dixon line, and convinced her that the two of them would climb the ladder of success together. Yet, there was only enough room on the airplane of success for him. Everytime Juanita tried to establish an identity outside of the home, he forbade her from doing so, even using his police powers to circumvent every effort she made. Eventually, helpless and defeated, she gave up all together. On the outside she seemed normal, but on the inside, she knew that she had married a monster in which she vowed never to love.

They never had children and he never questioned why. He said it was all God's will, but she knew differently. She knew that she had strolled into a private doctor's office with another man who pretended to be her lawful wedded husband, after terminating an earlier pregnancy because she believed the father was the man she depised the most. Her actual husband was too busy to discover most of her secrets, and by the time he realized just how deceitful she had become, it was too late.

Juanita Pickney Bryant stared at the paperwork spread across her bed. It all made sense now. Ida Tilley once said Sheriff Bryant had two lives. That one piece of information rang in her ear like an echo. When she did some checking on her own, she found out exactly what it meant. Now, holding the evidence in her hands of both the police report and the medical records, the truth came shattering down all around her like a rushing wind...her sister's killer and her husband were the same hellacious beast. On that day, she willingly traded a spot in Heaven for an eternity in hell just to destroy Charles Nathaniel Richards-Bryant, once and for all.

1992

Beulah stood in the doorway as her husband drove away. She sat down on the painted forest green glider and rocked back and forth. A lot of things happened to her that not even her alleged supernatural powers could explain. Exhausted, she stared into space and then fell sound asleep in the warm afternoon glow.

At some point that afternoon she was awakened by the sound of a brick colored Lincoln Town Car that ripped through the gravel bringing enough smoke to set an actual fire. She stood up and walked over the edge of the front porch.

Frank Wilcox walked up the steps but did not say a word. His eyelids were moist as he stared at his friend with a sense of hopelessness etched across his face.

"I promised myself I would never kill a man for as long as I lived. I'm over fifty now, and I've kept that promise." He sat down on the bottom stair and moaned. "So far."

Beulah walked down the stairs and stroked his salt and pepper curly locks. "What is it, old friend? You know you can tell me anything." She sat down on the step above him.

"Charles Bryant beat a child out of my sister's womb! I just found out yesterday. I've been driving around all night. I've searched all over and he's gone without a trace. I want him dead, Beulah. I want to have the pleasure of killing him with my own hands."

"My brother, as your mother would say, you're a day late and a dollar short." She leaned against Frank. "I know how you feel finding out about it all these years later. That's the way it was supposed to be. Your life would have been totally different had you known. Your sister knew what she was doing. She thought she would never see the likes of the man who nearly killed her again, but like a bad dream, he just kept coming back into her life."

"You knew about this too?" He spoke just above a whisper. "It seems I'm the last person to find out."

"It even took me a while to figure out who Charles Bryant really was, and you know that generally does not happen. That man was pure evil. It all caught up with him in the end. Just trust me. He already got what he deserved." She leaned back, wrapped her arms around her knees, and rocked back and forth.

"What do you mean, he got what he deserved?"

"You'll never get to him now, Frank. Someone already took care of that."

"Who? I just heard he retired and moved to Florida? How is that getting what he deserved? I know he was involved in Edgar Carter's death regardless of how he denied it. How is justice served if the only punishment that man got was a forced retirement and a divorce?"

"Oh, he got more than that. Seems somehow the person he least expected did him in, and in a big way. Yes, a big way!" She looked out onto the horizon and smiled. After a few minutes, Frank turned around and faced Beulah. "Where is he?"

"Long gone."

"Just tell me where."

Beulah stood up and walked up the stairs to the front door, went inside and returned carrying an old newspaper. "Read it for yourself," she instructed as she handed it to him.

The title read, "Human remains identified from burning truck found on Route 336 in Ridgeland." His eyes drifted into the text that read, "Dental records matched a Charles Nathaniel Richards, who was thought to have been killed in an automobile accident in Atlanta sometime in 1962. However, medical tests showed Richard's dental records matched that of the former Jasper County Sheriff, Charles Bryant. Bryant, who retired and moved to Clearwater, Florida, apparently never moved into the house he purchased in September last year. Authorities in Ridgeland and Florida have not been able to locate his ex-wife for questioning."

1988

The first time adult Ida Mae Tilley stepped into a church structure was two days after Mary's installation as pastor. Since everyone knew her suspicions about churchfolk, no one said anything when she and Timetheous sat on a wooden bench under the oak tree whiled the open windows broadcast the services on the inside.

That summer, Mary decided to move the congregation back outside to join Ida. She never explained why such a faithful member chose to remain outside of the confines of the church. She truly believed that over time, something would drive Timetheous and Ida Tilley inside. It had done so for Buelah Chaney, and she prayed the same would happen for those two.

There was a knock on the back door. The church housed four administrative offices located in back of the sanctuary near the cafeteria, media room, bookstore, and daycare. The back door was for clergy only. Ruth looked at the security camera above her head and saw them. She continued writing and waited. When the knocking continued, Ruth pushed the intercom and told one of the volunteers to let Pastor Brown know that someone was at the back door.

Mary was kneeling at the baptismal pool when she heard the knocking. She assumed it was Mother Ruth, the only other board member that entered through the rear door, so she continued praying.

Daisy Lyons shared an office with Ruth. She was in the kitchen at the time. She looked around and, when the knocking continued, she walked toward the back door.

"I'll get it," she said, as someone approached her from behind.

"I have told you about sneaking up behind me, Micah Brown." She turned around, laughing.

"It's only a sneak if you are alarmed. You handle surprises with ease. No one can ever sneak up on you." He walked ahead of her toward the rear door.

Micah opened the door and spoke to the individuals at the door. When he did not move to the side to let them in, Daisy became alarmed.

"Everything okay?" she asked.

Micah turned around. "You tell me." He stood to the side so that she could see Timmy and Ida Tilley standing on the back porch.

"Hey, y'all. Is everything all right?" Daisy asked.

Micah moved and Timmy walked past him to face Daisy.

"Hey, Daisy. We dropped by to have a word with Pastor Brown if she's in." He appeared nervous.

"Well, come on in. I'll take y'all to her office. You both standing there like you are guests. This is your church home even if you never come inside," she teased.

"Well, it took a lot of convincing, but we are heah now," Ida boasted.

"We are delighted that you dropped by." Daisy walked ahead and then yelled out, "Ruthie, surprise!"

Ida gave Timmy a suspicious, then reassuring look. He was holding a wide-brimmed straw hat with both hands as they walked down the corridor.

Ruth ran outside of her office toward Daisy's voice. She stopped in her tracks when she spotted the two of them and declared, "Well, God in Heaven, it's really gonna rain now!"

1991

Dexter Wilcox tiptoed down the hallway to their bedroom. He was carrying two dozen red roses, a box of chocolates, and a diamond ring secured in his front pocket. He opened the bedroom door, spotted his wife in a deep sleep, and stepped inside.

Buelah heard the door knob as he turned it. She kept her eyes closed.

He walked over to the bed and placed the flowers and chocolates next to her. "Happy Valentine's Day, sweetie," he cooed.

"So now we are celebrating holidays?" She did not open her eyes.

"It's the first time I've been home on a holiday." He sat on the bed and removed his shoes.

"Dex, has it really come to this after all these years?" She pushed her body up onto the pillow beneath her. "You wait until I'm an old woman, and you're an old man to get romantic!" She let out her classic holler.

"Well, Sarah, the Bible says it's never too late."

"For what? I have been happy with what we have since the day you landed on my doorstep. Don't tell me you're going to change on me now?" She reached out to grab him.

He lay in her arms smiling. It was a while before he started talking and when he did, he released a river of information that not even Buelah Chaney knew.

"Usta love another girl from this area. That was before I joined the military, before I met Hannah," he started out slowly.

"Yeah. What happened to that relationship?" Buelah's fingers played in his thick salt and pepper hair.

"She run off and married another man. I heard they had a couple of kids. I saw her one day. She looked so sad. By the time I looked for her again, she was long dead. Some say she died from a broken heart." He looked up into Buelah's intense black eyes and changed the subject.

"I told Mark I'm through with life as a travelling musician. I've played every major venue in this country. That was my dream. Now I just want to feel like a husband. I'm just sorry it took me all these years to really appreciate what I had waiting at home all the time."

He reached into his pocket. "Oh. I almost forgot. Will you marry me, Buelah Chaney?" He opened the small velvet covered box to reveal a two carat princess cut diamond ring.

"Old man! I married you a long time ago, don't you remember?" She stared at the ring. "Besides, where do you expect me to wear such a large diamond to? I'm either here or at the church with Ruth and the others."

"That's all going to change now. Daddy's home." He took the ring out of the box and placed it on her finger.

"Dexter Wilcox, you don't have to make up the years you spent away from me. I'm a wise woman. I understood your pain better than you did. I married you because you needed a reason to pursue your dreams of becoming a musician."

"Did you love me?" He looked startled.

"Nope. Never did," she teased.

They laughed non-stop for a few minutes.

"I'm serious, Chaney, the first thing I want to do is renew our wedding vows in front of the entire town. I want them to know that you belong to me forever." He looked at her and winked.

"I'm not so sure that's a good idea, old man," she said.

"And why? You keeping secrets?" he asked.

"Shucks no! Folk don't pry into my business like that. They are too afraid of the consequences. I tried to tell Ruth and them that I was married a long time ago, but they couldn't believe anyone would still be married to me as much as I traveled back then,"she said.

"Well, now we have a chance to do something that shows the softer side of you," he said.

"That's what I'm afraid of, old man. I like my reputation as a root doctor. It used to bother me when my mother was alive, but I've learned to make the most out of it."

"You saved me! That's my testimony. Whatever powers you have, saved my life." He kissed each of her soft palms.

"Love saved you, old man. Good old-fashioned love." She bent down and kissed him. "Oh, what about the girl? I still want to hear that story." Buelah had a serious look on her face.

"Chaney, you are just trying to see if you knew her."

"And? What's your point? I never said that I wan't nosey."

"Okay. This will count for one of my stories that you make me recite everytime I come home," he said.

"Well the man can't help it if he can tell a great story. Spill the beans, I'm all ears."

"Her name was Winifred. We were childhood playmates. She was younger by a few years. One of her brothers was killed by the Klan, so they say. No one knows for sure. Anyway, we called ourselves courting when she became of age. It was about two years before I went in the service. It was my first time being in love so I was very protective of her. So protective that I refused to dishonor her. I made up my mind that I was going to marry her when I returned home. Then I changed my mind, decided do it sooner but she came to me, out of the blue, and called things off."

"Why?" Buelah asked.

"I don't know. I guess it wasn't meant to be. At the time, I was devastated. I thought she would change her mind, but she didn't. By the time I ran into her again, I was married."

"That's when she seemed sad?"

"Yeah. Something was strange. She had two kids with her. The daughter was still in her arms. The son was about three years old. Her husband seemed pleasant, but I could feel something else was going on between them. She almost seemed scared of him."

He looked around. "One day I was in the convenience store with Herbert Gray and some woman came in there looking for Winifred. Old man Gray said she moved away some time ago. After the woman left the store, he told me that Winifred's husband found out that she had a child by another man right before they got married. Seems he confronted her and when she admitted it, that son of a gun blew his brains out right in front of her and the kids."

"Oh, God! What was Winifred's last name?" Buelah was perplexed.

"She was a Foley. They some kin to the Habershams. I forgot her married name." He looked at her.

Buelah sat up in the bed. "It was Richards," she said slowly.

1996

Mary, Ida, Ruth, Daisy, Pauline, Mable and Samantha huddled together in prayer. It was the ninth anniversary in the new church, and the fortieth anniversary of the Prayer Circle. There was a lot to be thankful for and a lot of memories that flooded each of their minds.

As women, they each represented a different spectrum on the wheels called life. Each had their own unique stories to tell and a destiny to fulfill. Prayer brought them together, and continued prayer helped make their dreams become a reality, for it confirmed to each of them that nothing in life could hold them back.

Absolutely nothing.

Tragic events united them and created the circumstances that sealed their fate forever. Mary knew she was led to Jasper County all those years ago; Ruth vowed to leave but never could, and Ida found it to be the home she loved more than any other place in the world.

They each had lived good lives. Some would even call them great, but they knew in many ways that, despite what they had been able to accomplished, God was not finished with either of them. There was still a lot of work to be done.

By 1993, Mary Brown Wilcox, now known simply as Mother Brown, and Ruth Garrett, had both become world renown as women in minsitry. They spent a tremendous time on the road, either speaking at conferences, or preaching to other congregations. In 1995, they took their first voyage to West Africa to lay the foundation of an international Oak Tree Tabernacle of Prayer in the city of Accra, the capital of Ghana. It was near completion. Finally, the Prayer Circle that God told Ruth to start all those years ago in her backyard, had become a worldwide ministry.

Named Associate Pastor on his fortieth birthday, Micah Raymond Brown stepped into his mother and father's shoes and became responsible for managing the day to day activities of the church. His wife, Pauline, and their two daughters, Ramona and Rose, spent practically every hour right next to him. Eventually, they built a home directly across the street from the church.

Daisy Lyons led all outdoor prayer activities held under the oak tree. She called it her outreach ministry and she governed everything as if it were a political campaign. Folks from all around, when passing through Coosawhatchie or exiting Route 462 toward Hilton Head Island, read the billboard advertisement for The Garden of Eden. It eventually garnered thousands of visitors a year.

Frank Wilcox finally settled down after the church officially opened. He sold the Herman's franchise to Jacob and Laurence Harrison Garrett, Ruth's two older sons. They kept the name, but added gas stations throughout the south called J & G Service centers, which stood for James and Gus, the fathers they both adored.

Benjamin Harrison, who Ruth officially adopted when he turned sixteen, graduated from college and moved to Detroit to build cars for the Ford Motor Company. Homesick, he returned to the Low Country, opened a car dealership in Hardeeville, and took over the media ministry of the church. Eventually, he produced two Christian television shows: Oak Tree Ministries Presents, and Pastor Lauren, a show hosted by none other than his sister, Evangelist Lauren Harrison Denver.

Dexter and Beulah Wilcox celebrated their twenty-fifth anniversary in style. Patterned after parties by Pastor Roy, decades before, guests were treated to a three day affair that culminated on Sunday afternoon, as they served as Master of Ceremonies for Pastor Brown's second anniversary.

Buelah promised herself that she would keep the secret about Winifred Richards to herself. It was best to leave some secrets buried deep down below the earth. That was the place she was sure could evoke no further pain on the people who still remained among the living.

In its fourty years, the circle had not been broken. Every woman, touched by the power of God through that enormous oak tree, could testify that life had dealt them severe blows. There were losses and tears shed that changed each of them in both small and great ways. It is what made them stronger; it was what finally liberated them, and, for a new wave of women ministers, the tragedies each endured, made them unstoppable.

Epilogue

Spring, 1997
Oaktree Tabernacle of Prayer, Coosawhatchie, South Carolina

Mary stood watching a nervous Timmy and Ida Tilley sit down in her office. She looked at Ruth, who stood next to the doorway unsure if she should come all the way inside.

"Do you mind if Sister Ruth joins us?" she asked.

"No. Ruthie can come in." Ida turned around and looked at her cousin. "Anythang I ever got to say can be said around huh."

Ruth stepped in the office and waited for Pastor Mary's instructions before taking her seat.

"Ruthie, come sit next to me so we can face our two favorite family members," Mary said as she picked up the Bible on her desk. "I have a feeling we might need the Good Book here." She took a seat.

"Thank you for seeing us on such short notice," Timmy said.

"You don't need to give us advance notice. You both are welcomed anytime," Mary assured him.

"We got something on our minds that we need to discuss with you. I just felt like it could not wait until Sunday," he said.

"That's why our doors are open everyday," Ruth interjected. "I never held with churches only being open on Sundays. Folks need God every day."

Ida grabbed Ruth's hands. "You knew this day would come. Thank you for never giving up on us."

"That's because you never gave up on me." She winked at them.

"Well, I guess I better start." Timmy looked directly at Ida. "Y'all know Ida don' give her life to Christ and I want to do the same thang. She was mostly sitting under that oak tree waiting for me to get my head straight. I tell ya, it was hard to totally surrender to God. I have been doing my own thing, running clubs and other businesses all my life. I guess a part of me thought I never needed church." Tears filled his eyes.

"Oh, it's more than church, brother," Ruth nodded.

"Yeah, Ruthie, it is," he smiled.

"So you come to give your life to Christ? That's great news." Mary stood up and clapped.

"I did. I confessed that I needed the Lawd and then I came heah to have prayer," he said.

"You did the right thing. You confessed with your mouth and believed in your heart, and guess what, son? You are saved!"

"Well, great God! I knew what you wanted the minute you walked in the back door." Ruth proclaimed. "I saw it in your eyes last Sunday."

"Yeah, Ruthie, I was meaning to come talk to yuh, but I wanted to give it some time first. The Lawd was courting me, sho' 'nough." He laughed, relieved to have it said aloud.

"Well, let's pray and seal the deal," Mother Brown yelled.

After they prayed, Ida Mae Tilley held Timetheous for a long time and shed a bucket of tears. Ruth and Mary stood by watching quietly.

"Would you two like some privacy?" Mary finally asked.

"No. We are so filled with joy, I tell yuh!" Ida stood wiping her eyes.

They each hugged Mary and Ruth and turned to leave. As they walked down the hall, Ruth could see that Ida wanted to say something more.

"Cat got your tongue, Ida Mae?" she whispered.

"No, Ruthie. How come you always know when something has not been said?" She turned and looked at her.

"Chile, it's written all over your beautiful face."

Ida and Timmy stopped walking and turned around to face the two women.

"We need a favor," Timmy blurted out.

"Anything." Pastor Mary said. "Anything your hearts desire."

"We want to get married," Ida said slowly.

"What? Come again. You want to now get married in a church?" Ruth looked puzzled.

"No, Ruthie. We just wants to get married period. Right this minute," Timmy said.

"You two been married for years."

"No. I never wanted to. I just knew it wouldn't last. I thought the pain in my life took away my ability to love someone again. I told Timmy until I could love myself, I could not marry him. When I finally started to love myself, we were too embarrassed to go down to the courthouse and make it official. We kept talking about it, but we never made one move." She started to cry.

"Now you know all of my shame, Cousin Ruth. I finally run out of secrets."

"Oh, hush now, Ida. The Lord knows all of our secrets and he still loves us!" She kissed her on the cheek.

Mary stood rocking back and forth. "Well, I do declare, I told you I needed to hold onto this here Bible. We have a wedding to perform!" She grabbed Ruth and hugged her tight.

"Daisy!" she yelled at the top of her lungs. "Come quick! We need ourselves a witness!"

The End!

Book Club Discussion Questions
The Prayer Circle- Book One

1. Un-forgiveness appears to be a major theme in the novel, particularly with the Wilcox Family. Discuss how the unwillingness to forgive affects Eula Mae, Ida, Frank and Mark Wilcox.
2. Each of the main characters possesses unique characteristics. Compare and contrast Ruth, Ida, and Mary's greatest attributes. What do you feel are their greatest strengths?
3. Race Relations is one of the underlying themes in the novel. Discuss the ways some of the characters dealt with racial relations or behaved in the presence of Caucasians.
4. After reading Mary Brown Carter's story, why do you think she hid the physical abuse in her marriage to Edgar Carter for so long?
5. The childhood religious experiences of many of the characters greatly impact their adult lives and choices. Discuss some of the most memorable religious experiences detailed in the novel and the impact those experiences had on that particular character.
6. Ruth Fields Harrison Garrett struggles to free her mind from the mental disorder of Schizophrenia. Discuss the interplay between Ruth's illness and her supernatural powers. What experiences do you believe were real as opposed to those caused by her illness?
7. Each of the main characters harbors some deep dark secret which eventually erupts during the course of the story. Discuss the impact of those secrets on Ruth, Ida, and Mary.

8. Why do you think Mary struggled so much with her calling into ministry? Discuss how this is evident in the telling of her story. What distinguishes Mary's inner torments to preach the word of God from the internal struggles of both Ruth and Ida?
9. Ida Mae Tilley adopts her mother's hatred towards the church. Based upon her story, do you believe their anger towards the church is for the same reason? Why?
10. Maternal influence plaques each character. Discuss how the relationship each has with their own mothers eventually influenced their adult lives? How does that influence make the characters perception of society alike or different?
11. The three main characters all suffer substantial losses at a young age. Describe how those particulars losses shaped their adult years.
12. In discovering their identities, each woman learns to shelter her pain by becoming involved in something else. Discuss.
13. The relationship between Mary Brown and Frank Wilcox spanned decades. Although she originally questioned his character, what do you think finally drove Mary into Frank's arms?
14. Why do you think Ruth never told anyone about the piece of fabric she discovered lodged in Edgar Carter's throat?
15. Beulah Chaney played guardian angel to Ruth Garrett several times, particularly while Ruth was institutionalized. Why do you think there was always a kindred spirit between these two women?

CPSIA information can be obtained at www.ICGtesting.com
Printed in the USA
BVOW050407241011

274267BV00002B/7/P